LA

Julia Williams grew _____ _____ London, one of eight children, including her twin. Coming from a large family, Christmas was usually a chaotic affair, and her earliest memories of the festive season include tales of her parents' drinking sherry with the milkman at four in the morning, that deliciously exciting sound of rustling paper in the dark, always wishing for snow and never getting it, the inevitable satsuma in the stocking, watching *The Wizard of Oz* – again – and fighting for the last chocolate in the Quality Street tin. Since she's grown up and had a family of her own, she wonders with awe how her parents managed to always make Christmas so much fun without any apparent signs of stress . . .

To find out more about Julia go to her website at www.juliawilliamsauthor.com or visit her blog at www.maniacmum.blogspot.com.

By the same author:

Pastures New
Strictly Love

JULIA WILLIAMS

Last Christmas

AVON

AVON
A division of HarperCollins*Publishers*
77–85 Fulham Palace Road,
London W6 8JB

www.harpercollins.co.uk

This paperback edition 2011
1

Copyright © Julia Williams 2009

Julia Williams asserts the moral right to
be identified as the author of this work

A catalogue record for this book is
available from the British Library

ISBN-13: 978-1-84756-339-2

Set in Minion by Palimpsest Book Production Limited,
Grangemouth, Stirlingshire

Printed and bound in Great Britain by
Clays Ltd, St Ives plc

Mixed Sources
Product group from well-managed
forests and other controlled sources
www.fsc.org Cert no. SW-COC-1806
© 1996 Forest Stewardship Council

FSC is a non-profit international organization established to promote the
responsible management of the world's forests. Products carrying
the FSC label are independently certified to assure consumers that they
come from forests that are managed to meet the social, economic
and ecological needs of present and future generations.

Find out more about HarperCollins and the environment at
www.harpercollins.co.uk/green

For Ann Moffatt and Rosemarie Williams,
Granny Dreamboats both.

Prologue

Marianne sat back in the comfort of Luke's brand new BMW M5. Every inch of its sleek leather interior screamed luxury, while the latest technogizmos pronounced its top-of-the-range, worthy-of-praise-from-Jeremy-Clarkson status. She glanced at Luke, who oozed confidence with practised ease as he drove with one hand on the wheel. Marianne sighed happily . . .

'What?' he said, laughing at her.

'Just pinching myself,' she replied. 'I still can't believe all this is real.'

'You are daft,' said Luke grinning, before he accelerated into the wind.

It wasn't the first time she'd had to pinch herself since she and Luke had got together. His charm and looks had entranced her from the start, even though she had felt thoroughly out of his orbit. In fact, Luke was so far removed from the sort of man she tended to fall for, the strength of her feelings had taken her by surprise. But there was something mesmerising about the combination of hazel-brown eyes and fair hair, which swept back off a strong, classical-looking face.

Under normal circumstances Marianne would never have met someone like Luke, but, thanks to Marianne's two rich friends, Carly and Lisa, who still seemed to earn ridiculous amounts of money in the City, even with the credit crunch, she had found herself on a skiing trip during February half term. Her teacher's salary wouldn't usually have stretched to that, but at the last minute Carly had pulled out and generously donated her space to Marianne, who then spent a dizzyingly intoxicating week hitting the slopes and revelling in an après-ski environment she could hardly have imagined being part of in her normal life.

She'd met Luke on the first day when, overcome with nerves, she'd fallen flat on her back in front of a group of more experienced skiers. Their laughter hadn't been unkind, but Marianne was already feeling like a fish out of water in the company of these sophisticated beautiful people. She was so far removed from her own world, and they knew it. Now she felt that she'd proved herself for the ugly-duckling klutz she undoubtedly appeared to them.

Luke was the only one who hadn't laughed. Instead, he'd swept her up in those strong arms and offered to teach her to ski. Throughout that week he'd treated her with tenderness and affection, combined with infinite amounts of patience at her obvious lack of skiing ability. Marianne had been hugely grateful for his kindness. The fact that Luke was incredibly good looking, charming and clearly fancied the pants off her had also been a great help. He made her feel like a graceful swan, even though she knew the ugly duckling was hidden away somewhere, underneath the ski gear. Being with him was a magical, dazzling, life-changing experience.

Since then, Marianne felt like her feet hadn't touched the ground as Luke whisked her into a world so completely alien to her own. He took her to Henley for the Regatta, to Wimbledon for Finals Day, to Silverstone for the Grand Prix, for weekends away in the country at exquisite hotels

2

where she felt like a film star. Every day with Luke was an adventure, but today he had surpassed all her expectations.

He'd rung the previous night. 'Fancy a weekend at my parents' place in the country?' had been his opening gambit. Marianne's heart had leaped with anticipation. With Luke it was always feast or famine – he was either frantically busy at the weekends, or impulsively spiriting her off somewhere exciting. Which was wonderful but sometimes Marianne wished they could put their relationship on a bit more of an even footing.

Did this mean that finally he was going to introduce her to his family? He'd met her parents twice now. She'd been nervous as hell on both occasions, but Luke was his usual charming self, and professed himself delighted by Marianne's rather tame suburban home. Her parents had been charmed, and her mum, who was desperate for grand-children, had to be restrained on at least one occasion from asking outright when Luke was going to join the family.

Marianne had expected a reciprocal invitation, but so far it had been unforthcoming. Luke, it seemed, was happy to meet her family, but evasive about his own. She knew he'd got money, knew he worked for the family firm in property development – 'building eco towns' was how he put it – but, apart from that, the crumbs of information he'd scattered had been few and far between. Perhaps if she weren't so dazzled by his brightness, she would have asked more questions earlier. Besides, if he wanted to tell her things, she surmised, he would. She didn't want to pry.

They were driving through winding country lanes, the late summer sun warming the car and casting long shadows on fields ripe with corn and bursting with abundance. Cows wandered contentedly through fields, and birds sang in hedgerows. It was the countryside of her dreams. Of her imagination. As a child Marianne had been obsessed with

3

stories about children having adventures in the country-side: The Famous Five, Swallows and Amazons, the Lone Pine Club all seemed to lead much more exciting lives than she did in the dull North London suburb that she called home. Marianne's favourite television programmes, *The Waltons* and *Little House on the Prairie*, provided further confirmation that her ideal future involved a cosy country cottage, being married to a man who adored her, having several rosy-faced children and, of course, heaps of animals. Their square handkerchief of a garden not allowing for pets, Marianne had been determined to make up for that as an adult.

Growing up in a grey London street, Marianne had always felt stifled and hemmed in by the city. She was never happier than when she was out on a long country walk, breathing in the fresh air and feeling at the mercy of the elements. It had long been her dream to live somewhere like this.

'This is fabulous,' Marianne said. 'What a wonderful place to live.'

'It's okay, I suppose,' said Luke dismissively. 'But I get a bit bored being a country bumpkin.'

'Really?' Marianne was incredulous. She couldn't under-stand why anyone coming from here would ever think about leaving.

'Nearly there now,' said Luke, manoeuvring the car round an incredibly slow tractor, before putting his foot down and racing through the lanes at an exhilarating speed. The wind whipped back her hair and the sun shone bright on her back. It felt fantastic to be alive.

And then, suddenly, there it was. They came round a bend, and there before them, in the middle of a vast lawn – across which *peacocks* were wandering – was an imposing Tudor house, complete with two wings, Elizabethan towers, black and white timbering and pretty gables. Marianne felt her jaw drop. Finally she was seeing Hopesay Manor, home to the Nicholas family for generations, and where Marianne's future might lie.

'*This* is the family home?' she squeaked.

Luke glanced across at her in amusement.

'Didn't I say?'

'Not exactly,' said Marianne. She'd imagined Luke living in a huge house, of course. But she'd thought it would be a rockstar kind of house, with its own pool and tennis court in the back garden. But this, this was a mansion. Vast didn't quite cover it.

'Well, it's not technically where I grew up. My parents have a pad a bit closer to Hope Christmas. Hopesay belongs to my grandfather. Not that he's here much. Silly old sod still insists on globetrotting, even at his age. I don't think he's been back here for more than a day or two for years.'

Luke said this with unaccustomed savagery and Marianne was taken aback by his sudden vehemence.

'Don't you get on with your grandfather?'

Luke smiled. 'Oh, the old bugger's okay, I suppose. He's just a bit blinkered about the way the world works these days. Insists we have duties to our people, as he puts it. He likes to think we live in some bygone feudal age, when everyone doffs their cap to Sir. He can't see the world's changed.'

'What does he think about your eco towns then?'

'He doesn't know anything about them,' admitted Luke. 'I'm the only one interested in the business side of things in this family. My mum and dad are more into playing bridge and drinking G&Ts than anything else. They're pretty shortsighted too. I run the show in his absence. If he doesn't like the way I do things he should turn up at board meetings more.'

He swept the car into the circular gravel drive in front

of the house and they got out and crunched their way up the path to the house. The large oak door was about twelve foot high and looked immensely imposing. Marianne could just about make out an inscription carved in stone above the door. Something about being happy and owing it to God.

'What does it say?' she asked, squinting up to try and see better.

'Oh, nothing important.' Luke dismissed her question with a careless wave, and lifted the brass door knocker and banged it really hard. That, too, was unusual, Marianne noted, as it seemed to depict a man – or was it a man? – wearing some kind of long robe and crushing a serpent underneath his feet. Marianne wanted to ask but, put off by Luke's evident lack of interest in anything remotely connected to the house, she fell silent. Luke impatiently banged the knocker again, and eventually a rather dusty-looking retainer, who could have been any age from fifty to a hundred, came and opened the door.

'Ah, Mr Luke, sir,' he said. 'It's been a while.'

'Hello, Humphrey,' said Luke. 'This is my friend, Marianne.' Why doesn't he say girlfriend, Marianne thought, with a disappointed lurch of her heart. 'I just thought I'd show her round the old pad before we go to see the folks.'

Humphrey nodded, and disappeared somewhere into the bowels of the house, while Marianne stood and looked at the vast hallway in awe. Compared to the suburban London semi that she called home, this was massive. The hallway was panelled in dark oak, and pictures of people in old-fashioned dress lined the stairs, which swept upwards to an imposing landing above. The black and white tiled marble floor echoed as she walked on it. She felt fantastically overexposed in such a huge space. Marianne's stomach contracted. This was so different from where she grew up. How could she possibly ever fit in here? Surely now Luke had her on his home territory it was only a matter of time before he saw it too?

'Jeez, it's dark in here,' said Luke, and opened some shutters to let in the evening light. Motes danced in the beams cast by the setting sun, dazzling Marianne as she stood, silently drinking it in.

'Well, what do you think?' said Luke.

'It's fantastic,' murmured Marianne.

He drew her to him, and her heart thumped erratically as he kissed her on the lips. Marianne felt a familiar flutter in her stomach. She had never desired someone as strongly as she desired Luke. It terrified her how much she wanted him. Suppose he didn't want her as much?

'There's a four-poster in the master bedroom,' he said mischievously.

'We can't,' she protested. 'Not here.'

'There's no one here but us,' said Luke. 'Who's to know?'

'Er – your butler?' She went out with a man who had a butler? This felt so surreal. Any minute she was going to wake up.

'He won't say anything. Besides, he's as deaf as a post so you can be as noisy as you like,' said Luke, with a grin on his face that was impossible to resist.

He dragged her giggling by the hand up the stairs, pointing out various ancestors en route: 'The original Ralph Nicholas, went with Richard I to the Holy Land; Gabriel Nicholas, hid in the priest hole under Edward VI and lived to tell the tale; Ralph II saved Charles II at the battle of Worcester, nada, nada, nada . . .'

'How can you be so dismissive?' said Marianne. 'I mean, in my family the height of historical interest is the time when Great Aunt Maud stood next to George VI at Windsor Park. I come from a noble line of labourers and serfs. This is . . . just . . . incredible. I'd love to have this kind of ancestry.'

'You wouldn't if you knew my family,' said Luke, with a grimace. 'With power comes responsibility, manners maketh the man. We have a duty of care. We even have a Latin family motto, *Servimus liberi liberi quia diligimus*, which translates as: "Freely we serve, because we freely love". Having that shoved down your throat from birth is pretty stifling.'

'Oh,' exclaimed Marianne. They had come to the landing, and Luke flung open the window shutters to reveal a land-scaped lawn complete with fountains, walled gardens and, in the background, a deer park. 'This is amazing. You're so lucky.'

'I *am* lucky – to have found you,' he said, and her heart skipped a sudden beat. *This* was why she was with him. For the way he looked at her as if she was the only woman in the world. For the way he made her feel so incredibly special. All her doubts and anxieties disappeared as Luke took her hand and knelt down. 'I wasn't going to do this now, but seeing you here looking so incredibly sexy, I can't resist.'

Oh my God, Marianne thought, was he going to . . .?

'Hang on, I've forgotten something . . .' Luke ran over to a set of curtains which was lying in a corner and unhooked a curtain ring. He came running back, fell back down on his knee, and said, 'Now, where were we?'

Marianne stood motionless as he kissed her hand, slipped the curtain ring onto her engagement finger, and said, 'Marianne Moore, will you marry me?'

'Yes,' she whispered. She didn't have to think for a second; this was what she'd wanted her whole life, to be with a man she loved and live in a wonderful place like this. 'Yes, of course I will.' And suddenly she was in his arms, and they were running through the house shrieking with delight.

A sudden slam of the door brought them both to their senses.

8

'What was that?' said Marianne.

A bell rang impatiently from the hall, and they ran to the banisters to look down.

A smallish, elderly, dapper man stood in the hallway looking rather cross.

'Grandfather?' Luke's face was a picture of shock and dismay.

'Luke, my boy, is that you?' the man said. 'I can see I haven't come home a moment too soon.'

Part One

I Gave You My Heart

Last Year

December 22

Sainsbury's was heaving. Catherine, already feeling hypo-critical that she was here at all, felt her heart sink as she saw the hordes of people ravaging through the super-market, frantically grabbing things from the shelves as if they were in the last-chance saloon and they might never have the chance to shop again. For God's sake, she felt like saying, as she saw people staggering past with trolleys full to the brim with hams and turkeys, mince pies and brandy butter, and the inevitable bottles of booze, it's not like we're all going to starve, is it? Then she berated herself. After all, *she* was here too, wasn't she?

But only for the necessary items, things she'd forgotten, like brandy butter and Christmas pud. Mum had prom-ised to make both, but uncharacteristically for her had forgotten, so Catherine was grumpily facing the seething hordes, all of whom looked as miserable as she felt. She wondered if she should give up and try and make them herself. It's what the bloody Happy Homemaker was always telling people to do.

No, Cat, she admonished herself. There were still pres-ents to wrap, a turkey to defrost, vegetables to prepare, a house to make ready for the guests (and one which would unscramble itself as fast as she tidied) – she *really* didn't have time to make a Christmas pudding. Not even that

13

one from her Marguerite Patten cookbook, which could actually be made the day before. The Happy Homemaker could go stuff herself.

'That sounds like an eminently sensible idea to me.' A little old man in his seventies, wearing a smart gabardine coat, doffed his hat to her as he walked past with a basket under his arm.

'I beg your pardon?' Cat looked at the man in astonishment. She must have been wittering on to herself again. She had a bad habit of doing that in supermarkets.

'I was just observing that you could for once let yourself off the hook,' said the man. 'Christmas isn't all about perfection, you know.'

'Oh, but it is,' said Catherine, 'and this is going to be the most *perfect* Christmas ever.'

'Well, I certainly hope so,' said the man. 'I wish you a very happy and peaceful Christmas.' And with that he was gone, disappearing into the crowd while Catherine was left pondering how on earth a complete stranger seemed to know so much about her. How very, very odd.

Catherine took a deep breath and ploughed her trolley into the fray. Christmas muzak was pumping out, presumably to get her into the spirit of the thing. Not much chance of that, when she had felt all Christmassed out for months. Bugger off, she felt like shouting as a particularly cheesy version of 'Have Yourself a Merry Little Christmas' blared out. Look at all these people. Do any of them look bloody merry?

Christmas seemed to start earlier and earlier every year, and, now she had children in three different schools, Catherine had been obliged to sit through as many Christmas performances (one year she really was going to get Noel to come to one of these things if it killed her), which varied from the sweet but haphazard (her four-year-old's star turn

14

as a donkey), through the completely incomprehensible (the seven and nine-year-olds' inclusive Nativity, which had somehow managed to encompass Diwali, Eid and Hanukkah – an impressive feat, she had to admit), to the minimalist and experimental concert put on at the secondary school her eleven-year-old had just started. One of the reasons Catherine had wanted a large family was so she could have the big family Christmas she'd always missed out on by being an only child. Catherine had always imagined that she'd love attending her children's carol concerts, not find them a huge chore. And no one told her how much work it would be preparing Christmas for a family of six, let alone all the hangers-on who always seemed to migrate her way, like so many homing pigeons, on Christmas Day.

'Next year, remind me to emigrate,' Catherine murmured to herself, as she propelled herself through the mince pie section. Bloody hell. Once upon a time people had bought (or most likely made) mince pies. Now Sainsbury's had a whole section devoted to them: luxury mince pies, mince pies with brandy, mince pies with sherry, deep-filled, fat-free, gluten-free, dairy-free, probably mince-free for all she knew. The world had gone mad.

'Me too.' The woman browsing the shelves next to her gave a wry laugh in sympathy. She looked at Catherine curiously. Oh God, no . . .

'Aren't you—?'

'Yes,' sighed Catherine, 'I'm afraid I am.'

'I'm such a huge fan,' said the woman. 'I keep *all* your recipes. I don't know what I'd do without your lemon tart.'

'Thanks so much,' said Catherine, guiltily hoping the woman wouldn't notice what she had in her shopping trolley, otherwise her cover as the provider of all things home-made was going to be well and truly blown. 'I'd love

15

to stop, really I would, but unfortunately I'm in a tearing hurry. Places to go, people to see. I'm sure you'll understand. Have a wonderful Christmas.'

Catherine felt terrible for rushing off. The poor woman had seemed nice and it was churlish of her to react like that. But couldn't she have five minutes' peace just to be herself and not the bloody awful persona who seemed to be taking over her life? She went to join one of the many huge queues that had built up as she'd wandered round the store, and caught sight of the latest version of *Happy Homes* by the tills. There she was resplendent in a Santa costume and hat (why, oh why, had she let herself be persuaded to do that shoot?), next to a headline that bore the legend, 'The Happy Homemaker's Guide to the Perfect Christmas.'

Any minute now someone in the queue was going to make the connection between the Happy Homemaker and the harassed woman standing behind them, and realise she was a big fat fraud. Catherine didn't think she could stand it. She glanced over at the serve yourself tills, where the queues looked even more horrendous, and people were indulging in supermarket rage as the computers overloaded and spat out incorrect answers or added up the bills wrong.

Catherine looked in her trolley. She had been in Sainsbury's for half an hour and all she had to show for it were two packets of mince pies, a bag of sugar, a Christmas pudding, and no brandy butter. At this rate she would be queuing for at least half an hour before she got served, by which time every sod in Sainsbury's would probably discover her alter ego.

Furtively looking each way up the shop, Catherine pushed her trolley to the side of an aisle and, feeling rather as she had done aged fourteen when she used to bunk off to smoke behind the bike sheds, she abandoned it. They could manage without brandy butter for once. And no one liked Christmas puddings anyway.

As she fled the supermarket, 'Have Yourself a Merry Little Christmas' was still pumping out. Bah humbug, she thought to herself.

Gabriel sat in the lounge, head in his hands. The fire had long gone out and, as the wintry evening drew in, dark shadows were springing from every corner of the normally cosy room. He should make up the fire again. Warm up the place before he went to pick up Stephen. Never had his family home felt so cold and barren.

Stephen.

Oh God. What was he going to tell Stephen? Thank goodness he'd been at the rehearsal for the Village Nativity all afternoon. Thank goodness he hadn't witnessed the latest painful scene between his parents. Gabriel had tried to protect Stephen from the truth about his mother for the best part of seven years, but even he would have had difficulty today.

'You don't understand. You've never understood,' Eve had said, her eyes hard and brittle with unshed tears, her face contorted with pain. It was true. He didn't understand. How could he understand the pain she went through every day, the mental anguish of feeling forever out of sorts with the world and unable to deal with the reality of it?

It was her very fragility that had drawn him to her in the first place. Eve had always seemed to Gabriel like a wounded bird, and from the moment he'd met her all he wanted to do was to care and protect her. It had taken him years to see that, whatever he did, he couldn't protect her from herself. Or from the painful places her mind journeyed to.

'Please let me try,' Gabriel had pleaded. 'If you always shut me out, how can I help you?'

Eve had stood in the house that she had always hated with her bags packed and ready – she'd have been gone without a scene if he hadn't popped back because he'd forgotten to tell her that he was taking Stephen round to his cousins' house after the rehearsal for the Village Nativity, to help decorate their tree – and looked at him blankly.

'You can't,' she said simply. She went up to him and lightly stroked his cheek. 'You've never got that, have you? All this,' she gestured to her home, 'and you. And Stephen. It isn't enough for me. And I can't go on pretending it is. I'm sorry.'

Tears had pricked his own eyes then. He knew she was right, but he wanted her to be wrong. For Stephen's sake as well as his own. Gabriel had spent so many years trying to reach Eve, it was a default way of being. He hadn't wanted to face the truth. There were no more excuses. He was never going to be able to give Eve what she needed. She was a world away from him, and always had been.

'What should I tell Stephen?'

Eve stifled something that sounded like a sob.

'You're a good man, Gabe,' she said. 'Too good for me. You deserve better.'

She kissed him on the cheek, and fled the house towards the waiting taxi, while Gabriel stood in stunned silence. He'd known this moment had been coming from the minute he took her under his wing. She was a wild bird, and he'd always felt that eventually she would fly away and leave him. But not like this. Not now. Not just before Christmas.

Gabriel had lost track of the time while he sat alone in the gathering gloom. It was only now that he was beginning to notice how cold it had suddenly got. How cold it

18

was always going to be now that Eve had gone. He wondered what he was going to do. Whether he'd ever see her again. And what the hell he was going to say to their son . . .

Noel Tinsall stood nursing a pint at the bar in the tacky nightclub the firm had booked for this year's Christmas party, listening to Paul McCartney blasting out what a wonderful Christmas time he was having. Noel was glad someone was. He wondered idly when it would be decent to leave. Probably not wise to go before Gerry Cowley, the CEO, who was strutting his deeply unfunky stuff on the dance floor, leering at all the secretaries. It was only eight o'clock. The party was barely started yet, and already he could see some of the junior staff had drunk more than was good for them. He wouldn't be surprised to find a variety of embarrassing photos doing the rounds on the Internet in the next few days. What was it about the office Christmas party that made people behave so idiotically? Bacchanalian excess was all very well when you didn't have to face your demons at the water cooler the next day.

'Hey, Noel, you sexy beast, come on and dance.' It was his secretary, Julie. Or rather, not his secretary anymore. Not since that jumped-up toerag Matt Duncan had got his promotion. Now Noel had to share a secretary. A further subtle means of making him feel his previous high standing in the office was being eroded. Time was, when people jumped to his beat. Now they jumped to Matt's. Perhaps it was time to get a new job.

Noel hated dancing, but also found it nearly impossible to be rude to people, so before long he found himself in the middle of the dance floor, surrounded by sweaty, writhing bodies, and unable to escape the feeling that everyone was laughing at him.

'You're dead sexy, you know,' Julie was shimmying up

to him, and grabbing his tie. 'Much more than that silly tosser Matt.'

No, no, no! They had always had such a professional relationship, but she was clearly pissed and coming on to him. Not that she wasn't incredibly attractive or anything. And not that Noel wasn't sorely tempted for a moment. Would Cat even know or care if he were unfaithful? Sometimes he didn't think so. Julie was lovely, uncomplicated and she was available. It would be so easy . . .

What on earth was he thinking? Noel shook his head. Definitely time to go.

'Sorry, Julie, I've got to get back,' Noel said. 'Catherine needs me. Kids. You know how it is.' Catherine probably wouldn't care if he were there or not, judging by the notice she took of him these days, but Julie didn't need to know that.

Ducking her alcohol-fumed kiss, Noel made his way out of the club, and into the welcome crisp air of a London December evening. It was still early enough for the third cab he hailed to be miraculously free, and before long he was speeding his way towards Clapton, secure in the knowledge that, despite the amount he'd imbibed, he'd got away without making an idiot of himself.

The cab drew up outside his house, an imposing Edwardian semi down a surprisingly leafy street. The Christmas lights he'd put up with the kids the previous evening flickered maniacally. One of them had no doubt changed the settings again. He bounded up the steps and let himself in to a scene of chaos.

'I hate you.' Melanie, his eldest daughter, came blasting past him and flung herself up the stairs in floods of tears, followed swiftly by his son, James, who shouted, 'I so hate you too!'

'Nobody hates anyone round here, I hope,' he said, but

he was ignored and the house rang to the sound of two slamming doors.

'Don't want to go to bed. Don't WANT to!' his youngest daughter Ruby was wailing as Magda, their latest inefficient au pair, tried to cajole her off the floor of the playroom where she lay kicking and screaming. Noel noted with a sigh that the bookshelf had fallen down *again*. He wasn't quite sure he was up to dealing with that, so he poked his head in the lounge and found Paige, his middle daughter, surreptitiously scoffing chocolate decorations from the tree.

'Where's your mother?' he asked.

'She's on the bloody blog,' said Paige calmly, trying to hide the evidence of her crime.

'Don't say bloody,' said Noel automatically.

'That's what Mummy calls it,' said Paige.

'And don't steal chocolate from the tree,' added Noel.

'I'm not,' said Paige, 'Magda said I could.'

'Did she now?' Catherine came down the stairs looking frazzled. 'Come on, it's your bedtime.'

She kissed Noel absent-mindedly on the cheek before going into the playroom to calm down not only the howling Ruby, but also a semi-hysterical Magda, who was wailing that these children were like 'devils from hell'.

Noel stomped downstairs to the kitchen, got himself a beer, and sat disconsolately in front of the TV. Sometimes he felt like a ghost in his own home.

'Angels! I need angels!' Diana Carew, formidable representative of the Parish Council, flapped about like a giant beached whale. It was hard to see how someone so large could actually squeeze through the tiny door of the room allocated for the children to sit in while they awaited their turn to go on stage, but somehow she managed it.

21

Marianne suppressed the thought as being bitchy, but it was hard to take her eyes from Diana's enormous bosoms. Marianne had never seen anything so large. And it gave her something to smile about while she sat freezing her arse off in this godforsaken tiny village hall watching the Hope Christmas Nativity taking shape, knowing damned well that any input from her was not actually required. In the weeks leading up to the nativity, Marianne had become grimly aware that she was only on the team because every other sane member of the village, including her colleagues at the village school, had already opted out.

Everyone, that was, apart from the very lovely and immensely supportive Philippa (or Pippa to her friends). Marianne had only got to know Pippa in recent weeks, since she'd been co-opted into helping on the Nativity, but she was fast becoming Marianne's closest friend in Hope Christmas and one of the many reasons she was loving living here. Pippa was bearing down on her now with a welcome cup of tea and a barely suppressed grin. Together they watched Diana practically shove three reluctant angels on the stage, where they joined a donkey, two shepherds, some lambs, Father Christmas and some elves, who were busy singing 'Have Yourself a Merry Little Christmas' as they placed gifts at Mary and Joseph's feet.

'I have to confess,' Marianne murmured, 'this is a rather, erm, *unusual* retelling of the Nativity. I can't recall elves from the Bible.'

Pippa snorted into her tea.

'I'm afraid the elves are here to stay,' said Pippa. 'Diana does a slightly altered version every year, but the elves always feature. It dates back to when she ran the preschool in the village. And it's kind of stuck. Everyone's too frightened of her to tell her to do it differently.'

'Are there actually any carols involved in this?' Marianne

asked. So far, on the previous rehearsals she'd been roped into, the only thing remotely carol-like had been 'Little Donkey'.

'Probably not. At least this year she's dropped "Frosty the Snowman",' said Pippa. 'Mind you, it took the Parish Council about three years to persuade her that really, it didn't *actually* snow in Bethlehem on Christmas Day. She loved that snow machine.'

Marianne hooted with laughter, then quietened down when Diana hushed her, before continuing to marshal the children into order and berate them when they'd got it wrong. She was quite formidable. And her version of the Nativity was sweet in its way. It was just . . . so long. And had so little to do with the actual Nativity. Marianne liked her festive season – well, festive. There was a purity about the Christmas story that seemed to be lacking in everyday life. It was a shame Diana couldn't be persuaded to capture some of that.

The natives were getting incredibly restive and parents were beginning to arrive to pick their offspring up. Diana looked as if she might go on all night, till Pippa gently persuaded her that they still had the dress rehearsal to have another run-through of everything.

Marianne quickly helped sort the children out of costumes and into coats and scarves. The wind had turned chill and there was the promise of snow in the air. Perhaps she might get a white Christmas. Her first in Hope Christmas, with which she was falling rapidly in love. Her first as an engaged woman. This time next year she would be married . . .

Nearly all the children had been picked up, but there was one small boy sitting looking lonely in a corner. Stephen, she thought his name was, and she had a feeling he was related to Pippa somehow. Marianne hadn't been in the village long enough to work out all the various

23

interconnections between the different families, many of whom had been here for generations. Marianne didn't teach him, but the village school was small enough that she'd got to know most of the children by sight at least.

'Is your mummy coming for you?' she asked.

The little boy looked up and gave her a look that pierced her heart.

'My mummy never comes,' he said. 'But my daddy does. He should be here.'

Poor little mite, thought Marianne. Presumably his parents had split up. He couldn't have been more than six or seven. Perhaps she should go and let Pippa know he was still here.

Just then she heard a voice outside the door. A tall man entered, wearing a long trenchcoat over jeans and a white cable-knit jumper. A thick stripy scarf was wound round his neck. This must be Stephen's dad.

'Daddy!' Stephen leapt into his dad's arms.

'Woah,' said the man. He turned to Marianne and looked at her with deep brown eyes. Soulful eyes. She shivered suddenly. There was such pain in those eyes. She felt she'd had a sudden glimpse of his soul. She looked away, feeling slightly uncomfortable.

'Sorry I'm so late,' he said. 'Something came up.'

There was something about the way he said it that made Marianne feel desperately sorry for him. He looked as if he had the weight of the world on his shoulders.

'Is everything all right?' Marianne nodded at Stephen who was clinging to his dad's side for dear life.

Stephen's dad stared at her, with that same piercingly sad look his son had.

'Not really,' he said. 'But it's nothing I can't handle. Come on, Steve, I'll race you to your cousins'. I think it's going to snow tonight.'

24

'Can we build a snowman?'

'Of course,' said his dad. He turned back to Marianne. 'Thanks again for looking after him.'

'No problem,' said Marianne, and watched them go. She wondered what was troubling them so deeply, then dismissed it from her mind. Whatever their problem was, it was no business of hers.

This Year

Chapter One

Marianne stood in the kitchen fiddling with her drink, looking around at the shiny happy people spilling into Pippa's cosy farmhouse, an old redbrick building with a slate roof, oozing tradition and country charm. Marianne had fallen in love with this kitchen and its wooden beams, battered old oak table and quarry-tiled floor. It was all so different from the pristine newness of her family home, and exactly the sort of house she'd hoped she and Luke would live in when they were married. *When they were married*. What a distant dream that now seemed.

If it wasn't for Pippa, who had been like a rock to her this last week, she'd never have come. She wondered how soon she'd be able to leave. It was strange how numb she felt, as if she was detached somehow from those around her. There was ice running through her veins. The life she had hoped for and looked forward to had fizzled away to nothing. She had no right to be here, no right to join with these happy relaxed people. Her new year wasn't a new start but a reminder of everything she'd lost. How could her life have altered so abruptly – so brutally – in just a week? She should be in Antigua with Luke right now, just like they'd planned. Instead . . .

Don't. Go. There. Marianne had been determined not to

cry tonight. She knew she was the subject of a great deal of gossip. How could she not be in such a small place? It was the downside to country living of course, and one she didn't relish now. But Pippa had persuaded her to hold her head up high and come out tonight to her and Dan's annual New Year's bash. So come she had. She wouldn't have done it for anyone but Pippa, but the way she was feeling right now, Pippa was the only good thing left about living in Hope Christmas. Not that she was going to stay here much longer. Not after what had happened. As soon as school started next week, she'd look for a new job and go back to London where she belonged.

Marianne watched the crowds surging in and out of the comfortable farmhouse, which seemed Tardis-like. Pippa and Dan had the enviable knack of making everyone feel welcome – Dan was on hand pouring bubbly for all the guests while Pippa worked the room, making sure that the grumpy and irascible (Miss Woods, the formidable ex-head teacher of Hope Christmas primary, who had stomped in with her wooden stick, declaring her antipathy towards New Year: 'Never liked it, never will,') were mollified with mulled wine; the shy and retiring (Miss Campion, who ran the post office, and Mr Edwards, who played the organ in church) were encouraged to fraternise; and the party animals (including Diana Carew, those enormous bosoms taking on a life of their own on the dance floor) had room and space to throw some shapes in Pippa and Dan's new conservatory.

'More fizz?' Dan was suddenly at her side refilling her glass. Was that her third? Or fourth? She probably should eat something. She hadn't eaten properly all week, and the bubbles were going straight to her head. She was starting to get a slightly surreal floating feeling. Perhaps she was going to be all right after all. No one had paid her any attention yet, so perhaps she wasn't the hot topic of discussion she imagined.

Or maybe not. Marianne wandered into the hall, where three people in animated conversation suddenly went silent as she approached. Feeling uncomfortable, she left, only to hear one of them cattily hissing, 'Well, to be honest, it was never going to work was it, the lord of the manor and the teacher?'

Blinking back tears, Marianne knocked back her champagne and grabbed a bottle from Dan, who looked rather taken aback. Marching up to Pippa, she said, 'Fancy getting absolutely bladdered?'

'Are you sure that's such a good idea?' said Pippa cautiously.

'Never been surer,' said Marianne as the strains of 'Girls Just Wanna Have Fun' filled the room. 'My mum always says hold your head up high and sod the consequences. Come on, let's dance.'

An hour later, all danced out, and having moved on from champagne to vodka and orange, Marianne's emotions had lurched from deep misery to a wild ecstasy that bordered on the unhinged. So what if her engagement was over? She was young, free and single again, it was time she took control of things. There must be *some* decent men at this party.

Having worked her way around the entire confines of Pippa's house and discovering that, no, there really weren't any decent men there, Marianne's cunning plan to start the New Year was beginning to look a little shaky. Perhaps it was time for plan A – an early night. Marianne was heading for the hall when the doorbell rang. No one appeared to be taking any notice, so she went to answer it. Standing

28

there was a dark-haired man who looked vaguely familiar. He had the most amazing brown eyes.

'You'll do,' said Marianne, grabbing him by the hand and dragging him into the conservatory.

'Er, I'd better just tell Pippa and Dan I'm here,' he said, before she could get him onto the dance floor.

A wave of sobriety suddenly hit Marianne. What was she doing? She never ever behaved like this. What must this stranger have thought of her? But a more reckless side of her said, so what? It was New Year and her life was in tatters. She quickly brushed her embarrassment to one side, grabbed herself another vodka and orange and started dancing wildly to 'I Will Survive'.

Someone shouted, 'It's nearly midnight.' Suddenly, without warning, her sense of joyous abandon deserted her. Midnight. The countdown to New Year. Everyone singing 'Auld Lang Syne'. Suddenly Marianne couldn't bear it. She stumbled out into the garden, barely noticing that the temperature was below freezing. The alcohol coursing through her veins was keeping her warm. She sat down on a bench, and stared up at an unforgiving moon. The Shropshire hills loured out of the darkness at her, appearing gloomy and oppressive for the first time since she'd been here. She looked back into Pippa's warm, friendly house, full of bright lights and cheerful people. Everyone was having such a good time and she was out here in the cold on her own, sobbing her heart out.

The back door opened and a shadowy figure came towards her.

'Anything I can do?' it said.

'10, 9, 8 . . .'

'Nothing,' sobbed Marianne. 'My life is a disaster, that's all.'

'7, 6, 5 . . .'

'Well, if you're sure. Only . . . you seemed . . . sorry, forgive me. None of my business. I'd better go in. You know.'

'4, 3, 2, 1 . . . HAPPY NEW YEAR!' Screams and shouts came from inside. Marianne suddenly felt hatred for all these people she didn't know who were having such a good time, and suddenly she couldn't bear this stranger's kindness. She didn't want kindness. She just wanted Luke.

'Yes, you'd better,' she spat out.

'Oh.' The man looked slightly put out.

'I hate everything,' said Marianne, attempting to stand up, before falling back in the rose bushes. Her unlikely hero came to help her up. She sat up, looked into his deeply attractive brown eyes, and promptly threw up on his feet.

Noel sat at his desk wading through emails, most of which were completely irrelevant to him. Did he *really* need to be on the Health and Safety Committee's minutes list? There were emails about three leaving parties at the end of January, he noted, people yet again leaving for 'personal reasons'. The credit crunch was hitting his industry hard; building was always the first thing to go. And without anyone buying all those shiny flats in city centres, there wouldn't be any need for new eco-friendly heating systems designed by the likes of him either. Gerry Cowley had been muttering under his collar for weeks before Christmas about the business needing to be leaner and trimmer. In the past, Noel felt he could have relied on his reputation as the brightest engineer GRB had ever employed, but then Matt had joined the firm. Matt, with his lack of dependants, bright-eyed young-man's energy, and brown-nosing abilities. There was someone heading for the top if ever anyone was. And Noel had a nasty feeling that it would be at his expense.

30

No point thinking about what might never happen. Noel could almost hear his mother's voice. It had been her favourite phrase when he was growing up. Way back when they'd had some kind of relationship, before she'd turned into the mother-in-law from hell and, according to the kids, Granny Nightmare. Not that he'd ever had an easy relationship with his mother. Noel had spent most of his childhood feeling that somehow he'd disappointed her. Particularly after his younger sister was born, who apparently could do no wrong. He envied Cat her relaxed relationship with her mother, Louise, who was Granny Dreamboat in every way possible.

Cat. Something was happening to them. He felt like the sands were shifting beneath him, and the world was changing without him. Ever since Cat had started the blog, and the Happy Homemaker thing had taken off, Noel felt Cat had had less and less time for him. All she seemed to focus on was her work and the children. The money it brought in was undoubtedly welcome, particularly when his own job was looking increasingly dodgy. But when a whole week had gone by and he'd barely seen Cat, let alone spoken to her, he wondered if it was all worth it. Sometimes Noel wondered if there was any place in Cat's heart left for him anymore. And, after the way he'd behaved on Christmas Day, he wasn't sure he blamed her.

This was no bloody good. Time he pulled himself together and got on with some work. Noel started to check through the plans he'd drawn up before Christmas for the air-con system at a nearby leisure centre and sighed as he saw the notes from the architects querying why he couldn't match their exact specifications. When would they learn that the real world didn't operate in shiny boxes and out of plush offices but in the mathematical parameters that physical laws allowed you?

31

A head popped round the corner. Matt Duncan, looking mighty chipper with himself.

'Have you heard?'

'Heard what?'

'Davy Chambers has copped it.' Matt drew a finger underneath his throat, with barely concealed glee.

Shit. Dave Chambers was going? Dave was part of the furniture at GRB. If he was going, *no one* was safe.

Noel shivered. January seemed to have set in both chill and drear. He had a feeling a cold wind was blowing over the horizon.

So, Christmas over, turkey stuffed, cooked and eaten, house full of plastic toys – mainly broken – children back at school. It's time for a spring clean. Yes, I know, technically we're still in winter, but post-Christmas, full of New Year's Resolutions, is as good a time as any to clear out the rubbish and it's always good to start the year as you mean to go on . . .

Catherine stopped typing and looked idly out from her eyrie-like study at the top of the house as a half-starved crow flapped and flopped its way across the frosty attic roof. Bloody blog. Bloody Happy Homemaker. Some days she wished she'd never started it. It had begun as a piece of fun, posted between Ruby's feeds, something to keep her sane while she worked out what to do about her career.

Catherine, whose idea of domesticity involved the minimum amount of cleaning compatible with reasonable hygiene requirements, had struck on the idea of an ironic take on the life of the twenty-first-century housewife – or homemaker, a term Catherine utterly loathed. She'd sat down and typed sarcastically:

So, here you are, once a busy, successful businesswoman,

tied to the home with a squawling baby and a stroppy toddler. Is it possible to be a twenty-first-century homemaker and survive, sanity intact? By applying the same management skills to your home life that you did to your work, I believe that not only can you survive, but that you can actually embrace *the challenges being at home throws you. A happy home is one organised with military precision, which is why every Sunday evening we sit down as a family and work out our timetable for the week. A colour-coded copy sits on the freezer, so I can keep track of Kumon lessons and French club and when the baby needs her next set of jabs. I've even perfected my own clocking-in system. It works for me. It can work for you.*

So had the Happy Homemaker been born and, to her astonishment, had been an instant hit. Unfortunately a lot of her readers failed to get the irony and took her far too seriously. Somehow she had stumbled into some kind of zeitgeisty thing where women appeared to be sitting at home with their offspring, willing to be lectured at by a complete stranger about how to run their homes. Soon she was getting several hundred hits a day, and achieving a massive following. Her blog became so popular it even got mentioned in the broadsheets, much to Cat's wry amusement.

Before she knew it, she was doling out domestic advice on a near daily basis, and soon the Happy Homemaker was attracting attention in the wider world, not least from Bev, her old boss from *Citygirl* magazine, where she'd been features editor till the arrival of Ruby had finally convinced her that her home/work balance was all wrong. Bev rang her one day and offered her a regular feature at *Happy Homes* magazine, which involved both time in the office and at home. Coming as it had at a moment when Catherine had been worn out with the demands of a toddler and going stir crazy on the school run, she had jumped at the chance. She'd organised herself an au pair, an office at the top of the house, and had looked forward to reclaiming part of her old life.

If only things were that simple. No one else at *Happy Homes*, including Bev, had the domestic ties she did. A couple of the girls had one kid certainly, but four? No one she knew apart from her and Noel had four children. They must have been quite insane.

Initially Cat had thought that going back to work now that the kids were older was going to be a piece of cake. But as the success of the Happy Homemaker grew, so did the pressures. She was constantly in demand in the media, writing articles for the broadsheets, appearing on radio shows, and even making the odd TV appearance. If she had no domestic ties this wouldn't matter. But while she enjoyed the attention her newfound success was bringing her, not to mention the cash, particularly after years of feeling like a second-class citizen who got pocket money, Cat was struggling with balancing it against her family responsibilities, and was particularly conscious that she was giving Noel a lot less attention than he deserved.

And although the kids were older now, they seemed to need her more than ever, particularly Mel, who was struggling to make the transition from primary to secondary school, and Ruby who had started her first day at school without her mum holding her hand – that bloody Christmas edition photo shoot had put paid to that. Catherine had always managed to take her children on the first day of school, but in Ruby's case she'd failed. In fact, she felt she was failing Ruby a great deal. She never had time to read with her (though, thankfully, Paige was a good substitute) and she'd only just scraped into her (admittedly dreadful) Nativity just before Christmas. When she worked late, she missed Ruby's bedtime. Her children were growing up and, at the moment, it felt like they were doing it without her.

And in the meantime she lectured others on how to run their homes, bring up their children and generally cope with day-to-day living. How ironic that she couldn't manage to retain the slightest bit of control over her own situation . . .

Gabriel held Stephen's hand as they walked down the frosty lane on a crisp clear January morning.

'Look, Daddy, a robin!' said Stephen excitedly. Their breath blew hot and steamy in the cold sharp air. It was a shock to the system to emerge from the warm cocoon of family and friends that Pippa and Dan had been providing him with for the last fortnight. He would have been lost without them. Gabriel's parents, who were his default support network when trouble brewed with Eve, had set off on a much anticipated round-the-world trip to celebrate their retirement. Ironically their retiring had been what had brought him back to Hope Christmas, to take over the farm and try to expand the business with Dan and Pippa who were setting up a service to provide organic farm produce. And it was coming to live in Hope Christmas that appeared to have triggered Eve's latest depression.

Gabriel sighed. He still didn't know how he was going to face the future, but he supposed it was a good thing to be forced back into the real world now that Christmas was finally over. Not that sheep were always that accommodating about the Christmas season. He and Stephen had spent a large proportion of the previous week checking on the pregnant ewes. Luckily Stephen saw going out in the snow as an adventure, and being busy had given Gabriel less time to brood.

Gabriel sincerely hoped that going back to school would be a good thing. Eve hadn't contacted them now for nearly a fortnight and, though Stephen had stopped mentioning it, he knew by the way that he would sigh sometimes, or wander off in the middle of a game, that his son was hurting deeply. He only wished there was something he could do beyond the practical to make it better.

'He's got you,' Pippa had said. 'And us. He knows his mother isn't steady, but he also knows you *are*. So long as you can provide security and love, he'll be fine.'

Wise, wonderful Pippa, with more than enough troubles of her own to cope with, but always there to catch you when you fell. Gabriel would have cracked under the strain if it hadn't been for the support of his favourite cousin. Although Pippa was more like a sibling than a cousin, growing up as they had on neighbouring farms, spending a blissful childhood scrumping and fighting and fording streams together. Pippa, a year older, had always been the grown-up, there to bandage his wounds or salve his wounded pride when he'd come off the worse in a playground fight. And she was still doing the same thing. He'd be lost without her.

The robin hopped away and Stephen ran on ahead down the lane, pretending he was an aeroplane. It was good to see him so carefree for once. He was far too solemn usually, and Gabriel continually worried about the effect that events would have on him. Whatever Pippa said, it wasn't going to be easy for him coping without his mother. Flaky and all as Eve was, she did love Stephen, and it was clear that he missed her badly.

As indeed Gabriel did. He felt a sudden constriction in his throat. If only he could have done more for her. If only she'd let him. If only . . . But one of the things he was coming to realise with painful clarity was that, however much he loved her, it wasn't enough, it was never going to be enough. Eve's problems were too big for him to mend. Sometimes if you loved someone, you just had to let them go.

Chapter Two

The Saturday before school had started, Marianne walked with a heavy heart from the little cottage she rented at the south end of the village, down Hope Christmas High Street. Even passing Diana Carew's house wasn't enough to cheer her up. Diana's garden was filled with a huge plastic Santa and several gnomes, and her house was a blaze of flashing reindeer even during the daytime. Marianne turned the letter in her hand over and over again. It was the means by which she could flee Hope Christmas, go back to her old life. A life that didn't include Luke. Was that what she wanted? Could she *really* bear that? Once she left, there would be no turning back. But the thought of never seeing him, never touching him, never hearing him laugh or seeing him turn on that dazzling smile that had made her feel like a million dollars. Never to do any of that again. How could she stay here and be reminded every day of what she'd lost?

Part of her wanted to run home to her mum and escape the pain of walking down the High Street every day and risking bumping into Luke or running into his mother on the rare occasions she strayed into Hope Christmas to visit the beauty salon. All Marianne had to do was post this job application to the primary school in Hendon, where a teaching friend from her London days assured her they were crying out for good staff, and then she could look forward to being back home where she belonged. She had to accept it. Luke had been a mistake. Moving to Hope Christmas an even bigger one.

It was a grey dull day. The clear skies of late December had given way to a glowering gloomy January, with dark snow clouds obscuring the hills for most of the day completely, in keeping with her mood. Marianne had never felt so cold in her life. It was a cold that sapped her strength and seemed to reach somewhere into the core of her being. Even the sight of Miss Woods, the erstwhile head of Hope Christmas primary, whizzing precariously down the High Street on her mobile scooter, flag flapping in the breeze, failed to amuse. Although watching Miss Woods hit a corner too fast and oversteer to compensate, causing the large plastic canopy that covered her mean machine to wobble alarmingly, did draw a small smile. There *would* be things to miss in Hope Christmas, and the eccentricity of characters like Miss Woods was one of them.

Vera Campion at the post office was another. Always there with a ready smile behind the counter, offering hope and cheer to all the inhabitants of the village, especially the elderly, her shy kindly nature – not to mention her short-sightedness – reminded Marianne of a mole. One who was a force of great good for the whole village.

'Marianne, how lovely to see you,' Vera greeted her, but her smile didn't look quite as genuine as normal. 'What can I do for you today?'

'A book of first-class stamps, please, Vera.' Marianne handed over the money and looked at Vera again. She seemed very agitated. Marianne wasn't normally one to interfere in other people's lives, but Vera had been immensely kind to her since she'd come to Hope Christmas, and Marianne didn't like to see her like this. 'Vera, I hope you don't mind me prying, but are you okay?'

'Oh dear,' said Vera. 'Is it that obvious? I've just heard that they want to close me down. It's a government initiative, they say. We're not profitable enough apparently. From the summer all postal services are to be moved to Ludlow.'

'But that's terrible!' exclaimed Marianne. 'How will all your old folk get their pensions?'

Vera's 'old folk' formed the core of her customers, and she protected their interests with the fierceness of a mother hen.

'Exactly,' replied Vera. 'And what about the village as a whole? Along with the pub, the post office is the centre of our community. Without it we'll be lost. But they say that with the building of the eco town, which is nearer to Ludlow, people won't want to come here for their post, they'll just get in their cars and drive instead.'

'Very eco friendly,' remarked Marianne. 'Isn't there anything you can do?'

'I don't know,' said Vera. 'But I do know I'm not going down without a fight. Mr Edwards said I should start a campaign.'

Vera blushed at the mention of Mr Edwards. It was not a very well kept secret in Hope Christmas that she nurtured feelings for the church organist but whether he was the only person in the village not to know, or whether he was too shy to approach her, so far Vera's passion remained unrequited.

'That's a great idea,' said Marianne.

'Perhaps you could help?'

'Oh, I'd love to,' stammered Marianne. 'But I'm not sure how much longer I'm going to be here.'

'Are you leaving us then?' Vera looked disappointed and Marianne felt a pang that someone actually cared. Despite what had happened with Luke, she had started to put down roots here. Luke hadn't been the only draw for coming to the country. From the moment Marianne had first come to Hope Christmas she'd fallen in love. The village, with its quaint high street with pretty little shops full of knick-knacks and fabulous old-fashioned bookshop, its square complete with farmers' market, and its tumbledown workers' cottages was everything she'd hoped for from living in the country. The friendliness, the warmth of the school she taught in, the kids she taught – and Pippa, she would miss Pippa. And the longer she'd stayed the more she loved it. It *would* be hard to tear herself away.

'Maybe,' said Marianne, trying to sound vague. The post office wasn't just the hub of the village, it was the main source of gossip. She didn't really want the whole world to be discussing her business.

Making a hurried excuse, Marianne rushed out of the shop, meaning to march straight to the post box and post her well-worn envelope.

'Oh—' Someone was coming in as she was coming out. And they got rather entangled.

'Marianne, my dear, how lovely to see you.'

Oh lord. Did Luke's grandfather *have* to walk by just now? A reminder that getting out of Hope Christmas was going to be essential for her sanity if she was ever to get over Luke.

'Er, hello.' Marianne still hadn't quite figured out how she should address her erstwhile grandfather-in-law – wasn't he a lord or something? – and now they weren't to be related by marriage, she felt even more awkward.

'How are you, my dear?' The kindness in Ralph Nicholas' voice took her by surprise.

'Not too bad, thanks,' said Marianne.

'If it's any consolation, which I know it won't be,' Ralph continued, 'I think my grandson is an utter fool for letting you go, and I've said so.'

41

'Erm, thanks.' Blimey. That was unexpected. Luke's mum, who had always looked as though she were sucking lemons when she met Marianne, couldn't have appeared more relieved by the turn of events if she'd tried.

'I hope the actions of one Nicholas won't be enough to drive you out of town,' Ralph was continuing. 'I think the school would struggle to replace such a talented teacher as you. I thought that you wanted to make a difference.'

Now he'd touched a nerve. Marianne had got so fed up teaching in London schools where the class sizes had seemed impossibly large. Coming to teach in Hope Christmas village school had been a joy. For the first time in her teaching career she really felt she had the time to do the job she loved properly.

'I did – I do,' said Marianne. 'Actually, I *was* thinking of moving on. I've got a job application to post.'

'Pity,' said Ralph. 'I think you could do a lot of good in this village. Not least by helping poor Vera out. Still, if you're determined to leave . . .'

He looked at her so directly and clearly, she almost felt he was stripping her soul bare. Which was absurd as she barely knew him. But she felt her resolve crumble a little. She did like it here. Maybe she shouldn't rush off home the minute something went wrong. That's what her mum always expected her to do.

As if mirroring her thoughts, Ralph added, 'And don't you think it would be better to face out the situation, rather than running away from it? After all, *you're* not the one who's done anything wrong.'

He smiled at her and doffed his hat, before continuing into the post office and greeting Vera. 'Ah, Vera, a packet of your finest Werther's Originals if you please.'

Marianne stared after him open mouthed. Perhaps Ralph

was right. Perhaps she should stay. Help Vera with the campaign. Keep teaching the kids she loved. Pay Pippa back for being such a good friend. Show Luke what he was missing . . .

She turned the envelope over once more, then crumpled it up and stuffed it back in her pocket. She still hadn't quite made up her mind, but maybe Hope Christmas deserved another chance. And, maybe, so did she.

'Cat, are you in?' Noel walked through the door on Friday night and was met by an eerie silence. The hall light was on, but the rest of the house was dark. Odd. He didn't recall Cat saying that the kids were doing anything tonight. Mind you, she was always accusing him of not paying any attention to their activities, so perhaps she *had* mentioned it and he'd forgotten.

He went down the stairs to the basement kitchen, turning on lights as he went. The house was as quiet as the grave without the children. Much as the constant noise and chaos grated on him sometimes, it was better than this funereal silence. Where was everyone?

There was a note on the kitchen table in Cat's writing.

Noel,

I tried you on your mobile but it was switched off again. (Funny how such a simple sentence could bristle with so much hidden antagonism. Cat was always on at him to turn his mobile on, but he hated being in constant communication with the world, so turned it off unless forced not to. And, whenever he did ring, Cat always seemed to be engaged so he'd long given up trying.) *Magda cut her finger chopping up vegetables* – Noel's eye was suddenly drawn to a pool of blood on the floor by the sink – *so I've taken her to hospital.*

*Mel on sleepover, Regina has everyone else. Back as soon
as I can get away.
Love Cat
x*

Right. So now, instead of settling down with a well earned
beer and a rerun of *Top Gear* on Dave, Noel was going to
have to drag the kids away from Regina, their saintly and
wonderful neighbour, probably feed them, put them to bed,
then wait on his tod till Cat and Magda made it back from
Homerton, which from their many experiences of family
trips to Casualty could be anything up to several hours.
He'd been looking forward to curling up with Cat on the
sofa. Magda was normally out with her disreputable Russian
boyfriend, Sergei, whom Noel darkly suspected was part of
the Russian mafia. Bloody Magda. She ruined everything.
Her life seemed to be one perpetual crisis – if she wasn't
homesick, she'd had a row with the boyfriend. She had to
be the most useless (and sulky) au pair they'd ever had.

Noel left a message on Cat's mobile and then went next
door to round up his children.

'Noel,' said Regina warmly, letting him in, 'do you fancy
a drink? The kids are all fed, and Ali's just come home.'

'Regina, you are an angel sent from heaven, thank you
so much,' said Noel. 'It's been a hell of a week.'

He poked his head into Regina's playroom where two of
his offspring were sharing a sofa with Regina's two youngest,
watching *MI High*.

'James?' he asked.

'With Joel on the Wii,' said Regina.

Satisfied that everyone was quite happy he made his way
down to the basement kitchen, which was a mirror image
of his own and Cat's, and sat down with his neighbours,
reflecting how lucky he and Cat were to have such good

44

mates on their doorstep. Life with four children and a working wife would be impossible otherwise.

'Thanks for this, you two,' he said, as he sipped his beer. 'And sorry to dump on you. *Again*. I don't know what we pay Magda for. It's certainly not to look after the kids. She's more of a liability than all of ours put together.'

'No problem,' said Regina. 'Cat's helped me out more times than I care to mention. It's what friends are for.'

Noel stayed for one more beer, before regretfully deciding he'd better get his charges home. It took him half an hour to round everyone up, and Ruby was only persuaded to go if he promised piggyback rides, but eventually they were through their own front door. Noel made a unilateral decision to dispense with baths that night, and packed the little ones off to bed while he went to prepare something for Cat, Magda and himself to eat.

Top Gear was over by the time he'd finished cooking and cleaning up the mess Magda had left behind. He felt a smidgeon of guilt at the thought that she might actually have hurt herself, but quickly put it away. Magda had cried wolf on so many occasions, he doubted very much that it would turn out to be more than a scratch. He chased James up to bed and turned over to *Have I Got News For You*. There was still no word from Cat. How long did it take to stitch up a finger?

He rang Cat's mobile again but got no reply. In the end, he ate alone in front of the news. He had just dozed off when the phone rang.

'Sorry, I only just got your message,' said Cat. 'We've been stuck in A&E forever and Magda was so hysterical I couldn't leave. But she's being bandaged now, so I hope we won't be too much longer.'

'Oh, okay,' said Noel, feeling somewhat disappointed. 'Your dinner's in the oven.'

'Thanks. I'm really sorry about this.'

'It's not your fault,' said Noel. 'Bloody Magda.'

'Very bloody at the moment as it happens,' said Cat. 'I've never seen so much, in fact.'

'That's not fair. Now I feel guilty,' said Noel. 'Is she going to be okay?'

'Don't,' said Cat. 'She's going to be fine. I, on the other hand, am going completely bonkers. I'll try not to be too much longer.'

'I'll try to stay up without falling asleep,' said Noel. A depressing feature of his mid forties was his uncanny ability to nod off on the sofa. He barely ever saw the end of films anymore.

'If I'm not back in half an hour, go to bed,' said Cat.

'I'll keep it warm for you,' he replied.

'You'd better,' she laughed, and the phone went dead.

Noel breathed a heavy sigh. All thoughts of a cosy evening were gone forever. It was nearly eleven, he may as well go to bed right now, otherwise he definitely would be asleep on the sofa by the time she got in.

Cat went back inside the brightly lit A&E department and sat down on the incredibly hard chair she had spent most of the evening on. Did the person in the NHS responsible for chairs have a particularly sadistic streak, she wondered? Every chair she had ever sat on, in every hospital she'd ever been in, had been incredibly uncomfortable, and usually she'd had to sit on it for hours. She glanced at her watch. It was gone ten thirty. What a waste of a bloody evening. She'd been planning to spend it cuddled up with Noel on the sofa, conscious she'd spent far too many evenings glued to the computer of late.

Trust Magda to manage to slice her finger to the bone. Cat hadn't realised any of her knives were sharp enough.

If it had been anyone else, anyone at all, Cat would have felt sorry for her, but Magda's litany of woes and trauma had left her all empathised out, and, while she had felt duty-bound to sit her down and wrap up the finger after Magda had come round from fainting at the sight of her own blood, Cat had taken her to the hospital while gritting her teeth. It was the only decent thing to do, but for once Cat wished she didn't always feel obliged to do the decent thing and had the audacity to tell Magda to either get useless Sergei to take her in his shiny motor, or send her off in a taxi. In the end, Magda's look of woe, and the sudden flash-forward she'd had to Mel in a few years time, hurt and alone in a foreign country, had been enough to make her rearrange her life at lightning speed. Sometimes having a conscience was a damned inconvenience.

Twenty minutes later Magda emerged, her finger bandaged thickly, her arm in a sling, milking the moment for all it was worth by flirting outrageously with the house officer who'd been unfortunate enough to be assigned to her. He looked so completely overwhelmed, Cat immediately felt sorry for him. Magda was a force to be reckoned with.

'Doctor says I must not work for week,' announced Magda. 'Very bad for finger. Cleaning. Ironing. I must not do.'

'I bet he does,' murmured Cat, thinking frantically ahead to the next week. How many meetings did she have? And could she cancel any of them? She had a feeling Magda's poorly finger was going to prevent her from doing anything remotely like the job Cat had been paying her to do for the last six months. She wished she had the nerve to sack Magda, but trying to find a replacement at short notice was going to be nigh on impossible. Cat was having enough trouble juggling all the demands on her with the cookery book she

47

was working on, as well as the blog and the regular column. She simply couldn't afford to lose Magda – even a useless au pair was better than no au pair. She'd just have to bite her lip and put up with it.

Cat drove silently through the drably dark inner-London streets, not having the energy to strike up a conversation. Even at this late hour it was hideously busy. Cat screamed to a halt behind a night bus disgorging revellers who'd obviously been living it up in town, reminding her of how her life used to be when she wasn't weighed down with the cares of the world. How she envied those young men and women spilling out onto the streets, living their carefree lives of partying and a kebab before bedtime.

Once that had been the way her weekend was too. Once a lifetime ago. Now it was reduced to trips to Casualty with useless au pairs and returning to find the house in darkness. Magda declined the offer of the food Noel had prepared for them and disappeared to her room to hold excitable conversations in Latvian.

Cat sighed. She didn't feel all that hungry now. She put Noel's cold offerings in the fridge, and made her way upstairs. Deep snoring from her bedroom indicated that Noel was already in the land of nod. They had so little time together. And now they'd lost another precious evening. Sometimes Cat worried they would end up having nothing to say to each other by the time the children eventually left home.

She went into the children's rooms, picking up toys, smoothing over duvets and, in Ruby's case, planting a kiss on her cheek. Paige and James both thought they were too big for kisses, and, though once or twice she'd stealthily managed to sneak kisses on them when they were asleep, James had a tendency to roll over and shout 'Gerroff!' and Paige had been known to sit up in a semi-wakeful state and balefully declare, 'You do not kiss me, *ever*!' before falling back to sleep again. Cat stood and looked at them and allowed a blissful contentment to steal over her. Despite the stresses of her day, the sight of her children asleep could never fail to lighten her heart. As an only child she'd always longed for the hustle and bustle of a big family. At moments like this it actually felt worth it.

Satisfied that her children were all well, she snuck back to her husband and undressed silently in the darkness. Noel's snoring had slowed down to more rhythmic breathing. She knew from past experience that he was so deeply asleep he'd need a bomb to wake him up. The feelings of contentment dissipated as she climbed into bed next to him. Noel moved towards her in his sleep, but otherwise didn't stir. Cat shut her eyes feeling defeated and lost. One day her life would run on an even keel. One day . . .

Gabriel strode through the frosty fields that clung around the edges of the hills surrounding Hope Christmas, a cold wind whipping through him. One of his sheep had gone missing and he'd been up early looking for her. Pippa, as ever, had stepped into the breach with Stephen but, having found his errant sheep stuck flat on her back in a ditch, her pregnancy making it difficult for her to get up, Gabriel was now in a hurry to get back so he could at least take Stephen to school. Some days he found the weight of responsibility so crushing he didn't know how much longer he could stagger under it.

'If you still had a proper job . . .' Eve had been wont to cry. She never fully understood what had prompted him to 'drop everything', as she put it, and leave his comfortable job as a marketing consultant, which he had loathed, to retrain at agricultural college so he could take over the running of the farm from his father. How to explain that it was in his blood? He'd grown up farming sheep and had only left it behind because his parents feared for the future of their industry and had wanted him to have a job with more security. But Gabriel had never really taken to city life and had always known that one day he'd go back. When his parents announced their retirement it seemed like the perfect time to do so. He'd loved it from the first, but Eve had never settled.

'If you could be a proper wife . . .' had often been on his lips, but he'd never been cruel enough to say it. Eve, his poor little Evie, couldn't help who or what she was. She'd never been cut out for country living and found the life oppressive. Everyone had warned him he couldn't change her, but Gabriel had been too stubborn to listen, and now he was paying the price.

Where was she? How was she managing without him? He hadn't heard from her in weeks and the sense of loss was still so raw that the pain caught him short sometimes, and he'd find himself blinking away sudden tears that came when he least expected them. Shit. He had to be stronger about this. Stephen needed him. Gabriel couldn't afford to let him down.

Mind you, sometimes his son showed such astonishing strength, Gabriel had to pinch himself to work out who was the child and who was the parent. Stephen seemed to have a knack for knowing just when Gabriel was hurting most, and would sometimes come up and hold his hand, and say, 'It's okay, Dad' in a way that tore at Gabriel's heart. It was at such moments Gabriel's sympathies for Eve's suffering would evaporate and be replaced with cold, harsh fury. How could she have done this to them?

The fury returned briefly as Gabriel strode across the frozen wastes of the land thinking of the life that he'd so badly wanted to share with her. It didn't seem fair. None of it did.

'I think you'll find life isn't very fair,' a voice greeted Gabriel, as he approached the stile leading to the lane that ran down the side of his house.

'What?' Gabriel jerked himself back to the real world to find himself staring into the welcoming smile of Ralph Nicholas, out walking his dog. Where had he sprung from so suddenly and silently?

'Jeez. I must be going mad,' said Gabriel. 'I'm talking to myself now. Sorry.'

'No matter,' said Ralph. 'I know you have a lot to deal with.'

'How?' Gabriel was a little more belligerent than he meant to be. He was uncomfortably aware that his family situation was the talk of the town and hated being the centre of attention. He'd barely ever spoken to Ralph Nicholas, who hardly spent any time in Hope Christmas anymore. How on earth did he know what was going on in Gabriel's life?

'There's not much that happens in this village that I don't know about,' said Ralph. 'Incidentally, do you think it unfair when a fox gets one of your sheep?'

'No,' said Gabriel, 'because I do everything I can to prevent that. If a fox catches a sheep, it's usually bad luck.'

'And if you've done everything you can to help your wife,' said Ralph, 'don't you think you should just accept there's nothing you can do for her? Some people cannot, or will not, be helped. It's just bad luck.'

Gabriel looked at Ralph in astonishment. How had this relative stranger plumbed the depths of his heart so conclusively? He'd never even talked to Pippa about how he really felt about Eve.

'I feel I've failed her,' said Gabriel slowly. 'I wanted to look after her and I couldn't.'

51

'But you can look after your son,' pointed out Ralph. 'I've always found a new hobby very helpful for a broken heart.'

'I don't have time for hobbies,' said Gabriel.

'Well, maybe it's not a hobby you need,' said Ralph. 'But perhaps you could use the considerable talents you have for protection into something that you *can* do something about.'

'What do you mean?'

'Look around you,' said Ralph, encompassing Gabriel's fields and the hills they bordered with a sweep of his arm. 'We take all this for granted. Assume the immutability of it all. But nothing stays the same forever. In case you hadn't noticed, Hope Christmas is under threat. There are moves afoot to change all this.'

'What's that got to do with me?' said Gabriel. 'What can I do?'

'I'd say the post office is as good a place to start as any,' said Ralph. He whistled loudly and his dog, a grey wolfhound, came lolloping up to them. 'Best be off then,' he said.

Gabriel walked on down the lane, shaking his head. He'd heard Ralph Nicholas was eccentric, but not that he was so utterly barking. What did that mad old man know anyway? No one was planning to do anything to Hope Christmas. Why would anyone want to destroy something as beautiful as this? Ralph Nicholas must have got it wrong. And, even if he hadn't, Gabriel had enough problems right now without worrying about the future of his village.

Gabriel strode on down the lane to Pippa's house, where Stephen was contentedly munching his Cheerios.

'Shall I take them in today for you?' he asked his cousin, who was looking distinctly harassed.

'Would you?' she said. 'Lucy isn't too well today. It would be a great help.'

'It's my pleasure,' said Gabriel, and it was. He chased

Stephen and his cousins down the lane to school, whooping and laughing as he pretended to be a monster chasing after them, and a pale weak winter sun emerged from behind the cold grey clouds. It gave him heart somehow. Maybe his future wasn't so bleak after all.

Chapter Three

'Ah, Mrs Tinsall. Thank you for taking the trouble to ring me back.' The voice of the school secretary boomed down the phone, bristling with disapproval that she was speaking to a mother who actually went out to work. Cat had taken advantage of a break in proceedings during the discussion of the cover design for the June issue of *Happy Homes* to check on her messages and clocked to her dismay that she'd missed a call from school. It always panicked her when the school rang.

'No problem,' said Cat, her heart racing. Why was the school ringing her at 3.45? Mum had offered to go and get the kids for her so that she could go to the meeting, Magda claiming her injured finger prevented her from carrying bags and holding the children's hands to cross the road. 'Is dangerous, Cat-er-ine,' she'd said in the annoying singsong voice she always used when she wanted to get out of something. 'I do not want to be danger to the children.'

'I have your children sitting in my office,' said the secretary, 'and I was just wondering if someone was planning to come and pick them up any time soon.'

'*What?*' Cat went cold all over. It was her worst nightmare. It would take her at least an hour to get back, even if Bev (who was gesturing to her to wind up the call) let her go.

'I'm so sorry,' she was gabbling now. 'My mother was supposed to come. Oh God. Erm. I'll try and ring her. See where she is.'

'I'd appreciate it if you did,' said the secretary, not noted for her diplomatic skills, 'I'm not paid to babysit your children.'

Cat put the phone down and said to Bev, 'I'm really sorry, this won't take a minute, can you excuse me?'

Bev rolled her eyes. 'Don't be long.'

Cat went into the corridor and punched in her mum's number. She was shaking like a leaf. Suppose Mum was ill? Or had had a fall? She was normally fit and healthy, but Cat had to remind herself from time to time that her capable mother was now seventy-three. Something *must* have happened to prevent her from picking the children up. She never made mistakes like that.

On the third ring, her mother picked up. 'Hello,' she said.

'Mum, are you okay?'

'Well, of course I am,' said Mum. 'Why wouldn't I be?'

'I was worried about you,' said Cat, trying to remain calm. 'You haven't picked the kids up from school.'

'*What?*' said Mum. 'That was today? I thought you wanted me to do it tomorrow.'

'No, Mum,' sighed Cat, 'I rang last night and said today.'

'You said tomorrow,' replied Mum tetchily.

'I did?' said Cat, convinced that she hadn't got it wrong.

'Yes, you definitely said it was tomorrow,' said Mum. 'I even wrote it down.'

'Sorry, my mistake then,' said Cat, trying to make light of it, but seething inside. She felt guilty about feeling so cross with Mum, who rarely let her down, but panic was making her agitated. 'Can you get there now? The school are pretty frantic and I'm stuck in a meeting.'

'I'll be there in ten minutes,' her mother promised.

Cat rang back the school, mollified the secretary, and went back to her meeting with relief. It was hard enough juggling work and home commitments without disasters like that befalling her. Thank goodness it was so rare, otherwise she'd *really* be in trouble.

'Glad to see you're more cheerful.' Pippa walked into Gabriel's kitchen pushing Lucy's buggy, followed by Stephen and her two boys, Nathan and George. She'd offered to return his favour from the morning and pick the kids up from school. Gabriel had accepted gratefully as he'd spent the morning fence-mending and had got seriously behind on his domestic chores.

Gabriel paused from whistling 'Always Look on the Bright Side of Life' and realised with a jolt that since his meeting with Ralph Nicholas that morning he had been feeling a lot more chipper. He'd gone to work with a will and being out in the fresh frosty air had invigorated him. Even coming back to an untidy, silent house hadn't caused him as much internal wrestling as it normally did. He'd got down to tracking down the socks that always mysteriously vanished under Stephen's bed with an enthusiasm he hadn't felt for ages. Maybe Ralph was right. He just needed to focus on the stuff he *could* do.

'Good day at school?' he asked his son, who nodded his assent before running off to watch TV with his cousins.

'Cup of tea?' he asked his cousin. 'You look tuckered out.'

'I am a bit,' said Pippa. 'Lucy's a lot better now, but we did have a bad night with her.'

'I don't know how you cope with three of them,' said Gabriel.

'Well, what else am I going to do?' said Pippa laughing. 'Slit my wrists? By the way, have you seen this?'

She shoved a leaflet in his hand.

STOP POST OFFICE CLOSURES NOW!!
SAVE OUR VILLAGE!!
PUBLIC MEETING THURSDAY 7.30pm

'Oh, *that's* what he was talking about,' exclaimed Gabriel.
'Who?'

'Ralph Nicholas,' he replied. 'I met him this morning and he was wittering on that I should try and do something about the things I can do something about, not get hung up on trying to help Eve.'

'He's right,' said Pippa. 'I'm going to the meeting. Poor old Vera's beside herself. They want to close her down and move the postal services to Ludlow.'

'But that will be a disaster,' said Gabriel. 'How will people get there? There's only one bus a day.'

'Exactly. You should have heard Miss Woods going on about it today. They could probably hear her in Ludlow.'

Gabriel laughed. Pippa was such good company. It did him good to be around her.

'So, what do you think? I could get Mum to come and babysit for my lot and Stephen could stay over if you like?'

'We-ell . . .'

'Oh, come on, Gabe, it's hardly like you've got a busy hectic social calendar now, is it?' teased his cousin. 'You need to get stuck into something else for a change. It'd help take you out of yourself. Plus it is important. Just think how this place will change without its post office.'

Gabriel stared out of his kitchen window at the bird table Eve had been insistent they'd bought. It had started off, like so many of her interests, as a burning enthusiasm and she went out every day for several weeks to show Stephen the different varieties of birds that were attracted to the garden. But, after a while, she lost interest, and though Gabriel still left food out, it was as if the birds knew she

57

wasn't there any longer. Apart from a lone robin who was pecking at some crumbs, very few of them now came to the garden. But it was time he stopped dwelling on stuff like this and got on with the business of living. Ralph and Pippa were both right. He needed an outside interest.

'Okay,' he said, 'you've twisted my arm. Where do I need to go?'

'Noel, you haven't forgotten your mum's coming on Sunday, have you?' Catherine said before yelling up the stairs to Mel: 'I haven't finished talking to you, young lady!'

Noel walked in on Wednesday evening to the usual chaos. The little ones were arguing over the DVD control, Magda was sobbing hysterically in the corner because Sergei had ditched her – again – James was hardwired into his Playstation and looked like he wasn't going anywhere any day soon, and, as Noel opened the door, he'd heard the telltale thumping of feet on the stairs and slamming of a bedroom door that indicated that Mel was in another of her moods. Though, as Cat often said to him, when wasn't she these days? He couldn't remember the advent of going to secondary school causing the amount of trauma it was evidently causing his eldest but, as his wife frequently pointed out to him, It's Different Now.

'Yes, I had actually. Damn, can't we put her off?'

Cat gave him a withering look.

'You know we can't. I've been making excuses to her since Christmas.'

'Oh, bugger,' grumbled Noel.

'It would be nice if *you* talked to her for once in a while,' said Cat. 'She is your mother, not mine.'

'Yeah, well, you got the lucky straw in that department,' said Noel, unknotting his tie. 'I'd trade Granny Dreamboat for Granny Nightmare any day of the week.'

'Hmm. I'm not so sure of that,' said Cat. 'Granny Dreamboat didn't pick up the children from school today.'

'You're joking,' Noel was stunned. His mother-in-law was always so reliable.

'I'm not,' said Catherine. 'She got the dates mixed up apparently.'

'That's not like her,' said Noel.

'No, it isn't,' said Catherine, frowning slightly. 'Oh, well, no harm done, I suppose.'

A sudden crash from the playroom and a wail had them scurrying.

'That damned bookshelf—' Every week Noel mended the bookshelf and every week someone managed to make it collapse again.

'Can you deal with that?' Cat asked. 'I need to sort Mel out.'

'Oh?'

'Girl talk,' said Cat firmly.

'Right,' said Noel. 'Yes. Bookshelves it is.'

Of late Mel had spent a lot of time huddled with her mother having sobbing fits. It always seemed to be related to women's things. Noel didn't like to ask, or think about that. To him, Mel was still his little girl. The thought that she might be growing up made him very uneasy. His daughter was becoming a woman, and he was feeling tired and old. Sometimes it felt as though the best part of his life was over.

Marianne ducked into the back of the village hall, panting a little. One of the things that had annoyed Luke about her when they were together was how she never managed to get anywhere on time. He did have a point. Since she'd arrived in Hope Christmas, Marianne found it nigh on impossible to walk down the High Street without finding someone to chat to, so she was generally late everywhere. She felt a smidgeon of guilt when she saw Pippa already in the front row. How did she do that? There she was with her three children and much more frantic life than Marianne had, and *she* was never late. Marianne felt a familiar downturn in her emotions. Luke had had a way of criticising her that made her feel pathetic and useless. Could she never get anything right?

There were two empty seats at the back, so she sat down on one of them and hoped that the formidable Miss Woods and Diana Carew wouldn't be taking notes as to who was there or not. Diana Carew, who had of course taken charge, her reading glasses hung about her neck and perched on top of her enormous bosoms, was booming down the microphone about the need to fight back for the sake of their community. Vera, looking more than ever like a frightened mole, got up to speak while Mr Edwards (did anyone ever call him by his first name?) shot her encouraging looks.

'Thank you all so much for coming,' Vera squeaked. 'I've been looking into our options and it seems that we might be able to take our case to the courts and try and stall things for a while. We could also try and diversify. That seems to have worked well in other communities. They've combined their pub with the village shop and post office. That's something we could consider. Thanks to Mr Edwards—' Vera blushed, 'we now have a website, which you can find at www.soshopechristmaspostoffice.com, and I believe he's also set up a petition on the Number 10 Downing Street website, so please do tell all your friends. Miss Woods has kindly drafted us a letter that you can send both to our local MP, the council and the Post Office. We have copies at the front here, or you can download them from the website.'

Vera sat down to a roar of applause, before Diana threw things open to the floor and a lively debate ensued.

'I'm not sure that we really need to go chain ourselves outside the Houses of Parliament—' Diana was saying to a rather enthusiastic teenager, who'd clearly just learnt about the suffragette movement, when the door opened and someone sidled in and grabbed the seat next to Marianne.

'Is this seat taken?'

Of all the seats in the room, why did he have to pick the one next to hers? Marianne stared up into the eyes of the very same stranger whose feet she'd been sick on at New Year.

Chapter Four

'Have I missed anything?' Gabriel whispered. He felt incredibly awkward. He knew the new reception teacher from school, of course he did, but he'd barely spoken to her till New Year's Eve. When first she'd flirted with him, and then she'd thrown up on his feet. He could only imagine how mortified she must be feeling right now. Probably best if he didn't mention any of that.

'Not much,' Marianne whispered back, blushing a little. On their previous encounter he hadn't noticed how pretty she was. Her dark curls fell down her back and her bright blue eyes were alive with intelligence. He felt a pinprick of interest in her, which took him by surprise. 'They've set up a website now and have asked us all to write letters to our MP and the Post Office and so on. That's about it. And now we're getting to the point in the evening where we enter a circular debate in which nothing gets resolved.'

Gabriel sat back to listen and had to conclude that Marianne was right. There seemed to be a division already forming between one group – led by a rather forthright Miss Woods – who seemed to think direct action was called for – 'I'll travel down the motorway on my scooter if I have to!' she declared – and another led by Diana Carew, who felt that it would be unseemly to be campaigning in such a public way. 'We don't want Hope Christmas to become synonymous with thugs,' she kept saying, which elicited a harrumphing response from Miss Woods.

Seeing things seemed to be getting out of control, Mr Edwards took the opportunity to leap to his feet and announce that that wrapped it up for now, but that a steering committee was being formed to tackle the issues head on and anyone who wanted to join it was welcome to sign up.

The meeting ended in noisy confusion as people broke off to chat in animated groups.

'So, are you going to join up?' Gabriel nodded towards the front of the hall where a small crowd, including Pippa and Dan, had gathered.

'Not sure,' said Marianne, who looked ill at ease. 'I'm not much of a committee person . . .'

'You shouldn't have chosen to come to live in a village like Hope Christmas then,' said Gabriel, grinning.

'That was clearly my first mistake,' said Marianne, smiling.

She was relieved to see Pippa come bounding up to them both. 'Come on you two, we need some voices of reason on this committee if it's not going to develop into a mad bunfight between Diana and Miss Woods.'

'Pippa, you are a bugger,' said Gabriel. 'I said I'd come along, I didn't say I'd get involved.'

'Now you know that's not the attitude, cousin of mine,' cajoled Pippa.

'Oh my God. You two are related?' Marianne was utterly mortified.

'Didn't you know?' said Pippa. 'I thought you two knew each other. Marianne, my cousin, Gabriel. Gabe, this is Marianne, she teaches reception at the school.'

'We've met,' said Gabriel.

'Have you?' Pippa looked puzzled.

Marianne was now the colour of a tomato.

'New Year's Eve, your house,' she muttered. 'I was sick on Gabriel's feet.'

Pippa roared with laughter. 'Oh my God. Gabe, you never said!'

Gabriel felt almost as embarrassed as Marianne. 'I didn't think it was polite to, and I think you're embarrassing your friend.'

'Oh, Marianne, I didn't mean to offend you. Come on. Let's go to the pub, so you two can get to know each other properly. Honestly, he doesn't bite.'

It's a kind of magic... That's what I always think about baking. You take four simple ingredients, flour, eggs, butter, sugar, and look what you can achieve with them, anything from fancy cakes to shortbread. And when I was a kid, watching my mother bake was also somehow quite magical...

Catherine paused from what she was typing and sighed. How was it that the words in her head, which seemed so magnificent, always seemed so dull when transferred to the page? Maybe it would be better if she wrote the recipes first and added the linking bits in later? She pulled a sheaf of material out. Granny Dreamboat's Perfect Victoria Sponge, Auntie Eileen's Fabulous Fairy Cakes... she'd stolen recipes from around the family and planned them all for this book, which was meant to be a celebration of basic good, honest home-baked cooking, aimed at the generation of women who'd always been too busy for the kitchen.

It was also in part meant to be a homage to her own mother, a way of saying thank you for all the help and support. Ever since she was tiny, Cat could remember her mum cooking in the kitchen, and following her round, eager to learn how to cook herself. It had only been the two of them, when Cat was growing up, and they had bound their love in the kitchen preparing pastry and roast dinners. So it had seemed appropriate to write a cookbook based on her mother's recipes. Catherine paused for a moment. Was it her imagination, or was Mum being rather tetchy of late? It was unlike her to make mistakes, and she'd been quite vociferous in blaming Cat about the day she hadn't picked the kids up. Yet when Cat had sneakily peeked in Mum's calendar she saw Mum *had* written the right day down. Cat had also spotted a pile of unpaid bills in the kitchen, but, when pressed, Mum had insisted she was up to date on all that stuff. The episode had left her with a slight feeling of unease.

She was probably worrying unnecessarily. Noel certainly thought she was. Maybe Mum had just got a bit behind with her bills. Catherine turned back to the screen, her mind utterly blank. Funny that. It was always so easy writing a blog post or an article for *Happy Homes*. But this? This was like panning for gold in a river where you knew you were only ever going to find lead.

It didn't help that she'd only come up here to start working at nine, and she was absolutely knackered. Mel and James needed to be chased into bed so much later now. She'd practically had to prise them away from watching Dave. Magda, who had reluctantly agreed she was fit enough to cope with childcare duties once more, was out with the boyfriend – the bust-up as usual only lasting as long as it took to send a reconciliatory text message. Noel was out at yet another leaving do. From what he was saying about work, which wasn't much, there seemed to be an awful lot of redundancies at the moment. Reading between the lines, Catherine could tell he was worried. She wished he'd talk to her about it, but he seemed unwilling to, and she didn't like to push it.

Sometimes it felt as if a vast chasm was growing between

them. Cat worried that Noel didn't seem to be as pleased with her success as she might have hoped. She even thought he might resent it slightly. But then he'd come home, muck about with the kids, give her a hand with the tea and it was as if there was no division at all. Maybe it was like that for everyone when they had kids, but sometimes (and she felt guilty for even thinking it) Cat longed for the days before they'd had children, when they only had themselves to please. Life had seemed so much simpler then.

Nowadays she was so exhausted coping with the various needs of the children, the demands of Magda, and the difficulties of her job, she had very little left to give Noel. He deserved better from her, she knew that. But it was so hard to give of yourself, when you had nothing left to give.

How she wished her life was as easy and straightforward as the Happy Homemaker's. *She* wouldn't be reduced to trying to write a cookery book late at night, when the children were in bed. Oh no. The sodding Happy Homemaker would have been up at six to do the housework or prepare that day's dinner. She'd have sorted out reliable childcare so she wouldn't spend her days fretting about arrangements she wasn't sure would be met. She'd be able to effortlessly organise her work life so it didn't impinge on her home life, and no doubt *she'd* always be up for dynamic sex in exciting new positions with her husband at any time of the day or night.

There were times when Catherine really hated her creation, and increasingly she was becoming drawn to the idea that she should actually kill the Happy Homemaker off. The only thing stopping her was the financial reward that her alter ego brought them. If Noel's job *was* in jeopardy, Cat couldn't really do her in. Even if, as Cat sometimes suspected from the bitchy comments that occasionally got left on her blog by people who clearly didn't get the joke, thousands of women up and down the country would rejoice to know the *true* state of affairs chez the Happy Homemaker . . .

Marianne settled down in the corner of the Hopesay Arms feeling completely idiotic. How come she hadn't picked up that Gabriel was Pippa's cousin? She'd been so embarrassed about what had happened on New Year's Eve she hadn't told anyone about it. She rather liked the fact that Gabriel hadn't told anyone either. Well, she would like it once she got over the embarrassment. In the meantime, she was squeezed at the end of a large table, feeling out of place and awkward, listening to Vera talking to Mr Edwards in a pink and enthusiastic manner. It was so crashingly obvious that Mr Edwards had the hots for her as well. Marianne had never seen a couple so well suited and yet so shy of each other. She felt almost voyeuristic. But she'd rather be cramped down here than sitting anywhere near Gabriel, whose mere presence made her feel like a prat.

'You are *so* not going to hide in the corner.' Pippa came marching over and dragged Marianne up to their end of the table. Marianne was about to protest but, realising that Vera and Mr Edwards were oblivious to her departure, decided there was no point.

'I can't talk to Gabriel,' protested Marianne. 'I was sick all over his feet.'

'I wondered what had happened to you on New Year's Eve,' said Pippa. 'The trouble was, I was so pissed by the end of the night, I couldn't remember anything about it. Though I do recall Gabe saying something about having sick on his shoes, I just thought it was his.'

'Yes, well, now you know,' said Marianne, 'and you've embarrassed me enough for one evening. So I think I need to go home *right* now.'

'What you need,' said Pippa, 'is to lighten up and meet

new people. Coincidentally, my lovely cousin needs to do exactly the same thing. So you are going to get to know him and find out that he isn't at all ogrish, and thinks it's quite funny that you threw up on him.'

Pippa pushed Marianne into the seat next to Gabriel before disappearing to the bar. This was excruciatingly awful.

'I'm sorry about this,' Marianne said, thinking it couldn't get any more awkward. 'I had no idea Pippa was so bossy. She seems to have decided we need to bond or something. But it's quite all right, we don't. After the last time we met, I can quite see that you wouldn't be at all interested in talking to me, so I'll just finish my drink and head on home.'

'Don't do that,' Gabriel said. He looked at her with those lovely brown eyes and Marianne had to swallow hard. 'I once went back to a girl's room and did the very same thing. We've all done something silly under the influence.'

'In my defence,' said Marianne. 'It was a bit of an intense night. I hadn't meant to get so drunk, and I certainly didn't mean to come on to you like that. I was on the rebound.'

'I'll try not to take that as an insult,' laughed Gabriel.

'Oh God, sorry, I didn't mean it like that,' gabbled Marianne. 'It's not that you're not attractive or anything—'

'Glad to hear it,' said Gabriel with a grin.

'—but I was feeling a bit desperate and so was behaving quite out of character. It's just not me to be like that.'

'I know,' said Gabriel. 'And I do understand. I've been there too. I'm sorry to hear about you and Luke Nicholas.'

Marianne suddenly glimpsed the pain she'd seen in his eyes at Christmas. She wasn't one for village gossip but she had picked up that Stephen's mum had left them. She felt a burst of solidarity with him. Things hadn't worked out the way they'd hoped for either of them.

'And I'm sorry to hear about your wife,' she replied.

'Probably for the best,' mumbled Gabriel.

'I don't believe that,' said Marianne. 'As a fellow member of the Lonely Hearts Club, I can tell you're lying.'

'And you'd be right,' said Gabriel. He raised his glass. 'Here's to being friends and Lonely Hearts together.'

'To friends and Lonely Hearts,' echoed Marianne and clinked her glass against his. 'To never falling in love again and a pox on heartbreakers everywhere.'

Noel put his key in the lock, and turned it. Damn. Didn't seem to be working. He blinked myopically down at his keyring, which mysteriously had found itself a twin. Oh. Hang on.

'Wrong key,' Noel slurred. 'That's it.' He stood swaying on the doorstep, got the key in the lock, turned, and hey presto.

'Ssssh,' he said to the wall as he fell against it. 'Mustn't wake everyone up.' Cat had been most insistent on that point, after he'd come home from someone's leaving do the previous week and sung 'Pinball Wizard' so that the whole house had heard. He couldn't help it if the DJ had been a *Tommy* fan.

Noel reached out for the light but the bulb popped. Bugger. He fumbled his way down the corridor towards the stairs that led down to the kitchen. There was usually a stash of new bulbs in one of the kitchen drawers.

As he got there he heard a noise. He paused at the top of the stairs.

There was a bang and a muffled shout.

There was definitely someone down there.

Noel crept back to the family room and rooted round in the dark for a suitable implement. He grabbed something long and hard. That would do.

Taking a deep breath and feeling emboldened by the

69

alcohol firing through his veins, he crept back down the stairs again.

Nothing. There was no one there. He must have imagined it.

Noel was about to head upstairs again when he heard the dustbins crash outside. Noel paused, his heart in his mouth. Now what was he supposed to do? It was all very well coming over all Neanderthal and protecting your family in theory. He wasn't quite so sure that he'd really like to put it into practice. Particularly now, when he'd started sobering up rather fast.

He crouched tensely in the dark. There were muffled sounds coming from outside. It clearly wasn't a cat. Then he heard the kitchen window opening. Feeling sick to the pit of his stomach, Noel flung himself into the larder. Some hero he'd turned out to be.

Suddenly there was a loud crash and lots of shouting.

Noel came roaring out of the cupboard with his weapon held aloft.

Light flooded the kitchen.

Cat was standing sleepily in the doorway. 'What the—?'

Noel sheepishly put down his weapon – a plastic cricket bat – to see Magda and her boyfriend sitting helplessly on the floor.

Chapter Five

'What the bloody hell is going on?' Catherine stood in her dressing gown feeling a combination of bewilderment, fury and embarrassment. Sergei and Magda were arguing frantically in Russian and Noel was standing waving a plastic cricket bat in the air.

'I thought we were being burgled,' said Noel.

'I sorry, Cat-er-ine,' – God, that singsong whine again, how Cat hated it – 'I forget key. I not want to disturb. So Sergei say, climb in through window.'

'Did he now,' muttered Cat.

Sergei was looking as apologetic as a wannabe Russian mafioso would allow himself to look. 'It was my fault,' he said. He flashed Cat a smile that was clearly meant to be winning, but which reminded her so much of Vladimir Putin, she felt utterly repulsed. 'I didn't want to make Magda trouble.'

Repressing the comment that Magda could make trouble all by herself, Cat grudgingly accepted his apology.

'It's very late,' she said. 'So, Sergei, I think it's time you went home.'

'Oh,' Magda looked stricken. Oh God. *That* Look.

'What's the matter?' said Cat. She glanced at Noel who clearly was having the same horrified thought she was.

'Sergei, he have nowhere to go,' said Magda. 'He fight with landlord, and now he homeless.'

71

'Well, he can't stay here,' said Noel. They'd always been very strict with their au pairs – they could do what they wanted outside the house, so long as they respected Cat and Noel's rules within it.

'Please No-el,' Magda pleaded, 'he has no bed tonight. He can stay here, please?'

Cat looked helplessly at Noel. It was gone midnight and, if Sergei really had nowhere to go, it was a bit harsh to throw him on the streets. She felt herself weakening. Shit, she always weakened in the face of Magda's dogged persistence. The trouble was, if she didn't give in, she was treated to hours of Magda sobbing and right now it was too late and she was too tired to cope with that.

'All right,' she said. 'He can stay, but just for tonight. I want you to promise me you'll find Sergei somewhere to live in the morning.'

'Oh, thank you, thank you, Catherine, you are very nice person,' said Magda, hugging her with such effusiveness Cat began to think that it might have been better to brave the tears.

She and Sergei quickly disappeared upstairs, as if worried that Catherine might change her mind.

'Well done,' said Noel. 'You're always the one saying we should be tough on Magda.'

'Don't,' said Cat. 'It's late, I'm knackered, and I couldn't cope with the thought of Magda's hysterics.'

'Good point,' said Noel, finally putting down the cricket bat and going to shut the kitchen window firmly. 'I can't believe you left this unlocked.'

'I didn't,' protested Cat. 'I'm sure I locked it after tea, before Magda went out . . . Oh, bloody hell, you don't think she left the window open deliberately so she could sneak Sergei in?'

'I wouldn't put it past her, would you?'

'Bugger that girl,' groaned Cat. 'I am damned if she's going to pull the wool over my eyes again.'

'Do you think it's a secret Russian mafia plot to steal all our valuables?' said Noel anxiously. 'Perhaps I should take the bat to bed with us. Just to be on the safe side.'

Cat looked at him.

'Don't be daft,' she said. 'Sergei's harmless enough. I think if he is a villain he's probably a pretty inept one, or he'd have managed to break into the house properly. Come on, let's go to bed.'

They turned out the lights and headed upstairs, Noel pausing to put the bat back.

'I can't believe you thought that a plastic cricket bat would work,' said Cat, giggling as she climbed into bed. Suddenly she could see the funny side, and the vision of her husband defending their home by swinging a kid's toy bat above his head made her feel a sudden burst of affection for him. She cuddled up close to him. 'What were you going to do, hit the burglar over the head saying "Biff, kapow!" like some kind of cartoon superhero?'

'I hadn't thought that far ahead to be honest,' admitted Noel. 'I just grabbed the first thing to hand.'

'Well, Superman, do you fancy grabbing what's to hand right now?' Cat said suggestively.

Noel grinned.

'Okay, Lois. If you insist,' he said.

Marianne was out walking early on Saturday morning. Now she'd finally come to terms with the fact that she was staying in Hope Christmas, she'd taken to exploring the hillside paths around the village at the weekends. The countryside was stunning, and she was constantly discovering new and unexpected valleys as she followed the sheep paths that crisscrossed the countryside. Often she saw no one apart

73

from the sheep and the odd solitary buzzard flying high in the sky. Even on glowering grey days, of which there'd been many of late, Marianne found it exhilarating to walk here. But on a bright sunshiny day like today, there was nothing like a brisk walk to dispel her wintry gloom and brush away the cobwebs. And she found that it stopped her sitting inside and brooding about Luke, who had been spotted in and around Hopesay Manor recently, according to Pippa. There were rumours afloat that his eco town idea was causing some kind of controversy now, and that he wasn't seeing eye to eye with his grandfather about the project. Marianne knew very little about his plans, but Pippa had snorted when she'd told her where the proposed site was, a low-lying valley a couple of miles from Hope Christmas.

'He's got to be bonkers to build out there,' Pippa had said. 'It's known as the Lake District round here. It floods nearly every year. Even if we have a drought year, the ground's always soggy in winter. I wouldn't buy a house there if you paid me.'

Seeing Luke's plans through Pippa's eyes was doing Marianne good. She had been so seduced by his good looks and easy charm, she'd failed to see a certain ruthlessness in Luke. People in Hope Christmas certainly didn't seem to be all that excited by his eco town or even to like Luke very much. Marianne was beginning to think that just maybe she'd had a lucky escape. And ever more so on days like today, when she climbed over a stile at the top of the steep hill she'd climbed and looked down the valley towards Hope Christmas.

The hillside was scattered with sheep baaing gently in the bracken, and a fresh wind whipped at her hair and made her catch her breath. It felt gloriously wonderful to be alive, to be alone here on the hillside, the only person revelling in the beauty of her surroundings, watching a red

74

kite circling up ahead and listening to the chattering of the rooks in the trees behind her. She had a sudden absurd impulse to run down the hillside, like Laura in *Little House on the Prairie*. It felt like a long time since she'd been so content.

Deciding, in the end, that she was more likely to catch her foot in a pothole and break her neck, Marianne instead made her way down the hill in a sedate manner. Recent rain had made the ground muddy, so she'd probably been wise not to run. She'd just rounded a bend in the path when a black and white collie came bounding up towards her, panting and barking. It came up to her and submitted to her petting. A minute later a little boy came running up. 'Benjy!' he called, 'I've got your stick.' He was followed by Gabriel.

'Oh, hi,' said Marianne, feeling suddenly shy.

'Hi yourself,' said Gabriel. 'You know Stephen, and this is our dog, Benjy. We're out checking on the pregnant sheep. It'll be lambing time before I know it, and I need to start thinking about getting them inside.'

'Don't they lamb on the hillside?' asked Marianne.

'They can do,' said Gabriel, 'I just prefer to get mine indoors.'

'How big's your flock?' said Marianne.

'Not that big,' said Gabriel. 'I've recently taken over my parents' farm. Since the foot and mouth outbreak they'd really downsized and had half the flock they used to. Pippa, Dan and I are planning to expand the business and produce our own beef and lamb and sell that along with the vegetables we grow locally. Dan farms the cattle and I farm the sheep.'

'It sounds lovely,' said Marianne. 'I'm such a townie, I know nothing about farming.'

'Well, maybe I should show you,' offered Gabriel.

'Maybe you should,' said Marianne, smiling.

'Da-ad, come on,' said Stephen, 'I want to go looking for monsters.'

'Oh, and that's the other thing we're doing,' said Gabriel. 'Going on a monster hunt is about the only way I can get Stephen out sometimes. Pippa's brilliant, but I can't always rely on her as a babysitter.'

'It must be tough,' said Marianne with sympathy.

Gabriel gave her that familiar sad look.

'We manage,' he said.

'Da-ad.' Stephen was clearly getting impatient.

'Right, I'd better . . .'

'Yes, of course.' Marianne waved them goodbye and set off down the hill, a small smile playing on her lips. Of all the reasons to stay in Hope Christmas, getting to know Gabriel North better was probably as good as any . . .

'Mum. Let me take your coat,' Noel greeted his mother with a perfunctory kiss. As usual, a feeling of dread came over him when she walked through his front door. Would the kids behave themselves? Would Magda do something shocking? (On her previous visit at Christmas his mother had gone on and on about the horror of meeting Magda in the bathroom exposing her bare midriff.) Would he show her yet again how much he'd failed her in the son department?

Mum hadn't always been so bitter. She'd always had a sharp tongue, true, and Noel and his brother, Joe, had been left in no doubt that their sister, Kay, was the favourite, but when his dad died things had started to go badly wrong. It hadn't been Noel's fault that Dad being ill had coincided with Cat's first pregnancy. He'd done his best to balance the two sets of demands, but it had been incredibly hard being in London and his parents being in Stevenage, and Noel was conscious at times he hadn't been the conscientious son he'd wanted to be. The only comfort at the time had been presenting his mum with her first grandchild, but, instead of taking the event as a positive, she'd turned it into a negative in a way that only she knew how. From the first, Cat had dubbed her Granny Nightmare. She'd barely stayed five minutes to look at her new grandchild, she never offered to babysit when she came to stay and, when the others had arrived in quick succession, had made sarcastic comments about living beyond your means. If it weren't for Cat's incredible generosity and insistence that he should keep on good terms with his mother, Noel might have been tempted to cut her out of his life altogether.

Noel knew from Kay that his mother had felt let down that he hadn't been around more to help sort out his dad's estate, but at the time he'd been the only member of the family tied down with children of his own. Besides, he hadn't expected her to sell up and move out of the family home so quickly. In his darker moments he thought Kay had engineered things so that their mum would give her some cash as a down payment on her first flat, but Cat had accused him of being paranoid.

The final nail in the coffin had been the discovery that, in his mother's determination to cut loose and start again, she'd got rid of all Dad's war memorabilia – including his medals – without telling him or Joe. How she could have done that was beyond him. Noel had always been aware that his parents didn't enjoy the happiest of marriages, but that seemed spiteful beyond belief. The resulting row when he'd told her so had taken several years to recover from. And it was only now (mainly at Cat's insistence) that he was beginning to see a bit more of his mother again. Every time she came, he hoped she wasn't going to stay long. But, for someone who exuded displeasure at her surroundings from every pore, Granny Nighmare also seemed quite happy to ensconce herself *in situ* for days and sometimes weeks at a time.

'I see you've still not mended that shelf,' were his mother's first words on entering the playroom. One day he really would get round to fixing it.

'I'm afraid it's not really a priority at the moment,' said Noel between gritted teeth. 'Why don't you go down to the kitchen and see Cat, while I put your bags upstairs?'

He knew it was a copout, that he was being unfair to Cat, but somehow her toleration of his mother outreached his own and, within seconds of seeing her, she'd already got him riled.

He dug the children out of their respective foxholes – instinctively they'd all vanished when their grandmother arrived – and went to put his mother's things in the spare room. Cat had spent hours cleaning it, and had even found a vase to put daffodils in, but Noel knew from bitter experience there was bound to be something wrong with the room. The only thing his mother seemed to tolerate about coming here was Ruby. Which was ironic as, being the youngest, she was also the most hard work and the one most likely to have a tantrum.

Noel made his way downstairs with a heavy heart. He could already hear his mother quizzing poor Melanie about her school grades (not, as it happened, as good as they should have been, but she'd had problems settling into her new school), and picking on James for not being sporty like his Uncle Joe. It was going to be a very long week.

'I saved you a seat,' Gabriel whispered to Marianne as she snuck in at the back of the second public meeting about the post office campaign. Impressively, Vera had managed to inveigle the MP for South Salop to come and speak on their behalf. He'd given an impassioned speech about the future of rural post offices and promised to raise the matter in the House. Gabriel had his doubts as to whether Mr Silent, a backbench Lib Dem, could actually make any impact, but at least he'd turned up, which was more than the MP from the neighbouring constituency had done – but then it was his government's policies which were leading to such closures, so he probably wouldn't be seen anywhere near a meeting like this.

No one from the Post Office had come either, which was no surprise. To Gabriel's amusement, Vera had installed a cardboard cutout of Postman Pat. Someone was filming the meeting and planning to put it on YouTube. Very droll.

'Have I missed anything?' Marianne whispered.

'Only John Silent's fight 'em on the beaches speech,' said Gabriel.

Vera had now got up and was thanking them all for coming again.

'I've got good news and bad news,' she began. 'The good news is that we have nearly 15,000 signatures on our Downing Street petition,' (this raised a cheer) 'the bad news is that I can't get hold of anyone from the Post Office to come and meet with us and discuss a compromise. So we've decided to take the issue to them. And we're planning a trip to London to visit the Post Office headquarters, as well as presenting our petition at 10 Downing Street. We'd like as many of you to sign up for this as possible, of course. Thanks to Ralph Nicholas, who has several friends in the media, we're hoping to get some national coverage to raise our campaign further.'

'Blimey,' said Marianne, 'that sounds impressive.'

'Good for Vera,' whispered Gabriel. 'I never knew she had it in her.'

'Well, you know what they always say about the quiet ones,' said Marianne. The room was so packed her and

Gabriel's chairs were so close together their knees were nearly touching. She shifted a little in her seat to move away from him. She didn't want him getting the wrong idea.

The meeting soon broke up, with people going to sign up for the London trip and promising to write more letters of protest. Marianne found herself agreeing to take minutes of the next meeting, while Gabriel, having confessed to an interest in Photoshop, discovered he was now going to be running an entire poster campaign.

'Honestly, this village is hopeless,' said Gabriel. 'Give an inch and they take a mile.'

'That's what public service is all about,' sniffed Miss Woods, as she stumped by with her stick. 'We need more altruism in this world, not less.'

'True,' said Marianne, laughing. She picked up her coat and started heading for the door.

'You're not staying for a drink?' Gabriel felt a sudden stab of disappointment.

'Oh, um,' Marianne looked awkward. 'I hadn't really given it any thought.'

'It doesn't matter if you've got plans,' Gabriel said in a rush. 'It's just everyone else is going and I thought—'

'No, I don't have any other plans,' said Marianne, 'a drink would be lovely.'

They made their way into the Hopesay Arms, the friendly local, which was cram-full of regulars and so busy it was three-deep at the bar.

'I'll get these,' offered Gabriel. 'What's your poison?'

'Half of lager, thanks,' said Marianne. 'I'll look for a table.'

'This is cosy,' said Gabriel when he arrived eventually at the fireside table that Marianne had found.

'Oh, I didn't want you to think . . .' Marianne blushed. 'This was the only place I could find.'

'Here's fine,' said Gabriel. He sipped at his beer, and there was a momentary awkward silence, before he said: 'So, how does Hope Christmas compare to London, then?'

'I love it,' said Marianne. 'Even though I grew up in London, I've never really felt like a city person. From the moment I came here I felt like I'd come home. Does that sound odd to you?'

'Nope,' said Gabriel. 'I moved to London for work originally, then stayed for Eve's sake, but my heart was never there. Not really. I always felt I was living in the wrong place, having the wrong life. Now . . .' he paused for a moment.

'Now?' she prompted.

'Well, even though Eve's gone and everything,' said Gabriel, 'at least I feel I'm living the life I'm meant to be living. Does that make sense to you?'

'Perfect sense,' said Marianne.

The evening flew by, and, before Gabriel knew it, it was nearly eleven.

'I'd better go,' he said. 'I've got the teenage daughter of my neighbour babysitting and she's got school in the morning. I'd better let her get home.'

'Oh, I assumed Pippa must be babysitting,' said Marianne.

'She couldn't. She and Dan were meeting a possible new supplier tonight.'

'I'd better be off too,' said Marianne. 'It's way past my bedtime.'

'I'll walk you home,' offered Gabriel.

'There's no need,' protested Marianne. 'Honestly, I'm a big girl.'

'And I'm a gentleman,' said Gabriel. 'And, as your fellow Lonely Heart, I insist on walking you home whether you like it or not. I have to protect you from any potential lotharios out there intent on breaking your vow of chastity.'

'All right then,' said Marianne, 'if you insist.'

They got their coats on and made their way down the High Street towards Marianne's cottage. It was a bright starlit night and the moon was full, the kind of night that was made for lovers, Gabriel suddenly thought. And whereas in the pub the warmth of the fire had led to a kind of cosy intimacy with Marianne, out here in the cold he was suddenly pulled back into the reality of both their situations. They really were two Lonely Hearts offering one another companionship. That was all. They walked the short distance back to her cottage in near silence. The intimacy from the pub seemed to have vanished somehow.

When they got there, Gabriel felt suddenly awkward. Suppose she thought . . . ?

'Must get in, early start and all that,' Marianne gabbled. 'Thanks for a lovely evening.'

She almost dived into her cottage. Gabriel was relieved. She clearly hadn't been expecting anything. Which was good. As he had nothing to offer her. Nothing at all.

Chapter Six

'More wine, Angela?' Catherine waved the bottle in front of her mother-in-law almost with bated breath. So far this was the first meal since her arrival that hadn't been peppered with snide comments and sharp asides to Noel. It helped that Magda had gone out for the day, so Angela couldn't harp on about why Catherine had to work and needed an au pair (especially such a lousy one) anyway. Thankfully, though Sergei had outstayed his welcome by two days, Catherine had managed to chuck him out before her mother-in-law's arrival. Seeing as Angela had yet to forgive Cat and Noel for the year they'd lived in sin, she'd have been horrified to discover Magda cohabiting with her foreign boyfriend in the same house, corrupting her grandchildren, even if she appeared to heartily dislike said grandchildren.

'No, thank you, Catherine,' sniffed Angela. 'I don't like to overindulge in the middle of the day.'

But it doesn't stop you knocking back a bottle of sherry in the evening, thought Catherine uncharitably, and shot Noel a knowing look. He raised his eyes to heaven in the helpless manner he always employed when his mother was around. Cat wished he'd stand up to her more.

'I'll have some more, thank you,' said Cat's mother, whom they'd invited over to help dilute the toxicity of Angela's presence. 'I think I'm past the age where I care about overindulging.' She flashed an understanding smile at her daughter, as if to say, *You're doing fine.* Cat smiled back. Not for the first time she felt incredibly grateful to have such an easygoing, wonderful and utterly generous mother.

The meal continued in silence until Ruby and Paige started kicking each other under the table.

'Stop that you two!' hissed Cat, trying not to draw Angela's attention, whose views on children's behaviour at the dinner table were more than a little Victorian. Luckily, Angela had chosen that moment to quiz James about which school he might be thinking about going to, a thorny subject as Noel and Cat were keen for him to try for a grammar school five miles away, which had a much better reputation than the local boys' school, while James of course wanted to go where his friends were going. They'd already been through this once with Melanie, but her friends had roughly divided in half as to where they went, which had softened the pill of saying goodbye to her best friend somewhat.

'She started it!' said Paige, sticking her tongue out at Ruby.

'Did not!' said Ruby. 'Paige, you're a fucking shit!'

The silence at the other end of the table was so deafening Cat felt as though she'd entered some awful time capsule where things were frozen in perpetuity. *Oh my God.* Where on earth had Ruby learned language like that? She battled the urge to laugh. Really it wasn't funny.

'Ruby! You do not say words like that ever!' Cat shouted as sternly as she could. Great, now Angela would have all her worst fears about how terribly her grandchildren were being brought up confirmed.

'James does,' whined Ruby.

'Don't tell tales,' Cat and Noel said automatically. 'Go to your room at once.'

Ruby stormed out of the room sobbing, while Cat and Noel scolded their son, who took himself off to the lounge, kicking the door as he went, complaining about how unfair the world was.

'Angela, Mum, I'm so sorry about that.' Cat tried and failed to recover her poise. 'I had no idea they even knew words like that. It's so difficult nowadays to stop them learning this stuff. I know it was different when we were young.'

'I have to say I am a bit surprised,' said Cat's mum, with an asperity that was unusual for her. 'I thought rather better of your children.'

'Oh, piffle. It's not as if children have only just learnt to swear,' said Angela. To Cat's utter amazement, she was grinning. 'I seem to remember being called in to Noel's school because he'd been writing rude words in the boys' loos. Do you remember, Noel?'

Noel looked as though his teeth were set on edge.

'I don't think you've ever let me forget it,' he said.

Cat let out the breath she'd been holding without realising. That had been a close call but miraculously – presumably because the guilty party had been Ruby-Who-Could-Do-No-Wrong – Angela didn't seem at all fazed by the incident. So much so that within minutes she was insisting that Ruby came back and sat down again, and even went into the lounge to try and persuade James to come back.

'Wonders will never cease,' Cat remarked to her mother later, as they were loading the dishwasher.

'What's that, dear?' Her mother was looking a little distracted, looking at a teatowel as if she'd never seen one before.

'Angela, earlier,' explained Cat. 'I thought she'd be apoplectic about Ruby swearing like that. I couldn't believe she'd seen the funny side.'

Mum looked at her in a bemused fashion.

'Sorry, when was that?' she said.

Cat looked at her, puzzled.

'You know, earlier on,' she said. 'Ruby said a rude word and we told her off, and then rather than Angela being angry she told a funny story about Noel. Surely you can't have forgotten already?'

'No, no, of course not,' said her mother, but she had a slightly perplexed look on her face. 'Right, where do you want these?'

She lifted the washed plates from the table where Cat had left them.

'In the cupboard they normally go in,' said Cat.

'Which is?'

'That one,' said Cat, pointing to the relevant cupboard. 'Mum, are you all right?'

'Never better, dear,' said Mum brightly. 'Oh, of course, silly me. They go in here, don't they?'

'Yes,' said Cat, with a prickle of unease. Was it her imagination, or was her mother becoming more and more forgetful?

'Have you seen this latest about the new eco town?' Pippa was practically exploding as she sat at her kitchen table reading the local paper.

'No, what?' Gabriel had just dropped by to pick up Stephen. He'd been out in the fields since early that morning, tracking down his flock, ready to bring them indoors for lambing. Most of the farmers round here left their sheep on the hillside, but Gabriel preferred having his under cover: when, as had occasionally happened, he'd bred from different stock, the occasional large lamb was born, causing complications that were more difficult to deal with out on the hillside. A couple of sheep were still missing though. He was going to have to go out again tomorrow.

'That bloody Luke Nicholas,' said Pippa, practically spitting with venom. 'Can't think what Marianne can ever have seen in him.'

'Why, what's he done?'

'Just announced that his eco town is going to have a brand new supermarket up the road, which conveniently his company is also building. I bet some money's changed hands with a dodgy councillor over that. It says here that the supermarket is going to be donating a new leisure centre for the eco town. No wonder they got planning permission.'

'A leisure centre doesn't sound very green and, come to that, nor does a supermarket,' said Gabriel.

'Not unless they harness all the energy from the exercise bikes to power the place,' snorted Pippa. 'The whole thing is mad. We don't need a new town this close to Hope Christmas. Besides, I'm sure that land he's building on used to be designated a flood plain. Do you remember that Christmas a couple of years ago when it rained so heavily? The fields round there were waterlogged for weeks.'

'Doesn't it all still have to be approved, though?' said Gabriel. 'Surely he can't just steamroller the thing through?'

'Why shouldn't he?' said Pippa. 'He's got money and influence, hasn't he? I tell you, that bloody town is going to kill Hope Christmas stone dead. What with that and the post office, I despair, I really do.'

Something stirred inside Gabriel. Something that Ralph Nicholas had said to him weeks ago about keeping hold of the things you loved. He looked out at the hillside, towering over the house in the gathering gloom. Gabriel had lived in Hope Christmas for most of his life, and he realised, somewhat to his surprise, that he loved it with every fibre of his being. He couldn't bear the thought of it being under threat. He'd been so preoccupied with his own personal problems

87

he'd given less thought to those of the people around him. Hope Christmas was built around a community that in many cases just about eked out a living. Losing the post office would be a blow, but the eco town could prove the nail in the coffin.

'Can't we challenge it somehow?' he said. 'I seem to remember reading somewhere that there are a lot of protests about eco towns elsewhere. Maybe we should try and find out a bit more.'

'Ooh, Gabe,' teased Pippa, 'you're becoming quite the environmental campaigner, aren't you?'

'Well,' said Gabriel, 'I think you're right. If we don't act now, it might be too late. Maybe it's time to widen our campaign to saving Hope Christmas itself.'

'What do you propose to do, then?' said Pippa, her interest piqued.

'I'm not sure yet,' said Gabriel. 'But I think I might just pay Ralph Nicholas a visit. I wonder how much he knows about what his grandson is up to.'

Noel sat in the boardroom at a budget meeting feeling something akin to despair. Matt Duncan was doing a great brown-nosing job agreeing with everything that Gerry Cowley was saying, however stupid it might be. It also appeared Noel was more out of the loop than he'd thought, as Matt seemed to have access to figures and documents that Noel hadn't ever seen. That had meant that Noel had been unable to answer half the questions asked about this year's sales projections. He'd looked like a real tit. Which is what Matt was after, presumably. Noel half expected Gerry to morph at any moment into Alan Sugar, point at him and say, 'With regret, my friend, you're fired.' Not that he was getting paranoid or anything, but it was clear the writing was on the wall.

Luckily, for the time being, no one was paying too much

attention to him as Karl Dear, the finance director, was having a row with Alan Thompson about the budget his department had been given. Alan was arguing that without sensible funding he couldn't actually build the new freezer stores that Asda had commissioned, and did GRB really want to lose that account, while Karl was patiently and patronisingly telling Alan that no one was immune to the wintry storms blowing over the economic wastelands left behind by the credit crunch, however big the deal they'd wangled. So he was just going to have to compromise like the rest of the company.

Noel was busy doodling on his sketch pad. One of the projects he'd got involved in recently had been to design the heating systems for a new eco town, up in Shropshire. Eco towns were hot property at the moment and everyone was vying for a piece of the action. The company were hoping that if they could make this one work it would lead to more of the same, so the stakes were very high indeed.

There had been talk originally of creating sustainable housing from old workers' cottages close to the village of Hope Christmas, but that had been eschewed in favour of the brand new shiny eco town that the likes of Matt Duncan were keen to build. Noel had been unfortunate enough to have spent an evening in the company of Matt and Luke Nicholas, who ran the local building firm tasked with creating the new town. Having spent a glorious morning strolling around Hope Christmas, which Noel had instantly fallen in love with, Noel couldn't for the life of him see why an eco town was even needed so close to such a wonderful place.

Hope Christmas was already eco friendly. Its shops and restaurants sourced their produce from the local farmers, who held their own market in the village square every Thursday. There was a fabulous bookshop and a great antiques market, which was a real treasure trove. Why anyone needed to replace it was beyond Noel. The whole thing had seemed like a huge waste of money to Noel, and he hadn't made himself popular by saying so.

Noel still felt sure that the cottage route would have been a better fit for this, but he knew throwing suggestions around like, 'Prince Charles has done a good job of this kind of thing in the Duchy of Cornwall', wouldn't get him anywhere. Prince Charles' vision of sustainable developments that incorporated the notion that keeping the existing communities alive might actually be a good thing didn't cut any ice in Matt's shiny world. He was after the glory and so, suspected Noel, was Luke.

The meeting was breaking up, with nothing very much resolved. It was clear that economic conditions were causing nearly all the company's projects to be scaled down, except for the eco town, as Noel realised when he looked through the figures once again when he was back at his desk. Now why didn't that surprise him?

Marianne felt hesitant as she drove up the drive of Hopesay Manor. She hadn't been back for two months. Not since that dreadful night on Christmas Eve. She'd only glimpsed Luke once in the street since. As usual with Luke, his business seemed to be taking him up and down the country, and it seemed that he was rarely at home, preferring to spend more time in his bachelor pad in London.

Marianne had some stuff of his to return. She could have taken a chance that Luke was away and dropped it round at his place, but she couldn't bear the thought that the blonde bimbo was still hanging about, although Pippa reckoned he'd moved on to the next one by now. On Christmas Day Marianne had toyed with throwing most of his possessions in the lake at the front of Hopesay Manor, but she hadn't quite been able to bring herself to. And then she'd hoped that, by keeping them, maybe Luke would have to call round to pick them up. Pathetic, she knew, but she couldn't help that sneaky little hope that he'd still come back. Terrible thing, hope, it kept you going against all the odds, even against the constant battering that Pippa was prone to giving Luke, who as far as Pippa was concerned was systematically trying to destroy all that was good about Hope Christmas.

It was hope that had brought her here now. Hope that if she gave Luke's things to his lovely charming grandfather, maybe Ralph could smooth the way not only for a meeting, but also for the happy-ever-after reconciliation that Marianne knew she shouldn't be contemplating, but couldn't help thinking about. So, here she was, standing like an idiot in front of that imposing door. The first time she'd come here had been the best day of her life. The last time, the worst. What would happen to her here today?

Taking a deep breath, Marianne lifted the large door knocker. She realised looking at it now that she'd made a mistake before – it wasn't a man squashing a serpent, it was an angel. The wings spread round the circle of the door knocker. How unusual.

The sound of the brass knocker ringing against the door echoed ominously, making Marianne feel more nervous than ever. It seemed aeons before the door opened and Humphrey appeared. His face was implacable and, if he felt any surprise at seeing her, he didn't betray it.

'Erm – is Sir Ralph in?' Marianne was feeling like a total idiot now. What on earth had possessed her to come?

'I'm afraid he isn't, madam,' replied Humphrey. 'Is there anyone else you'd like to see?'

'Oh, er, no, it was nothing, really.' Marianne felt herself floundering. 'I'd better go—'

'Who is it, Humph?'

A familiar voice called from inside the house. God, no. She could picture him at the top of the stairs, just as he'd been that day. Her heart was hammering and she felt vaguely sick. She wanted to leave, but her feet seemed to be rooted firmly to the spot.

'Oh, it's you.' Automatically, her heart skipped a beat, but Luke was standing at the door looking down at her as if she was something unpleasant on his shoe.

'I've brought – I've still got some of your things,' stammered Marianne. 'I thought you might like them back.'

'Put them in the hall,' he said dismissively and turned to go. How could he be so cruel?

'Don't you . . . ?' Marianne was speechless. Part of her was shocked to the quick that he could be so unkind, and another part was furious with him. After what he'd put her through. After the promises he'd broken.

'Will there be anything else?' That charming smile, that mocking look. Once it had entranced her, now it was breaking her heart.

'No, nothing.' The fury had abated, as suddenly as it had come, and Marianne was just feeling incredibly sad and foolish. What had she expected? After the way he'd treated her at Christmas, it was hardly as though Luke was going to welcome her back with open arms, was it?

She dropped the box she was holding onto the marble floor of the porch, and it was with satisfaction that she heard something crack. She hoped it was the very expensive bottle of aftershave he'd left in her bathroom, which she'd wedged next to a couple of shirts Luke liked. Hopefully they were now ruined.

She went to the car and got the other boxes, and left them on the porch. Luke had gone back into the house, and Humphrey slowly picked up the boxes Marianne was

92

dumping one by one. This was it then, she thought as she put the last box down. All her hopes and dreams of the future were now definitely over. She might have made a life for herself in Hope Christmas, but Luke couldn't have made it any clearer that she'd be living it on her own.

As she walked back to her car to go home, an old Land Rover drove up and Ralph got out of it. In a rapid glance he assessed the situation.

'It might seem painful now,' he said, 'but at least you're making a clean break. It will get better in time.'

Marianne looked at him bleakly.

'I know,' she said. 'And I am getting better. But this . . . this was hard.'

'Most things that are worthwhile generally are,' said Ralph, patting her on the arm. 'But this too will pass. You'll see.'

He whistled and his dog jumped out of the car and followed him back into the house.

Marianne turned to take one last look at the house. Her hopes of a life with Luke were dashed. But Ralph was right. This would pass, eventually. Things, after all, could only get better.

Chapter Seven

Noel sat in the first-class carriage of the Virgin train speeding for Shrewsbury opposite Matt Duncan, who was getting carried away on a wave of blue-sky thinking about forward projections by which they could rationalise their objectives. Noel was too polite to suggest he stop bullshitting and actually do some proper work for once. Besides, he knew that wouldn't get him anywhere. Blue-sky thinkers were the future. Hard-grafting, precise engineers like him used to coming up with plans that actually worked were the past. Never had he felt more like a dinosaur.

Noel sighed and pretended to look at his own laptop, as if it could make this sow's ear of a development into a silk purse. There was something he didn't quite like the smell of here. Whether it was the smarminess of Luke Nicholas, who was meeting them at Shrewsbury to take them on site, or the self-satisfied air that Matt always projected whenever he talked about the eco town, but there was something about the whole project that made Noel uneasy. He dimly recalled seeing a comment in the files from one of the original architects about the suitability of the site, but there had been a falling out with that particular architect and no one seemed to know anything more about it.

'This is us.' Matt gathered his things together as the train slid into Shrewsbury station. They got out and made their way to the entrance where Luke Nicholas was waiting for them. Noel sighed again. A whole day with these two goons. He didn't know how he was going to stand it. At least he'd managed to get out of an overnighter, pleading that Cat needed him at home – which she did, it being half term. Not that he'd be much use to her by the time he got back late this evening, but it was better than nothing. He hated staying away from home at the best of times, but the thought of spending a night in a hotel with Matt Duncan was too much to bear.

'Hi again.' Luke held out his hand to greet them, and was interrupted by a distinguished voice saying, 'Well, Luke, me boy, aren't you going to introduce us?'

Luke said, 'Oh, yes, of course. Matt Duncan, Noel Tinsall, meet Ralph Nicholas, my grandfather. As head of the family firm, he thought he'd like to come along for the ride.'

Noel detected a hint of irritation in Luke's voice but he covered up smoothly. His grandfather tipped his hat, and said, 'Luke, I hope I'm not going to be in your way here, just wanted to see what you're up to.'

'And it's a pleasure to have you, Grandfather,' said Luke in a manner that indicated anything but pleasure. 'Gentlemen, if you please.'

Noel followed them to the car, a faint smile playing on his face. He'd had the distinct impression that Luke's granddad was up to something. This might turn out to be a very interesting day indeed . . .

'So that's that then?' Pippa was helping Marianne stick crêpe flowers onto paper plates for the forthcoming Easter Bonnet Parade. She was using the half-term break to get them ready early, knowing that once school had started she wouldn't have much time. Besides, Easter was early this year, it would be upon them before she knew it. In theory the children were supposed to make their own for a competition but, despite it being her first Easter in Hope Christmas, Marianne had had enough experience of dealing with small children having temper tantrums because they hadn't won, and their parents berating her for the extra stress involved in making the bonnets, to make her take the easy option. There were only twenty children in her reception class and she'd become a dab hand at making crêpe flowers over the years. Besides, she found arts and crafts therapeutic and today, every time she picked up the scissors, she was also viciously imagining what she would do to Luke next time she saw him.

'Yes,' Marianne put down her bits of paper and sighed. 'I know, I know. Don't tell me, I was completely bonkers to even think he'd have me back. You don't have to tell me I've made a fool of myself. I've been kicking myself for being so pathetic ever since.'

'Don't,' said Pippa. 'We've all been there. It's a well known psychological condition known as the Heathcliff effect. However much the bastards kick us when we're down, we can't help creeping back for more.'

'What, even you?' exclaimed Marianne. 'I can't imagine you ever being as pathetic about a bloke as I've been about Luke.'

'Even me,' grinned Pippa. 'In that faraway time before I met Dan, I kissed my fair share of toads. I was just lucky that eventually one of them turned out to be a prince.'

'Oi, who are you calling a toad?' Dan had just come in on his way to take the boys swimming with Stephen. Lucy was sitting quietly in the corner 'making' some Easter bonnets of her own.

'Well, at least I got the most handsome one in the pond,' said Pippa, laughing and kissing Dan smack on the lips. Marianne felt a wistful pang as she watched them. It must be so lovely to have that relaxed, secure relationship with someone. Would it ever happen for her? Since the debacle with Luke, she was beginning to wonder if she even wanted it to. Being alone did also mean being safe from further heartache.

'Right, we're off,' said Dan. 'Come on, boys.'

The boys, who'd been happily playing on the Playstation, leapt up and disappeared in a flurry of excitement.

'It'll happen for you one day,' said Pippa, as if reading her thoughts, as she waved goodbye to her family.

'You think?' said Marianne, feeling sadder and bleaker than she'd done since her break-up with Luke. 'Sometimes I think I'll never meet the right person.'

'Never say never,' said Pippa. 'Besides, I don't just think. I know. Somewhere out there, there's someone for all of us. You just have to believe that one day you'll find him.'

Marianne went back to sticking flowers on paper plates. It was all right for Pippa, it had already happened for her. She stared out of the window as the sun set across the magnificent hills rising from the valley floor, casting vivid oranges, pinks and purples in the sky. It was so wonderful living here. She just wished she wasn't doing it all alone.

Gabriel was driving his flock down the country lane that led past the rain-sodden fields where the proposed eco town was to be built. The land fell sharply to the left and plateaued out into large, flat and very soggy fields through which ran a stream that was usually full in spring. The fields, he'd belatedly realised, bordered the edge of his land. He'd only discovered this in conversation with Ralph Nicholas, who seemed as unenthusiastic about the new proposal as Gabriel did. Gabriel had called into Hopesay Manor to see him and over a glass of whisky Ralph had confided that he had originally planned for there to be renovation work on the cottages at the corner of his estate. Somehow, in his absence, this had escalated into a full-blown new eco town which, far from supporting the community as Ralph had intended, threatened to destroy it.

'Can't you do anything?' Gabriel had asked.

'Unfortunately the board have all got behind this,' Ralph said, 'and though I'm technically its chair they don't actually have to do what I say.'

'So, what can we do?' Gabriel had wanted to know. Which was when Ralph had deemed it wise to show Gabriel his old map collection.

'Useful things, maps,' Ralph had said. 'You never know what they're going to throw up.'

Poring over the old charts, Gabriel had discovered an old bridleway, down which he was now herding his sheep, as was his ancient right from time immemorial, written into the laws of Old Salop. And, if he'd timed it right, his sheep-herding should just about coincide with the arrival of Luke Nicholas and his posh engineering folk from London, whom Ralph had assured him were site-visiting today.

Gabriel turned a corner and saw a car coming towards him. A sleek BMW M5 driven by Luke Nicholas. Good old Ralph. Gabriel watched the car slow to a halt as his herd of pregnant sheep baaed and fought their way round it.

Luke got out of the car looking furious.

'What the bloody hell is going on? This is a private road.'

'I'm sorry,' Gabriel tried to look surprised. 'Since when?'

'Since forever,' said Luke. 'This land and this road has been in my family for generations as I'm sure you well know. Now get your sheep out of here!'

'Well, that's funny,' said Gabriel, emphasising the strength of his Shropshire burr and scratching his head. 'Because my family have been using this as a right of way to herd our sheep for generations. I'm only getting my flock off the hillsides ready for lambing. You can't stop me exercising my ancient rights.'

'Oh, can't I?' Luke was angrier than ever. 'We'll see about that. Oh shit!'

Casting another furious look at Gabriel, Luke tried to wipe the sheep dung from his foot in as dignified a manner as possible. Gabriel did his best to keep a blank look on his face as he whistled to Benjy and shooed his sheep past Luke's car.

Luke was bound to find a way round the ancient right to roam thing, his sort always did. But in the meantime, as Ralph had pointed out to him, they'd bought themselves a little more time, and with any luck put Luke on the wrong footing with his friends from London. Gabriel grinned as he passed Luke's car, from where Ralph directed a broad wink at him, and drove his flock baaing and stumbling their way down the road towards home. If nothing else, it had been worth it to see the look on Luke's face . . .

The secret to a happy half term is organisation . . . trilled the Happy Homemaker into Cat's computer. The Happy Homemaker always trilled. She was that kind of woman. God, how Cat loathed her, particularly as she was listening to the chaos downstairs as Magda screamed, 'James! You must come and tidy your room now. Your mother said!' and she could hear the dulcet tones of Ruby and Paige fighting – again. Melanie was mooching miserably in her room, no doubt texting her friends to say what a terrible life she had, following her parents' inexplicable refusal to let her go and see the latest must-see action adventure film, which, sadly for Melanie, had a 15 certificate. Cat might have relented, but she'd seen a clip of it last time she'd been at the cinema and there'd been a torture scene that had made both her and Noel wince.

If you keep the children organised and busy, you will auto-matically find the days progress smoothly with few fights and arguments. As it is often difficult at this time of year to guar-antee outside activities – Cat shivered and wrapped herself more tightly in her fleece. One day Noel would keep his promise and redo her study with some insulation in it – *try to organise visits indoors. Go to a museum or visit an aquarium or a waxworks museum.* Cat scrubbed the last sentence – she knew it would bring forth the normal response in her comments section about it being all right for people who lived in London, as if living in the capital were some kind of crime. The bloggy world was in the main a benign place, but there were some odd people out there and occasionally they took delight in surfacing on her blog. She wrote instead, *If you aren't lucky enough to have a nearby museum, why not try bowling, or go swimming at your local leisure centre? And, failing all else, you could do worse than spend a rainy afternoon playing games like Scrabble or Monopoly . . .*

'Except, I'm sure in *your* house your children would be well behaved enough not to squabble over every bloody move,' Catherine said out loud. How much easier to live in the world of the Happy Homemaker whose children would always obligingly play games together beautifully, create wonderful art and craft collages, spend hours playing poohsticks in the park . . . Cat had to hand it to herself, she couldn't have created a more perfect and unrealistic picture of parenthood if she'd tried.

The chaos downstairs seemed to have died down, which was a relief, as Cat didn't think she could cope with yet another lecture from Angela about her failings as a parent. Her mother-in-law, despite her stay coinciding with half term, hadn't yet managed to offer to do anything useful with the children, although she had at least taken to going out on a cultural tour of duty of the capital. Somehow Cat didn't think the kids would have been all that wowed by the prospect of visiting the National Gallery – they found Tate Modern or being dragged round the Tower of London enough of a chore.

Cat went back to the Happy Homemaker again. What other pearls of wisdom could she dispense? Were there any about dealing with stroppy teenagers and mums who were losing their marbles? Mum seemed so distracted of late. Recently she'd not only forgotten a recipe for a raspberry cheesecake that Cat had wanted to include in the book and which Mum had made countless times over the years but, to Cat's dismay, she'd nearly had her electricity cut off for not paying her bill.

Mum had made light of it, but Cat was beginning to worry that she was hiding something from her. Maybe she had some kind of financial worry that she was too proud to mention? There was no point trying to talk to Mum about it, though. Knowing her as well as she did, Cat knew that if there was a problem she would be keeping it from Cat so as not to 'worry' her. Maybe Cat should ring Auntie Eileen instead. If anyone knew if Mum was having money worries, it would be her. Cat picked up the phone and dialled the number. It was probably nothing, but at least she could put her mind at rest.

Chapter Eight

Noel stumped his way through a sodden, windswept field and wondered who on earth could have thought this god-forsaken place was a good location for an eco town. As soon as the sheep had gone (which had caused him much silent laughter), and they'd got out of the car to inspect the site, the rain had come down in sheets. Of course, he hadn't thought to bring wellies or a decent overcoat, and he was soaked through. Only Ralph Nicholas seemed prepared in his oilskins and ancient galoshes. It was almost as if he knew it would happen. And yet, no rain had been forecast . . . His grandson and Matt looked even more ridiculous than Noel felt, both of them having eschewed something as sensible as a coat for expensive suits – Luke's probably came from Savile Row – and shiny shoes. At least Noel's had some kind of tread in them, which had so far stopped him from going arse over tit in the mud.

He realised as soon as he stood in the field what the problem the architects had mentioned was, and wondered why Matt hadn't seen fit to comment on it. If, indeed, he even realised what it was. The fields where the proposed town was to be built were in a flat valley surrounded by bleak-looking hills, though Luke had been quick to assure them everything looked different in the sunshine. But most importantly it was a valley, with a river running through it, a river that came off the hillside and sloped downhill towards the fields. They were, if he wasn't mistaken, standing on a flood plain. It was a disastrous place to do any building on.

'Erm, Matt, can I have a word?' Noel found himself shouting over the wind and it took three attempts before Matt heard him.

'Sorry, what's that?' Matt looked as though he were turning blue from the cold.

'I think this is a flood plain,' shouted Noel. 'I'm not sure that anything should be built here, let alone a village.'

Matt looked at him in incomprehension.

'It can't be!' he yelled. 'Luke assured me himself this was perfect building land.'

'Look at it!' Noel said. 'The fields are so wet you could grow rice in them. Would *you* want to live here?'

Matt had no answer for that, and Noel trudged back to the car. This was madness, it could only be Matt's inexperience and determination to look good in front of the CEO that had kept the project going so long.

But when they got back to the posh manor house that Ralph Nicholas apparently owned, and where they were treated to an incredibly lavish three-course meal, Noel discovered to his dismay that Matt had no intention of discussing the issue of the site's suitability. Instead, he and Luke seemed to be formalising plans for work to begin.

'Whoa, don't you think you're jumping the gun a bit?' Noel said as they waited for their puddings. 'I'm not sure that that site is incredibly suitable for building on.'

'Why ever not?' Luke directed a charming smile at him. 'I know you didn't see it at its best today, but every house will have stunning views, with a decent garden, not to forget the magnificent playing fields we're planning and the wonderful leisure centre, which will be the heart of our new community.'

It was clearly a well-practised spiel, but it cut no ice with Noel, who'd heard enough of this kind of guff to last him a lifetime.

'Oh, I'm sure you're right,' said Noel. 'It will be a wonderful development, but you're building it in the wrong place. It's got a sodding great river running through it, which at the moment looks as if it's about to burst its banks. How often does that happen?'

For the first time that day Luke looked slightly uneasy. 'We *have* had an unusual amount of rainfall for the time of year,' he conceded.

'The fields are flooded,' said Noel. 'Is this a common occurrence?'

'Well, er . . . It certainly doesn't happen *every* year . . .'

'Oh, come now, Luke,' said his grandfather, from the far end of the table. 'We both know those fields flood regularly.'

'So it *is* a flood plain?' said Noel. 'In the government draft planning statement it clearly states that eco towns are not to be built in areas where flooding is a problem.'

'No, of course it's not a flood plain,' said Luke, who quite clearly had never read any government guidelines about anything. 'I'd never propose such a thing. There is, I grant you, a problem with flooding from time to time, but we've looked into it and we think by building barriers further upstream, or possibly diverting the river, we can prevent this from recurring. Once the water is pumped out of the ground we should reduce the risk of dampness.'

'Thereby increasing the risk of subsidence,' interrupted Noel. 'It's clay – once it dries out it will crack up. No, I can't accept that this is a decent site to build on. It goes against all the government guidelines. I'm afraid I'm going to recommend to GRB that we don't proceed.'

There was a stunned silence. Noel got up to get his coat. 'Coming, Matt?' he said.

'I think I just need to go over a few things with Luke,' said Matt hurriedly, looking pale.

I bet you do, thought Noel, as he was shown to the lobby where he waited an uncomfortable half an hour before a cab appeared to take him to the station. He had a horrible feeling that he might just have marked his card for good. Despite this being a really bad investment, he'd seen enough dodgy constructions in his time to know this would probably go ahead with or without his intervention. The company couldn't afford in these straitened times to turn down such a potentially lucrative deal. This time he'd *really* blown it.

Marianne was walking in the rain. There was something satisfyingly cleansing about Shropshire rain: even when it was cold, there was an invigorating quality to it that walking through rain-drenched London streets lacked. If she was suffering from the Heathcliff effect, she may as well act like a Brontë heroine and catch consumption or something. She'd always found the idea of that very romantic as a kid, although as an adult it seemed somewhat less appealing. And, given that Luke wasn't exactly likely to rush to her bedside stricken with guilt and laden with red roses, there wasn't much point getting a terminal disease.

But walking in the rain was a good purge of her spirits. Despite her assurances to Pippa that now she'd really accept things were over between her and Luke, Marianne actually felt worse than ever. The way Luke had looked through her, like she meant nothing, nothing at all, had cut her to the quick. He used to look at her as if she set his world on fire.

He'd told her that she meant everything to him, that a life without her wasn't worth living. And he hadn't meant one single solitary word. Whereas she had. She'd really believed she and Luke were destined to be together forever. Walking out in the pouring rain, her thoughts churned over and over to no helpful purpose. And she realised with a jolt that she was crying, really crying for the first time in months. Great racking sobs were coming out of her, and she found herself shaking violently. How was she ever going to get over this? It was the greatest betrayal of her life.

She didn't notice at first she'd strayed into the edges of Gabriel's land. Slowly but surely she was beginning to work out the geography of the area and, as she walked down footpaths that meandered through the farms dotted about the hills, she was beginning to know which farms were which, and whose sheep belonged to whom. Gabriel's, she knew, were a medium-sized sheep with black faces known as Shropshires, but only because Pippa had told her. She also recognised the telltale blue brand mark that signified they belonged to Gabriel's farm.

Only not today. She'd been so preoccupied that she'd failed to notice there weren't any sheep on the hillside at all. Where were they all? Ever since she'd been here, a feature of her walks had been the sheep who wandered across her path willy-nilly or fled up the hillside at her approach. She'd been spooked by the sheep at first, as she found the way they suddenly ambled in front of her on the paths a bit unnerving, but had gradually got used to them and now a walk wasn't complete if she hadn't said hello to a few sheep on the way. But today there were none.

A noise caught her attention. A bleating sound that didn't seem quite right. It was coming from a little way down the hill and, as Marianne walked down the steep path that led to the fields, the noise became more urgent and panicky.

Maybe there was a sheep in trouble. She scrambled to the edge of the path, and looked down. In a dip in the hillside was a sheep, bleating frantically. A very pregnant sheep. Somehow it must have fallen over the edge and got stuck. The poor thing kept trying to get up and collapsing again. Hang on . . . Marianne cast her mind back to a nature programme she'd watched a while back, from which she'd learnt that when sheep are about to give birth they keep standing up and sitting down. As if on cue, the sheep stood up and its waters broke. Holy cow. Now what was she supposed to do?

Catherine was sitting down in the lounge with a well-deserved glass of wine by the time Noel got home. She was exhausted. Magda had gone out for the evening and Cat had had a fraught teatime during which Melanie had left the table in tears because Paige had 'looked at her in a nasty way'. The advent of hormones and secondary school had rendered her eldest daughter sensitive in the extreme. Cat didn't know what had got into her, but was struggling to come to terms with the fact that the little girl she loved was approaching womanhood faster than her mother would like. A few more years and she'd be leaving home, her life just beginning, while Cat's would be contracting. She felt an oddly jealous pang when she thought of the future that Mel had before her. Was that normal, she wondered, or was she going to turn into a bitter old hag as her daughter shone young and bright and beautiful in front of her? She hoped not. For the first time in her life when she read Ruby fairy tales, she was starting to sympathise with the wicked stepmother more than the beautiful princess. That couldn't be right.

At least all the fraughtness had stopped her thinking about the rest of her utterly stressful day. It had started badly when she'd turned up to see Mum for a cup of coffee, and been confronted with a furious rant about Cat interfering in her business.

'How dare you ask Auntie Eileen if I had any money worries?' Mum said. 'I'm not a child. I have managed my own finances pretty successfully all these years, you know.'

'I know,' said Cat, 'it was just with you having your electricity cut off, and seeing all those red bills last time I was here, I was worried about you.'

'How dare you spy on me!' Mum was bright red in the face. Cat had never seen her like this before. She backed down at a million miles an hour.

'I'm so sorry, Mum, I didn't mean to pry. I was concerned, that's all.'

'Well, there's no need to be,' retorted Mum. 'I made a mistake. It's not like I can't cope.'

'I've never said you couldn't,' said Cat. 'But are you sure you've got enough money?'

'Of course I have,' Mum looked perplexed. 'You know I have a good pension.'

'So there's nothing wrong?' said Cat.

'Repeat after me, "Everything is fine",' said Mum. 'Cat, you worry too much and you don't need to worry about *me*.'

So that was that. But the niggle of worry remained. She sipped her glass of wine and cuddled up to Noel watching the news. She didn't mention her concerns about Mum, as Noel had already made it clear that he thought she was overreacting. Maybe she was. In every other way her mother was perfectly fine. Cat tried to convince herself that there was nothing to worry about, but the growing knot of anxiety in her stomach told her she hadn't succeeded.

Gabriel was scouring the hillside in the rain. One of his ewes was missing. In the palaver of getting round Luke's car,

108

he hadn't noticed. He only realised his mistake when he got back to the farm and herded the sheep into the shed. She must have wandered off. It was one of the ewes who was close to lambing. Gabriel knew he should have had them all in by now but since Eve had left he had found it increasingly difficult to juggle everything, and now he was cursing himself for his lack of planning. Though there were rarely problems with Shropshire sheep at lambing time, this particular ewe had been rather large and he suspected she was carrying triplets. If something went wrong she might die on that hillside, and he couldn't risk that happening. So now he was out searching for her with all the kit he needed in case she gave birth: rubber gloves, string, Vaseline, were all stowed away in his backpack.

He heard a shout and saw Marianne scrabbling towards him.

'I think one of your sheep might be about to give birth,' she was calling.

Gabriel raced towards Marianne, who showed him where the ewe was stuck. It was an awkward clamber, but Gabriel managed to lower himself down onto the ledge where the sheep was.

'There, there, girl,' he said, patting the sheep on the back. He gently eased his way round behind her and, after putting on his rubber gloves, had a feel to see what was going on.

'Damn,' he said, 'it's a big one, and I think there's a smaller twin. Marianne, there's some string in my backpack, can you get it for me?'

Gabriel felt inside the sheep again and found the lamb's front legs. He pulled them towards him, and looped the string around the legs. Gently he pulled the lamb out in time with the contractions. It slipped back for a moment, and he had to loop the string around its legs again. Eventually he could feel it coming and teased it out of the ewe. It flopped out onto the ground and didn't move. Oh no. Please, not that. This happened sometimes, but not often. Gabriel grabbed some grass and tickled the lamb's nose to try and get it to sneeze. Nothing.

'Is everything all right?' Marianne climbed down beside him, looking worried.

'Wait a sec,' said Gabriel. He picked the lamb up by its hind legs, swinging it gently to try and get it to breathe. Still nothing.

The ewe, sensing something was wrong, bleated her distress. Gabriel patted her again.

'Sorry, old girl, there's nothing I can do,' Gabriel felt her pain. He hated losing lambs. The miracle of birth was one of the most precious moments of his job, and it was heart-breaking when it went wrong.

'Oh, Gabriel,' Marianne looked just as gutted as he was. He was shot through with gratitude that she seemed to understand so instinctively how painful it was. Eve never would have noticed at all.

'It's not over yet. There's still another,' he said, and went back to the sheep, who was moaning in pain. The second lamb was coming out legs first. Damn. He hoped they wouldn't lose this one too.

'It's coming out backwards,' said Gabriel. 'Marianne, I may need some help. Can I brace myself against you? I can't risk turning it around or I might strangle it with the cord.'

Slowly but surely he lined the lamb's legs up and, by dint of gentle rocking and timing the sheep's contractions correctly, he eased the lamb out. He could feel Marianne's breathing keeping pace with his own. As the lamb slid to the floor, he thought, *Oh no, not again* – but this time the lamb bleated loud and strong, and within minutes was sucking at his mother's teat. Elation and relief surged through him and without thinking he flung his arms round Marianne.

'Thanks,' said Gabriel, 'I couldn't have done that without you.'

'I'm just glad I was here,' said Marianne, flushed and grinning. 'I've never seen a lamb being born. That was magic.'

Gabriel looked at her and grinned back. She was so pretty, he thought. It always took him by surprise when he was with her.

'Yes, it was, wasn't it?' he said, but he wasn't just thinking about the lamb. Sharing the experience with Marianne had been magical too. She hadn't batted an eyelid, had reacted calmly in a way he could never have imagined Eve doing.

On impulse he hugged her again.

'You were brilliant,' he said.

Marianne whooped for joy.

'I wouldn't have missed it for the world,' she said. 'It's our special spring surprise.'

They stood looking at the lamb, now suckling from its mother. A red kite soared high above them in the bright blue sky, a gentle breeze blew on the pink and purple heathers. Gabriel squeezed Marianne to him. For the first time in a very long while, he felt that all was right in the world.

Part Two

You Gave it Away

Last Year
December 23

Gabriel could hear the bird's frantic cheeping before he saw it. It was a bright, sunny day and he'd been walking in the woods. He frowned. Hadn't it been snowing earlier?

Suddenly the skies went grey and he was filled with an urgent sense of foreboding. The bird's cries became more frequent and desperate. Gabriel knew it was vitally important that he reach the bird. Had to try and help. But couldn't think why or how.

'Daddy!' A shout came from behind him. What was Stephen doing here? He was meant to be at home tucked up in bed. The anguish in his son's voice tore at Gabriel's heart. He should go to his son.

But the bird . . .

Why was the bird so important?

Couldn't he help them both?

The bird was too far away. He could just about see it now, caught in barbed wire, but he couldn't ignore his son's cries, which were getting louder and more persistent.

'Daddy, Daddy, Daddy!'

Gabriel ran in the direction of Stephen's voice, but the wood seemed different today. Less open, more hostile. Dark twisted trees crouched menacingly above him, small spiteful bushes barred his way. Soon he was lost, and frantic. Where was he? Where was Stephen?

'If you love something, let it go.'

'It can't be—'

Eve was there in front of him, blocking the way towards Stephen.

'Eve!' he called out in anguish. She looked at him with such sadness in her eyes, and then she was gone. But there was Stephen, a small sobbing bundle calling his name . . .

Gabriel woke with a jerk, blearily aware that he was cold and stiff. It was midnight, and his tumbler of whiskey was half full, though the bottle beside it was nearly empty. He had vague memories of sitting drinking it, wallowing in nostalgia, but had no idea how long he'd been asleep. He did know that he had a thumping head. The fire had gone out in the grate and through the gap in the curtains he could see it was still snowing. He should go to bed.

'Daddy.' A small shadow appeared in the doorway.

'Stephen.' Gabriel felt uncomfortable. He didn't want his son to see him in this state. Stephen had seen enough that he shouldn't have already.

'Why aren't you in bed?' said Stephen. 'I had a bad dream, and woke up and couldn't find you.'

'I'm sorry.' Gabriel felt worse than ever. 'I fell asleep down here. Come here.'

Stephen climbed onto Gabriel's lap and snuggled against him.

'You're cold,' he said accusingly.

'You're warm,' said Gabriel. 'You can cuddle me and warm me up if you like.' He held his son tight, and kissed him on the top of his head. Maybe Eve had been right. He couldn't help her, but he could look after their son.

'I wrote a note to Santa, Daddy,' said Stephen.

'You know he might not have enough Wiis to go round, don't you?' Gabriel always made a point of damping down

116

Stephen's wilder expectations at Christmas, which were usually, it had to be said, generated by random promises that Eve made and never kept, like the time she'd promised him a trip to Disneyland Paris that had never materialised.

'I don't want a Wii anymore,' said Stephen solemnly. 'There's only one thing I want. Do you think if I'm really really good Santa will give it to me?'

Gabriel's heart sank.

'It depends what it is,' Gabriel said carefully.

'Shh, it's a secret,' said Stephen. He held out a crumpled bit of paper. 'Can I put this by the fireplace for Santa?'

'Of course,' said Gabriel. 'Now really, it's time you were back in bed.'

Stephen put his letter by the grate and allowed himself to be carried back to bed.

'I miss Mummy,' he said, as Gabriel tucked him in.

'I know,' said Gabriel. 'I do too.'

Stephen looked at him expectantly. This was the point at which he should say something reassuring like, *It's okay, Mummy will be home soon*, but Gabriel couldn't bring himself to. Painful as this was for his son, how could he lie and promise something that wasn't going to happen?

With a heavy heart, Gabriel went back downstairs to tidy up. He paused in the lounge and picked up the letter Stephen had written.

Dear Santa,
I have been very god. Can my mummy plees come home for Xmas.
Yours sinserly
Stephen North

Gabriel sat back down on the sofa and wept.

* * *

The traffic on the North Circular was predictably dreadful. Magda's flight was at three so Cat had planned to leave at ten, partly to give herself plenty of time, and partly to get rid of her sulky au pair at the earliest possible opportunity. She hadn't, of course, factored in Magda's ability to take three times as long as a normal person to get ready. By the time she had finally emerged from her bedroom with enough bags for half an army, it was nearly ten thirty. Although that still gave them over two hours, Cat wasn't convinced that they'd make it through London in time, but she was getting to the point where she was past caring. At least Magda was out of her hair for Christmas.

Magda had only been with them since September and she was already shaping up to be the worst au pair they'd ever had. If Catherine could see a way to reduce her workload slightly (unlikely since the Happy Homemaker had taken over her life), she might think of dispensing with an au pair again. But she needed Magda, otherwise her working day would be reduced by at least three hours, and she couldn't afford that at the moment.

Nor, for that matter, could she afford to spend the best part of a precious day just before Christmas ferrying her rubbish au pair to the airport. Magda had originally planned to go to her boyfriend, Sergei, for Christmas Day, but that was before a frantic phone call from Latvia from which it transpired that her mother was desperately ill – dying even – and Magda needed to get home. Catherine hated herself for being dubious about how ill Magda's mother really was, but she couldn't help thinking it was incredibly convenient that this mystery illness had arrived just before Christmas, considering that Magda had spent months moaning that she didn't have enough money to get home for the festive season. But, of course, this being a crisis, Cat had felt duty-bound to cough up the money for a plane ticket. She had done it with the strictest of provisos that on her return Magda would be repaying the money out of her wages, but Catherine had the feeling that somehow Magda would wriggle her way out of that one.

Still, at least Magda had opted not to talk on the journey, preferring to sit in the back listening to the Cheeky Girls on her iPod. Mind you, the downside of that was that Cat had to listen to her slightly out-of-tune rendition. Too bloody right she was a cheeky girl.

The traffic started moving again and Cat felt a bit more hopeful. Maybe she'd be back by lunchtime. She didn't trust Noel to get through all the jobs she'd left for him. Magda's bed had to be washed and aired ready for her mother-in-law's arrival and the playroom desperately needed a tidy – the kids were all on tidywatch for that one, though if left to their own devices they would make things worse rather than better.

As she made her way on to the M4, Catherine was busy running through lists in her head: presents for mothers, check; presents for kids, mainly check, but Noel was going to have to go out on a frantic last-minute search to get a Baby Annabel who had mysteriously appeared at the eleventh hour on Ruby's list (being the youngest she generally got hand-me-downs, and Cat felt for once she really ought to get a decent present that she actually wanted); present for the husband, uncheck. She'd drawn a complete blank this year for Noel. Apart from a book she knew he'd like, some socks and a couple of CDs, she'd barely got him anything. Which was most unlike her. But things had been so busy recently and, what with working more or less full time now, she'd had less time to shop than normal. Feeling incredibly guilty, she did a last-minute dash round the shops in Heathrow and came out with a leather manbag, which she wasn't even sure Noel would like and which was far too expensive. But that's what last-minute, desperate Christmas shopping always entailed – buying something hideously expensive that you'd see reduced the next week in the sales. She hoped he'd understand. After all, Christmas was for the kids.

'Your mother doesn't like me.' Marianne was fixing in a pearl earring as she got ready in her cosy little cottage for the Nicholas family annual Christmas lunch, held at Hopesay Manor. This would be only the second time she'd been there, and she hadn't met Luke's grandfather since their embarrassing encounter with him in the summer. She'd endured enough of her prospective mother-in-law's snobbiness over the last few months to be sure that she wasn't being welcomed into the bosom of the family with open arms though.

'Don't be daft.' Luke was staring in the mirror as he adjusted his tie. 'She thinks you're great.'

Marianne's heart gave a little lurch, the way it always did when Luke was near. He was so gorgeous and he was hers. Sometimes she had to pinch herself. And sometimes the insecure part of her worried that it couldn't last, and one day he would leave her. Despite Luke's denials when she raised the subject, she couldn't help the gnawing anxiety within her, which made her feel that she was way out of her depth in his family. After all, how many men really married women their mothers so obviously disapproved of?

'Do I look all right?' Marianne gave a twirl in the little velvet black dress she reserved for all occasions when she didn't know what to wear. She felt rather self-conscious though. Was it too short for Hopesay Manor?

'You look fine,' said Luke, who seemed more interested in making sure his own appearance was okay.

120

'You barely looked at me.' Marianne gave him a friendly poke.

'You look lovely,' said Luke, kissing her on the top of the head. 'Come on, we should go.'

Marianne followed him into the car, her insecurities rising. She was nervous, couldn't he see that? But it was almost as if he didn't care.

Things got worse when they arrived and she realised her clothes were all wrong. All the other women were wearing twinsets and pearls and she was in a cocktail dress. Luke's mother didn't say anything, but her eyebrows rose to the ceiling when she saw the length of Marianne's skirt.

'My skirt's too short,' she hissed at Luke.

'Not for me,' he said, giving her a lascivious look before diving off to talk with one of the directors of the family firm.

Marianne was left standing on her own in the magnificent drawing room. There were about thirty members of the extended Nicholas clan and their friends, but not one of them came anywhere near her. She was too nervous to start a conversation with any of them, so instead concentrated on looking at the picture above the magnificent fireplace, which featured a rather dashing Cavalier on a horse.

'My ancestor, another Ralph Nicholas.' Luke's grandfather was suddenly standing beside her with his twinkling smile.

'I can see the family resemblance,' said Marianne. It was uncanny how alike the man standing beside her was to this portrait of a man from four centuries ago. 'What happened to him?'

'Oh, family legend has it that he helped Charles II escape, and in gratitude was knighted on his return.'

'You certainly have an interesting family,' said Marianne. 'Mine is quite dull by comparison. Labourers and dock

121

workers back to the time of the Conquest. I don't think we even have a convict who went to Australia to liven things up.'

'I'm glad you think so,' said Ralph. 'It's rather a pity that my grandson can't be persuaded to take more of an interest. But that's the trouble with youth. It's wasted on the young.'

Marianne laughed. She was glad to see her future grand-father-in-law didn't seem to have held the awkwardness of their initial encounter against her.

'Now, we can't have a lovely young thing like you standing all by yourself,' continued Ralph. 'Let me introduce you to the rest of the family.'

He gently steered her in the direction of some younger cousins, who certainly seemed a lot less stuffy and pompous than the rest of the family; but Marianne soon discovered that an inability to talk about trust funds and holidays in Antigua were a bit of a conversational stumbling block, and she was immensely grateful when Luke announced it was time to leave.

'Shall we go and have a festive drink in the pub?' Marianne said when they got back, but Luke looked at her blankly.

'Sorry, babe, I've still got some shit to sort out, no rest for the wicked and all that.'

'Oh.' Marianne felt crestfallen. 'I will see you later though, won't I?'

Luke looked vague.

'I'm not sure about tonight,' he said. 'I'll call you.'

And with that he was gone, leaving Marianne on her own, kicking off her shoes, taking off her pearl earrings and feeling terribly alone.

'Daddy, Daddy, Dadd-eee!!!' It's nearly Christmas!!!' Ruby was jumping on Noel's bed with all the glee of a four-year-old two days before the big day. He would have liked to feel as enthusiastic as she did, but the stonking hangover he'd got from the previous night wasn't helping any.

He looked at the time. Damn. It was nearly eleven thirty. He hadn't meant to go back to bed after Cat had left, but it had been so tempting. Cat had left him a depressingly daunting list of things to do and, knowing how exacting her standards were, he also knew he'd been set up for failure. Living with the sodding Happy Homemaker was a pain in the proverbial sometimes.

Noel climbed out of bed, threw some clothes on and went downstairs to discover the lounge in chaos, with bowls of cereal littered about and three out of four of his children still in their pyjamas watching *Harry Potter*.

'Come on you lot, up and out,' he said. Despite a great deal of moaning, Noel eventually managed to get them into some semblance of order, and got a reasonably good system of teamwork going whereby the little ones searched in all the small gaps under sofas and behind cupboards for missing toys, while the older two sorted everything out into the relevant boxes.

In the meantime, Noel tackled the huge pile of washing that had developed overnight apparently. What were they paying Magda for exactly? He even got the broom out and swept the kitchen, which was a first for him, but he knew Catherine was always moaning about how no one did it apart from her.

'I'm hungry.' James appeared at the kitchen door, looking hopeful.

'You're always hungry,' said Noel. He'd only just started – if they stopped for lunch now he'd never finished.

'I'm starving,' said Melanie, 'when's lunch?'

'Not yet,' said Noel, 'we've got too much to do.'

'I'll make everyone eggy bread if you like,' offered Melanie.

'Brilliant, yes. That would be great,' said Noel. He carried a load of washing upstairs and dumped it in his and Cat's bedroom and then gingerly went into Magda's room to see how that was looking.

For someone who seemed to have packed most of her possessions to take away with her, Magda's room was surprisingly messy. Where did she get all this stuff? Perhaps he should leave it to Cat, he felt like a dirty old man poking around in here, but his mum was due at four and they had at least to have got clean sheets on the bed.

He stripped Magda's bed, and picked up the three half-empty coffee cups on the floor. He decided to leave the lacy knickers and bra draped across the chair. Funny though, he could have sworn Cat had a set just the same.

He marched downstairs feeling quite triumphant, only to discover the kitchen full of smoke and the children bickering.

Cat, of course, chose that moment to arrive back from the airport and, blithely ignoring all the things he had been doing, immediately started haranguing him about the things he hadn't.

Christmas had barely begun and already he was feeling like Scrooge . . .

This Year

Chapter Nine

'Oh God,' said Marianne as she watched Diana Carew, bursting with self-importance, march down the aisle of the church to the altar to where her reception class were perched precariously, clutching their Easter bonnets, ready to burst into 'All Things Bright and Beautiful' when the vicar gave the nod. 'I didn't realise Diana ran the Easter Bonnet Parade too.'

Pippa, who had helped walk the children up from the school, grimaced. 'Hadn't you worked out by now that Diana runs *everything* in Hope Christmas? Without her the place would fall apart. Don't worry, she doesn't get her hands on this service the way she does the Nativity. You won't be seeing any elves and mice today.'

Marianne stifled a giggle. The memory of last year's Nativity in all its awfulness was still imprinted on her brain.

'Are you sure she doesn't want one of the children to dress up as the Easter Bunny?' grinned Marianne.

'Don't even think about it,' warned Pippa. 'I swear she's telepathic. She'll probably suggest it at the next Parish Council.'

But it turned out that Diana wasn't interested in talking about the Easter service that the Hope Christmas primary school always put on in the last week of the Easter term.

'Ah, Marianne, Philippa, I'm glad to get you two together,

I just wanted to check that you were still all right for the Post Office trip next Wednesday? You weren't at the last meeting so I wanted to make sure.'

Marianne and Pippa both muttered excuses. Diana was incredibly good at wrong-footing people but, ignoring their discomfort, she went on, 'We're going to picket the main sorting office in London and then go on to Downing Street. Dear Ralph Nicholas has found us a TV journalist who's going to film the whole thing. It should be terribly jolly. I do hope we'll be seeing you both?'

'School finishes on Tuesday,' said Marianne, 'so I should be able to get there. I'm going down south to visit my parents anyway.'

'I'll do my best,' said Pippa. 'It just depends on the children.'

'Oh, bring them too,' said Diana. 'The more the merrier. Besides, children are *such* good PR!'

She bustled off in a self-important manner to accost Miss Woods, who had hobbled her way down the church aisle and was grumpily looking for a seat, leaving Marianne and Pippa in fits of giggles, which they had to repress quickly as the reception class was getting restive.

Marianne calmed them down and went through once more with the two eldest members of the class what they were going to say, while reassuring the youngest member, who was having the collywobbles. She turned to face the front as the organ started to play and the vicar came forward to welcome the congregation, mainly made up of parents, grandparents and siblings.

She caught sight of Gabriel, who slipped in from the back and squashed his way onto the end of a pew. She smiled and he gave her a small nod of recognition, which filled her with an immediate warmth. She hadn't seen him since the day they'd delivered the lamb together, but she was pleased to see him now. Seeing him in action on the hilltop had given her an increased respect for him. She was glad that they were becoming friends. In fact, for a moment on the hillside, when he'd hugged her after the lamb was born, she'd experienced a slight fluttering feeling as if their friendship could develop into something else. But she hadn't heard from him since, so maybe she'd been imagining things . . .

'Hi, Mum, I was just checking you're still all right for Friday.' Cat was in the kitchen leaning against a worktop and idly flicking through the calendar. Noel had been invited to a charity do at a posh hotel in London through work. He hadn't been all that keen to go, but Cat, whose life of late seemed to alternate between working and picking up children from school, was determined she wasn't going to miss out on the one chance she'd had in ages to wear a glamorous frock.

'Friday?' her mother sounded a little put out. 'What's happening on Friday?'

'You're babysitting for us,' Cat said. 'Remember? Noel and I are going to a charity ball.'

'You are?' her mother sounded quite dumbfounded. 'Well, I'm sorry, darling, but I won't be able to babysit on Friday. You know it's my bridge evening.'

'I thought that was next week,' said Cat in exasperation.

'No, it's this week,' said Mum firmly. 'I know I told you.'

'Like you knew you had to pick the kids up,' muttered Cat crossly.

'Did you say something?'

'Nothing important,' Cat lied, feeling immediately guilty. Cat was aware they relied on her mother to a huge degree. She couldn't help it if she'd double-booked. Maybe it was Cat who'd got the day muddled up. She had so many balls to

127

juggle, what with work, the kids' activities and Noel's increasingly frequent business trips to deal with the eco town in Shropshire, it was no wonder she dropped one occasionally.

'Well, I'm sorry I can't help, dear,' continued her mother. 'I could do next Friday though.'

'It's all right, Mum, I expect I can get Magda to babysit,' said Cat, trying to repress the irritated thought that there was no bloody use her mum babysitting next Friday when the ball was this week.

At that point Magda came in, sulkily bearing a pile of washing. She made a great show of pushing past Cat as she went to load the washing machine. As always when Cat was working at home she felt like a stranger in her own house. Magda had the knack of making it seem like she, Cat, was the intruder, and a martyred air that said, *If you can find time to talk on the phone, surely you can find time to pick the children up.* She'd been keeping up the sulks ever since Cat and Noel had dictated that under no circumstances was Sergei to move in with them.

Cat put the phone down and offered Magda a placatory cup of coffee. Maybe that, and the offer of some extra cash in hand, would be enough to persuade her to babysit on Friday. Maybe.

Gabriel squeezed into his pew with a sigh of relief. He'd just made it in time. The ewe he'd been lambing had conveniently delivered ten minutes before he was due to leave, and Sam, a local farmer, had offered to keep an eye on mother and baby while Gabriel went to Stephen's Easter service. Stephen's class were deemed too old for Easter bonnets, which was just as well as he'd reacted in horror when teased about it, but he'd been asked to sing a solo after the sermon so Gabriel, who felt ambivalent about going to church at the best of times, had felt duty-bound to turn up.

128

The service commenced and proved to be Hope Christmas' usual mix of the homely (the reception class duly made everyone go 'aah' when they got up and recited a prayer of their own – Gabriel grinned and gave Marianne the thumbs up when they sat down), the bizarre (Diana Carew bounding in as though she had allegedly nothing to do with proceedings and exhorting everyone to join with her in prayers for the mission in Africa where her sister was currently working – the vicar looked slightly startled, but covered it up admirably), and the dull. The vicar couldn't help having a monotone, Gabriel supposed, but it was damn hard keeping awake when you'd been up all night lambing. And he couldn't help suppressing the odd yawn as Richard (he never wanted you to call him anything else) earnestly exhorted him not to forget the importance of the Paschal season and the sacrifice of the Lamb of God. Gabriel smiled wryly to himself – everything seemed to be about lambs at the moment.

Gabriel was counting down the minutes till Stephen's party piece. He'd been surprised when Miss Peterson had sent a note home to say that Stephen had a solo, having had no idea that his son was even vaguely musical, but one of the very nice, if occasionally misguided things about the village school, was their belief that every child had a talent that should be encouraged. Having witnessed the humiliation of footballers with two left feet, and actors who could barely deliver a line, Gabriel wasn't always sure of the wisdom of this approach. He just hoped Stephen wasn't going to get too upset. He'd been in bits on Mother's Day and refused to do a reading in assembly.

Gabriel suddenly jerked awake, hoping no one had noticed him dozing off in the dying moments of Richard's sermon, and realised that his son had made his way to the microphone at the front of the church. He swallowed nervously, but smiled encouragingly at Stephen, who stared past him in steely determination as if he couldn't focus on anything but the back of the church. Stephen stood with his hands in his pockets looking as if he were about to do anything but sing. Gabriel longed to tell him not to slouch. He hoped this wasn't going to be too dreadful. Marianne, meanwhile, had moved to the piano by the side of the altar and played a single note.

Stephen took his hands out of his pockets, pulled himself straight, and launched into a hymn that Gabriel half remembered from childhood.

'Now the green blade riseth from the buried grain,' Stephen sang. Gabriel was aware his jaw had dropped to the floor. His son had the voice of an angel. How was it that he had never known? The purity of the notes he was hitting was astonishing. Gabriel listened with a lump in his throat, as his son sang poignantly of the wheat that lay in the dark earth and the love that springeth green. The courage of his boy. The joy of him. How could Eve have walked away from that? The hymn was religious, Gabriel knew, but all it reminded him of was the death of his marriage, and the pain his wife had caused them. Tears prickled his eyes as the hymn came to an end.

When our hearts are wintry, grieving, or in pain,
Thy touch can call us back to life again;
Fields of our hearts that dead and bare have been:
Love is come again, like wheat that springeth green.

Stephen sang with a pathos to break the hardest of hearts. There was absolute silence when he'd finished. Gabriel smiled at his son through his tears. He watched Marianne putting her arm around Stephen and giving him a hug as she walked him back to his seat. Maybe hope and love could after all come again.

* * *

130

Noel stood gloomily at the bar, wishing he were anywhere but here. At least Cat was with him at a work do for once. The only reason he'd come at all was because it had been made patently clear to him that everyone who was anyone at GRB was expected to go to the charity ball to raise money for eco towns in The Gambia. ('It's a global village,' had become Gerry Cowley's mantra recently.) Noel suspected it was because if they didn't go en masse, the very lucrative contract that House the World were offering might get snapped up by one of their rivals.

Since his trip to Shropshire, Noel had been expecting to be given his marching orders but, while no one had paid any attention to his suggestion that the site of the eco town was completely wrong, neither had anyone given him a hard time about it. Noel was half convinced that Matt was keeping Noel's feelings about the project under wraps so Noel could do the donkey work on the calculations. It was becoming rapidly clear to Noel that Matt was a shit engineer who flew close to the wind at every available opportunity. But presumably even he had to get the calculations right, so now Noel was feeling even more disempowered as he realised that he had simply become Matt's whipping boy. Was there no end to this downward spiral of humiliation?

Apparently not. As he approached their table with the drinks, he was mortified to see that Matt was cosying up to Cat, who seemed to be lapping up his every word. Noel sat down moodily and sipped his pint. Cat barely seemed to notice his return, though she quickly tucked into the wine he'd bought her.

'Hi, darling,' she said. 'Have you heard this outrageous joke Matt's just told me?'

'No,' muttered Noel ungraciously, but Cat barely seemed to notice, leaning forward to laugh at the next thing Matt said, and drinking far more quickly than she normally did.

'Do you have to drink quite so much?' he hissed in her ear, as she stumbled up to go to the loo.

'Don't be such a killjoy,' said Cat. 'Come on, after the next course they've promised dancing. We haven't been out together in ages, let's have some fun.'

But Noel wasn't in the mood for fun. He hated these charity dos. The endless phoniness of people outdoing each other in their outrageous bids for bits of celebrity tat, the excessive amount of money spent on food and booze, when, particularly in this case, half the money spent on the event could probably build an eco town in The Gambia. Maybe it was time he moved on. Did something else. Got away from all these people he was beginning to hate. Yes, but then what?

'Come on, big boy.' Julie was standing before him, looking resplendent in a far too tight little black number. Little being the operative word. 'You owe me a dance from the Christmas do.'

'I do?' Noel glanced over to where Cat and Matt were still in full flow. She barely seemed to know he was there. Well, two could play at that game.

'Sure do,' said Julie, and dragged him on the dance floor, where she proceeded to throw both of them around wildly. Next thing he knew, Cat was next to him with Matt.

'What are you playing at?' she snapped at him. 'You look ridiculous. She's young enough to be your daughter.'

'No more ridiculous than you with your toyboy,' Noel spat back.

'Oh, for heaven's sake,' Cat sighed. 'It may have escaped your notice but Matt has just disappeared into a corner with one of your secretaries.'

Noel looked over to where Cat was pointing and saw Matt all over a buxom girl from Accounts. He felt wrong-footed but wasn't going to admit it.

132

Meanwhile, Julie seemed to have sensed she wasn't welcome and had disappeared, leaving Cat and Noel glaring at each other. Bryan Ferry was just admonishing them to stick together, when Cat said, 'I've had enough of this. You've been like a bear with a sore head all evening. I want to go home.'

'Good,' said Noel. 'I'll call us a taxi.'

Ten minutes later they were speeding home, neither of them speaking, the atmosphere feeling as poisonous as Noel could ever remember. Why had he ruined a perfectly good evening? He and Cat hadn't been out together for ages. They'd spent a fortune and had a rotten time.

They arrived home in silence and were shocked by the sound of music playing at top volume from their lounge.

'What's that bloody girl doing now?' Noel growled.

'How the hell should I know?' said Cat. 'I'm not her keeper.'

Noel strode into the lounge and flung open the door to tell Magda to turn the music down.

'Oh my God—'

Magda was splayed across the sofa, and Noel was mesmerised by the sight of Sergei's firm buttocks bouncing up and down on top of her.

Chapter Ten

Cat moved swiftly to the CD player and turned Amy Winehouse off.

'What the hell do you think you're doing?'

Magda sat up and for once had the grace to look rather sheepish.

'I did not know you would be back so soon,' she said. She pulled her satin slip up to cover the bits Cat would rather she hadn't seen, while Sergei hurriedly zipped up his trousers. Without a word he pushed past Noel and ran out of the front door.

'It's immaterial what time we got back,' said Cat, trying with great restraint to keep her voice steady. 'You shouldn't have been shagging Sergei here anyway.'

Magda rapidly went into an orgy of explanation, which went something along the lines of how difficult it was for her and Sergei to find any privacy now he had nowhere to live. Cat felt tired and fed up. Her evening out with Noel had been an utter disaster and now this. Magda was now sulkily getting dressed and Cat got another flash of her silk camisole, which looked remarkably like one of Cat's . . .

'What gave you the right to steal my clothes?' The bloody cheek of the girl. She'd pinched Cat's underwear! God knows what else she was wearing that belonged to Cat.

'You have so many nice things,' whined Magda. 'I am poor. You do not understand.'

'I understand you're a thief and a liar, and not to be trusted,' said Cat. 'I shall be calling the agency in the morning. And I want you out of here by the afternoon. Is that understood?'

At this Magda let out a great wail.

'But I have nowhere to go. And now I don't have Sergei. He will finish with me for sure. And I need money for my sick mother. Please, you can't sack me.'

Cat felt herself relenting. Magda was after all very young. Perhaps, if she'd been in the same situation in her early twenties she might have taken similar advantage. (No you wouldn't have, her inner voice admonished sternly.) Besides, if she got rid of Magda tomorrow there'd be no back-up plan. She'd be left without childcare. And she had a busy week ahead of her.

Cat looked at Noel, who was still standing in stunned silence.

'Well?' she said.

'Your call,' said Noel. 'But if she really is down on her luck . . .'

Lord, he was such a soft touch, although of course that was one of his most endearing qualities.

Cat turned to Magda.

'Okay,' she said. 'This is your very last chance. You can count tonight as a verbal *and* written warning. I shall be ringing the agency to tell them what has happened, and if there is any repeat of this, I mean ANY at all, you'll be out on your ear.'

'Oh, thank you, Cat-er-ine, thank you,' said Magda effusively, the tears on her face miraculously drying. 'I promise it won't happen again.'

'You bet it won't,' said Noel with feeling.

135

Magda gathered her things and disappeared up to her room, while Cat busied herself putting the room to rights.

'Fancy a nightcap?' said Noel.

'I think I need a triple after that,' said Cat. 'I also feel the need to fumigate the room. Honestly, it could only happen to us.'

She looked at Noel and they both burst out laughing, the tension of the evening dissipating as if by magic.

'Give you something to blog about,' said Noel, as they made their way down to the kitchen.

'I don't think so,' said Cat. 'I'm sure the Happy Homemaker's au pair would *never* behave like that.'

The rain was still coming down in sheets as Gabriel strode across his land. There'd been a storm earlier in the week and one of his fences had come down. It shouldn't take him long to mend, but he was soaked through and just wanted to get home and dry. He'd never known a wetter spring. Gabriel had hoped that if the weather improved he'd be able to get the lambs back out on the hillside, but they were still too small to withstand this onslaught. In fact, though Gabriel was quite hardened to the weather conditions, even he felt like curling up in front of the fire toasting marshmallows and drinking hot chocolate with Stephen while they watched CBBC together. He'd been most envious of Pippa who'd offered to take Stephen for him again, and was busy making hot chocolate as he left.

Still, sooner looked at, sooner sorted, as his dad always said. He put his head against the wind and rain and soldiered on, wishing his parents hadn't chosen this particular time in his life to go and find themselves. He missed his father's wisdom and his mother's comfort. Sometimes, even with all the help Pippa gave him, he felt horribly alone.

It was pretty bleak on the hillside today, so Gabriel was

surprised to see a figure coming towards him. Who on earth would be mad enough to be out in this?

As the person approached he realised it was Marianne. Her cheeks were flushed from the exercise and her dark hair curled softly under her woolly hat. She managed to look lovely even in all-weather gear.

'Hi,' he said. 'What brings you out in this dreadful weather? I don't need any assistance lambing today, you know.'

'I'm not sure,' said Marianne cheerfully, who looked if anything even wetter and muddier then he did. 'Unless it's a ridiculous subconscious desire to end up with pneumonia. It wasn't that bad when I left.'

'Where are you headed?' said Gabriel.

'Well, I was going to nip round to the next valley and then back home,' said Marianne, pointing to the path that stretched behind Gabriel and up the hillside. If you could call it a path – it was more of a boggy stream at present. 'I just wanted to make the most of my last day here before I disappear for a fortnight but, judging by that horrendously muddy path, I think I may just call it a day and go home.'

'You're going away?' Gabriel felt a pang of regret. He'd got used to seeing Marianne about the place.

'Only for Easter,' she said. 'I'm going down to this demo at the Post Office, and then on to my parents' for the Easter weekend. I'll probably visit friends in London as well, but I may come back sooner if I'm bored.'

She smiled at him and his heart gave a sudden lurch. Good lord, could he possibly be feeling what he thought he was feeling? A stab of guilt shot through him. Technically he wasn't free, he shouldn't even be thinking about anyone other than Eve, wherever she was. But Eve wasn't here and Marianne was.

'I'll miss you,' he said simply, and realised for the first

time the truth of it. He would miss her. Marianne was fast becoming a necessary part of his life.

Marianne clambered onto the coach a little breathless and late. She'd overslept, having had a restless night. She couldn't put her finger on why. Part of it was to do with going home for the first time since Luke had dumped her – she'd been putting off dealing with her mother's over-solicitousness – and part of it, she had no doubt, had been to do with her rather unsettling encounter with Gabriel on the hillside yesterday.

Marianne had gone for a walk to blow away the cobwebs, having been cooped up all day with a bunch of over-excited reception children who'd eaten far too many chocolate eggs and been made doubly hyper by being kept in for play by the wet. She'd gone out for one of her usual hikes, setting off in a light drizzle that swiftly became a torrent, and she was soon soaked through. Somehow she didn't mind though. There would be plenty of time to stay indoors in London; right now, right here, she felt elemental, and close to nature. It felt fabulous.

Marianne had been lost in her thoughts when she'd run into Gabriel. He'd appeared over the brow of the hill, looking for all the world like some kind of dashing hero. Mr Rochester, eat your heart out. She'd always preferred him to Darcy.

It was with a jolt that Marianne had realised that just meeting Gabriel like that was having a funny effect on her. Her back had felt all tingly and her legs had turned to jelly. And when he said he'd miss her in that lovely Shropshire burr, her heart had given a springlike leap of joy. Suddenly she'd realised she was going to miss him too.

'Penny for 'em?' Pippa had squeezed into the seat next to Marianne and was doling out food to the children.

'Oh, nothing,' said Marianne, 'just thinking.' She daren't

mention Gabriel to Pippa. Dearly as she loved her friend, it was obvious that Pippa was itching for the chance to play matchmaker.

She stared out of the coach window as it left Hope Christmas and everyone cheered. When she'd come here she'd been so much in love with Luke. And then he'd broken her heart. But over the last few months she'd come to love Hope Christmas and the people in it more than she'd ever loved Luke. She wondered how much she could let that include Gabriel. Could she think about a relationship just yet? And more importantly, should she? Gabriel had a lot of baggage, even if he were interested: she wasn't sure it would be wise to get involved. But, then again, Marianne thought, as the coach pulled away from the Shropshire hills and the sun broke out through the clouds, what had wisdom got to do with love?

Noel was cutting through Mount Pleasant on his way back to work after rather more of a liquid lunch than he'd intended with an old school friend, when a demonstration caught his eye. There was a TV crew and a bunch of people holding banners. They appeared to be protesting against post office closures and, weirdly, when he got up close he realised they were holding banners saying 'KEEP HOPE CHRISTMAS ALIVE! HANDS OFF OUR POST OFFICE!'

'That's such a coincidence,' he said out loud.

'No such thing as coincidence.'

To his surprise, Ralph Nicholas was standing to one side of the group, looking on with a mischievous gleam in his eye.

'What are you doing here?'

'Can't have my local post office closing down, can I now?' said Ralph. 'It's bad enough that my beloved grandson and your chums are seeking to destroy what remains of our local environment with their wretched eco town schemes. If the post office goes, Hope Christmas will surely die.'

Noel thought back to the pretty village in which he'd stayed on his various site visits. Every time he went up to Shropshire he'd fallen a little bit more in love. He'd even started fantasising about living there. If only Cat could be persuaded to leave London. If only he could find himself a job up there. If only the grass were greener and there were gold at the end of the rainbow.

'That's a great pity,' said Noel. 'It looks a lovely place to live.'

'It is,' said Ralph. 'You should come and stay properly. See for yourself. Then maybe persuade your company not to get involved in my grandson's harebrained schemes.'

'If I had my way, we wouldn't be building the eco town,' said Noel. 'But sadly my clout isn't what it was. No one wants to listen to me anymore.'

He felt maudlin when he said it. He was approaching his mid forties, washed up, his career going nowhere, his wife paying him little attention. What was there left?

'There's plenty left,' Ralph said briskly, as if somehow he'd read Noel's mind. 'If you do ever decide to come to the country, you can always give me a call. My company could do with a decent engineer.'

'Oh, thanks,' said Noel. He rather liked this eccentric old man. 'Good luck with your campaign by the way.'

'Don't forget to sign our petition,' said Ralph, tipping his hat at Noel before going off to engage the manager sent out by the Post Office to discuss the situation with him.

Noel did as he was asked and then walked back to the office.

Move to Hope Christmas? Get a new job as Ralph's engineer? It was a fantasy and he knew it. Let's face it, he had no more chance of moving than of flying to the moon.

Chapter Eleven

'Okay, peeps, listen up.' Beverley had gathered the troops together for the bi-monthly forward planning meeting. 'I know we're all in Easter Bunny land right now, but it's time to give some thought to the Christmas issue.'

There was a collective groan round the table. Every year, agreeing upon the contents of the Christmas issue seemed to get harder than ever.

'Now, now, folks, that's not what I expect,' said Bev. 'Come on, let's do some brainstorming. I've ordered sandwiches for lunch so we can keep going as long as possible.'

'I could do top ten make-up tips for the party season,' offered Abi, the new fashion editor, who looked to Cat both depressingly young and even more depressingly thin.

'Hmm, we've done that every year since forever,' said Bev, 'as has every other mag out there. Can you come up with a twist?'

'Well, I suppose I could funk it up a little,' said Abi. 'Maybe how to be a Christmas fashion victim with a difference? Marrying clothes and colours you wouldn't normally expect. Your little black dress with some glitz and sparkle perhaps?'

'Now you're talking,' said Bev.

Was she? Really? Cat for the life of her couldn't see the appeal. The more Abi talked about the strange things she wanted to join up together, the more Cat had a vision of what Melanie was likely to wear to the next school disco – Mel and all her friends tending to go for a mix-and-match approach. Still, maybe Abi was right and that's what the fashion brigade were after these days. Presumably, being twenty-something, she was far more in the know than Cat.

'We could do a piece on what celebs are getting up to at Christmas,' said Rosie, the entertainment writer. 'You know, Angelina and Brad are going for the traditional roasting chestnuts round the fire approach, you could do the same.'

'Hmm, might work, depends on the calibre of the celebrities, I guess,' said Bev.

'What about an article on Christmas bling?' offered Abi. 'You know, Swarovksi crystals, black Christmas trees – that kind of thing.'

'Didn't you do something similar last year?' Bev asked Cat.

'I'm afraid I did,' said Cat, still groaning at the memory of having to extol the virtues of glass Santas perched atop a snowy table decoration for the reasonable price of £40. 'But I could do a credit crunch version if you like. Can't afford Swarovski, but still want your Christmas to bling? How about a cheaper alternative?'

'That's a possibility, I suppose, depends how tacky cheap bling is,' said Bev. 'Keep working, people.'

After an hour there were a dozen or more ideas on the table, but nobody felt inspired by any of them.

'It all feels a bit old hat,' said Bev, looking critically through the list. 'We've got our usual fashion list, our usual celebs list, our usual what to buy your husband for Christmas list. It doesn't feel fresh. I want fresh. And different. Cat. We haven't heard much from you today. What's the Happy Homemaker's take on Christmas?'

Cat thought back to her own last disastrous festive season

and repressed a shudder. 'You probably don't want to know,' she said. 'Only, I was thinking . . . Nah. Forget it. It's probably a stupid idea.'

'Forget what?'

'It's just, well, I guess we all remember the Christmases of our childhood, and I don't know . . . they seemed simpler somehow. Look at all the stuff we've got down here. Five different ways to stuff a turkey; fill your home with festive garlands; bring some sparkle to your Christmas table. Doesn't it seem, I don't know, a bit too much? Why do we need a brand new Christmas tablecloth and matching napkins each year?

'Since when has Christmas been spoilt because we couldn't get the requisite number of baubles on the tree? And do the kids really need every single electronic gizmo going? When I was a kid you were just as happy with a board game and a book and a satsuma in your stocking. Why does Christmas have to be such a frenzy of consumerism?

'Couldn't we turn it around and go for a simpler approach? What with us being now officially in recession and all, and people not having so much money to spend, why not get back to the true spirit of Christmas?'

'What, like *A Christmas Carol* type of thing?' smirked Rosie.

'Well, yes, a bit, I suppose,' said Cat. 'I could do a piece on how to do Christmas lunch on a budget, Abi could do one on reviving fashions of yesteryear. Rosie, your celeb piece could be about celebs who keep it simple, maybe?'

'It could work, I suppose,' said Bev. 'Yes, I'm beginning to like this. What else could we have?'

'Could we give something away to the family who achieved the simplest Christmas?' said Abi.

'Or donate some money to charity?' offered Clare, Bev's assistant.

143

'What about finding the perfect Nativity?' said Cat. 'God knows I've been to some dire ones in my time. Last year, all I wanted to hear was a decent carol. Maybe we could give a prize to the school or parish that comes up with the Nativity play that is closest to the spirit of the season?'

'That's a brilliant idea,' said Bev. 'We'll put it on the front cover. Were you planning a break over the summer holiday? If so, cancel it!'

'What do we want?'
   'To save our Post Office!'
'When do we want it?'
   'Now!!!'

Diana was doing such a good job directing the action, Marianne felt that the rest of them might as well not be there. She was darting about, geeing everyone up, thrusting leaflets into the faces of every beleaguered soul who was going in or out of Mount Pleasant. Unfortunately, though a representative had come out to politely take their petition, there hadn't been too much interest. The TV crew that had pitched up as they arrived had interviewed Vera (much to Diana's chagrin, Marianne had noticed with amusement), but had pushed off, having received a tip-off that someone famous was about to leave The Ivy.

   People were beginning to mill around aimlessly in the street, not knowing quite what to do.

'I think we should chain ourselves to the Post Office building,' said Miss Woods. 'Someone must have a strawberry-thingy with them to send a message to that film crew, to get them back here again.'

'I'm not sure that's such a good idea,' began Vera tactfully, before being swept out of the way by a self-important Diana, her bosoms going before her like a magnificent ship, clearly enjoying herself hugely.

'Right, come on now.' Diana bustled up clapping her hands. 'It's time we were moving on. Next stop Downing Street.'

Within seconds the crowd had been marshalled and cajoled into order. You had to hand it to Diana, Marianne thought. She and her enormous bosoms did manage to get things done.

Marianne and Pippa made their way back to the coach, trying to stop the boys making bunny ears behind Diana, though they were both hard pressed not to dissolve into laughter.

'How lovely to see you looking so cheerful,' Ralph Nicholas said, as Marianne waited to board the bus.

'Well, I can't sit around feeling sorry for myself for the rest of my life, can I?' replied Marianne.

'True,' nodded Ralph. 'I'm pleased to see you getting so involved as well. Much better than festering at home.'

'Well, it's all down to you I'm here,' said Marianne. 'I'm glad you suggested it. And that you persuaded me to stay in Hope Christmas. It's not quite how I planned things, but it's not as bad as I feared.'

'Ah well, as one door closes another one opens,' said Ralph. 'You never know what the future holds, which I always find rather exciting, don't you?'

'I've never looked at it like that before,' confessed Marianne, climbing on the bus. 'But you know, I think you could be right.'

Noel was sitting at his desk looking at the mountain of paperwork he had to deal with, contemplating whether he should commit a slow hara-kiri, when Julie came in looking sombre.

'Gerry wants to see you,' she said.

'Oh?' Noel felt his stomach drop to his boots. The cull

at GRB had been going on for months. He knew his days were numbered – surely the only reason that he hadn't gone by now was his ability to cover up Matt's inadequacies. Presumably now that the eco town was well under way, Matt was going to leave him out in the cold, and it was his turn to discover that GRB were going to dispense with his services. Feeling like a condemned man, and aware that ten pairs of eyes were fixed firmly on his back, Noel got up and took the long walk down the corridor towards Gerry Cowley's office. Noel wasn't given much to empathy, but he knew exactly what all the other buggers were thinking. First off it would be a gleam of sympathy for his plight, rapidly replaced with guilty relief that it wasn't them having to face the music.

He knocked on Gerry's door, feeling like a guilty schoolboy. Crikey, he was forty-four. Far too old to be feeling like this.

'Ah, Neil, sit down, sit down,' Gerry said expansively as Noel walked in.

'It's Noel,' said Noel. How many times over the years had he had to say that? All the bloody work he'd put into this company. All those years. He was a good engineer. Damned good. One of the best GRB had ever had. And now he was being put on the scrap heap. He'd been in the same job for fifteen years. Noel had forgotten how to even look for a job. He didn't even have a CV anymore. What on earth was he going to do?

'As you know, these are difficult economical times,' said Gerry.

Noel felt sick. He'd allowed himself a brief flash of hope when Gerry had invited him to sit down – previous redundancy victims had all reported not being allowed to sit – but the mention of the economy was a sure sign of what was coming next.

'And in these challenging times we all have to cut our cloth to fit,' continued Gerry. He paused. Noel felt like screaming, this was excruciating. 'We have to make sacrifices. Some of them painful.'

Go on, Noel felt like saying, just spit it out, but he remained silent.

'You're our best engineer,' Gerry said abruptly. 'And, from what young Matt says, you're doing a grand job on the eco town.'

Noel grimaced. Was this a good moment to say that the eco town was being built in exactly the wrong place? Five years ago when his stock was high at GRB, he could probably have got away with it, but now? He contented himself with a muttered thank you.

'Well, I'd better not beat around the bush any longer,' said Gerry. 'While I appreciate everything you've done for the company . . .'

'You're going to have to let me go,' finished Noel. Considering how many redundancies Gerry must have doled out this year, he seemed remarkably inept at dishing out the bad news.

'Oh.' Gerry looked surprised. 'Well, I'm not exactly letting you go. But I have to be honest, Neil, we are going to have to make some sacrifices.'

'What kind of sacrifices?' muttered Noel.

'The thing is, though, old boy,' Gerry continued in a conspiratorial manner, as if he was doing Noel a huge favour, 'you cost us too much money. Young Matt isn't a patch on you as an engineer, but he's much much cheaper. We don't want to lose you, naturally, but in order to keep you, I'm afraid to say you're going to have to take a substantial drop in salary.'

Noel went cold all over.

'How substantial?' he said.

Gerry named a figure that left Noel reeling. He resisted the impulse to say he was sorry that his mortgage company couldn't generously offer to lower his mortgage to accommodate GRB's needs, but then Gerry dangled the inevitable carrot.

'Of course, if you do a good job on the eco town, things will probably look very different. Hopesay Holdings have considerable interests around the country and abroad. If this project goes well, GRB could be on to a winner. So, if you deliver, Neil, who knows – there might be a big fat Christmas bonus with your name on it.'

Noel left Gerry's office feeling curiously lightheaded. He'd spent months anticipating losing his job, but what Gerry was offering was worse. He didn't even have golden handcuffs anymore, just very tarnished brass ones. The trouble was, with the job market so uncertain, Noel wasn't in any position to bargain and Gerry knew it. The drop in salary couldn't have come at a worse time for them, with their mortgage rate being fixed while interest rates were tumbling. But at least he was still in a job. For now at least.

'Daddy, Daddy, I think one of the ewes is ill.' Stephen came bursting out of the sheep barn as Gabriel walked up with a barrel of food for his flock. He'd left Stephen there looking at the new lamb who'd been born last night. The mother had seemed a little feverish afterwards, but she had seemed more settled this morning. He hoped so. He couldn't really afford the vet's bill at the moment.

Gabriel followed his son back into the barn, where he saw the mother lying listlessly on her side while her lamb forlornly tried to suckle from her. Gabriel leant down and stroked the sheep. 'There there, old girl,' he said, reaching for a pulse. It was faint, and unsteady. He had a bad feeling about this. Even if the mother recovered, she clearly couldn't feed her lamb at the moment.

'Is she going to be all right?' Stephen looked anxious.

'I don't know.' Gabriel was trying to dress it up as best he could, but growing up with animals had left Stephen no stranger to what could happen to them. There was no point pretending the ewe was going to get better if she wasn't. He felt in his fleece for his mobile. 'I need to call the vet.'

'Daddy, look.' Stephen grabbed Gabriel's arm.

Oh no.

The sheep, who had been breathing erratically and in a laboured way, gave a sudden wheezy gasp, and then her head flopped to the floor. Her lamb, whose distinctive black tail made it instantly recognisable, baaed pitifully, its little wobbly legs making it seem more vulnerable than ever.

'Is she . . . ?'

Gabriel put the phone down. He'd need to ring the vet later, but for now there was nothing more he could do for the ewe.

'I'm sorry, Stephen, but I think she is,' said Gabriel.

Stephen flung himself into Gabriel's arms, sobbing hysterically.

'Woah.' Gabriel held his son tight. How strange, when the boy scarcely mentioned his mother now, that watching the ewe die had caused so much distress.

'Can we look after the lamb?' Stephen raised a tear-stained face to his father. 'Can we?'

Gabriel swallowed. Did he really want the lamb in the house? By rights, he should give it to the ewe who'd lost the twin, she had plenty of milk for both. He looked at Stephen's expectant face. He couldn't let him down.

'Of course,' he said. 'I'll fix a box for it in the kitchen, and you can look after it.'

'Can I?' Stephen's face broke into a huge grin and he hugged his dad even harder. 'Daddy, you're the best.'

Together they prepared a box of hay, and Gabriel gently lifted the lamb into it and carried it back to the house. They settled it down in the kitchen and Gabriel found a baby's bottle he kept for the purpose. Soon Stephen was snuggled up on the sofa giving his new pet a bottle.

'He's just like me,' Stephen declared, 'he hasn't got a mummy either. But I'm going to be his mummy now.'

Gabriel didn't know whether to laugh or cry.

Chapter Twelve

'You're too thin.' Marianne's mother stood in the kitchen, looking her daughter up and down as if she were a prize cow. It was the only about the millionth time she'd said so. Marianne sighed. There was a reason she'd delayed coming home. And, after the first rapturous moments of welcome, the joy of a decent meal she hadn't cooked herself, and the luxury of a bath in water that didn't take three hours to heat up via the ancient immersion heater, she had quickly fallen back into suppressing her irritation at her mother's fussing. She loved her mother dearly but, even though Marianne had left home years ago, somehow her mother still failed to recognise her daughter's ability to be independent. Marianne had found her stifling growing up but, now she was an adult, she rebelled against it even more. She felt so hemmed in at her parents' house, she longed for the freedom of the place she was beginning to think of as home. Back there, in a few short minutes, she could be striding out in the Shropshire hills, whereas here the only place to escape to was the drab local park, with its miserable patch of green, graffitied play area and confining borders. Marianne invariably came back from a stroll around the park feeling worse than when she'd left.

'You'd hate it if she didn't make a fuss,' her father always said, and to a degree it was true. But Marianne felt faintly depressed by the thinly veiled disappointment as another chance for her mother to plan a wedding had disappeared, and the prospect of grandmotherhood seemed to be fast disappearing into the distance. Marianne's only brother was a permanent student who was currently travelling the world finding himself. He was about as likely to procreate as an amoeba, though Marianne frequently teased him about leaving a girl behind in every port.

'I'm not too thin, Mum,' said Marianne. 'I've put on half a stone since Christmas.'

Mum sniffed, as if to say, likely story, and Marianne decided to ignore her. She knew her mother only wanted what was best for her, but it was hard enough coming to terms with a broken heart without feeling that her every emotion was being scrutinised by the maternal equivalent of Sherlock Holmes.

'Leave the girl alone,' said her dad, coming in from the shed. Lord knows what he did in there, but the shed, a shadowy feature of her childhood, seemed to have become his second home since retirement. 'She looks perfectly healthy to me.'

Marianne shot him a grateful look. Dad had always been her champion, and helped deflect delicate situations with her mother. He had far more empathy than his wife did, and always knew just when to speak and when to keep quiet, whereas Mum always seemed to feel a silence was there to be filled.

'So, there's no chance of you getting back with that chap?' Mum said. Nothing like the direct approach.

'No,' said Marianne. 'I think there's *very* little chance of that.'

She thought back to the last few months without Luke. It had been hard but, to her surprise, she suddenly realised that she wasn't now as heartbroken as she had been, and was thinking about him less and less.

'Well, plenty more fish in the sea then,' said Mum. 'Anyone else in mind?'

'Give over, Mum,' protested Marianne. 'I've only just come out of one relationship, I'm in no hurry to rush into another.'

'Hmm,' said her mother in disbelieving tones. 'Well, at your age you should get on with it. No time to lose . . .'

The more Marianne protested, the less her mother seemed to believe her.

But then again, as Marianne went to load the dishwasher, and got a sudden flash of Gabriel's face, perhaps it wasn't altogether true . . .

Cat was on her way home from work. She was running late and feeling guilty because she'd promised to get back and help Mel with some science homework that was proving tricky. Science was really Noel's department, but more and more of late he'd been distracted and she'd found it really hard to get him to engage with the children. Cat suspected there was a problem at work, but Noel seemed very tight-lipped about whatever it was and she'd given up trying to prise the information out of him.

Mel had emailed Cat at work with a panicky 'Mum, Homework. Tonight!!!!' email at lunchtime, and Cat had promised she'd get home in time to help her. An increasingly common feature of their relationship of late, Cat wryly noted, was that Mel expected Cat to drop everything for her. Of course, Cat compounded things by always doing exactly that, but she could still remember the uncertainty of her first year at secondary school and didn't want Mel to feel she couldn't ask for help.

The only trouble was, of course, her work life was rarely accommodating of her home life. Just as she was about to leave, one of the subs had queried a line in her last feature on 'How to Detox Your House', and Bev wanted her urgent opinion on the October cover layout, and suddenly it was gone six and she still hadn't answered her emails. She rang Magda to say she was running late, and tried Noel who, judging by the list of missed calls, had been urgently trying to call her. But when she rang back all she got was a 'This mobile is switched off' message, and his work answerphone was proclaiming he was away from his desk. She was about to leave when her mobile rang. Mum. She'd better answer that.

'Hello?' Cat gathered her bag over her shoulder, and headed for the door. The phone went dead. Odd. She rang back and got a busy tone. Damn. On the way down the corridor she kept trying her mother, and continually got the engaged tone. Well, it can't have been that urgent.

The phone rang again as she headed down the road to the bus stop.

'Catherine, there you are,' her mother sounded a bit flustered. 'I've been trying to ring you for hours.'

'I've been trying to ring you,' said Cat, 'but you were engaged.'

'Because I was trying to ring you,' said her mother.

This was going nowhere. 'Was it anything in particular? I'm just on my way home.'

'Oh, nothing,' said Mum. 'Just. This is a bit daft. Can you remember? Do I need flour or eggs in an apple pie? I've got Auntie Eileen coming for dinner, and I keep looking at the ingredients and they both look wrong.'

Cat frowned. Mum was the best cook Cat knew. How strange that she should have forgotten how to make pastry.

'Well, I've never made pastry with eggs,' she said, trying to laugh it off. 'But you do need flour.'

There was a pause.

'Well, of course you don't use eggs in pastry. At least not if you're making shortcrust pastry. Why on earth did you think you did?'

It was on the tip of Cat's tongue to make an acid remark about why her mother had bothered to ring her then, but she paused. There was something very odd about the tone in her mother's voice. In fact, the whole conversation was very odd.

'Mum, are you all right?'

'Never better, dear,' said her mother. 'I will be seeing you all for lunch on Sunday, won't I?'

'Yes, of course,' said Cat.

'Well, bye then,' said her mother, and put the phone down, leaving Cat feeling unsettled. *Was* there something wrong with her mum? And if so, what, if anything, could she do about it?

The last of the ewes had finally delivered her lambs, twins again, but this time neither had died. Gabriel settled mother and babes and made his way back to the kitchen where a sleepy Stephen was sitting with Pippa as he fed his pet one last time before bed.

'Everything all right?' Pippa nodded in the direction of the barn.

'Fine, thanks,' said Gabriel. 'And thanks for looking after Stephen, again. I feel bad about always asking you.'

'Well, you shouldn't,' said his cousin briskly. 'That's what families are for, to help each other out. Besides, if you hadn't had the kids for me on Saturday, Dan and I wouldn't have been able to get out for that meal.'

'True.' Gabriel felt he did little enough for his cousin, so the least he could manage was the occasional sleepover if it helped her and Dan out. 'Stephen enjoyed it anyway, so it was no hardship.'

'I'd best be off,' said Pippa, gathering her things. 'I don't really like leaving Dan to deal with everyone at bedtime.'

'No, of course not,' said Gabriel. 'Are you going to the Monday Muddle on Easter Monday?'

'Wouldn't miss it for the world,' grinned Pippa. 'Besides, Diana Carew said I could have a stall to showcase our produce, didn't Dan tell you?'

'I don't think so,' said Gabriel. 'Mind you, I've been so busy recently everything's going in one ear and out the other. Still, that's great. The Monday Muddle's a brilliant opportunity to show people what we can offer.'

The Monday Muddle was an annual village event held every Easter Monday, along with a traditional market. Part football match, part free for all, the origins of it were lost way back in the mists of time, but everyone in the village turned out to see a football, reputedly two hundred years old and made of an old leather sack, alleged by some to have covered the head of a notorious highwayman, kicked high in the air. In the ensuing scrum, whoever picked up the ball was meant to run with it as fast as they could, without letting go, to the village pub. Miraculously, the event hadn't yet been cancelled by the health and safety brigade, which was remarkable considering how many people ended up injured in the scrum. The person who managed it was then bought pints by everyone else for the rest of the day. All the village men were supposed to take part, but Gabriel often declined.

'Daddy, you are going to go in for it this year, aren't you?'

Gabriel groaned. Stephen had pressured him into going in for it last year, and he had reluctantly agreed. He had never got over the trauma of doing the event in his teens when he'd been a total lightweight and Dan and all his cronies had inevitably sat on him. Dan in fact was still the undisputed champion of the event, being a broad six-foot-plus rugby player. Gabriel, with his wiry build, was fine on speed, but lacked the brute strength to win at such a physical event.

'No,' he said. 'You know I hate the Monday Muddle. Besides, Uncle Dan will beat me hands down, don't you think?'

'He might not,' said Stephen. 'You don't know if you don't try, do you?'

Raising his eyebrows at Pippa at having one of his constant sayings to his son parroted back at him, Gabriel saw his cousin to the door.

'Go on, give it a try,' she urged. 'You never know, you might even enjoy it.'

'I think you can safely say I won't,' said Gabriel, 'but just for you, I'll think about it.'

'I think Marianne's coming back for it too,' Pippa added slyly.

Gabriel's heart gave an unexpected leap at the thought of Marianne being there. 'I thought Marianne was away for the whole fortnight?'

'She was supposed to be,' said Pippa, 'but she's just texted me to say she's going mad at home, so I rang her and suggested she came back for Monday. She thought it might make the perfect excuse for coming back.'

'Oh right,' said Gabriel. Now he really didn't want to take part. The last person he wanted to see him making a fool of himself was Marianne.

'So now you have to take part, don't you?' teased Pippa.

'What do you mean?' asked Gabriel.

'Well, I told Marianne you would be,' said Pippa. 'And she said she couldn't wait.'

'Pippa, I could kill you sometimes,' sighed Gabriel. 'Don't you ever stop interfering?'

'Nope,' said Pippa. 'But it's for your own good, so one day you'll thank me.'

* * *

The pub was heaving. Noel was incredibly touched by how many of his fellow GRB sufferers were prepared to come along to cheer him up once the news spread about his change of circumstances. Feeling that he was in the worst of all possible worlds, Noel had seen no other option than to go to the pub. He'd rung Cat to say he'd be late, but kept getting her work answerphone and her mobile was switched off. So he rang Magda, who sounded utterly disinterested but at least promised to pass the message on to Cat. He tried Cat one last time. Still no answer. Leaving a message to say he was going to the pub, but not feeling able to say why, he snapped his phone shut and went to the bar and ordered another pint.

Four pints and no food later, Noel was feeling more than a little unsteady on his feet. He really should go home.

'Are you coming to eat?' Julie appeared by his side with a couple of her cronies.

'I think I'd better be off,' said Noel, aware that he was swaying and also aware that he was probably looking like an undignified, middle-aged twat.

'No, come with us,' commanded Julie, and suddenly he found himself swept up in a wave of youth, beauty and drunken enthusiasm. He tried to ring Cat again, but her mobile was still switched off, and he was so useless at texting sober he couldn't even begin to think about it drunk.

Hours passed and suddenly it was midnight and he was sitting dishevelled in a dingy nightclub, his tie undone, feeling a complete wreck. Really, it was time to go home.

'Come on, come and dance.' Julie was dragging him to the dance floor.

'I've got to go,' he protested feebly.

'No, you haven't,' said Julie. 'Come on, we're having fun.'

Fun. Yes. Noel remembered that. Last time he'd had any fun had been sometime in the Dark Ages.

He let himself go, for a minute forgetting all his troubles under the bright light dazzling his eyes, finding a strange drunken rhythm to the thumping rap of the dance anthem blaring out from the floor. He moved closer and closer to Julie. She was exceptionally pretty. And she'd always been so nice to him . . .

'I really like you, you know,' Julie shouted in his ear.

'I really like you too,' said Noel. He looked down at her. Julie. Julie, his sexy, sweet little secretary. She looked at him. His mouth suddenly went dry and then they were kissing, passionately, stupidly, frantically, as if there was no one left on earth to kiss.

Oh dear God, what was he doing?

Noel broke away in confusion.

'Sorry,' he said. 'Shouldn't have done that. Sorry.'

'I'm not,' said Julie, looking at him lasciviously.

Oh my God. Time to go. Now.

'Julie, you're lovely, but I can't,' Noel said. 'Sorry. Really I am. I didn't mean to be such a shit.'

He fled the dance floor, and ran out into the cold air. He turned his mobile on. Five missed calls from Cat. He leant against the wall of the nightclub gulping in the cool night air. What on earth had he done?

Chapter Thirteen

Catherine sat staring out into the dark garden, sipping a glass of wine and feeling furious. Noel had promised to come home early. It was a bank holiday. They had planned a family day out the next day. He was clearly in the pub because his mobile had been switched off all evening. She'd given up trying to reach it. The kids had all been riotous when she got home, Magda having apparently given them something with thousands of E-numbers for tea. Mel had forgotten all about the important science project by the time Cat had got in; instead, she was in floods of tears because she'd fallen out with her best friend on MSN. Despite Cat's dire warnings about being careful in online dealings, Mel still hadn't quite worked out that MSN wasn't the best place for sorting out disputes. The resulting hysterics had taken an hour to calm down, by which time it was too late to put Ruby in the bath, and James and Paige had managed to cause chaos in the lounge by setting up a complicated *Dr Who* game, which for some reason had required all of Cat's nicest, plumpest, whitest cushions being stuck end to end on the floor. By the time it had all been tidied away and the children chased to bed, it was gone nine.

She glanced at her watch. It was midnight already. Should she go to bed or wait up for him? It was ages since Noel had stayed out so late. And after last Christmas, when she'd made the mistake of confronting him about his late nights in the pub and been given short shrift, Cat was reluctant to give him a hard time. But really she was furious. Why was it okay for him to go out and have a drink with his mates, without a thought for her or the family, when Cat getting out for the evening involved military-style precision planning? And invariably, if she had managed to organise a night out, Noel would always swan in late, as if to make a point about her abandoning her duties for the evening. Long-held resentments bubbled under the surface. This was no good. She was feeling so cross now they'd be bound to have a huge row when he did get home.

Cat finished her drink, washed her glass up, and made her way up to bed. She was halfway up the stairs, when she heard Noel fumbling with the key in the lock.

She went down to open the front door.

'There's no need to wait up for me, you know.' Noel's tone was belligerent.

'I wasn't,' said Cat, trying not to rise to it. 'I was on my way to bed.'

'Oh.' Noel swayed in the hall. 'What time is it?'

'Late,' said Cat. 'You could have rung me.'

'I did,' said Noel. 'Your phone was switched off.'

'That was earlier,' said Cat. 'Where the hell have you been?'

'Well, that's bloody nice,' said Noel. 'How about a kiss when I come through the door?'

'Noel, it's nearly 1 am, I'm really knackered, you're really drunk. I think it's time for bed.'

'Good idea.'

'No,' said Cat. 'I meant bed as in sleep.'

'Sleep? Sleep?' Noel said. 'How can you talk about going to sleep?'

'Quite easily,' said Cat, turning back up the stairs. 'I'm going to bed, you can do what you like.'

161

'Oh, that's right, walk away,' Noel spat out with sudden venom, and Cat turned and stared at him in fury.

'What's that supposed to mean?' she said.

'You, you're not even interested in me anymore,' said Noel.

'That's not true,' protested Cat.

'When was the last time we had sex, then?' said Noel.

'I don't know,' said Cat, 'the other week, probably.'

'Two weeks ago,' said Noel. 'That's when it was.'

Cat had had enough. 'Are you keeping some kind of record?' she said incredulously. 'For heaven's sake, Noel, just grow up, will you?'

She was shouting now, much louder than she intended. But really, he was the sodding limit.

'You just don't fancy me anymore, do you? Why don't you say it?' Noel had gone from angry to bitter in a heart-beat.

'Where the hell did that come from?' asked Cat in exasperation. 'There's no point talking to you when you're like this. I'm going to bed.'

'Well it's true,' shouted Noel after her.

'Oh, save it,' said Cat, storming back upstairs. She was damned if she was going to sleep with him tonight. He could spend the night in the spare room.

'Can you two keep it down?' Mel appeared, yawning sleepily on the stairs.

'Sorry,' said Cat. 'Dad and I were just going to bed.'

She went into her bedroom and turned on the light. What was wrong with Noel? Why did he insist on behaving so badly? They had never really talked over what had happened at Christmas, and now here they were again, back in the same mess as before. What on earth was going to happen to them?

* * *

Marianne sat in a crowded pub with her oldest school friends, Lisa and Carly, whom she'd met to swap stories about old times and catch up on the new. The trouble was, after a perfunctory conversation about what had gone wrong in Marianne's love life, Lisa and Carly seemed utterly uninterested in anything else she had to say now she no longer had a rich boyfriend. Neither of them was exactly the country type and they couldn't understand why Marianne was still holed up in 'the back of beyond', as Lisa put it. In fact, when Marianne thought about it, they'd never been very interested in her really. Lisa with her big City job and succession of fund-manager boyfriends had always been dismissive of Marianne's life choices. 'What do you want to teach for?' she'd gasped in horror. 'Everyone knows teachers are poor.' Carly's job as a gossip girl about town was enough to keep her firmly wedded to the bright lights, big city. 'While there are parties to crash and drinks to blag, I'm your woman,' she was fond of saying. She, too, had barely asked about Marianne's life in Hope Christmas.

'I helped deliver a lamb, you know,' Marianne butted in on one of Lisa's interminable stories about what the recession was going to mean for her. (If you hadn't racked up so much debt on your three credit cards it mightn't be such a disaster, Marianne felt like cattily saying.)

'What on earth for?' Lisa looked incredulous. 'That sounds disgusting.'

'It wasn't,' said Marianne. 'It was rather wonderful actually. I met a friend of mine when I was out walking. He needed help with one of his ewes, and so I helped deliver the baby. Well, it was two babies, but one of them died.'

'You know a *shepherd*?' Carly broke off into peals of laughter.

'I bet he's called Gabriel,' said Lisa. 'Remember how we

163

all fancied Gabriel Oak when we saw *Far from the Madding Crowd* at school?'

'He is actually,' said Marianne, to hoots of laughter from her friends. 'Well, not a shepherd, but he does farm sheep.'

'Marianne, you never cease to amaze me,' said Carly. 'You'll be going all native on us next.'

'What's wrong with that?' said Marianne. 'Gabriel's nice. Living in the country's nice. I like it.'

'Don't you miss the town at all?' Lisa was utterly incredulous.

'Not much,' admitted Marianne. 'If anything, there I feel like I've come home.'

And, with a jolt, she realised it was true. Despite everything that had happened with Luke, she felt more at home in Hope Christmas than she'd ever felt anywhere in her life before. Marianne was overcome with an overwhelming rush of homesickness. Suddenly, she couldn't wait to go back.

Even though she'd hardly known Pippa any time at all, she'd been more of a friend to Marianne than these two had ever been. She might have spent her whole life in London and never realised what life was all about. Pippa had rung her to say that there was some traditional village football match going on on Monday. Her parents were flying out on holiday early on Sunday morning. Carly and Lisa had a host of wild parties to go to, to which she was invited, but where she knew she wouldn't feel welcome. What on earth was keeping her here?

Making her excuses, Marianne got up and left. Lisa and Carly made token noises about wishing she didn't have to go so soon but, as she left them gossiping over a drink and busily texting friends to find out where to go next, Marianne ruefully realised that they wouldn't really miss her any more than she'd miss them. Somehow, she'd clung onto these two friends from her past long beyond a point at which they really had much in common. It was time to live her life in the way she wanted to. A picture of Gabriel swam suddenly before her eyes. Pippa said he was likely to be taking part in this football match, which, if she was honest, was even more of a reason to go. It had been nice to see her family, but it was time to go back to where her heart now belonged.

Noel woke up with the light streaming in through the open curtain. His head was pounding and his mouth was dry. What was he doing in the spare room? He lifted his head up. Bad idea. The room lurched in a rather alarming fashion and he had a sudden awful thought that he might be sick. Crikey. It was a long time since he'd had a hangover that bad. The events of the previous day came flooding back to him. He'd had a paycut. Had he told Cat he'd had a paycut? Somehow he didn't think so. It didn't matter that it was something that happened to thousands of other people every day. It didn't matter that, as Gerry had told him in that hearty-fellow kind of way, it wasn't 'personal'. He, Noel Tinsall, had been utterly humiliated in the work-place. And at a time when he was feeling that his world was contracting, and there were fewer opportunities for him. Waves of self-pity and guilt swept over Noel. He didn't know where they were coming from, he just felt utterly locked in his misery. What would a woman as beautiful, intelligent and attractive as Cat want with someone as worthless as him? He couldn't blame her for hating him. He'd been an utter sod to her last night. His guilt about what had happened with Julie had made sure of that. God, he was making a mess of things. He was beginning to feel he had less and less to offer Cat. How would she react to the news of his paycut?

Suddenly Noel couldn't face the humiliation of telling

165

her. From the very first moment he'd seen her standing at the bar in their student hall of residence, Noel had been swept away by her beauty and vivaciousness. Over the years neither had been dimmed, but how did she really feel about him these days? Noel sometimes detected a look of exasperation in her eyes, which never used to be there. Was she losing interest in him? And if she was, how would the news that her previously successful husband was heading for the scrap heap go down?

No, he wouldn't tell her, Noel decided. What Cat didn't know couldn't hurt her after all. And, by the time the eco town project was finished, maybe he'd have found himself something else or, who knows, he might even get that elusive bonus Gerry had promised him.

The door opened and a frosty-looking Cat came in with a cup of tea.

'You are still planning to come out with us for the day, I take it?' she asked. 'Ten minutes and counting.'

Noel raised a smile he didn't feel. What he wanted to do was crawl back into bed and stay there for a very long time, but he'd promised the kids. He felt enough of a heel as it was. He couldn't let them down too.

'Be with you in five,' he said, trying a feeble smile.

'You'd better be,' said Cat, thawing a little.

'And sorry,' he added, 'about last night. Being so late and everything.'

'It's okay,' she said. 'Well, it's not okay, but I don't want it ruining today. Agreed?'

'Agreed,' said Noel. He felt relieved, as if he'd been given a reprieve. But for how long?

'Daddy, can I ring Granny Smith?' Stephen was bouncing on Gabriel's bed on Easter Sunday morning. 'I want to wish her Happy Easter.'

166

'Yes, of course.' Gabriel always questioned the wisdom of allowing his son to ring his maternal grandmother. If she knew where her daughter was she never divulged it, and in her strangely dotty way seemed to think that somehow it was Stephen and Gabriel who had caused Eve's problems, whereas, in fact, Gabriel could see now they had started long before Gabriel had ever met Eve.

'Guilt, that's what it is,' had been Pippa's assertion. 'She knows she cocked Eve's life up, but it's easier to blame you.'

But Gabriel couldn't find it in his heart to condemn his mother-in-law. Whether it really was Joan's fault for abandoning Eve with her own mother every time a suitable new lover came along that had caused Eve to be so needy and fragile, he couldn't say. What he did know was that Joan had suffered for it nearly as much as he had.

'Granny, Granny, the Easter Bunny brought me three Easter eggs,' Stephen was bouncing up and down on the bed, a bit bunnylike himself. How much chocolate had he already had? Gabriel had placed a chocolate embargo till after breakfast, but realised he had probably lost that battle already.

'We're going to church and the vicar said we'll have an Easter Egg hunt.' Stephen was explaining the day's events to his grandmother. 'And then we're going to Auntie Pippa's. Can you come and see us soon?'

Gabriel's heart sank. Stephen always asked this. And the answer was always a negative. But this time his son's face lit up. 'You can? That's brilliant!'

Oh. That was unexpected. But what followed was even more so.

'Who's there?' Stephen suddenly demanded. 'Who wants to talk to me?'

The look of expectation on his face suddenly turned to fury.

'Well, I don't want to talk to her!' He flung the phone on the bed, and ran out of the room crying.

'Stephen?' Gabriel looked at his son helplessly, then picked up the phone. 'Joan, what on earth is going on?'

'Is Stephen still there?' she asked. 'Only I've got his mother here, and she wants to speak to him.'

Chapter Fourteen

Gabriel stood in the bedroom, cradling the phone in shock.

'Eve's there?' He couldn't believe it. All these months with no contact, and suddenly here she was at her mother's. 'I thought you didn't know where she was?'

'I didn't,' said Joan. 'She turned up out of the blue last night.'

'Can I speak to her?' Gabriel asked, and then wished he hadn't. What was he going to say to Eve? How could he speak to her and not let rip the fury that had been building in him all these months since she'd gone? It was only now he was here, an inch away from having a conversation with his absent wife, having seen the devastating effect she was still having on his son, that he realised just how very angry he was. Maybe now wasn't a good time to speak.

'I'm sorry,' said Joan, 'she doesn't want to speak to you.'

'Oh.' Fury turned to disappointment. How was it that Eve could churn him up so much, and make him feel so very confused, and yet still a part of his heart reached out to her, still he wanted to make things right between them? Would he never learn?

'And Stephen doesn't want to speak to her,' said Gabriel. He wasn't entirely sure that this was true. Stephen was in shock and had certainly reacted in childish anger, but Gabriel knew how often his son had sobbed into his

169

pillow at night. Despite everything, he loved Eve. Gabriel suppressed a momentary feeling of unease – did he have the right to stop his son speaking to his mother? But then he thought about what she'd put them both through and anger hardened his heart once more.

'I see,' said Joan. 'And that's nothing to do with anything you've said to him, I suppose?'

'It has everything to do with the fact his mother is a flaky depressive who wouldn't understand commitment if it hit her over the head,' retorted Gabriel, his irritation at Joan's jibe reigniting his fury. 'I have done my very best not to badmouth Eve to Stephen. She's done all that herself.'

'She's very sick,' said Joan.

'I know, I know,' said Gabriel, familiar guilt piercing the anger. 'But I can't help her if she won't help herself. And she can't expect to just walk back into Stephen's life like this. Tell her to stay away. For both of our sakes.'

He put the phone down and walked down the corridor to Stephen's room to find him lying on his bed, sobbing his heart out.

'Was Mummy really there?' Stephen asked. 'Will she hate me for not speaking to her?'

Gabriel looked at his son and, unable to bear the look in his eyes, for the first time in his life, he lied to his son. 'No, sweetheart, Granny was mistaken. Mummy's gone away and she won't be back for a very long time. But I'm here, aren't I? And I think we've got an Easter Egg hunt with your cousins.'

Stephen smiled through his tears and reached out his hand to Gabriel, who closed his own over his son's tiny one, then held him in a fierce tight embrace.

'It's you and me now, Stephen,' he said. 'You and me, against the world.'

* * *

'You're early.' Cat's mum greeted them as they came through the front door of the Georgian house in which she'd brought Cat up single-handedly, once Cat's feckless father had left. Nothing much had changed for years. The grandfather clock, inherited from Mum's grandmother, still took pride of place in the hall, the shabby comfy furniture from Cat's childhood still retained its spot in the chintzy lounge, last redecorated circa 1990 – 'I don't care what other people think, *I* like it,' was her mother's response to Cat's frequent pleas to get her to redecorate – and the oak-panelled kitchen, all the rage in 1988, retained its peculiar charm because it was Mum's. Cat had learnt to cook here, on the Aga that stood in the corner. She'd invited friends back for coffee, had sat up having illicit late-night drinks with Noel when they were courting. Cat knew every nook and cranny of this kitchen, every one holding a memory precious to her alone. Despite having long since made a nest of her own, Mum's house would always feel like home to Cat.

'Sorry, Mum,' said Cat, looking at her watch, which proclaimed the time to be 12.30, 'but you did say midday. I thought we were late as usual.'

'Oh,' her mother frowned. 'I must be going mad, I could have sworn I said 1pm.'

'We can go away if you want and come back later,' joshed Noel, giving his mother-in-law a kiss. The children all piled in behind him, squabbling about who was going to get Granny Dreamboat's attention first.

'Now now, enough of that, Noel, I'm sure I can cope,' said Mum. 'Cat, if you could be an angel and just put the kettle on?'

'Mind if I'm terribly anti-social and go and watch the Grand Prix?' Noel asked.

'Get away with you,' said Mum. 'You've been using my

house like a hotel since you first met Cat. Why change the habit of a lifetime?'

Noel laughed and went into the lounge with the children, who made themselves at home, as usual finding the various games and books their granny had thoughtfully got out for them. Cat relaxed visibly. Noel had been like a bear with a sore head all weekend and wouldn't tell her what was wrong. After the events of Christmas Day, she'd been nervous about coming here. But, she reminded herself, *your* mum doesn't wind him up like his does.

'Anything I can do?' said Cat, as she sorted out cups and a teapot, her mother never letting her get away with anything as uncouth as teabags and mugs. She knew the answer would be no – her mother was so capable in the kitchen, Cat barely got a look in. It was quite remarkable she'd ever learnt to cook in the first place.

'You could chop the carrots, if you like,' said her mother. 'I haven't quite got there yet.'

'What, the greatest cook in the history of the universe has got behind?' Cat teased. 'I don't believe it. First you've forgotten how to make pastry, now this. You'll forget your own head next!'

'That is a ridiculous thing to say!' Mum snapped. Cat was completely taken aback.

'Sorry,' she said. 'I was only joking.'

'Well, don't,' said Mum tetchily. 'You seem to forget sometimes how old I am.'

'Only because you do,' laughed Cat, trying to lighten the tone. It was unlike her mother to be so stressed.

'All I'm saying is that you shouldn't be surprised if occasionally I can't quite do everything I used to be able to do,' said Mum. She looked rather wistful as she said this, and Cat had a sudden surge of panic. She did take her mother for granted, perhaps it was time she took care of *her* a bit more.

172

'I'm sorry, Mum,' she said. 'I didn't mean to be thought-less. It's just you're always so capable and in control it never occurs to me that you can't do anything.'

'Who said anything about can't?' said Mum. 'I'm not in my dotage yet.'

'I – never mind,' said Cat, turning away. Sometimes you couldn't do right for saying wrong.

'That was lovely,' said Noel appreciatively, as he passed over his empty plate later. It was so restful at his mother-in-law's, and a relief to get away from the tension he'd been feeling all weekend at home – tension, he didn't have to remind himself, caused by his appalling guilt at his own selfish behaviour on Thursday night.

Louise beamed at him with gratitude.

'I'm so glad you enjoyed it,' she said. 'I have so few people to cook for these days, it's a real treat to cook for you all. Though it's unlike the children to leave things on their plate.'

'The children have rather overindulged on chocolate,' said Cat guiltily. 'Sorry about that.'

'Which is why I didn't buy them any,' said her mother. 'I have devised a Treasure Hunt in the garden, though.'

'Treasure Hunt! Yay! Treasure Hunt!' James and Paige practically leapt from the table, Granny Dreamboat's Easter Treasure Hunt being the highlight of Easter Sunday as far as they were concerned. Ruby had only vague recollections from last year, and was sucking her thumb looking bored, while Mel was trying very hard to pretend that she was far too superior to let herself get carried away with anything so feeble. However, once in the garden, where, following weeks of rain, the spring sunshine was finally forcing its way out, she whooped and hollered with the rest of them.

'Is this all I get?' James came marching up to Cat looking

thunderous. Normally Granny Dreamboat was scrupulous in providing prizes that were suitable for her grandchildren, but even Noel could see that he was far too old for the Thomas the Tank Engine he'd found with his name on. Even Ruby would probably consider herself too old for that.

'Shh,' said Cat. 'Don't be rude. Granny's gone to a great deal of trouble for you.'

James looked mutinous and was soon joined by Paige, who didn't seem too impressed by her Barbie either. 'Doesn't Granny know I hate Barbie?' she whined, and Mel, who clearly thought that she was much too grown up for the Polly Pocket set that seemed to be hers, at least had the grace not to moan about it in front of her grandmother. Only Ruby seemed to be satisfied with her wooden pull-along duck.

'Oh dear.' Louise looked really put out. 'I seem to have muddled up their ages. How did I manage that?'

'It doesn't matter,' said Cat. 'It's easily done, we're always doing it, aren't we, Noel?'

Noel was staring into space trying not to think about Thursday night. Cat dug him in the ribs and he said, 'Oh, yes, all the time.' He was fond of his mother-in-law and didn't like to see her upset.

'Look, let me give them some money and they can get something more suitable each.' Granny Dreamboat thrust some money into Noel's hands.

'Don't be daft,' he said, 'it's good for the kids to learn disappointment once in a while. It's good for their souls.'

'Is it?' muttered Mel. 'Gee, thanks, Dad.'

'Yes, it is,' said Noel firmly. 'But, as I am such a nice, kind, wonderful father, if you all go and hide in the lounge for five minutes, I might just be able to arrange another Treasure Hunt.'

'Dad, you're the best!' Paige threw her arms around his neck and Cat gave him a grateful look.

'Yup, the best,' said Noel, feeling like a fraud. 'That's me.'

'Welcome back.' Pippa hugged Marianne and ushered her into her home. 'Have you had anything to eat? I'm just doing brunch for the sportsmen. You can be the first to try out my special new herby sausages.'

Marianne let herself feel overcome with the warmth and generosity of her friend.

'Oh, it is so good to be back!' she said. 'I love my parents dearly, but they were driving me insane.'

Pippa dragged her into the kitchen where Dan was frying sausages for what appeared to be half the men in the village. Marianne had a surreptitious look to see if Gabriel was amongst them and felt a surge of disappointment when she saw he wasn't.

'I thought you said Gabriel was taking part in this great event?' she asked in as casual a tone as she could muster.

'Gabriel? I tried my best,' snorted Pippa. 'He was persuaded to take part last year, but then Dan accidentally sat on his head. The Monday Muddle isn't his cup of tea. I've been trying very hard to make him change his mind, but I fear I'm wasting my time.'

'Oi, who are you maligning?' Gabriel came strolling in just then, holding Stephen's hand. 'I've decided to give it another go this year.'

Marianne's heart lurched, and she looked up to see Gabriel bearing down on her, his dark hair swept off his face, and his cheerful smile brightening his handsome face. Oh, it was good to see him too. She hadn't realised how much she'd valued seeing him around until she'd been parted from him for a while.

'Well, I'll be cheering for you,' said Marianne, with a

smile. God, she hoped it wasn't a girlish smile. Or that Gabriel wouldn't notice how hot and bothered she had suddenly become.

Gabriel smiled back, his whole face lighting up. He was gorgeous. She'd somehow failed to notice before – he was always so serious and intent, but when he smiled he was utterly *gorgeous*.

'Well, that makes two of you,' he said. 'Half-pint here is my other supporter.'

'Go, Daddy,' said Stephen solemnly, waving a flag he'd clearly made.

'Surely you've got more than that?'

'You haven't seen how bad I am at this,' said Gabriel.

'He is truly truly awful,' said Pippa. 'I, on the other hand, am married to the Monday Muddle King, so be warned. This game gets really dirty!'

'Right,' said Marianne. 'Crikey, they don't have anything like this in Cricklewood.'

'Well, you're in the country now, aren't you, my dear?' said Pippa, exaggerating her Shropshire burr. 'It's all differen' here, don't you know?'

Marianne laughed and gladly accepted the sausage bap that Dan shoved in her hand. She was starving.

'I think,' she said, to no one in particular, 'I'm going to enjoy this.'

'I'm not,' said Gabriel with feeling.

'You've only yourself to blame,' Marianne teased him. She leant back on the kitchen worktop: despite her sudden hormonal rush, she felt at ease and relaxed around Gabriel, he was such good company.

'I'm doing it for him,' Gabriel nodded at Stephen, who was in animated discussion with his cousins. 'He was so keen for me to enter this year. And he's had enough upset. I thought I owed it to him to give it a go.'

176

'No word from his mum still?' Marianne remembered how forlorn Stephen had looked on Mother's Day at church.

Gabriel looked awkward.

'Turns out she's staying with my mother-in-law. Stephen rang his granny yesterday, and Eve wanted to speak to him.'

'What did Stephen do?' Marianne asked, as a sudden cold shockwave hit her. Did this mean Eve was coming back?

'Ran off crying,' said Gabriel miserably. 'He said he didn't want to know her. He seemed so upset – I think I may have done something rather stupid. I have to tell someone or I'll burst.'

'What did you do? It can't be that bad,' encouraged Marianne.

'I think it probably can,' said Gabriel, 'I lied to Stephen and said Eve wasn't there. I was so cross with her for hurting him. At the time it seemed the right thing to do. But now. Now I wonder.'

Marianne looked across at Stephen who was now playing happily with his cousins in the garden.

'I'm sure it was the right thing. Anyone can tell you're a great dad,' she said. She thought back to the cruel way Luke had ditched her. Would she rather he'd carried on lying to her? On some days, indubitably yes. 'And sometimes, well, sometimes the truth hurts too much. Sometimes it's better not to know.'

Chapter Fifteen

Gabriel walked into the throng of men standing in a field on the outskirts of the village, feeling sick to his boots. It was only his feelings of guilt about Stephen that had led him to enter at the last minute. Gabriel had never been much of a sportsman, and had always hated the rough and tumble of the Monday Muddle. Until last year, he hadn't entered for at least a decade and, much as he liked Dan and his cronies, he wasn't looking forward to the inevitable ribbing he was going to get when he made a tit of himself as usual. Worse still, Stephen seemed convinced that he was going to be a hero. The thought of failing his son was worse than taking part. And yet, despite his anxiety, he couldn't also help feeling inspired by the fact that Marianne had said she would be cheering for him. She was so uncompli-cated, and spending half an hour with her in Pippa's crowded kitchen had been incredibly soothing.

Gabriel glanced round him. The field was full of gossiping villagers who were wandering through all the craft stalls and, by the looks of things, buying plenty. He could see Pippa doing a roaring trade in home-made chutney, while the local butcher in the stall next to her was nearly sold out of hot dogs already. There were the usual Monday Muddle regulars, plus a few first-timers (village rules stated at eighteen, 'when a lad can buy his first pint', every boy in the village was eligible to enter). There weren't too many newbies this year, but Gabriel spotted one or two youngsters he knew as the sons of various acquaintances. He was pleased to note that most of them looked sicker than he felt. The Monday Muddle also attracted people from neighbouring villages, plus the odd rambler who'd been staying in town over the bank holiday weekend and been persuaded when in his cups to take part.

The field was crowded with well-wishers and supporters. Gabriel glanced over at Pippa's stall again and got a welcome boost from the sight of Marianne, who grinned and gave him the thumbs up. Only five minutes to go till he met his doom. Stephen and his friends had taken prime position on the stone wall at the edge of the field, and Ralph Nicholas was striding across the grass bearing the ancient leather football that, legend had it, had been used in the Monday Muddle for the previous two hundred years. The sun was shining, which made a pleasant change from the weeks of rain, but there was still a nip in the air. Mind you, he wouldn't be feeling that once they all got going.

'Fancy a dram?' Dan came up with a half bottle of Scotch. It was *de rigeur* to have something to keep the cold away before the great event.

'Why not?' said Gabriel. 'I may need something to numb the pain when you bring me crashing to the floor.'

'No hard feelings, mate,' said Dan grinning. 'Hey up, I think we might be ready for the off.'

They looked up to see Ralph Nicholas standing on an old crate and addressing the throng.

'Welcome one and all to this year's Monday Muddle. Right, you all know the rules—'

'There are no rules,' roared back the crowd in a well-worn response.

'When I blow my whistle, the ball will be kicked into the

179

crowd and then it's every man for himself, and first one to bring it home via the usual route will be declared King of the Muddle.'

A hush descended. Gabriel swallowed hard. Why was he doing this, why?

The whistle blew. The ball flew high in the sky and disappeared into the middle of the scrum. Gabriel hovered around the edges while there was the usual toing and froing and head-stamping, before finally a newcomer from a neighbouring village emerged with the traditional shout of 'Mu-dd-dle!' – and they were off.

'Go for it, Daddy!' Stephen was yelling with all his might as Gabriel set off running down the muddy field. He ran past Marianne and Pippa, who were cheering and wolf-whistling wildly.

'Go, Gabriel, go!' Marianne yelled, and suddenly his heart lifted, and he was swept with a huge adrenaline rush. He ran, busting a gut, towards the front of the crowd, easily outstripping the more lumbering members of the village. Maybe he was going to enjoy this after all . . .

Cat was in the kitchen trying out recipes for her new cookery book. Mel had started off helping her but had quickly lost interest, while James and Paige had gone next door to play. Noel was sitting watching DVDs with Ruby. Really she should get them out in the garden, it was such a lovely day and Noel was going back to work tomorrow, but Cat was enjoying the rare luxury of having the time to cook properly.

While other aspects of domestic duty were an arduous chore for Cat, cooking wasn't one of them. She loved the joy of turning basic ingredients into a tasty meal, the almost sensuous pleasure of kneading pastry, the delight of producing something which the whole family enjoyed. Cat could barely

180

remember a time when she hadn't been able to cook, beginning young and shadowing her mother in the kitchen. Interestingly, of all her children, it was James who showed the same propensity. Maybe he'd be the next Jamie Oliver. Cat associated cooking with peace and harmony, with safety and security. The smell of baking always lifted her spirits, as it did now.

She checked on the scones she was cooking and returned to the beetroot soup she was making partly from memory. It was an old family recipe of her Auntie Eileen's, who'd got it from her Polish mother-in-law. Cat was working her way through various recipes that had been in the family for years. They included her mother's famous apple tart, Auntie Eileen's amazing meringues (which she miraculously made without a whisk, instead using two knifes to whisk the egg yolks), and her own grandmother's tasty Irish Stew.

'How's it going?' Noel walked in. Thankfully he'd got over whatever it was that was eating him on Thursday and was less sulky.

'Okay,' said Cat, testing her soup and pulling a face. 'Damn, I'm going to have to ring Auntie Eileen. I don't think I've done this right.'

'What on earth is it?' said Noel peering into the pan. 'It looks like someone's bled to death in the saucepan.'

'Ha, ha, very funny,' said Cat. 'It's supposed to be beetroot soup. I think I may have added too much paprika. Lucky you grew so much beetroot on the allotment last year as it looks like I may have to scrap this lot and start again.'

She poured away the soup and started washing up pans. She'd be rubbing beetroot stains out of her fingers for days at this rate.

'What's in the oven? That smells nice.'

181

'Granny Dreamboat's Fabulous Scones,' said Cat, 'and yes, when they're ready, you and Ruby can test some.'

'Ah, well, if it's Granny Dreamboat's recipe, it must be all right,' said Noel.

'Talking of Granny Dreamboat,' said Cat, as she started putting pans away, 'did you think she seemed okay yesterday?'

'What do you mean?'

'Just . . . well, the thing with the Treasure Hunt was a bit odd, wasn't it? She's never got the kids' ages wrong before, but it was as if she was buying them things from a few years back.'

'Well, maybe she was busy and made a mistake,' said Noel.

'Maybe,' said Cat doubtfully. 'It's just unlike her. And then there's little things, like the way she rang me the other day to ask how to make pastry. I mean, my mum, ringing me for cooking advice? Plus there was that business of forgetting to pay her bills. I thought she might be in some kind of financial trouble. But now I'm not so sure. She seems to be terribly forgetful of late.'

'So are you,' laughed Noel, 'you never remember anything I tell you.'

'True,' said Cat, as she took the scones out of the oven and deftly turned them onto a cooling tray.

'It's probably just her getting older,' said Noel. 'It's just because she's so capable you tend to think she's invincible. I think you're worrying unnecessarily. Mmm, these are delicious.'

'You're probably right,' said Cat, unconvinced.

'I know I am,' said Noel, kissing the top of her head and disappearing into the lounge with a plate of scones.

'Yummy, scones!' Mel appeared as if by magic.

'Trust you to come back when it's all cooked,' said Cat,

as she tidied up the kitchen. She'd been cooking so long it was nearly time to prepare tea. She tried to convince herself that Noel was right, that the small worrying lapses in her mum's concentration were just the signs of advancing old age but, deep down, she knew she was kidding herself.

'What happens now?' Marianne asked. The last stragglers of the Monday Muddle were heading off down the hill towards the stream, by which muddy back route the Muddlers would make their way back into town. Most of the onlookers had run off down the field cheering them, and she and Pippa were doing precious little trade now.

'Now we pack this lot up and go and find a suitable spot to cheer them on – the bridge over the brook at the end of Willow Valley is always a good place. Sometimes we pelt them with rotten eggs and flour, but I think the committee has vetoed that this year.'

'Blimey, I had no idea the country was like this,' said Marianne. 'It certainly beats a boring bank holiday in town.'

She didn't say she had particularly enjoyed the sight of Gabriel running swiftly through the crowd, looking rather more athletic than he'd let on. He wouldn't have looked out of place in *Chariots of Fire*.

They called Stephen, Nathan and George, and made their way via the road to the brook, where a crowd was starting to gather.

'When are they coming?' The boys jumped about impatiently.

'Soon,' said Pippa, 'be patient.'

A shout from someone near the stream indicated that the first runner was already on his way. The original catcher of the ball clearly hadn't kept it, as it was now in possession of one of Dan's friends. Dan was in hot pursuit, looking fired up and covered in mud.

'One year they'll do this event in the dry,' said Pippa raising her eyebrows. 'It took me ages to get his stuff clean last year.'

'Dad-dy! Dad-dy!' the boys were chanting and Stephen joined in. Gabriel was making his way down the path, covered in sweat, his shirt sticking to him in a way that made Marianne feel most peculiar, his lean legs spattered with mud. The legs. Oh my God. The legs did it. Marianne couldn't tear her eyes off them. Then suddenly the leader tripped and Dan and his friends leapt on top of him. To shouts and whistles, four men rolled in the mud like a bunch of school kids. The ball escaped down the bank and, swift as anything, Gabriel was down there scrabbling frantically in the water for the ball, which was in danger of heading off downstream.

'Way to go, Gabriel!' Marianne leapt to her feet, cheering. The scrummers belatedly realised they'd lost the ball and set off in pursuit of their prey, but their heavy frames, so useful in the scrum, were no match for Gabriel's fleetness of foot.

'I had no idea it would be this exciting,' said Marianne. 'Where to next?'

'If we hurry we should catch them just as they come into the village at the top end of the High Street,' said Pippa.

'Well, what are we waiting for?' said Marianne. 'I haven't had so much fun in years.'

Gabriel was on a high. He raced down the path like a bat out of hell. This was completely exhilarating. He'd never known the Monday Muddle could be so much fun. No wonder Dan and the boys were so obsessed with it. He'd been vaguely aware of the cheers when he'd grabbed the ball, but then, as he'd scrabbled his way up the bank, he'd heard Marianne screaming his name. Something about that had fired him up beyond anything he could possibly have imagined. Suddenly it became vital that he didn't just win this damned thing for Stephen, but for Marianne as well. He wanted to prove himself to her, to show her that he was different from the rest of the crowd.

He ran on, ignoring the mud and the hammering of his heart, the feeling that it might just burst out of his chest. Never had he pushed himself so hard physically, and never had he felt more joyfully, vividly, brilliantly alive. He was dimly aware of the bluebells in the woods as he ran past, of birdsong and sunshine, but that didn't matter because he was nearly at the gate that led to the High Street. He heard the crowd roar and it inspired him beyond anything he'd ever felt inspired to do before. He vaulted the gate without a thought, fired up by adrenaline and stupidity. He could do anything. Anything at all. Free running? He could be king. He was going to be King of the Muddle.

Or not.

As Gabriel leaped over the gate, his foot caught the top bar and the ground rushed headlong to meet him. The last thing he thought was, *That's going to hurt*, and then everything went black.

Chapter Sixteen

'Gabriel!' Marianne wasn't even aware she'd screamed his name, but she was transfixed at the sight of him coming tumbling over the gate. She ran faster than she knew she could up the hill to reach him. Her heart was pounding. He couldn't be hurt. He mustn't be. Not now—

Now *what*? Hang on a minute? What on earth was she thinking? Marianne paused for a moment, stopped short by the bolt of lightning that had hit her out of the blue. Suddenly it all made sense. Oh my God, she'd fallen for Gabriel, big time, and she hadn't even noticed. The revelation was cut short. Gabriel was hurt and needed her. Please, please, let him be okay.

'Gabriel, can you hear me?' Marianne reached him at last, kneeled down and leant over to check his pulse. Thank God for that first-aid course she'd done last year. She never thought she'd have to put the things she'd learnt into practice so swiftly.

Good, he was breathing. His pulse was racing, but then he had been exerting himself. He didn't look like he was going blue around the lips, but you never could tell. Gabriel was Marianne's first proper patient, she desperately didn't want to cock things up.

'Is there anyone medical here?' Marianne shouted above the rest of the crowd who'd followed her. She couldn't see any of the village GPs.

'I'm okay, I'm okay.' Gabriel was coming round. 'Am I dreaming?' he said, as he looked into Marianne's eyes. 'I think I've just seen an angel.' He lay back and shut his eyes. Marianne swallowed hard.

'No, but I think you're probably concussed,' she said.

'Nonsense,' said Gabriel, sitting up. 'I'm the King of the Middle, I mean, Muddle. And I'm going to win this thing. Have ball, will travel.'

'That's the spirit! Go on, my son!' the crowd roared.

'Get him!' shouted Dan, who was running down the path, followed by two other members of the pack.

'Not bloody likely,' said Gabriel. He stood up, staggered slightly, picked up the ball and, with a herculean effort, ran as fast as he could towards the village pub, followed by a host of besieging onlookers all chanting his name. Luckily it wasn't too far.

'Gabriel, be careful!' shouted Marianne, to no avail. What a bloody idiot. Why did he have to go all testosterone-charged on her? 'This is insane!' she wailed to no one in particular.

'Yup,' said Pippa, who had caught up belatedly, 'but this is perfectly normal for round here. You should see some of the injuries Dan's had over the years.'

They watched as Dan made some headway towards Gabriel who was beginning to stagger slightly. Just as it looked as if Dan was going to reach him, Gabriel put on another spurt of speed and, like a man possessed, roared up to the pub entrance and slammed the ball down on the table.

'I am the man!' he declared, before swaying sideways and toppling straight over.

Noel was reading Ruby a story. It had always been one of his favourite pastimes, reading his children to sleep. He loved

187

the way she cosily curled up next to him as he put on silly voices to *The Gruffalo*. He missed the others being young. Mel was so moody and difficult these days, it was hard to know where to begin. He felt guiltily relieved that she took out all her grumpiness on Cat, but sometimes he wished she'd cuddle up to him on the sofa like she used to when she was little. When James wasn't on the Playstation, he was kicking a football about. (Noel had a sneaking feeling he was a great disappointment in the footballing department, very rarely joining the other dads on the sidelines on Saturday – he usually used work as an excuse, but it was mainly because he couldn't stand the other football dads, or standing round with cold feet – and he and Cat frequently rowed about it.)

More and more, Noel felt like he was superfluous in his older children's lives. Although Paige still demonstrated a pleasing tendency to jump all over him as soon as he walked through the door, the older two frequently acted as if they didn't care if he were there or not. Cat had a different take on things, he knew, extolling the joys of older children, but Noel had a sneaking affection for the muddle and chaos of the early days of parenthood when, despite the lack of sleep, the house had felt cosy and comfortable and he had felt a sense of pride at the home he and Cat were creating. Now it often felt like he was a stranger in his own house, and the jobs he had to do (memo to self, mend that sodding shelf) were a constant reminder that he wasn't matching up to either his or Cat's expectations as a husband and father.

His thoughts strayed to the eco town and the one bright spot in his work landscape. Though the trips up north were growing more frequent, the upside was that Noel got to spend more time in Hope Christmas. He'd taken to staying in the Hopesay Arms, the village pub, which was so much nicer than the Travelodge on the nearest motorway. Noel had even stayed once when technically he could have got home. He'd felt guilty about it, almost as if he were having an affair, but, somehow, Noel just wanted to keep Hope Christmas as his secret.

He just couldn't resist the opportunity to wander the little streets, pottering round the quaint shops with their lopsided walls, low ceilings, and displays of geegaws and trinkets that he found incredibly enticing. The shop that drew him back most often was more of an emporium, being a three-storeyed house, crammed full of antiques – most of them rubbish, though Noel had spotted the occasional gem. He harboured wild fantasies of buying one of the tumbledown old farmhouses he'd spotted on the way out of Hope Christmas, and cramming it full of old knick-knacks purchased from the antiques shop, as well as books he'd acquired from the fabulous bookshop, where the book-sellers were now ordering books especially for him. But, somehow, in his head he could never see Cat and the children there. Cat was far too much of a townie to ever countenance a life in the country. It was a pipe dream, and Noel knew it. Besides, by the time Matt and Luke had finished with the eco town there wasn't likely to be anything left of the Hope Christmas he loved. Noel felt hopelessly guilty about the part he was playing in destroying this particular paradise for the sake of a parking lot, but he couldn't see a way out of it without losing his job. And, in the current economic climate, he could scarcely afford to do that.

Realising Ruby was asleep, he gently kissed the top of her head, put the book away and popped his head into Paige's room, where she had her nose stuck in a Jacqueline Wilson.

'Five minutes till lights out,' he said, before going down-stairs and chasing James off the computer and into bed.

Cat and Mel were watching *Pride and Prejudice*, eating popcorn. He didn't mind period drama, but wasn't quite in the mood, so, ignoring the disappointed look on Cat's face, he headed into the study and went online to see if there were any job opportunities out there. After a fruitless half an hour, he realised he was wasting his time. He'd try some agencies in the morning. He switched off the computer and went back into the lounge in time to witness Darcy whisking Elizabeth off into the sunset. Mel said goodnight and Cat cuddled up to him on the sofa while they watched a repeat of *Little Britain*. Noel was uneasy. He still hadn't got round to telling Cat about the precarious nature of his work situation. Somehow there hadn't been a right moment over the weekend. Perhaps he should tell her now.

'Penny for 'em,' Cat said, tucking into a piece of popcorn. 'You seem very preoccupied.'

'I'm fine,' he lied, 'just a bit tired.'

He'd tell her tomorrow. Maybe.

Gabriel lay on a stretcher in a hospital corridor, feeling woozy. This was ridiculous, he shouldn't be in hospital, he was perfectly fine. Trust Diana Carew to insist on calling an ambulance. The paramedic who had checked him over had decided he needed to go to hospital for observation. The adrenaline rush from earlier had completely deserted Gabriel, and he was now feeling like a total prat.

You are the King of the Muddle though, a sneaky voice in his head said very clearly. 'Yeah, and look where that's landed me!' Gabriel said out loud.

'Do you often talk to yourself?' Marianne was standing over him, looking amused.

'Only when my head hurts,' said Gabriel.

'You've only yourself to blame,' said Marianne. 'What on earth were you thinking?'

'I wasn't, much,' admitted Gabriel. 'I just got a bit carried away.'

'I'll say,' said Marianne. 'How are you feeling?'

'Everything hurts,' said Gabriel. 'Where's Stephen?'

'Down the corridor with Pippa and the other kids,' said Marianne. 'I said I'd come and find out what was happening.'

'I'm really glad you have,' said Gabriel. Despite the pain in his limbs, and the aching of his head, he felt a sudden dizzying sense of joy that she was here with him, right now. All the way down that path, it was a vision of Marianne that had been spurring him on. Suddenly life seemed worth living in a way it hadn't done for months. Suddenly he had a reason to get up in the morning with a spring in his step and joy in his heart. He had forgotten the rushing, intoxicating ecstasy of early love – if indeed it was love that he was feeling. Whatever it was, it was making him feel like jumping in the air and punching the sky. For the first time he imagined a future without Eve. And a future with someone else.

'Even though I think you're an utter pillock,' said Marianne, bursting his bubble, 'I'm glad you're okay.'

'Marianne, you say the nicest things,' said Gabriel with a grin.

'Don't,' said Marianne.

'Don't what?' said Gabriel.

'Look at me like that,' said Marianne.

'Like what?'

'Like that,' said Marianne. 'You're stopping me from being as cross as I want to be with you.'

'Well, don't be then,' said Gabriel. 'At least I won.'

'Yes,' said Marianne, with a sudden grin that sent his heart leaping skywards, 'yes, you certainly did.'

* * *

191

'Cat-er-ine! Cat-er-ine!' Cat was roused from a deep sleep by the sound of Magda sobbing and shouting hysterically.

'What on earth is going on?' Cat leapt out of bed, crossly noting that as usual a bomb could go off and Noel wouldn't even notice, flung a dressing gown around her and opened the door. Magda was standing before her, doubled up in pain, blood pouring from her stomach. Cat looked down and saw a bloody trail of footprints leading from the bathroom.

'I was at club, with Sergei. We dance,' said Magda, who was swaying alarmingly and looked incredibly pale. 'I had my belly button pierced today. It catch on Sergei's jacket and – oh my God, the pain! – it start to bleed. So I come home. But it won't stop bleeding. I am going to die.'

'You're not going to die,' said Cat firmly. 'Don't be ridiculous. And hold your finger over it to stop the bleeding. Where's Sergei now?'

'He is in kitchen. He not like blood.'

'Oh, does he not?' said Cat. 'Haven't you heard of A&E?'

'What?' Magda was leaning against the wall, panting heavily. Christ, she wasn't about to go into anaphylactic shock, was she?

'Let's have a look, shall we?' Cat gingerly removed Magda's hand from her bare midriff to see a stud hanging off a bit of skin, with blood pumping out. Resisting the urge to gag, Cat shoved Magda's fingers over the hole to attempt to stem the bleeding and took her back into the bathroom. She made her au pair lie on the floor with her legs in the air to stop her fainting and prevent the blood flowing downwards and, remembering a trick her Auntie Eileen (a former nurse) had taught her, she held the two pieces of skin together as tight as possible in the vain hope that they would knit back together again. After ten minutes she cautiously took her fingers away and realised that a clot

192

was beginning to form. Going to the first-aid cupboard, she got some steri strips out and stuck them over the wound, having first cleaned it as best she could with antiseptic wipes, ruthlessly ignoring the feeble moans emanating from Magda.

Sergei, meanwhile, had bravely managed to come up the stairs and see how his girlfriend was getting on. He took one look at Magda's bloodied stomach and promptly threw up.

'You're a fat load of use,' snapped Cat. 'Have you been drinking?'

'We both have,' said Magda.

'Great, just great,' said Cat. 'Right, get in the car, both of you. I'll take you to Casualty.'

Cat drove like a maniac through the darkened London streets, furiously thinking about how she was going to deal with this situation. She was so angry she didn't even care if Magda bled to death in the back of the car, she just wanted her gone. By the time they'd got to the hospital, she'd made up her mind about what she was going to do, even though she blanched at the thought of how she was going to manage it. She drew up outside the casualty department and then turned to them both and said, 'I want you to listen carefully. I am going to say this only once. I'm going to leave you here, but you can make your own way home. And, in the morning, Magda, I am going to ring the agency and tell them your services are no longer required. You can come and pack your things up and then you can go. Do you understand?'

'But Cat-er-ine—' began Magda.

'But Catherine nothing,' said Cat. 'You've had enough warnings. I've had it up to here with you and lover boy over there. I'd rather not have an au pair at all than have to put up with one as useless as you.'

193

It took Cat an hour by the time she'd got back from the hospital and, when she returned, she had to clean up the mess. The last thing she wanted was for the kids to see all that in the morning.

'What's happening?' Noel appeared in the doorway, looking sleepy.

'Magda nearly bled to death all over the floor, Sergei threw up everywhere and I've now sacked Magda,' said Cat, as she mopped the floor with a will.

'Oh, right,' Noel looked a bit bemused. 'Crikey, how did I manage to miss all that?'

'How indeed?' said Cat.

'Here, let me help,' said Noel, going to get another mop. It took them half an hour, but eventually all the mess was cleared up.

'It could only happen to us,' said Cat, who was so wired up she couldn't face going back to bed again.

'Oh, I don't know,' said Noel. 'I'm sure there must be a house somewhere which is more chaotic than ours.'

'You think?' Cat said, bursting into fits of laughter. 'Oh, crikey. How am I going to cope? I've just sacked the childcare.'

'Something will turn up, Mrs Micawber,' said Noel, going over to her and kissing her on the top of her head. He paused. 'Cat, there's something I've been meaning to tell you—'

'Yes?' Cat looked up at him, and was surprised to see a sombre look on his face.

'Mummy!' A sobbing little voice came from the kitchen door. 'I had a bad dream.'

'Did you, pet?' Cat picked Ruby up, and gave her a cuddle. 'What were you going to say, Noel?'

'It doesn't matter,' said Noel. 'Time for bed.'

Cat carried Ruby back to her room but couldn't settle

her, and inevitably she and Noel had an uncomfortable night with Ruby lying aslant across their bed. By morning they were both shattered. The alarm had just gone off when Cat heard a commotion downstairs. She came down to a bewildering sight. Sergei and Magda were struggling to bring a mattress through the front door.

'What the hell do you think you're doing?' Cat said.

'We make protest,' said Magda. 'This my home, you cannot throw me out. Sergei is coming to live here. He will help with children.'

'He will not,' said Cat. 'If you don't take that mattress out of my house right now, I shall call the police.'

Magda and Sergei ignored her and so Cat, without thinking about it, launched herself at the side of the mattress coming towards her and leant on it for all she was worth.

'Noel!' she called.

'What the—' Noel came flying down the stairs and, seeing what Cat was doing, leant against Cat. The suddenness of his arrival pushed the mattress back a little, but Sergei on the other side was putting renewed vigour into things, and suddenly Cat and Noel both found themselves on the floor.

'What's going on?' James appeared at the top of the stairs.

'We're trying to stop Sergei moving in,' said Noel. 'Come and help.'

'This is fun,' said James, who was swiftly joined by his siblings. For a few moments the mattress teetered back and forth before finally, with one push, they were able to expel it from the door. Now it was Sergei's and Magda's turn to end up flat on their back with the mattress on top of them.

'Now, just so we've got this clear,' said Catherine. 'Magda, I'm sacking you. You may come and pick your belongings up later. On your own. If Sergei comes near the place I shall call the police. Got it?'

'Got it,' said Magda sulkily.

Cat went back inside and high-fived her family. She might be left without childcare, but at least she knew the Tinsalls could be relied on to pull together whatever happened. And she would manage. Because she must. She didn't actually have a choice.

Part Three

To Save Me From Tears

Last Year
December 24

'Christmas Eve, it's Christmas Eve,' Noel could hear Kipper intoning in the children's playroom from his study where he was surfing the net. Ruby was sitting with a blanket, sucking her thumb and watching her favourite programme. Any minute now there would be ructions because Paige wanted to watch *The Snowman,* which was on for the zillionth time. Back in the dawn of time they had had a copy on video, but when James was a toddler he had 'posted' it in the video machine and it had never been the same again.

From the kitchen he could hear carols wafting up the stairs. Cat was peeling the vegetables for tomorrow over a cosy cup of coffee with his mum and, though Noel had offered to help, she claimed to be on top of things. Cat had a way of looking at him when she said that which made him feel like an insignificant worm. She always denied it but sometimes Noel felt there was a great female conspiracy going on against him. In the office he was feeling more and more sidelined, and at home he felt thoroughly useless. The one thing Cat was always nagging him about, namely to mend the shelf in the lounge, was the one thing he never seemed to get round to doing. He couldn't quite explain to himself why that was but being nagged reminded him of his mum, and the more Cat nagged, the less likely he was to do it.

Christmas always seemed to make things worse somehow. Sometimes Noel suspected this Happy Homemaker thing had gone to Cat's head somewhat. It was almost as if she felt she had to live the way her alter ego did. Instead of his real, gorgeous, homely wife, Noel felt he was getting the cardboard-cutout, dressed-in-a-Santa-outfit, slightly deranged version currently gracing the cover of *Happy Homes*. The Christmas lists had started appearing in September and she'd been shopping regularly since then. All the Christmas cards had been posted promptly on 1 December, the presents bought, wrapped and hidden in the loft by the end of November, the turkey ordered from the organic butcher on Clapton High Street three months in advance. She'd made the cake at half term, mince pies in November, and spent the previous week baking sausage rolls. Who on earth made their own sausage rolls anymore? *I do*, had been Cat's firm response. The money she was bringing in was, of course, incredibly helpful, but sometimes Noel wistfully wanted his old wife back.

She'd been such a frightening whirl of efficiency, Noel had felt almost gleeful when he discovered she hadn't managed to make a Christmas pudding. Apparently Cat's mum was supposed to do it but had forgotten. Cat had actually returned from Sainsbury's stressed and empty-handed a couple of days earlier, and hadn't taken kindly to Noel's roar of laughter when he'd heard that she'd abandoned the trolley mid-shop. Maybe there was something he could do. He looked at his watch and saw it was only just midday. Sainsbury's was bound to be a nightmare, but at least if he bought a Christmas pudding he might feel slightly less useless.

Noel went down to the kitchen to find his mother relating some hilarious anecdote from his childhood about him pooing his pants, which Cat clearly found very funny. It riled him how well Cat got on with his mother, who did nothing but find fault with him and the children.

'What's my lovely granddaughter up to?' Another bone of contention. Why did his mother insist on favouring Ruby so obviously? She'd done the same trick with his little sister when he was growing up and it still rankled.

'Watching Kipper,' said Noel, bracing himself for the inevitable comment about how much television the children watched. For once, it didn't come.

'If you don't need me, dear,' Angela said to Cat, 'I'll just go and see if Ruby wants company.'

'No, that's fine,' said Cat. 'I really don't need any help now.'

'So, nothing I can do?' Noel hovered, feeling like a spare part.

'Noel, you know the last time I let you loose in the kitchen it was chaos,' said Cat. 'I think everything's sorted. Apart from the sodding Christmas pud of course.'

'Well, I could hunter gather – like, go out in search of one if you want,' offered Noel.

'I think you'd be wasting your time,' said Cat. 'Besides, I need you here.'

'For what precisely?' Noel's irritation got the better of him. 'I've been hanging around all day. You need me for precisely nothing. I'm going to the pub.'

'I didn't mean—' Cat looked stricken, but Noel was too cross to stop now. He stormed out of the house in a state of ire. Honestly. She was the limit sometimes. It was bloody hard to live with someone who was so sodding perfect. A soothing pint was all he needed to calm his nerves.

The pub was thoroughly miserable. Lots of people had obviously come in on their way home from work and the place was packed. 'Wonderful Christmas Time' was blaring out from the loudspeakers. Yes, wasn't he just having one of those. After a solitary pint squashed between a drunk solicitor, who was attempting to chat up the barmaid, and a couple of brickies, who looked like they were settling in for the rest of the afternoon, guilt kicked in and Noel decided to call it a day. He headed out into the cold December afternoon and decided to wander up to the little minimarket on the corner to see if they happened to have any Christmas puddings. By some happy miracle, there was one small pudding still sitting on the shelf. At least he could do one thing right.

'Elves, this way! Fairies, that!' Diana Carew's voice boomed out across the village hall as half a dozen feverishly excited children rushed out of the changing rooms in costume. Marianne paused from administering face paint to an overexcited three-year-old who was going to be a puppy (since when were there puppies in the stable, she wondered). She had a headache and was not looking forward to the rest of her evening. Luke had refused to come to the Nativity, claiming family duties. She sighed. It would have been nice if he could have supported her in this one small thing. But apparently there was only so much time in his busy life and it didn't extend to attending the Village Nativity play.

Marianne knew the evening was going to be a disaster. Most of her reception class, who were playing a variety of angels, stars and animals, were so hyped up on the chocolate cake that Diana had foolishly provided they were going to be impossible to keep quiet. They were excited enough about Christmas as it was, and were overtired – clearly most of them had been having lots of late nights already – and the hour-and-a-half long performance was going to be beyond them. Lord knows how the preschoolers were going to manage, but that was Pippa's department.

She helped out a couple of days a week and had volunteered to look after the littlies, as she called them.

'That's me done,' Marianne said, following her small charge out into the hall.

'Wonderful,' boomed Diana. 'Right, we need our mice up on stage, and everyone else to be backstage. Chop chop. Your parents will be here soon.'

Diana's version of the Nativity had to rate as the most bizarre Marianne had ever seen. It followed the story of a little mouse who on Christmas Eve was sent to his room for not sharing his toys with the poor little mice who lived down the road. The mouse then encountered a magic fairy (with her half a dozen very tiny fairy companions, who did a rather long and baffling dance) who took him on a journey to discover the true meaning of Christmas, by way of Santa's workshop, some selfish children, a poor little matchgirl, Bob Cratchit, various animals, and who eventually found himself in Bethlehem. Mary (an insufferable child who turned out to be Diana's granddaughter) and Joseph got about ten seconds on stage and the only carol Marianne recognised was 'Little Donkey'. Despite various suggestions from the Parish Council to shorten it over the years, according to Pippa, Diana wouldn't be budged. So the Village Nativity was now set in stone as an event to be endured rather than enjoyed.

Marianne and Pippa were in charge of the backstage area, a small anteroom at the back of the hall. The children were herded in like excited puppies and Marianne's headache began to get worse, along with an anxious feeling that was growing in the pit of her stomach. She was going straight from the show to Luke's grandfather's for another Nicholas family gathering.

'So, are you all set for tonight?' Pippa said, while she absent-mindedly replaited a fairy's hair.

Marianne grimaced.

'Not really,' she said. 'I'm not looking forward to it at all. Luke's relatives are all so stiff and ghastly. I'll feel like a fish out of water.'

'Ralph Nicholas can't make you feel like that, surely?' said Pippa. 'He's a sweetheart.'

'Oh, he's fine,' said Marianne. 'It's just Luke's mother I have to contend with.'

'Ah, mothers-in-law,' said Pippa. 'What would we do without them? Actually, that's not fair, Dan's mum is a gem. I couldn't manage at all if she wasn't.'

A call came for the fairies to go on stage and Pippa and Marianne watched from the wings as the children yawned their way through the dance. Despite Diana's best efforts (she stood at the back doing every move with them – 'it's a wonder she doesn't leap on the stage,' snorted Pippa), two of the fairies bumped into each other, one sucked her thumb and another spent the whole time in tears. And there was still over an hour to go.

The play dragged on, a combination of folly and high farce, but eventually, to Marianne's relief, it was finally over.

'One down, one to go,' she said with a grimace, as she and Pippa got the children ready to meet their parents. People were shouting 'Happy Christmas' and there was much merriment about how long the show had taken. 'Even by Diana's standards, that was bad,' said Pippa. 'God knows where she's going to take it next year.'

Eventually all the children had gone and it was time for Marianne to go home and get ready. Pippa had rushed off in a whirl, grabbing her own children and getting ready for festive celebrations with various family members. Marianne envied her. She'd elected to stay here this Christmas rather than go home, but right now she was wishing for her own bed and a cosy family Christmas where she could be who she was without let or hindrance. She made her way down the lane to her cottage. Snow was falling gently. Oh well, at least being in the country she was in for a white Christmas.

Cat was feeling out of sorts. She'd spent all morning cooking in the kitchen with Angela and come out to discover that the children had trashed the house. Before his little strop, Noel seemed to have spent the whole morning on the computer and done little to help. Honestly. He was the limit sometimes. Couldn't he *see* that things needed doing? Why did she always have to point it out? It was that frustration that had spilled over and led her to make the bitchy remark earlier.

She was guiltily aware it wasn't altogether true. It was just that when Noel was in the kitchen, he seemed to fill the space and ruin the peace and tranquillity of her ordered way of working. There were occasions when he'd cracked open a bottle of red, put some music on and insisted on dancing with her as they cooked, when he actually made cooking more fun. But then there was the clearing up afterwards. She should probably lighten up a bit about that, but it was so hard when you always felt you had to take responsibility for managing everything.

It was also frustrating to be the only one to write all the cards (though Noel at least had consented to put them in the post) and he'd shown scant interest in choosing Christmas presents. She'd been so busy with doing the extraneous extra pieces for the family – and his family to boot. Why Great Auntie Priscilla had to have bedsocks, and Cousin Ivy's third grandchild needed a bath toy, Cat didn't know. But she did know that Noel never paid any attention to that kind of thing and it was Expected. So *she* had to do it.

There were also all the presents for the waifs and strays she'd somehow ended up inviting for Christmas: as well as Mum, there was Auntie Eileen and Great Uncle Paddy (who wasn't a real uncle at all but a friend of Cat's grandfather), plus Angela, who generally managed to put people's noses out of joint wherever she went, and Soppy Sarah (so called by the children for the way she went around weeping at the sight of small children and animals), their doolally neighbour for whom Cat felt terribly sorry. The trouble was, Cat could never bear the thought of anyone being on their own for Christmas, so somehow half the neighbourhood was now coming.

She still felt guilty about her rubbish Christmas presents for Noel. Mind you, if he wanted more than a couple of CDs, the latest Terry Pratchett and a manbag, he should give her more time to go shopping. Noel was so bad at presents himself, he probably hadn't got her anything at all. It had been known to happen.

The door opened, and Noel came in looking triumphant.

'I come bearing gifts,' he said, holding a Christmas pudding aloft.

'Fantastic,' said Cat, 'where did you get it?'

'I paid a small fortune for it at the minimarket,' said Noel, 'but I do think it was worth it.'

He kissed her on the top of the head.

'Sorry about earlier,' he said.

'Me too,' said Cat.

'I've got a special Christmas surprise for you later,' said Noel.

'Oh, what?'

'Well, it won't be a surprise if I tell you, will it?' said Noel. 'But I think you'll like it. Now come on, what else is there to do?'

'If you could get the kids cracking on their bedrooms,' said Cat.

'Consider it done,' said Noel, and was off shouting his way round the house, getting the kids fired up in a way that she never could.

She'd been wrong to be so negative. Noel always meant well. She should try and listen more. They were going to have a great Christmas. In fact, she wouldn't be surprised if it was the best one ever.

'Are you sure we're not putting you out?' Gabriel asked Pippa for the hundredth time, as he helped sort out Stephen's made-up bed on the floor of the boys' room. Stephen was bounding about excitedly, holding up his stocking and saying, 'Where can I put this, Auntie Pippa?'

Gabriel had been in two minds about letting Stephen take part in the Nativity, but it had kept him occupied, and now he was so excited about staying with his cousins he seemed, for the moment at least, not to mind too much about his mother's absence. Pippa had pointed out that his mum was so often out or away anyway that maybe it didn't make as much difference as they thought – but Gabriel knew that that didn't matter. Eve might not have been the best of mothers but Stephen missed her terribly. It was heartbreaking to see how much. Which was why Gabriel was determined his son should have a fantastic Christmas and was throwing himself into the spirit of things, even though he didn't feel like it.

'I'm the Ghost of Christmas Past,' he said, throwing a sheet over his head and chasing the boys around the room.

'Careful,' said Pippa. 'I really don't want to end up in Casualty on Christmas Eve.'

'Sorry,' said Gabriel, 'I got a bit carried away.' He felt a curious sense of dislocation, as if his feelings about Eve were on hold, but at the same time he felt almost giddy and intoxicated. He had the awful feeling that if he started laughing he might never stop.

'No worries,' Pippa touched him lightly on the arm. 'You okay?'

'I'll have to be, won't I?' said Gabriel.

'Come on, let's leave these rascals to go to bed and let's get you fed and watered,' Pippa said.

Gabriel followed her down to the cosy kitchen and tried to join in the cheerful patter going on between Pippa, Dan and Dan's sister and husband, who'd come over from a neighbouring village for the evening, but he found he couldn't settle. His mind was constantly on Eve, wondering what she was doing. He kept checking his mobile. Maybe she'd left a message but – despite the numerous texts he'd sent her and messages he'd left on her phone, there was nothing. At least if he knew she was okay, it would be something to tell Stephen.

His phone bleeped suddenly, and he nearly jumped out of his skin. He scrolled through his messages. It was from Eve's mum. Excusing himself, Gabriel put on his coat and went out into the front garden where the reception was better. Then, taking a deep breath, he rang his mother-in-law.

'Hi, it's Gabe,' he said. 'Any news?'

Earlier in the week, Joan had been adamant she'd had no contact with her daughter, but now she was texting him out of the blue.

'I've heard from Eve,' said Joan, 'and she said to tell you she's fine.'

'Where is she?'

'With friends,' said Joan.

'Have you got a number?' Gabriel nearly shouted down the phone.

'I'm sorry, Gabe,' said Joan, 'she expressly asked me not to give it you. She doesn't want to see you.'

It was what he'd been expecting, but Gabriel was unprepared for the sharp searing pain that swept through him.

'What about Stephen?' Gabriel asked. 'Surely she can't

not contact Stephen? It's Christmas Day tomorrow, for fuck's sake.'

'I don't know,' said Joan, 'she didn't say.'

'Please,' said Gabriel. 'I'll understand about not seeing me, but please ask her not to do this to Stephen.'

'I'll try,' said Joan. 'But you know she's not in a good way right now. She's very very ill. I'm not sure I can persuade her of anything.'

Gabriel hung up and stared out at the snowy hills. He looked back at the warm glow from the cottage, the upstairs light indicating that Stephen and his cousins were still wide awake. How were they going to get through tomorrow? For the first time, he had to face up to the truth. Eve had gone. And this time, she really wasn't coming back.

This Year

Chapter Seventeen

The sun shone as Gabriel took his ewes and lambs down the lane and out to pasture. He'd delayed getting them back on the hills because up until Easter Monday the weather had been so dreadful. But spring was definitely sprung, and it was a fine clear morning to be out on the hillside. He whistled as he made his way up the valley. He loved these early mornings here, the freshness of the air, the vast blue arc of sky above him, the gentle sound of sheep baaing, the rooks cawing in their rookeries, and the soft spring of the heather under his feet. And the colours on the hillside never ceased to amaze him, ever changing with the seasons. In summer he knew the soft pinks and purples of the heather would become lost in a blaze of glorious gold and green, and by autumn the hills would be red and orange, before fading to the muted soft greens of winter. He felt lucky to be here, at one with nature, enjoying the view.

And since the Monday Muddle he felt luckier still. Marianne seemed to be slotting into his life in a comfortable and easy way. If Stephen had a late club at school, she often walked home with him and stayed for a cup of tea. The three of them had driven over the hills to an isolated country pub for Sunday lunch and then a long yomp across the fields. It had felt natural and right and, when they'd swung Stephen between them, Gabriel had realised with a jolt that this was what he had always been missing with Eve. Precious family moments had been few and far between, either because Eve couldn't 'cope' with Stephen, so Gabriel had taken him out alone, or because, when she had come with them, invariably something would happen to create tension and he and Stephen would have to be on tenterhooks for the whole day. Gabriel tried and failed to think of a single day spent with his wife and son that had been this easy.

He whistled as he wound his way into the valley near the proposed eco town. He could see that work had started already but was amused to notice that the foundations of the proposed houses were deep in mud, and the new back gardens, which led down to the river, were awash. When would they learn? This was such a bad place to build, any fool could see it. Although the weather had perked up of late, the river banks were swollen, and the last few weeks in March had brought severe flood warnings that so far hadn't come to pass. But if they did, Gabriel was fairly sure the river bank wouldn't hold, and the eco town might get swept away before it had even been built.

A few hours later, Noel was standing in the same muddy field looking round him in dismay. By dint of fudging things so that the bulk of the houses in the eco town would be built on the hillside, while the communal areas would be in the spot where there were potential floods, as per the government guidelines, the project been allowed to go ahead.

Coming as he had from the rural beauty of Hope Christmas, it seemed more shameful to Noel than ever that they were tearing up this beauty spot for what was at best going to be a shiny new town with no heart and soul, and at worst was going to be a disaster, leaving both houses and GRB in a quagmire. The sun was shining but he was

211

standing in a swamp and the river was flowing dangerously fast. Even Matt Duncan had blanched when he'd arrived. The soil was so damp, and had been for weeks, work had ground to a halt on the site, the foreman having pushed his workers off and put them on another job that they could actually finish. Noel didn't blame him. In these financially turbulent times it made sense to get a job done so you could get paid. GRB's finances were probably so precarious at the moment, the chances of the builders getting paid on time were slight to say the least, and any delay meant GRB's credit controllers would be rubbing their hands with glee at the thought they could stall paying someone. Noel always failed to understand how credit controllers operated. Presumably they realised that their counterparts in the customers' firms were playing the same game? Sure, they were saving GRB money, but someone, somewhere, was making sure GRB didn't get paid, which in the end could be the difference between keeping your job or not.

Noel swallowed slightly. He still hadn't told Cat about the precarious nature of his situation, and though his heart wasn't in this eco project at all, he felt duty-bound to give it his best shot. Maybe then his job might be safe? And maybe that promised bonus would materialise. But somehow Noel doubted it. There was a chill wind blowing across the business map these days. If he lost his job, for the first time in his life Noel wasn't certain he'd get another one.

'How's it all going, chaps?' Great. Luke Nicholas came swaggering up in a Barbour and this time, Noel noticed to his amusement, wellingtons, looking every inch the country squire.

'We're having a few difficulties with the builders', explained Noel, seeing that Matt looked like he was going to fudge the issue once more. 'They're saying it's not possible to carry on building in this swamp, so they've downed tools and swanned off to another job.'

Luke's eyes narrowed, and a vein began to throb dangerously on his upper temple. Noel stared at it, fascinated. It seemed to be developing a life of its own.

'Not good enough, people,' he said. 'We have investors to keep happy here. Investors who need reassurance in these difficult times that this particular investment is safe.'

Wondering how on earth anyone was going to guarantee that the houses here would actually be sold now that the world's finances were in such a downturn, Noel simply said, 'What do you suggest we do?'

'Throw money at it,' was the succinct reply. 'Whatever the other job is offering them, double it. We've spent too much on this to back out now. And you two. You're the engineers. Find a solution. Presumably you can find *some* way of drying the earth out so the building can recommence. It can't be that hard, can it?'

'It's not quite as straightforward as that,' began Noel, thinking of the fact that they were building on clay, which was going to lead to subsidence problems anyway once the earth had dried out, but he knew he was wasting his time as soon as Matt chipped in with, 'That's fine, Luke. I'm sure we can work something out, can't we, Noel?'

Noel said nothing. There was no point. But he looked at the swamp again and knew the project was failed. No matter how much money Luke Nicholas thought he could throw at it.

Cat was ostensibly working at home on the Christmas issue but so far this morning she'd managed to put on three loads of washing, clear a space on the floor in the chaos that was Ruby's room and make herself three cups of tea.

213

Cat had forgotten how very difficult it was working from home and trying to juggle the competing demands of seeing what needed to be done in the house with that of an editor screaming for copy yesterday.

Since Magda's departure, Cat had been trying to wangle more and more days at home so that she could at least do the school run without relying too heavily on Regina. Regina had been fabulous, it was true, and would help out at the drop of a hat, but Cat knew it wasn't fair to expect it of her friend. She wasn't often in a position to pay back the favour – having to work like a demon in between sorting tea out and getting the kids to bed, Cat couldn't manage to cope with Regina's mob for tea more than once a week – and she was guiltily aware that in the school-mum-helping-each-other-out bank she was heavily in her friend's debt.

In the first couple of weeks after Magda had gone, Cat had asked her mum to help out, but things hadn't gone according to plan. Mum had needed to be reminded every day she was picking the children up from school and, when she got home, the children had started complaining to Cat that Granny Dreamboat was either paying them no attention, or getting cross with them for no good reason. When quizzed about it, Mum was incredibly vague, and Cat was beginning to realise she couldn't even rely on her mother to cook the children's supper when she got in. Nine times out of ten when she got home, Mum would have been 'just about to' put the tea on, the kids were starving and snappy with each other, and the house was in more chaos than Cat could have thought possible.

It was becoming increasingly clear to her that though her mother continued to be delighted to see her grandchildren, and frequently moaned that she didn't see enough of them, the reality was they were exhausting her. And after two more occasions when Mum had simply forgotten to turn up on the school run, Cat reluctantly came to the conclusion that her mother was no longer to be relied on. She pushed away the gnawing ache of worry that that was engendering in her. She had enough to deal with, without thinking too hard about the fact her mother appeared to be losing it. Besides, the thought of something being wrong with her clever, capable mother made her shrivel up inside. She wasn't ready to face it.

Particularly not at a time when both Noel and Mel seemed to be locked in their respective bubbles of misery. Noel had clammed up completely on her. He was taking quite a few days working at home (funnily it never seemed convenient for *him* to do the school run), but, whether at home or work, he seemed silent and morose. She couldn't even get him to row with her, which at least would have shown some spark of something. It was as though Noel had lost interest in her and the children. While Mel, Mel was becoming harder and harder work. Cat knew the transition from primary to secondary school had been difficult for her clever, sensitive daughter, but, whereas the other mothers she knew were reporting their children settling down into their new schools, Mel seemed more and more closed in on herself. It was Cat's secret fear that her daughter was being bullied, and she was keeping a weather eye on Mel's MSN account to make sure nothing untoward had happened. It caught at her heart to see her daughter so very unhappy and be unable to do anything about it.

Cat sighed. Maybe she should blog about Mel's problems. One of the bonuses of the blog, she'd found, was that talking about domestic problems she had (not that the Happy Homemaker often admitted to having problems) usually resulted in a wave of supportive posts from people who had been through similar. She'd do that now and get going on the magazine later. It was important that she keep her blog posts up, they'd become a bit sporadic of late.

It's every mother's nightmare. The thought that your child is being bullied and you can do nothing about it. But how do you know if you're child is being bullied? And what, if anything, can you do to prevent it?

Cat began to type and was soon lost in her words. It was one way to stop herself worrying.

Marianne raced late into the latest Post Office Meeting. Vera had called it at short notice, so Pippa and Gabriel had both said they couldn't make it and she'd agreed to let them know how it went.

How it went was very simple. Vera got up, looking ashen-faced, and said in a straightforward manner, 'I'm really sorry everyone, but our campaign has failed. Despite the petition and the picketing of Mount Pleasant, I heard today that my post office licence is being withdrawn. It's nobody's fault, really, they're just following government guidelines, but there's nothing more any of us can do. I really appreciate the help you've given—'

She stifled a sob and sat down again, looking stricken. Mr Edwards, who was sitting next to her, patted her hand sympathetically and handed her a tissue.

'That's outrageous!' Diana Carew boomed from the back of the hall. 'There must be something we can do.'

'Absolutely.' Miss Woods came up, banging her stick determinedly into the ground in a way only she knew how. 'Never say die, that's my motto. Can't we use the interweb a bit more? Set up a Spacebook account or something?'

'I couldn't agree more,' said Diana, and Marianne smiled at the sight of the two of them, for once on the same side, though really she didn't feel like smiling at all.

'Why don't we run our own community post office?' said

Miss Woods. 'I've been skiing the interweb and discovered all sorts of places where communities have kept their post offices alive by working together. We could move it here, to the village hall, and work together with the village farmers to sell some of their local produce. Pippa, you could use it as an outlet for your produce. See, I printed something off about a village in Somerset that did the very same thing.'

'What an excellent idea,' said Diana, who only looked a little put out that she hadn't thought of it herself. 'And what with the new eco town, we might get an injection of new blood into the area, so why don't we suggest to the developers they get involved too?'

Marianne stifled the thought that Luke wouldn't be at all interested in developing anything if it involved the word community. It was a good idea. Maybe it would work.

The meeting broke up in a muddle of excited talk and gloomy harbingers of doom declaring the scheme was doomed to failure. Marianne set off for Pippa's to tell her what had happened, but she paused before she got there and, without questioning herself as to why she was doing it, she walked further up the lane to Gabriel's house. Since the incident at the Monday Muddle she'd been seeing him regularly but, despite her epiphany, to her disappointment nothing had yet happened between them. Gabriel was an inscrutable kind of character, quite hard to read, but she thought he liked her. Trying to calm down her nerves, which were on edge, and her heartbeat, which was so erratic she wondered she hadn't gone into cardiac arrest, she walked down the path and knocked on his cottage door. Maybe she was making a mistake. Perhaps she should have told Pippa what had happened at the meeting and just run into Gabriel in the normal way.

The dark path flooded with light as Gabriel came to the door.

217

'Marianne, how great to see you.' His warmth seemed genuine.

'I just came—' She hesitated, suddenly feeling like a total idiot. 'I thought you might like to know how the meeting went.'

'And there was me thinking you were coming to see me,' quipped Gabriel.

'I was . . . I am . . . well, both.' Marianne blushed in confusion.

'Good,' said Gabriel. 'Come in and have a drink. I've been meaning to ask you anyway.'

'You have?' Marianne's heart skipped.

'Yes, I have.' Gabriel looked at her semi-solemnly, and then said, 'If only to see you go that spectacular shade of beetroot.'

Marianne felt her cheeks flame even more and her heart went into overdrive on the skipping front. He did like her. He did. She could scarcely breathe, she felt so overcome. From somewhere distant, she realised Gabriel was motioning her into the lounge.

'Stephen's in bed,' he was saying, 'make yourself at home.'

Marianne collapsed onto Gabriel's comfy battered old sofa and let out a sigh of nervous relief. She had the weirdest feeling she'd come home.

Chapter Eighteen

It seemed wrong to be looking up Christmassy stuff at this time of year, but Cat was busy composing an article to go along with the launch of the competition, so she was online, searching through references to Nativity plays of yore, and tracking down more ancient carols to give people a taste of what they were looking for.

Perhaps, she wrote, *in these more difficult times, this Christmas we can return to the simplicity of yesteryear and dispense with too much expense, fuss and nonsense. Perhaps it is time to remember an event, that took place two thousand years ago, in a stable in Bethlehem . . .*

Too corny? Probably, but she knew that was what Bev would want.

Cat glanced at her watch – it was gone nine already. Noel had rung to say that he would be late, his train being delayed at Nuneaton apparently. The little ones were in bed, and James and Mel were playing on the Wii – last Christmas' must-have, over-expensive item, which Cat had felt guilty getting for them at the time. Now, with the credit crunch and the scary amount of borrowing that she and Noel had found themselves embroiled in over the last few years, such purchases were looking self-indulgent to say the least. How had it come to this, she wondered. Cat and Noel had always tried to be careful with money, but then the family had expanded, they'd needed extra space to accommodate the au pair, been unable to move thanks to the craziness of house prices, and ended up borrowing a shedload of money to pay for the loft conversion they required. They'd borrowed it on the strength of the partnership Noel had been promised, but which had yet to materialise. The building trade was bound to be affected by the financial slowdown, and Cat was worried sick about Noel losing his job but, if he shared her concerns, then he was keeping things very close to his chest. Not that he seemed to want to share all that much with her nowadays.

Cat saved the document she was working on and went downstairs to chase James into bed. He and Mel were in the middle of a row because James had won at tennis again.

'He always beats me, it's not fair!' burst out Mel, before rushing off in floods of tears.

'She's such a bad loser,' sulked James, about to throw his nunchuck on the floor – but one glance from his mother stopped him.

'Yeah, well, maybe she is,' said Cat, 'but I don't suppose it helps you rubbing her face in it.' James was generally very self-satisfied when he won and Cat found it most annoying when she played him. With Mel in the sensitive state she was in, he was bound to wind her up.

'You could go easy on her,' said Cat. 'She's having a tough time of it at the moment.'

'I know,' said James in disgusted tones. 'Hormones.'

James had recently had his puberty talk at school and was now apparently the expert on all things hormonal.

'Yup,' said Cat, 'so you have to feel sorry for her really. Now apologise and get to bed.'

Cat followed her son up the stairs and heard him dart in and mumble a feeble apology to Mel before darting out again. Taking a deep breath, she knocked on the door. She was never sure how Mel would react these days.

'May I come in?' she said.

'Suppose,' was the sullen reply.

Mel was sitting against the wall, red-eyed, playing with her mobile phone.

'Anything in particular bring that on, or just everything?' said Cat, squashing up next to her daughter.

'No, nothing. Oh, everything!' burst out Mel. 'I hate being eleven. It sucks.'

'Sure does,' said Cat, 'but twelve will be better, you'll see.'

'It might be worse,' said Mel.

'What, worse than this?' laughed Cat. 'Surely not.'

This elicited a small smile from her daughter and soon Cat had her giggling away as if nothing had happened.

'There's nothing really wrong though, is there, Mel?' Cat asked gently.

'NOoo,' said Mel disparagingly. 'You always ask that, and I always say no.'

'It's only because I worry about you,' said Cat.

'Well, don't,' said Mel, closing in on herself again. 'I'm fine. I just want to be left alone.'

'Okay,' said Cat, 'but get straight into bed and no reading, it's late.'

She paused at the door, looking at her daughter, who looked so vulnerable sitting there. Vulnerable but belligerent.

'You can tell me if something's wrong,' she said.

'There isn't anything wrong,' said Mel, 'except that I want you to go away so I can get undressed.'

Cat laughed, that was a bit more like it. She just hoped that Mel wasn't hiding anything from her. She sighed. Such a short time ago, she'd been terrified by the responsibility of having a newborn baby. Now she worried about her almost teenage daughter being bullied. It was just as well

221

no one had ever told her what being a parent was really like, otherwise she might never have done it.

The last person Gabriel had expected to see when he went to answer the door was Marianne. He'd assumed it would be Dan, who sometimes called in at this time in the evening for a beer. It was automatic for him to ask her in. Gabriel had inherited a welcoming gene from his mother and not to have done so would have felt unnatural. One bonus he was discovering from Eve's departure was that he could invite friends round again. Eve had been wary of people and hated entertaining, so over the years Gabriel had suppressed the welcoming side of his nature. He went into the kitchen to sort out drinks while Marianne browsed through his CD collection. It seemed natural and right that she was here. Gabriel was very glad she'd come.

'What would you like to drink?' he called from the kitchen. 'Wine or beer?'

'Actually, would you mind if I had something soft?' said Marianne. 'I hate going to work with a heavy head. You wouldn't believe how bad it is trying to teach a bunch of five-year-olds with a hangover.'

'Yes, checking on the sheep early in the morning is equally unforgiving,' said Gabriel as he came into the lounge, scouring it for dirty mugs. 'Sorry about the mess. I try hard not to, but it's all too easy to slide into bachelor-pad chaos.'

'It's neater than my place,' said Marianne, laughing as she put down a KT Tunstall CD. 'Can I put this on?'

'Be my guest,' said Gabriel. 'Tea or coffee?'

'Coffee would be great, thanks,' said Marianne as she put the CD on.

'So, how did the meeting go?' said Gabriel as he sat down opposite her. The light from the lamps cast shadows across her face, but he could see from here the way her eyes lit up as she talked, and the natural spontaneity of her manner. Marianne was like a breath of fresh air in his cobweb-filled life. She was bringing light and dance back into the unparalleled gloom he'd been living in since – since, well, forever. Gabriel had never liked to analyse it too much, but now, with a bit of distance between him and Eve, he was beginning to see just how unhealthy their relationship had been.

'Not great,' said Marianne. 'Apparently the post office has got to go, but Miss Woods and Diana Carew are planning to join forces to set it up in the village hall instead. I have no idea if that is feasible or not but, hey ho, it will keep them happy.'

'Miss Woods and Diana agreed on something? Wonders will never cease,' said Gabriel.

'My sentiments exactly,' said Marianne. 'But joking aside, I do hope it will work. It would break Vera's heart to lose the post office. Not to mention causing a huge blow to the village community.'

'You really like it here, don't you?' Gabriel said. 'Don't you miss the city at all?'

'Sometimes,' said Marianne. 'But I fell in love with this place from the moment I arrived. I love its peace and tranquillity and the fact that I can go walking on the hills in all weathers. I feel hemmed in in the city. Here I feel free and alive and, well, happy, I suppose. I'm glad I was persuaded to stay.'

'I'm glad too,' Gabriel smiled at her shyly. He was glad, very glad. That Marianne had come into his life. That she was here now. He still didn't know quite where this was leading, but he was enjoying the newness, the uncertainty, and the sheer joy of getting to know someone as uncomplicated as Marianne appeared to be. Yes, after Eve, she was definitely a breath of fresh air.

* * *

223

Marianne was enjoying herself too. After her initial anxiety that Gabriel might not want her here, he had put her so much at her ease, she was relaxing into their normal cosy friendship again. She had never been this relaxed with Luke. Never. The whole time she'd been with him, Marianne realised with a jolt, she'd been on tenterhooks in case she said the wrong thing, did the wrong thing, or generally didn't live up to expectations. That was no way to live your life.

'Penny for 'em?' Gabriel's voice intruded into her thoughts.

'Just thinking about Luke, and realising I had a lucky escape,' said Marianne. 'Oh dear, does that mean I'm no longer a member of the Lonely Hearts Club?'

'You can be an honorary member,' said Gabriel. 'So what's changed your mind about Luke?'

'It's taken me a while,' said Marianne, 'but it's recently dawned on me that I was never ever going to fit in in his world. I can't believe I was so stupid as to think I could.'

'Yes, well, we all make mistakes,' said Gabriel. He looked incredibly sad when he said this, and Marianne noticed the quick glance towards the photo on the mantelpiece.

'Is that your wife?' she asked. She was treading carefully, but this seemed the moment for confidences somehow.

Gabriel walked slowly to the fireplace and picked up the picture.

'That's me, Eve and Stephen when Stephen was first born,' he said.

Marianne looked at the smiling couple, a small baby between them. It was hard to imagine that things could have gone so wrong.

'You look really happy there,' said Marianne. 'She's very beautiful.'

'Eve was high as a kite on diazepam when that picture

224

was taken,' said Gabriel. 'And two weeks later she was in hospital, having taken an overdose.'

'What on earth happened?' Marianne asked, shocked. 'Sorry. I didn't mean to pry. You don't have to say if you don't want to.'

'No, it's probably good for me to talk,' said Gabriel. He rubbed his stubble with his hands and put the picture back on the shelf. 'She was – is – lovely, Eve. But she's fragile. Very fragile. Her home life wasn't exactly stable and I knew she was prone to getting a bit down about things before I married her. I thought I could help her, you see.'

'And you couldn't?' Marianne prompted.

'It's like dealing with an alcoholic. You can't solve their problems, only they can do that.' Gabriel sighed, and looked as if he was in some very far-off, dark place. 'It was different when we met, of course. I was in London, earning good money in marketing. Eve was a secretary in the same company, and we just seemed to hit it off. She was so lively and vivacious and fun. It never dawned on me that anything was wrong.'

'What changed?' prompted Marianne.

'It was a while after we married when I realised she had a problem sticking at anything. I'd stayed with the same firm for five years during which time Eve had had six jobs. Then it was her mood swings. One minute she'd be on top of the world and then she'd be down in the dumps. I thought it was my fault, of course. I did everything I could to make her happy, but eventually she came clean and told me how bad her depression actually was. So we went to the doctor and she got some happy pills and she seemed all right for a while . . .'

'And then?'

'And then we had Stephen. I discovered afterwards that an event like that can trigger a psychotic episode in someone

225

like Eve, but I didn't know that at the time. Eve seemed morbidly depressed that something would go wrong with the baby and was crying all the time. I couldn't leave her alone with him for a minute as I didn't know what she would do. One day I came into the room and she was holding a pillow over his face. She kept crying and saying it was all for the best, this world was too cruel, that it would have been better if he hadn't been born. I took her back to the doctor, got her on stronger medication, and then a week later she tricked me into taking Stephen for a walk. When I got back I found her unconscious next to a suicide note.'

'That's terrible, oh, Gabriel, I'm so sorry,' said Marianne.

'It was,' said Gabriel. 'Eve was in hospital for months after that. Without my parents, who came down to stay with me, I don't know what I'd have done. Eventually she came home, and over time things got better. After a while I thought about coming back here. Mum and Dad were finding the farm too much and Eve had always raved about how wonderful it was up here. I thought she'd like it. I went back to agricultural college, sold our house and we moved back.'

'And did she like it?'

Gabriel sighed.

'At first Eve seemed better here, but she never settled to being a proper mother to Stephen. And I couldn't trust her with him . . .'

Marianne could see Gabriel was close to tears. Instinctively, she moved towards him and held his hand. He closed his own around hers and continued, 'We staggered along like that for years. Never going out because Eve didn't like difficult social situations. Never having people round because Eve couldn't cope. I was constantly on edge in case she did something dangerous, either to herself or Stephen. Of late, I had thought she was getting better.

But last winter, she lost the little job she'd had in the village shop and suddenly she hit a downward spiral. I was on the verge of suggesting she go back to the doctor when she walked out.'

'Where is she now?' Marianne asked.

'I have no idea,' said Gabriel. 'She was with her mother at Easter, but she wouldn't talk to me then.'

'What a terrible story,' said Marianne. 'So sad for all of you.'

'Worse for Stephen than me,' said Gabriel. 'At least I can understand Eve's ill, even if I hate it, but Stephen still doesn't get why his mother is so different from other mums. For a long time he didn't want to go to school because he was being picked on. In a way, it's been better for him since she left.'

'At least he's got you and Pippa,' said Marianne. 'That will stand him in good stead.'

'Do you think?' said Gabriel. 'I have to be both mother and father to him. And sometimes it's really hard.'

Marianne squeezed his hand tightly.

'Well, I think you're doing a fantastic job. He's lucky to have you.' She smiled at Gabriel, and suddenly he gave her the most dazzling smile back.

'Thanks,' he said. 'I can't tell you how much it's helping having you in my life.'

Marianne's heart did a sudden lurch. Did he – was it possible that he could – feel the same way as she did?

For a moment they sat looking at each other as if someone had pressed the pause button, then Gabriel moved as if to . . .

'Daddy!' A small voice was shouting from the top of the stairs. Oh my God. Marianne had forgotten for a moment about Stephen.

'I'd better go,' said Gabriel. Was it her imagination, or was he tearing himself away reluctantly?

'Me too,' said Marianne in some confusion. 'I'll let myself out.'

'Thanks for the chat,' said Gabriel. 'It really helped.'

He bounded up the stairs shouting to Stephen, 'What is it, you little rascal? You were supposed to be asleep hours ago.' Halfway up he paused, turned those deep brown eyes on her, and said, 'Call me.'

'Okay,' said Marianne as casually as she could muster but, as she walked down the garden path, her heart was singing.

Noel let himself into a house that seemed worryingly quiet. Since Magda had gone the noise levels had halved, it was true. (When she had been there, if she wasn't on the phone arguing with Sergei in excited Russian, she was playing her 1980s thrash metal music way too loud.) But he was still used to so much noise all the time the silence was slightly unnerving. The lights were all turned off so he switched on the hall light and poked his head in the lounge. No sign of Cat there. Nor in the family room. As he left it, he heard the familiar sound of books sliding off the shelf. That damned bookshelf. It seemed to sum up his life somehow. In his fantasy farmhouse the shelves were always intact, and everything he made fitted perfectly. How he wished he was there and not in this draughty London house with its poky little garden: it was a financial millstone around his neck.

Cat wasn't in the kitchen either. Noel went to the fridge and got out a can of lager. He looked around to see if Cat had left him something to eat. He'd planned to eat on the train, but the buffet car had been shut, and, while he would have liked to have had a beer, he and Matt had instead been trying to thrash out a solution to their mud problem, without much luck. If he thought there was any chance of getting a job somewhere, anywhere, else, Noel would hand in his notice tomorrow, before he finally got pushed.

Cat must be working. He went upstairs, pausing to look at the little ones, who were fast asleep. A light swiftly went off in James' room as Noel entered. He ruffled his son's hair and said, 'I saw you, you monkey. Sleep. Now.'

'Night, night, Daddy,' said James, looking sleepy. Hard to remember he was a nine-year-old, testosterone-filled boy during the day. James always looked angelic at bedtime.

Mel was definitely still awake, lying in bed listening to her iPod and immersed in a Darren Shan book.

'Sleep,' said Noel, 'otherwise you'll never get up in the morning. Where's your mother?'

'On the computer,' said Mel. 'She's been there all evening.'

'Right,' said Noel. 'I'd better go and chase her off then.'

He climbed up the stairs to the top of the house. Cat was crouched in the dark over a computer screen – the only light in the room coming from that and her desklamp.

'Oh, hello,' she said. 'I didn't hear you come in. I was just finishing this off.'

Cat barely looked at him when she said this, she was so deep in concentration. Sometimes he felt like she hardly noticed him.

'Right, I'll just go downstairs and get myself something to eat then,' said Noel.

Cat looked up, frowning.

'Haven't you eaten?' she said. 'I thought you were going to eat on the train.'

'I was,' said Noel, 'but the buffet car on the train was shut. What have you had?'

'I only fancied beans on toast,' said Cat.

No wonder Cat was so skinny, she ate like a bird these days.

'Oh, right,' said Noel. 'I'll just sort myself out something then.'

'I won't be long,' said Cat.

Noel went downstairs with a heavy heart. He'd been planning to tell Cat about his work situation tonight but she seemed so distracted, and he felt so shattered, now probably wasn't the best moment.

And when Cat did eventually come downstairs, she sat next to him for all of ten minutes on the sofa, before declaring herself too tired to stay up a moment longer and going to bed.

Noel cracked open another can of lager, and switched to ITV3 where an old Sly Stallone film was showing. When Noel was young, he'd imagined that hitting middle age would be a point in his life when he had all the answers. So how was it he was sitting here alone, worrying about the future and feeling more uncertain about life than ever?

Chapter Nineteen

Call me.

Marianne was on one of her periodic yomps through the hills. Now that spring was here she was enjoying these walks more than ever. The sight of lambs gambolling in the fresh green fields couldn't help but lighten the spirits and the blustery breezes when, after a determined scramble, she'd finally reached the top of the hill, made her feel gloriously, wonderfully alive. She looked back down the valley towards Hope Christmas. The houses looked like miniature dolls' houses nestling in the hills, which brimmed with purple and pink heathers. It was so beautiful. She was so happy here now, but perhaps she could be even happier.

Marianne knew she hadn't mistaken the look in Gabriel's eyes the other night. She knew that she hadn't imagined it, that he was feeling the way she was feeling. But, and it was a big but, should she, could she, take things further? Marianne would have liked to have been bold enough to proposition a man like Lisa and Carly would – their ability to pick up men never failed to astonish her. They had frequently admonished her in the past to live like a twenty-first-century woman, not like a nineteenth-century heroine, waiting 'like a lapdog', as Carly always put it, for some handsome swain to turn up. But Marianne couldn't help it. She liked the sensation of being courted. She wanted the romance of it. It wasn't her fault that nineteenth-century fictional heroes always seemed so much better than the real thing. No wonder she'd been such a soft touch for Luke. What a sap.

But now, here was Gabriel putting her off her stride, asking her to take the initiative. There was certainly a bit – what was she talking about, a lot – of her wanting to do so, but she was conscious that he wasn't free and that the situation with Stephen was delicate to say the least. She wasn't entirely sure that she wanted the responsibility of children just yet. Particularly that of a child with so many issues. As a teacher, Marianne had seen enough of the stresses caused by family break-up to know that taking on Stephen was not something she should do lightly. But all that aside, maybe she didn't have the courage to take that first step anyway. And then again, suppose she was wrong and he was only after friendship? She'd feel a total fool if that were the case.

'You won't know if you don't try,' she declared loudly, as she came over a ridge of the hill and started her descent into the next valley.

'That you won't.' Ralph Nicholas, who was coming up over the other side of the hill with his dog. For someone apparently so old, he was remarkably not out of breath. 'Which is precisely what I think about stopping that monstrosity my grandson seems intent on inflicting on us.'

He waved his hand behind him and Marianne saw for the very first time what her erstwhile fiancé had been up to over the last few months. She didn't normally walk out this way. The excavation work for the eco town was clearly under way. It was a scene of utter devastation. The ground was all churned up, trees had been torn down, and it looked like something from *The Lord of the Rings*.

'I had no idea it would be so destructive,' said Marianne. 'I thought eco towns were all about preservation, not destruction.'

'My thoughts exactly,' said Ralph.

'You know the Post Office Committee was planning to talk to Luke about encouraging prospective buyers of eco town property to support us, don't you?' Marianne said.

'Sadly, I fear, they'll be wasting their time,' said Ralph. 'Luke hasn't a sentimental bone in his body. He must take after his father.'

'They neither of them take after you, that's for sure,' said Marianne.

'Ah, well, that's because I adopted Luke's father,' said Ralph. 'I live in hope that it will turn out well in the end.'

'It may yet,' said Marianne. 'You never know. Luke might realise the error of his ways.'

'He might,' said Ralph, 'but I doubt it.' He whistled to his dog, who came bounding up covered in mud. 'I think you may find a friend of yours in the valley. There are an awful lot of sheep to keep track of on the hills this time of year, don't you know?'

He walked off whistling to himself with what Marianne could only describe as a twinkle in his eye. How could he possibly know what she was thinking?

Noel was sitting at home, working on the kids' computer in the playroom. He'd given Cat some guff about the pressures of an office move (depressingly he was going to end his days at GRB hot-desking) making it impossible to work in the office. Really it was that there wasn't enough work to keep him there. Although there was a second computer in Cat's office, she'd made it clear that she hadn't welcomed his intrusion into her workspace, so he'd come downstairs to the kids' computer, ostensibly to draw up the plans for the heating system for the proposed community centre, which was apparently going to be the hub of the eco town.

Having spent a very happy morning mooching about Hope Christmas on his last visit, Noel was now convinced that the designers of the town had utterly missed the point. There was a living, breathing community already there. People had begun to recognise him. The man who ran the antiques shop had taken to joking that Noel always came in yet never bought, and the woman in the estate agents', having seen him mooching outside looking at the pictures, had dragged him in and shown him a whole variety of properties, all of which he coveted. When Noel was in Hope Christmas he bought organic meat at the butcher's (he told Cat he'd got it in Smithfield Market), Shropshire honey that he pretended he'd picked up in Oxford Street, far too many books from the tiny bookshop with its informative and friendly booksellers, and used the internet facilities in Aunty Betty's Coffee Shop, where he had met an ancient crone who had got him to show her how to surf.

Noel had fallen in love with Hope Christmas, and yet he had barely mentioned it to Cat. He couldn't even explain to himself why he didn't want to talk to her about it, but it was like he was having a fantasy life, far removed from his normal stresses and strains. And, for now, he just wanted to keep it secret.

From what he had seen of the place, it seemed like the perfect place to live already, so who needed to create a new town so close by? The prices were going to be out of the range of most of the young people in the surrounding villages, even in these uncertain times. Noel wished more than ever that someone at GRB had listened to his suggestions about utilising existing buildings to create sustainable and affordable housing. Every time he visited the building site, he felt sick. A perfectly beautiful valley was being destroyed. And for what? Just so that Luke Nicholas and his cronies could line their pockets.

'Can you do the school run today?' Cat had crept up on him unawares. 'I've got a really urgent feature to finish by five.'

Noel pulled a face. He hated the school run, always feeling out of place among the mums comparing notes about PTA committee meetings and children's tummy bugs.

'I've got a fair bit on myself,' he began to protest.

'Yes, I noticed,' Cat said drily, nodding at the screen, which was displaying the fact that he'd just lost his third game of Spider Solitaire.

'I was only taking a break,' said Noel. 'Didn't you ask your mum?'

This time it was Cat's turn to pull a face.

'I just can't risk it, Noel,' she said. 'She's become so unreliable. I don't know what's wrong with her. But I daren't ask her to pick them up again in case she forgets. Last time it happened she was so upset, I decided neither of us could go through that again.'

Noel frowned. Cat had been mentioning problems with Louise for weeks – he felt guilty for not realising how bad things had got.

'Have you tried to talk to her about it?' he asked.

'You know Mum,' said Cat. 'She would never admit something was wrong. I tried to get her to go to the doctor, but she wouldn't. She says she feels fine, and I'm making a fuss about nothing.'

'She's probably right,' said Noel. 'Don't forget she is in her seventies now.'

'Seventy-three isn't that old,' said Cat, 'and, as she keeps telling me, she isn't senile yet. She never forgot anything till recently, but now it's really hard to get her to remember the simplest things. Yet when you talk to her about the war, she remembers everything, from collecting shrapnel in the streets to having lessons in the air raid shelters. Weird.'

'Very,' said Noel. 'It might just be a phase, you never know.'

'Yeah, it might,' said Cat, looking unconvinced and rather sad. It wasn't like her to make a fuss. Normally she did deal with all the domestic stuff. As he were here, perhaps he should pull his weight a little more.

'Okay. I'll go and pick the kids up, but can you do tea?'

'It's a deal,' said Cat.

She went back upstairs and Noel started another game of Spider Solitaire. He lost. Any more of this and he was going to end up feeling completely emasculated.

Gabriel was tacking a fence post in. Someone driving a digger from the worksite had accidentally run it into his property. Gabriel wanted to make sure the fence was back in place again before he lost any sheep. It was a lovely clear day and he was enjoying his work. He never felt lonely here, out on the hills, but was very much at home and in his element. If it weren't for Stephen, he'd be tempted to occasionally sleep the night in the old shepherd's croft on the top of the hill. Especially in summer. As a young man, he'd often spent time up here on his own with the sheep. He still missed that. Stephen loved being out here too, but he was still young enough to get bored after too long, so this morning Gabriel had left him with his cousins.

'Hello there.' Gabriel looked up from his tacking and swallowed hard. Marianne was standing before him, the sun playing through her dark curls, the wind ruffling them. He'd been an inch away from kissing her the other night. He wondered if she knew. She hadn't called him, so Gabriel had assumed she either didn't know how he felt or was avoiding him.

'Hi,' he said. 'I'm just mending this fence.'

'Yes, I can see that,' said Marianne. 'Do you need any help?'

'That's what I like about you,' said Gabriel, handing her a hammer, 'you're a doer not a chatterer.'

'Oh, I can chat,' said Marianne, 'but I can't help having a strong streak of practicality. My dad was most insistent that I learnt how to fend for myself in the DIY department from an early age.'

'Here, can you bang that post in?' said Gabriel.

They worked in silence for a little while and then Gabriel found himself unable to keep quiet any longer.

'You didn't call,' he said.

'I was going to,' said Marianne.

'I sense a but here,' said Gabriel.

'It's only, well – look, I'm going to be very honest.' Marianne's words came out in a babbling rush. 'I like you – a lot – but there's Stephen and Eve. What if she comes back? What if she doesn't? Does Stephen even want a stepmum? Do I want a stepson? And you've both been through so much—'

'You can stop right there,' said Gabriel. 'I think maybe it's time we both put the past behind us and said goodbye to the Lonely Hearts Club, don't you?' He flung down his tools and, pulling her into his arms with joyous abandon, he kissed her firmly on the mouth. 'Now, does that answer your question?'

'What question?' said Marianne, looking stunned.

'The one you were going to ask about whether or not you could put me through this. And the answer is, yes, you most definitely can.'

Cat was just typing the last words of her feature on 'How to Make the Most of Your Time' (honestly, why had she

237

created an alter ego who was so bossy?) when the phone rang. Cursing, she answered it. Didn't anyone understand about the pressure of deadlines?

'Is there a Mrs Tinsall there?' a voice with a strong Jamaican accent said. 'My name's PC Josephs, and I think I may have your mother here. She seems a little upset.'

Forgetting instantly all about deadlines, Cat said, 'Oh my God, is she all right? She hasn't hurt herself or anything, has she?'

'No, nothing like that,' said the voice, 'but one of her neighbours called us. She was found half an hour ago wandering up and down the street in her nightie. She didn't seem to know where she lived. Luckily her neighbour had a key, so we've got her back home and we're having a nice cup of tea. She's rather distressed though, and is asking for you.'

'I'm on my way,' said Cat, ice chilling her bones. All the fear and anxiety she'd been feeling for months was coming together in a hideous rush. She couldn't let herself think too much about it though, otherwise she'd be sick. Shaking like a leaf, she typed the last sentence and, ever the professional, sent it to Bev with a quick note to say she'd been called away urgently. She rang Noel who, typically, had his mobile switched off, and left him a message, then she got in the car and drove like a maniac to Mum's, trying to suppress the panic bubbling up inside her.

'I really don't know what all the fuss is about,' said Mum when she arrived, looking almost cross that Cat was there. 'I was just a little confused, that's all.'

'Mum, it's the middle of the afternoon,' said Cat, 'and you're wearing your nightie.'

'I felt like a little nap,' said her mother. 'And then I got up and forgot I was wearing it. I only went to the shop to get some milk.' She frowned. 'But then, it was very strange.

238

Like a shutter going down or something. I couldn't quite remember where I was. Luckily this kind young gentleman has been looking after me.'

'Oh, Mum,' said Cat. 'What are you like?' She tried to make a joke, but she'd never felt less like joking. There was no pretending anymore. Something was very very badly wrong.

Cat saw PC Josephs to the door, having prevented Mum from giving him a tip, and thanked him profusely.

'Don't you worry, love,' he said, 'it's my job. Can't have a nice lady like that meeting a mugger, can we?'

Cat laughed and shut the door. She leant against it heavily and took a deep breath. Time to tackle Mum and finally get her to admit they had a very big problem.

Chapter Twenty

'You know, there's really no need for you to come with me,' Mum said crossly as Cat came to pick her up. 'I'm quite capable of getting to the doctor's on my own.'

'Yes, but I think it would be a good idea to have someone to sit with you,' said Cat. 'Sometimes there's a lot to take in when you see a doctor. I know it helped me when I was pregnant having Noel there, there was always something I'd forget to ask.'

Mum still looked mutinous, but at least she got in the car.

'Now, have you got your keys?' said Cat.

'Of course I have my keys. Don't fuss,' said Mum. 'Why wouldn't I have them?'

Why indeed, thought Cat. One of the hardest things she was discovering about dealing with her mother lately was that she was so adamant about things, and so forgetful, that she really had no idea that there had been a problem in the first place.

They reached the surgery in good time and, having signed themselves in, sat in the large modern airy waiting room among young mums and babies – it was evidently baby clinic today. Cat thought back with a pang to how helpful Mum had been when Mel was born. She'd come in every day doling out tea and sympathy and taking over on baby duties when she noticed Cat drooping. How things had changed. These days Mum required nearly as much parenting as any one of Cat's children, and there was no one to prop her up when she drooped. Cat was ever more conscious of a baton being passed to her and it was one that she didn't want to pick up.

'Louise Carpenter.' Dr Miles' voice came over the tannoy.

Cat and her mum gathered up their things and went into the doctor's surgery.

'Hello, Mrs Carpenter, and what can I do for you today?' Dr Miles smiled at them both.

'Well, I feel a bit of a fraud really,' Cat's mum said, turning on a charm offensive. 'I don't think there's anything wrong with me really, apart from that I'm a bit forgetful. Only Cat would insist on me coming.'

'And how does this forgetfulness manifest itself?' said Dr Miles.

'It's nothing, really,' Mum said. 'Nothing at all. Just that I sometimes can't remember where I've put things. I'm sure it's quite normal at my age.'

Cat interposed quickly, 'Come on, Mum, it's a little more than that. You rang me up recently because you couldn't remember how to make pastry.'

'Did I?' Her mother looked doubtful. 'I find that most unlikely. Anyway, I'm sure it's nothing, and we're wasting the doctor's time. I'm sure she has really sick people to see.'

'No, of course you're not wasting my time,' said Dr Miles. 'Let's just run through some points about your general health and take your blood pressure, shall we?'

Cat admired the deftness with which Dr Miles teasingly pulled the story out of Mum, clearly not at all bamboozled by the 'I'm perfectly fine' approach. When it got to the description of what had happened the previous day, she paused and looked at Cat.

'Thank you, that's very helpful, Mrs Carpenter,' she said. 'I think I've got enough to build a good picture of what's happening now.'

'I'm sure I'm wasting your time,' muttered Mum, 'there's nothing wrong with me.'

'I'm sorry, Mrs Carpenter, but I think there does appear to be a problem,' said Dr Miles gently. 'Something seems to be going wrong with the hard-wiring in your brain, which is leading to these lapses of concentration. It may be that you are having TIAs – little strokes – which are shutting off the blood vessels in part of the brain, or it may be something else altogether. I need to run some tests to find out.'

'Oh?' said Cat, alarmed. 'What kind of tests?'

'They're nothing to worry about. Just a blood test and an MRI scan to find out if we can get to the bottom of what's happening,' said Dr Miles. 'I just want to make sure we've covered all the possibilities. Like I say, the most likely cause of your mother's problems is that she's having TIAs. But it's perfectly normal at her age, and I'm sure we can sort everything out.' She smiled reassuringly at Cat, who smiled back with a confidence she didn't feel. Whatever was wrong with her mother, Cat knew it wasn't going to be sorted out that easily.

'This feels a bit strange,' Marianne said as Gabriel ushered her out of the car and into the lobby of the country pub where he was taking her for a meal. It was ten miles from Hope Christmas. They'd both agreed that for Stephen's sake they should take things slowly, and, for the time being, secret. Marianne hadn't even said anything to Pippa about it, though she was dying to.

'What is?' asked Gabriel.

'It's really strange coming on a first date when I feel

I know you already so well,' said Marianne. 'I don't think I've ever done that before. I almost feel like I'm dating my brother.'

'Thanks a bunch,' said Gabriel.

'My brother isn't nearly as good looking as you,' said Marianne. 'It's just – well, this will take some getting used to.'

'In a nice way, I hope?' Gabriel said, giving her a little thrill as he took her hand.

'The nicest possible,' said Marianne.

They were ushered into a small lobby area with dark oak panels and a fire burning in the hearth. The early spring weather had turned cold and heavy rain was forecast for that evening. The friendly owner came over and gave them menus, and they ordered their drinks.

Marianne, feeling a little nervous, ordered a G&T, but Gabriel, who was driving, ordered a Coke. They perused their menus in silence before Gabriel declared he'd have the dover sole and Marianne plumped for duck.

'It's lovely here,' she said. 'I've never been before.'

'It's a well kept secret to all but the locals,' said Gabriel. 'Can't have outsiders coming here, can we now?'

'Oh, stop it,' said Marianne. 'Don't tell me I need to have lived in Hope Christmas for three generations before I'll be accepted properly.'

'Five at least,' said Gabriel solemnly. Marianne threw a beer mat at him.

'Cripes, we'd better duck,' said Gabriel. 'There's Miss Woods and, good lord, is that Ralph Nicholas with her?'

Miss Woods was indeed being helped up from her seat by Ralph Nicholas.

'This is a bit cloak and dagger, isn't it?' said Marianne, giggling from behind her menu.

'You still haven't cottoned on to how a small village works

243

yet, have you?' said Gabriel. 'By the time they're back in Hope Christmas, everyone will know we've had dinner together. And I'd rather Stephen found it out from me than from the village gossips.' Miss Woods had her coat on and was leaving the restaurant. 'Phew, I think we got away with it,' continued Gabriel.

'It's all right,' said a twinkling voice over their heads. 'I won't tell if you won't.'

Marianne wanted the ground to swallow her up. What would Luke's grandfather think of her?

'I think,' said Ralph, uncannily reading her thoughts again, 'you've made a much better choice this time around.' With that he doffed his hat to them, winked and was gone.

'Blimey,' said Marianne, 'I've gone weak at the knees.'

'And you haven't even had your entrée yet,' grinned Gabriel.

'Oh, do shut up,' said Marianne, laughing. Her nerves had vanished. She was with Gabriel, and there was nowhere else she'd rather be.

'How did it go with your mum?' Noel had gone out for the day, purportedly to work but, while he had gone into the office, there had been so little to do, he'd left fairly quickly, particularly when he spotted Julie making a beeline towards him. He'd wandered down Oxford Street and done some desultory window shopping but, despite the temptation to spend, had decided now really wasn't the time to inform Cat they'd just got a new LCD TV, and so eventually found himself in the pub. He'd rung up a couple of ex work colleagues, but they were all busy and had only been able to have a couple of pints each before shooting off, which only served to make Noel feel even more despondent than before.

'Tell you later,' said Cat, who was standing in the kitchen

folding the washing while simultaneously reciting the eight times table with Paige. He marvelled at her ability to do that. It was all he could do to get the washing out of the machine, let alone do maths homework at the same time. Something was bubbling on the stove.

'Something smells good,' said Noel.

'Shit, I nearly forgot about that,' said Cat, rescuing the pan before it boiled over. 'It's only spag bol. Mel!' She called up the stairs. 'Your turn to set the table.'

'Do I absolutely have to?' Mel clumped heavily down the stairs, looking for all the world as if she'd been asked to walk over hot coals.

'Yes, you absolutely do,' said Cat. 'Your littlest sister has done it three nights running.'

'It's so unfair,' sulked Mel, but a look from Noel stopped the rebellion in its tracks. Even Mel knew when not to push it.

'Crikey, you stink of booze, Dad,' she said.

'You've been to the pub?' Cat looked incredulous. 'It's all right for some.'

Noel looked away. How to say that he'd been in the pub because his job was dwindling away to nothing? How to let her know she was married to a man who was worse than useless? Who very soon might not be able to provide for their children? How to begin to say all that?

'So, how did it go?' Noel chose a quiet moment when Mel had gone off to call the others for tea and Paige had gone to put her books away.

'Okay, I suppose,' said Cat. She looked a little teary before saying, 'Dr Miles thinks she may have had a minor stroke, but she's going to run some tests to make sure. I just don't know how serious it is, or how worried I should be.'

'Oh, Cat.' Noel gave her a hug. 'Try not to worry. It might not be anything to worry about.'

'No, it might not be,' said Cat, but she didn't look convinced.

She pulled away from him wiping her tears away as the children thundered down the stairs for their tea.

Noel stared out of the kitchen window. It seemed there was never going to be a good time to come clean.

It was chucking it down as Gabriel and Marianne left the Feathers. The pathetic excuse for an umbrella that Gabriel had taken out with him had turned inside out in the wild wind that was whipping furiously across the car park, so Gabriel abandoned it and they ran giggling through the rain like a pair of school kids.

They were soaked through by the time they climbed into Gabriel's ratty old Land Rover, but he rooted around in the rucksack he kept in there for emergencies and soon produced a towel to dry them off slightly.

'Sorry it's a bit rough and ready,' he said.

'No sweat,' said Marianne, who genuinely didn't seem to mind the shabbiness of the interior, or the fact that it smelt of dog.

The rain was coming down so heavily, the windscreen wipers were barely making any difference. Flick, flack, flick, flack they went, making little impact on the sheets of rain pouring down the windscreen. Soon the windows were all steamed up despite Gabriel having the blower on full pelt. It felt oddly spooky in the car, driving down the dark road, barely able to see the white lines thanks to the huge puddles that lined their route. Gabriel slowed down to a steady thirty.

'Sorry, it's going to be a slow old drive home,' Gabriel said. 'The road to Hope Christmas is a bit hairy at the best of times but in these conditions it's going to be lethal. I'm sorry, I hadn't realised quite how bad it was going to be.'

'Do you want to ring Pippa, to let her know we're on our way?' said Marianne.

'Good idea,' said Gabriel, but just then the phone rang. 'Oh, that's her now,' he said. 'Great minds think alike. Pippa . . . you what? Are you all okay? We'll be there as soon as we can.'

'What's the matter?' said Marianne.

'The river's burst its banks and Hope Christmas is flooding. Pippa's got water coming through the front door. Bloody hell. They're closer to the stream than we are, but for all I know my house is flooding too, and Benjy's inside on his own. I know they issued flood warnings, but nothing like this has happened in living memory. I bet it's something do with that sodding eco town. They've been dumping silt into the river for weeks now. Damn. I daren't drive any faster than this. It's going to take ages to get home.'

The rain was showing no signs of letting up and soon Gabriel found himself slowing down to twenty. They passed an abandoned Land Rover at one point, but there were no other signs of life on the road. A few minutes later, a deer ran out in front of them, gave a a startled look into Gabriel's headlights, and ran off into the dark.

Neither he or Marianne spoke as they inched their way further towards Hope Christmas. Why had he decided to come out to the Feathers tonight of all evenings? Gabriel was cursing himself for not realising how bad the rain was going to be. But who could have predicted this? As he drove through Ash Bourton, the village before Hope Christmas, he could see the roads there were awash and people were sandbagging like crazy. A policeman put out his hand to slow him down.

'Where are you trying to get to?' he asked.

'Hope Christmas,' said Gabriel. 'How's the road?'

'You'll be lucky if you make it all the way,' said the policeman. 'They're telling me the High Street's flooded.'

247

'Well, we have to get back,' said Gabriel. 'I have a son . . .'

'Take it easy then, sir,' said the policeman, and waved them on their way.

'You okay?' Marianne gave Gabriel's hand a quick squeeze.

'I just want to get back,' said Gabriel. His stomach was a ball of tension and he realised he was gripping the wheel harder than it warranted. It was just as well he was, because a car coming in the opposite direction lost its grip on the road and was spinning towards them. Instinctively Gabriel swerved into the bank to avoid it, narrowly missing a tree. The Land Rover came to a juddering halt and he and Marianne were flung forward with the impact. Quickly establishing that everyone had escaped uninjured, Gabriel got going again. They were now a mile from Hope Christmas, but the distance seemed interminable. The rain continued to teem down and, as Gabriel crouched over the wheel, concentrating as hard as he could on what little he could see of the road ahead, he had the most peculiar feeling that he and Marianne were the only two people left on the planet.

Eventually, to his relief, the sign for Hope Christmas flashed up, and the road bent round to the left towards the High Street. Nothing could have prepared them for the sight that greeted them.

'Oh my God.' Marianne was stunned. 'What's – what's happened to the High Street?'

As they came down the valley into what should have been the High Street, all they could see was a torrent of water sweeping through the town. Half the cottages were submerged in water and where the village hall had been destroyed. A police officer was standing helplessly watching the devastation and talking urgently into his walkie talkie.

'I'm sorry, sir,' he said, 'you can't go on. As you can see, the road's impassable.'

'But my son – he's on the other side of the village with

248

his aunt, I have to get to him.' Gabriel couldn't see anything beyond his frantic need to get to Stephen.

'I'm sorry, sir, truly I am,' said the police officer. 'It all happened so fast, see. The river burst its banks and suddenly we had a flash flood. The emergency services were totally unprepared. But help is on its way. I might be able to get you across when they bring the boats in.'

'Is there anything we can do?' said Marianne.

'Maybe, when the water subsides, you can help me get people out,' said the policeman dubiously. 'But I don't know where they're going to go, because the village hall was swept away.'

Gabriel rang Pippa again and was relieved to hear that everyone was all right, although she and Dan were now bailing out their hall.

They waited for what seemed like forever before the firemen arrived with a boat. Gabriel put on his wellingtons, also handily stowed in the back of the Land Rover, and passed an old pair of Eve's to Marianne, before climbing into the boat and rowing across with the firemen. The firemen quickly established who was in need of rescue and who wasn't – several of the town's oldest inhabitants lived in the cottages – before taking them what was now in effect upstream to the lane leading to Gabriel's house.

They got to Pippa's house to discover Pippa and Dan bailing out for all they were worth.

'Christ,' said Gabriel. 'Are the kids okay?'

'All asleep upstairs,' said Pippa. She was wrapped in an old mac over her pyjamas and looked totally shell-shocked.

'Do you mind if I just check how things are at home?' said Gabriel. 'I left Benjy in the kitchen and I don't want him to be frightened. I'll try not to be too long.'

'No problem,' said Pippa. 'I don't think we're going anywhere for a while.'

'I'll stay,' said Marianne, wading across the muddy water to help Pippa.

Gabriel walked as fast as he was able to his house where he found to his relief that, while the flood waters were swirling round his porch, they hadn't made it into the house. He opened the door and called to Benjy who was barking wildly in the kitchen.

'Here boy.' Gabriel went to comfort his dog, but suddenly Benjy's ears pricked up. Above the wind and the rain came the sound of a lamb in trouble. Benjy barked again and, following his instinct, he shot off into the darkness to rescue it.

'No! Benjy, no!' Gabriel could only watch in horror as his sheepdog disappeared into the gloom.

Chapter Twenty-One

Marianne paddled her way towards Pippa, who was frantically filling buckets with foul-smelling water and pouring them out of the back of the house. Like Gabriel's cottage, Pippa's house was on a slight slope so the water was at least pouring through into the back garden. But the speed at which it was coming meant that, however fast she bailed out, it wasn't fast enough. Dan was in the back of the house trying to rescue as much stuff from the lounge as he could.

'Leave that,' he said to Pippa. 'It's a waste of time. I think we've got to go into damage limitation mode now.'

'If we just kept going—' Pippa's normal composure appeared to be cracking.

'Come on, love,' Dan put his arm around her, 'we can't do anything against this, we just have to save what we can.'

'Dan's right,' said Marianne. 'Come on, let me help.'

Soon they'd formed a human chain and were passing things up the stairs to the boys, who found the whole thing terribly exciting. Lucy, fortunately, had remained asleep.

They worked into the early hours of the morning, when eventually the flood subsided a little, leaving them with a house full of swirling, filthy water.

'I can't even offer you a cup of tea,' said Pippa, sinking exhaustedly onto the stairs. 'I daren't use the electrics.'

251

'Don't worry about that,' said Marianne. 'Where are you all going to sleep? You can't stay here.'

'There's room at my place.' Gabriel appeared, looking exhausted and dishevelled. 'I only got a bit of rainwater in the hall. Pippa, you and Dan can have my bed, I'll go on the sofa in the lounge. The boys can share with Stephen and Lucy can have the spare room.' He paused and looked at Marianne in a nonchalant kind of way. 'You can have the sofa bed in the conservatory if you'd like.'

Marianne kicked herself for even thinking about what she'd been thinking in such stressful circumstances, but knew he was right. This was hardly the time to announce their relationship to the world.

'I could try and get home,' said Marianne.

'Don't be daft,' said Gabriel, 'there's a river running through the High Street, remember?'

'Oh, yes,' Marianne had almost forgotten the difficulty they'd had in getting over here. Her little rented cottage was on the other side of the High Street. She had no idea whether it had been affected or not.

Pippa gave her a sideways look as if to enquire what was going on, but Marianne chose to ignore it. There would be plenty of time for explanations later.

'Right, let's get everyone out of here,' she said brightly in her best teacherish manner – Pippa was looking too stunned by events to make a decision.

'Yes, right,' said Pippa at last. 'You go ahead with the boys. Dan and I will come on with Lucy.'

Having sorted the boys out with appropriate waterproofs, Marianne and Gabriel trudged off up the path. The rain was still coming down in sheets, and the wind was tearing across the valley in eddying bursts that took their breath away. Gabriel was very quiet but, when they got into the house, he suddenly turned to Marianne. 'Don't say anything to Stephen just yet, but Benjy ran off in the dark. I spent about an hour searching for him, but it's no good. I think I've lost him.'

He looked so desolate, Marianne gave him a hug.

'Maybe he's sheltering somewhere,' she said. 'Come on, let's get these kids inside. We'll all feel better for a hot drink. I know Pippa and Dan certainly deserve one.'

Gabriel gave her a small smile. 'I hope you're right. We've had Benjy since Stephen was a baby. He'll be broken-hearted if anything's happened to him.'

'No use worrying about what hasn't happened yet,' said Marianne, trying to be more cheerful than she felt.

Once Pippa and Dan arrived, she helped Pippa sort the kids out, then they all went downstairs and Marianne made hot drinks for everyone.

'I think I need something stronger in mine,' said Pippa with feeling, so Gabriel produced a bottle of his finest malt and added a generous glug to everyone's coffee. Pippa and Dan soon retired to bed, but Gabriel and Marianne sat close to each other on the sofa, but not so close that anyone who walked in would notice anything untoward, and mulled over the events of the evening, as they listened to the interminable pounding of the rain on the conservatory roof and the whistling of the wind down the chimney.

Eventually, noticing Marianne shivering, Gabriel brought a duvet downstairs and, past caring whether anyone would see them, they cuddled up together underneath it, chatting softly and getting drowsier and drowsier.

'I should move,' said Marianne dozily.

'In a minute,' said Gabriel, pulling her closer to him.

She nuzzled up against him, thinking how long it was since she'd felt this comfortable. Really, she should get up in a minute. They didn't want Stephen to find them like that in the morning. But it was so cosy, listening to the fire crackling in the grate, and the last throes of the winds, which were finally dying down. The last thought Marianne had as she drifted off to sleep, leaning on Gabriel's shoulder, was that he smelt of pine cones and smoke, and how comforting that was.

Despite the late night, Gabriel woke early the next morning with the sun streaming through the lounge window. Typical. The storm had blown past and now it was so calm outside it was almost impossible to imagine that nature could be so destructive. Marianne was already up making tea in the kitchen.

'Couldn't sleep,' she said, coming over to him and giving him a kiss. He allowed himself the swift luxury of taking her in his arms. It felt so comforting after the events of the previous night to hold her there. He felt like he never wanted to let go.

'I'd best be out looking for Benjy,' he said. 'And I need to check all the sheep are okay. I think they were on high enough ground, but it was such a sudden storm, some of them might not have had time to get away.'

'I'll come with you,' offered Marianne.

They set off up the valley, which was incredibly muddy. Looking back down the lane, they could see the flood waters were starting to subside.

'Pippa and Dan are going to have their work cut out,' said Marianne. 'I'll have to go and help them later.'

'What about your place?' said Gabriel.

'With any luck the other side of the village isn't affected,' said Marianne. 'It didn't look so bad when we came in from that side last night. Anyway, it's not as if I own the place, is it? And I haven't really been there long enough to accumulate much stuff. If I was flooded, I doubt I've lost anything of major value.'

254

'I'm not sure I'd be so sanguine about it,' said Gabriel.

'They're only things,' said Marianne. 'They can be replaced.'

They carried on walking, calling out for Benjy, but there was no response. Gabriel found most of his flock, huddled together for shelter in a little dip near the top of a hill. Apart from a little dampness, they seemed fine. But there was no sign of Benjy anywhere.

They were on the verge of giving up, when they heard some frantic baaing near the spot where they'd helped the ewe give birth.

Gabriel went scrambling over the slippery rock face, with Marianne following behind.

'Oh, no.' Gabriel stopped short at the ledge on which Marianne had found the pregnant ewe trembling and bleating piteously.

'What?' said Marianne, who couldn't see what Gabriel was looking at.

'There,' said Gabriel.

Below the ledge, there appeared to have been a mudslide. At the bottom of it lay the body of a dead ewe, and beside her lay Benjy, his neck clearly broken.

'Have you seen the news?' Cat was standing watching BBC News 24 with a steaming cup of tea in her hand.

'No, why?' Noel came downstairs, still knotting his tie. He didn't feel much like going into the office today, but he couldn't face another day fudging things with Cat at home.

The newscaster was talking about flooding up north. There had been warnings issued the previous night, but apparently it had been much worse than was predicted.

'Isn't Hope Christmas where you've been doing your eco town thing?' Cat said.

'Oh my God.' Noel stared in horror at the screen showing

a river running through Hope Christmas High Street. It was a scene of utter devastation. Noel felt like someone had ripped a hole out of him. The damage would take months to repair. The reporter cut to an interview with a local resident.

'We're lucky to have with us Ralph Nicholas, who owns a large estate here. I understand that you've been putting locals washed out of their homes up in your manor house?' the reporter was saying.

'Yes, indeed,' said Ralph. 'It was the least I could do. Unfortunately we lost our community hall in the flood, so people had nowhere to go. Luckily my house is on a hill and I have plenty of room.'

'And from what I gather, people were out till all hours helping rescue elderly folk trapped in their houses.'

'We're a close-knit community here,' Ralph was saying. 'Folk do tend to help one another. Although not everyone wants rescuing.'

The report then cut to a picture of an old woman leaning out of the top of her house, waving her stick at some firemen who were asking if she needed help.

'Hitler didn't bomb me out of this house, so a little rainwater isn't going to hurt me.'

'When I'm old I want to be like her,' said Cat. She turned the TV off. 'What's this going to mean for your project?'

'A lot of money and a big clear-up operation, I expect,' said Noel. 'That's terrible. Hope Christmas is a lovely place. You'd love it.' It was the first time Noel had ever mentioned what he thought of it, and he felt a spasm of guilt. His mobile rang. Great. Matt Duncan. Ever the harbinger of doom.

'Yes, I've just seen it,' said Noel. 'I doubt very much there's any point us going up there today. From what I've seen on the news, the place looks a complete mess.'

'Luke Nicholas is adamant we have to get up there as

soon as we can. I think he's worried someone might blame the excavation work we've been doing.'

'Well, I'm no expert on the causes of flash floods, but there was a lot of silt dumped in the river, and diverting part of it probably hasn't helped,' said Noel. He wasn't at all happy about the destruction he'd seen on the TV, but part of him couldn't help cheering at the thought that some of Luke Nicholas' chickens might be coming home to roost at last.

'So we may need to do some damage limitation then,' said Matt. 'I need your arse over here right now, so we can start trawling through the files. I do not want any of this coming back to GRB.'

Noel, who rather hoped some of it would come back to Matt, promised to be in the office as soon as he could.

He grabbed a bit of toast, kissed Cat and left. Every cloud had a silver lining. Maybe now Gerry Cowell would see Matt for the bullshitter he really was.

Cat dropped the kids off at school, checked her watch to see if she had time to quickly nip into Mum's before her monthly schedule meeting with Bev and, deciding she did, drove round like a demon to her mother's house.

'What are you doing here?' Her mother looked distinctly displeased to see her.

'I just thought I'd pop in to see how you were,' said Cat.

'I am not an invalid,' said her mother with dignity. 'I am just having a little trouble with my memory at the moment. I'm sure I'll be better soon.'

'I'm sure you will too,' Cat said diplomatically. She didn't want to distress her mother. Of late, any kind of disagreement seemed to set off a reaction. 'But can't a daughter come and have tea with her old mum anyway?'

'Less of the old,' said her mother. That was more like it – this was the mum she knew and loved.

But then she was gone again. Walking into the kitchen, her mother paused, looked perplexed, and stood staring blankly into space. It was as though for a moment the lights had all gone out. Cat didn't know much about strokes, but she wasn't sure this was how they manifested themselves. She had a ghastly insight into what the future might hold.

'Mum,' she said, and then Mum was back.

'Oh, Cat, dear,' she said, 'how nice of you to call in. Would you like a cup of tea?'

'I'd love one.' Cat sank into a seat at the kitchen table. This was terrifying. She was losing her mother before her eyes.

For the next half an hour though, it was as though nothing was wrong. Mum asked after the children and Noel. She talked about the flooding that she'd seen on TV. Everything seemed as normal as could be.

'I'd better go,' said Cat eventually, getting up. 'I've got a meeting at work.'

'Cat—' Mum sat looking incredibly sad and wistful.

'What?' Cat was gathering her bag and surreptitiously clocking her watch. She was going to be late if she wasn't careful.

'Thank you for taking me to the doctor yesterday,' said Mum. 'You're right. I do forget things. I forget things a lot. I have been for a long long time. I just didn't want to admit it to myself.'

Cat sat down again and held her mother's hands.

'Oh, Mum,' she said. 'We'll get through this, whatever it is. I promise.'

'You're a good girl, Cat,' said Mum. 'You always have been.' She paused, and Cat suddenly realised her mother was very afraid, and very vulnerable. 'We need to think about the future, Cat. I don't know how much longer I can be trusted to run my own affairs. So I want you and Noel to have power of attorney.'

258

'We can talk about all that later,' said Cat, tears pricking her eyes.

'I may not have later,' said Mum. 'I've got the forms here. You take them and talk it over with Noel.'

'Whatever happens, Mum,' said Cat, 'I won't leave you.'

'I know,' said Mum, patting her daughter's hand. 'But you must promise me that if I get really bad, you'll sell this place and put me in a home.'

'I could never do that,' said Cat, horrified.

'Never say never,' said Mum sadly. 'My mother started out like this and ended up with dementia. I couldn't cope. You won't be able to either.'

'You never said.' Cat was incredulous.

'It was a long time before you were born,' said Mum, 'and, to be honest, it was something that absolutely terrified me before. So I couldn't talk about it. But now, I'm going to have to.'

'It might not be dementia,' Cat said. 'The doctor never said you had dementia.'

'She didn't have to,' said Mum. 'I know something's wrong. And I don't think I'm having strokes. It's like a blank screen comes over me, and I can't remember where I am or what I'm supposed to be doing. It was just the same with my mum. It's a terrible, terrible disease, but we have to face what's going to happen to me.'

'I don't want to,' said Cat, the tears now flowing freely.

'I know,' said Mum, tears shining bright in her own eyes. 'And I don't want you to have to go through this either. But we can't all have what we want. So come on, chin up. You've got a meeting to get to.'

Mum saw Cat to the door, and they hugged fiercely.

'You promise?' Mum said, as they said goodbye.

'I promise,' said Cat.

Chapter Twenty-Two

Gabriel was still feeling shell-shocked about Benjy when he and Marianne got back to his cottage. They'd had to leave the bodies there for the time being. He needed to go back with the Land Rover and get them at some point, but for now he had to work out what to say to his son. Stephen was going to be devastated.

The opportunity wasn't going to come straightaway, somewhat to Gabriel's relief, because he and Marianne walked back into bedlam. The boys were all whooping about like lunatics, and Lucy was sobbing because they'd been teasing her. Even calm Pippa was having trouble keeping control.

'Where's Dan?' Gabriel asked.

'He went down to inspect the damage at our place. You wouldn't believe it, but everything was peaceful till about five minutes ago.'

Gabriel quickly had the boys sitting down in front of the TV, made Pippa a much needed cup of tea, and then sat down next to Lucy. He was immensely fond of his godchild, and he could usually raise a smile.

'What's my favourite girl doing down in the dumps?' he said, and then proceeded to pull funny faces at her till she was giggling away happily.

'That was amazing,' said Marianne. 'You've a real gift with children.'

Gabriel shrugged, and gave her a rather sad smile, 'Looking after people seems to be something of a speciality of mine. Talking of which . . . I really need to find some time with Stephen to explain about Benjy.'

'Do you need any help?' He was touched by Marianne's concern. When Eve had been around she always left all the difficult stuff to him.

'I think this is something I need to tackle alone,' he said. 'But God knows what I'm going to say.'

The office was buzzing when Noel got there. He noticed to his satisfaction that even Matt's smooth exterior had been ruffled by events up north.

'Thank God you're here,' he said. 'I've had Luke Nicholas on the blower five times already. *Five* times. What does he think I can do from here? Work a bloody miracle?'

Noel muttered something placatory and then got to work to find out what the damage was on the site. According to the site foreman, half the foundations were now so water-logged it was going to take weeks – possibly months – before building work could resume. It wasn't as if they'd been dry to begin with. But the local authorities were pumping water out of Hope Christmas, so there was a possibility that the pumps could be borrowed, ensuring the worst of the water could be got rid of. Quite how they were going to dry every-thing out to meet the incredibly demanding schedule, Noel wasn't quite sure.

He went back through the files and dug out his ori-ginal plans for revitalising the buildings on the Hopesay Manor Estate. He looked through them again. He felt suddenly angry that the building work had gone ahead despite his objections. He couldn't prove that the flood was a result of the silt being dumped in the river, but given that, according to the reports, Hope Christmas itself hadn't flooded for a hundred years, Noel couldn't help feeling that somehow the work they'd been carrying out was partly responsible. Apart from being morally wrong, it was a flagrant breaking of the stringent government guidelines for the building of eco towns. Matt should really get it in the neck for this.

He printed off the plans, wrote a quick report on the situation in Hope Christmas, promising to visit the site next week for an update, and left both on Gerry Cowley's desk. You never know, maybe Gerry would have a change of heart now. Surely even he would see that pursuing the eco town option now was throwing good money after bad?

'Oh my word.' Marianne and Pippa gingerly entered her farmhouse to see filthy water still swirling through the house and out of the back door. Dan had gone back to Gabriel's place to take over with the kids and start making the inevitable phone calls to insurers. The flood waters had receded somewhat, leaving a muddy, gloopy mess on the floor, but carpets were ruined, the wiring was sodden, the plaster was peeling off the walls, and the skirting boards were warped.

'It's so much worse than I thought,' Pippa said bleakly. 'I know it's stupid to be so upset, but look at it. That's our life. In tatters.'

She wandered desolately through to the lounge, where she picked up a broken photo frame and showed it to Marianne.

'Our wedding day,' she said simply.

'Oh, Pippa,' Marianne hugged her friend hard. Why did the worst things happen to the nicest people? 'Soonest done, soonest mended. As my granny used to say.'

'Has your granny got a phrase for every occasion?' said Pippa with a weak grin.

'Pretty much,' said Marianne. 'Look, why don't I carry

262

on here for a bit? It's mayhem at Gabe's place and the kids need you.'

'"Gabe"? I knew it! I knew it!' Pippa was practically dancing in delight. 'Now that has really cheered me up. I thought there was something going on between you last night, but I didn't like to ask.'

'Yes, well, last night was hardly the moment for confidences,' said Marianne. 'And now isn't the moment either. We've just found Benjy's body in the valley. Gabriel's devastated and he doesn't know how Stephen's going to react.'

'Oh my God, poor, poor Stephen,' said Pippa, forgetting her own troubles for an instant. 'He's had so much to deal with as it is. He doesn't need this.'

'What's she like?' Marianne said hesitantly, as she gathered up some soggy bits of carpet, ready to dump outside. She wasn't sure she really wanted to talk about Eve but she couldn't contain her curiosity . . .

'Who, Eve?' Pippa rolled her eyes. 'She's pretty, very pretty. And when she's on form, she's funny and lively and inventive. I can see why Gabe was attracted to her, but she's always been flaky as hell. Not at all cut out to be a farmer's wife. I've never met anyone so sensitive.'

'Gabe said as much,' Marianne said. 'I gather she had a lot of problems.'

'And then some,' said Pippa. 'You do have to feel sorry for her. Life hasn't been kind to Eve at all. Her dad left when she was small and, from what I can gather, her mum had a series of boyfriends and didn't show her the slightest interest. You could say she has security issues. Gabe's been amazing, considering all she's put him through. But in the end, it's better all round that she's gone. It wasn't doing Stephen any good, Eve sometimes at the school gate, sometimes not. I can't tell you the number of times I've had to pick that child up at the last minute because Eve was having a funny turn and couldn't come. It broke my heart to see how sad he was. I hope she can sort her head out, but equally I hope she doesn't come back and mess about with Stephen's anymore. That kid's been through enough.'

Marianne felt her original worries about getting involved with Gabriel resurfacing. Was she biting off more than she could chew here? Suppose she just added to Stephen's problems? To take her mind off things, she picked up a broom Pippa had brought in from the kitchen and started sweeping the remnants of sludge and slimy water towards the patio doors.

As if sensing her thoughts, Pippa said hurriedly, 'Oh my God, I hope I haven't put you off.' She scooped the muddy debris up with a dustpan and brush and started chucking it out into her swamp of a garden. 'I think the best thing that could possibly happen to Stephen is to have some kind of stability in his life. I'm sure you being around can only help.'

'If he can cope with it,' said Marianne, working away with a will. 'And that's a very big if. And now's probably not the time to go there. Anyway. You need to get back to the kids. I'll carry on here.'

'Haven't you got stuff to do?'

'Not really,' said Marianne. 'School's closed and I'm sure my cottage is fine, I may as well stay and help you out.'

'I don't know how I can ever repay you,' said Pippa, as she put the dustpan and brush down. 'You're a star.'

Marianne rolled her eyes.

'Ever since I came to this village, you've looked after me. This is the least I can do.' She waved the broom at Pippa. 'Now get away with you, before I sweep you away with this broom.'

Cat logged onto the blog. The post about bullying had evidently hit home. There was a flood of sympathetic messages offering advice and helpful comments. On the increasingly frequent occasions she considered giving up the blog on the grounds that, as well as hating the persona she'd created, it took too much of her time and energy, Cat would often have a response like this to a post and it made it all worthwhile. Sure there were some nutters out there (one or two frequently left annoying messages in her comments section, but she usually ignored them), but in the main she'd found the blogosphere a friendly place. Sometimes it felt like being part of a warm and cosy family, far removed from the messy domestic situation in her real life. There were times, in fact, when she felt that a virtual life might be more satisfying than an actual one. Certainly at the moment she could do with living the fantasy.

She scrolled down through the comments. 'Talk to your daughter, let her know she has nothing to fear from confiding in you,' opined *MommyintheUSA*, while *TwoKidsNoHusband* advised, 'Get in touch with the school. The sooner they know, the sooner they can nip it in the bud.' All good, sound, helpful advice. The only trouble was it was hard to get Mel to talk – she clammed up at the slightest hint of a question about school. Cat was about to sign off, when a new message popped up. *Anonymous*. Hmm. That didn't always mean trouble, but people who wanted to cause trouble in the blogging world weren't usually too keen to leave their names.

'Your daughter is a lying bitch and so are you.' Nice. Where did these people get off on such nastiness? Cat deleted the comment and closed down the blog. She concentrated on writing her recipe for Granny Dreamboat's Winter Warmer, a beef stew replete with winter vegetables and pearl barley. Even in summer, writing this gave her a warm and tingly feeling. Not that it felt like summer, the storm from up north having made its way southwards. It had rained so much today, it was a wonder there was any more rain left in the sky.

Cat looked at her watch. Nearly school pickup time. She started tidying things away when an instant message pinged up on the screen.

One of Mel's friends no doubt. Perhaps on a day off sick and bored trying to instant message her friends.

She opened the message, to a stream of abuse. 'I saw what you wrote on my Bebo page. You are a lying bitch and so is your mum.'

There was a picture of a rather tarty-looking twelve-year-old whose MSN legend bore *Inyourfacebitch*. How very very unpleasant.

With a sinking heart, Cat typed back: 'This is Melanie's mother, who are you?'

'Go away bitch,' was the charming response.

'Does your mother know what you are doing?' Cat typed back.

Her erstwhile correspondent beat a hasty retreat out of cyberspace.

What the hell had that been all about? Cat went into Mel's Bebo account. She had been most reluctant to allow Mel to set one up and had only done so on the condition she had full access to it at all times. She was horrified by what she saw. Her daughter apparently considered a girl at school called Juliette (nicknamed by Mel as 'Screwliette') a lying bitch, and everyone should apparently know what a slag she was. Reeling with shock at the language her eleven-year-old was using, Cat sat back absolutely stunned. There she'd been assuming that Mel was being bullied, but it now looked very much as if her daughter was the one doing the bullying.

Chapter Twenty-Three

Marianne walked down the High Street a week after the flood on her way to the dentist's. People were slowly trying to get back to normal, but it was going to take weeks, if not months, for the cottages on the High Street to dry out again. She walked past Miss Woods' house to see the ex-head of Hope Christmas primary berating the workmen who'd come to clear out her ground floor. In front of the house was a pile of what looked like junk, an ancient fridge-freezer, an old sofa, an aged TV set, but, Marianne thought sadly, it probably wasn't junk to Miss Woods. That detritus was her life. It was shocking to realise just how destructive nature could be.

'I'm sorry about your house, Miss Woods,' Marianne said, narrowly avoiding the stick that was waving at a poor workman who hadn't put a bit of old carpet properly in the skip.

'Don't be,' said Miss Woods. 'It's all old junk anyway. Now I can get myself a new plasma screen on the insurance. And a better computer for surfboarding the interweb. My dial up connection was just so slow. I fancy going Hi Fi.' She paused to tell the workmen off. 'Just what do you think you are doing with that sideboard? It's not to go in the skip, it belonged to my grandmother.'

'What do you think will happen about the village hall?' asked Marianne. Now that the floods had subsided, the

267

true extent of the damage was revealed. The doors were smashed in, one half of a wall had collapsed, and at least two of the windows had been swept away in the flood.

'I expect we'll have to have Parish Council meetings at Diana Carew's place, God help us,' said Miss Woods. 'But at least it might mean the Nativity will get cancelled.'

Marianne grinned. Last year's Nativity still gave her nightmares, and Diana had already begun dropping big hints about how invaluable her help had been, and would she possibly like to get involved in this year's.

'Do you think Diana will ever let that happen?' said Marianne. 'It seems like the Nativity is her baby.'

Miss Woods sniffed. 'Well, high time someone else took it over, I say. I don't think I can stand another year of hearing those bloody elves singing "Wonderful Christmas Time".'

'I don't blame you,' laughed Marianne. 'You should have tried getting them to rehearse it.'

'Perhaps you could take over?' suggested Miss Woods. 'In the old days we used to have a Nativity based on an old Shropshire mystery play, but sadly Diana is too much of a philistine to know what a mystery play is.'

'I don't dare even think about suggesting it,' was Marianne's firm response. No way was she getting embroiled in a feud between the two women. She made her excuses and left, marvelling at the small ways the community of Hope Christmas was pulling together in the crisis. At the butcher's, three burly farmers who supplied him with their meat were helping gut the shop floor, which had been ruined; at the small Parish Centre next to the church, a notice declared free hot meals for anyone affected by the floods till their kitchens were back in order; and, passing the post office, Marianne noticed Mr Edwards helping load Vera Campion's worldly belongings into his van.

'Mr Edwards has very kindly offered me lodgings,' Vera explained pinkly. 'With the post office closing anyway, I didn't have anywhere else to go. And at least this way the insurance is going to give me a bit of a breather while I decide what to do next.'

'It's the least I can do, Vera,' said Mr Edwards. 'I can't have my favourite girl struggling alone now, can I?'

'Oh, Albert.' Vera blushed bright crimson. Feeling like she was spying on them, Marianne went on her way.

By the time she'd reached the dentist's, conveniently placed at the top end of the village so it had escaped the flood, Marianne felt as though she'd said hello to half the inhabitants of Hope Christmas. As she went to sit down in the waiting area, she spotted Ralph Nicholas.

'Ah, my dear, how are you?' he said warmly. 'Didn't lose too much in the flood?'

'No, I was incredibly lucky,' said Marianne. 'I feel so sorry for everyone who's been affected.'

'It's going to take a long time for the village to recover, it's true,' said Ralph, 'but every cloud has a silver lining, I generally find.'

'Oh?'

The receptionist called Ralph's name. Tapping his nose, he smiled at Marianne and said, 'I'd take a look at page 43 in this month's *Happy Homes* if I were you.' And with that he was gone.

Marianne saw the magazine on the table. Idly she picked it up and it fell conveniently open at page 43.

Fed up with the commercialisation of Christmas? Longing for a return to simpler days? Then enter our competition to find the Nation's best Nativity. A prize of £10,000 to the community or school that puts in the best suggestion.

Marianne laughed out loud. Perhaps she should suggest it to Diana Carew. She could only imagine how well *that* would go down.

'Can you explain to me what all this is about?' Cat hadn't confronted Melanie with the evidence of her misdoings straightaway. She'd been so shocked by what she'd found and had needed time to mull it over. Besides, the last thing she wanted to do was accuse her daughter unnecessarily. Maybe, as Noel had pointed out to her, there might be some rational explanation. It could just be a schoolgirl prank that had got out of hand. Perhaps. After a long chat over a coffee with Regina, she'd decided to tackle the problem head on. So, with the rest of her offspring in bed and Noel away in Hope Christmas, trying to sort out the disaster that was the eco town, now seemed as good a time as any.

'Where did you get this?' Mel blushed a furious red and snatched the offending bits of paper out of her mother's hands.

'Your charming friend Juliette left an offensive message on my blog, and sent you some nasty comments on your MSN account,' said Cat. 'She told me you'd written some stuff about her on your Bebo page. I couldn't believe it when I found this. What on earth are you playing at? I didn't even know you knew language like that. After all the things I've told you about being careful about what you say online.'

'She deserved it.' Melanie looked mutinous.

'What did she do?' said Cat. 'It must have been pretty bad for you to have written all this stuff. Come on, Mel, this isn't like you. What's going on?'

Mel said nothing for a moment and then she burst out: 'It's all your fault!'

'My fault? Why on earth is it my fault?' Honestly, the logic of children.

'Why did you have to write on the bloody blog about my training bra?'

'What's that got to do with anything?' Months ago, Cat had written a jolly little piece about the traumas of dealing with preteens and, in this specific instance, the sheer embarrassment for Mel engendered by buying her first training bra. The Happy Homemaker blog was peppered with such stories of domestic life, it was one of the reasons people seemed to like it. But Cat had always been very careful not to mention her children by name – Mel's moniker on the blog was the Mean Teen (James was the Token Boy, Paige the Drama Queen and Ruby the Wild Child).

'Juliette's mum reads your blog all the time,' said Mel. 'All my friends' mums do. And then Juliette read it too, and printed it off and showed everyone in the class. It was so humiliating.'

Cat felt a cold bucket of water wash over her. Never in a million years had it occurred to her that one of Mel's friends might read the Happy Homemaker and make the connection with her. 'I am so, so sorry, Mel. Really, truly I am. I never ever meant for this to happen. But you should have said.'

'I didn't know what to say,' said Mel. 'I was too angry.'

'You do know that this,' Cat pointed to the paperwork in Mel's hand, 'isn't the way to deal with it though, don't you?'

'I suppose,' said Mel sulkily.

'So, what we're going to do is ring Juliette's mum up and you are going to go round there and apologise.'

'Do I have to?' Mel looked horrified.

'Yes, sweetheart, I'm afraid you do,' said Cat. 'It was wrong of me to mention the training bra on the blog, and I am very very sorry. But I will not tolerate a child of mine behaving like this. Got it?'

'Got it,' mumbled Mel.

'Now give us a hug, and we'll say no more about it,' said Cat. She kissed her daughter on the top of her head. 'And can you forgive your old mum? Sometimes grown-ups get it wrong too.'

'I suppose,' said Mel and slunk off up to her room to do whatever it was she did there when she was having an emotional crisis.

Cat went down to the kitchen and poured herself a large glass of red. Bloody hell. How could she have been so stupid? Cat had tossed off that little blog piece in a moment of light frivolity, never thinking for one moment about the repercussions for Mel. It was a lesson to her to be a bit more careful on the blog from now on. If indeed she should even carry it on. Somehow Cat felt she'd reached a turning point. The Happy Homemaker was starting to ruin her home life. She had a feeling that the days of her alter ego were numbered.

Noel was attending a bad-tempered meeting at Hopesay Manor. He'd come up to Hope Christmas the night before, but thanks to the flooding hadn't been able to stay in the cheerful pub he favoured. Instead he and Matt had been holed up in a faceless Travelodge on the outskirts of Ludlow where, remarkably, there was no evidence of flooding at all.

They'd gone to visit the building site first thing, and even Matt had been shocked by the devastation. The pumps had been utilised and the worst of the water had gone but the grey-brown sludge that had been left behind needed to be cleaned out, and the stench was foul. A couple of dead sheep had been swept down the valley, their corpses left in the mud. Noel, having taken numerous photographs and measurements, couldn't imagine how anyone could conceive that this was still a viable concern.

Luke Nicholas apparently could.

'I'm sure this is a problem we can resolve,' he was saying smoothly, several shareholders having expressed concern about the company's liabilities. 'Our investors are really keen to carry on with the project, and accept that this is a little local problem that can easily be sorted out.'

'You've built on a flood plain!' Noel said in exasperation. 'Your little local problem will be repeated if you don't do something to sort it out.'

'I think we have a solution to that,' Luke turned to Matt, 'don't we?'

'There is a way, if we divert the river away from the eco town, that, should the situation arise again – which let's face it is extremely unlikely, there hasn't been a flood this severe in over a hundred years – the village will be safe. I don't see why we can't proceed as normal.'

'Apart from being contrary to government guidelines, which clearly state you shouldn't do anything to create flooding elsewhere, which diverting the river is highly likely to do. This is mad,' said Noel. Several shareholders seemed to agree, but they were overruled by Luke's suave assurances that everything would be done to meet government requirements, and that in the end all would be well. Noel left the meeting feeling more disgruntled than ever. How could he carry on working like this? It was sapping all his strength and integrity.

He left the meeting in an angry mood and walked out of the office buildings on the edge of the estate where the Nicholas family organised their day-to-day business, passing as he did so the small tumbledown cottages that he had hoped to persuade GRB to invest in.

'Now *they'd* make proper sustainable housing, don't you think?' Ralph Nicholas was striding towards him with his grey wolfhound following on behind.

'I said as much the first time I came here,' said Noel gloomily, 'but no one wants to listen to me.'

'I'll listen,' said Ralph. 'Here, take my card. Show me some decent plans, and who knows? Maybe I can persuade my daft grandson and his cronies to change their minds.'

'Maybe,' said Noel, 'but I doubt you'll get anyone at GRB to see sense.'

'You know,' said Ralph Nicholas, 'it's a big wide world out there. I could use a decent engineer if you ever thought about decamping to the country.'

Noel looked at him incredulously. 'Are you serious?'

'Never been more serious,' said Ralph. 'This isn't my only property in the area. And I'd like to invest in decent homes for the people who live round here. Particularly after the flood. Would you be interested?'

'I'd come like a shot, but I doubt I could get my wife to move,' said Noel. 'She's a real townie.'

'Pity,' said Ralph. 'But if you ever change your mind . . .'

'You'll be the first to know,' said Noel. It was so tempting. He'd love to come up here, buy that fantasy farmhouse and start again. It would be a much better life for the kids too. Noel wasn't keen on the thought of James in particular going to the local comp, where stabbings seemed to be the norm. But how could he ever persuade Cat to leave the bright lights and big city? It was never going to happen and he knew it.

Gabriel poured the last bit of earth onto Benjy's grave, and placed the small wooden cross Stephen had made on top of the mound of earth. Stephen had insisted they bury Benjy in the garden, so 'he would feel at home'.

Stephen stepped forward, looking a little self-conscious in front of his cousins and aunt, whom he'd insisted on coming. Gabriel had thought about asking Marianne too, but as he still hadn't divulged the nature of his relationship with her to his son, he decided in the end that it might spell trouble.

'To Benjy,' read Stephen. 'You always came when I threw you sticks. You were always up to tricks. You were my friend and we had fun. Now it seems your days are run. I'll always miss you.'

He wiped a tear away from his eye, and Nathan giggled. Pippa punched him in the ribs and he shut up. Then, one by one, the children solemnly put a handful of earth on Benjy's grave.

'Do you think dogs go to heaven?' Stephen asked.

'Of course they do,' said Pippa, giving him a hug. 'There's a special doggie heaven where they get to chase sticks, and hide bones, and munch on treats every day. Isn't that right, Daddy?'

'Absolutely,' said Gabriel. He was relieved to see that, for the moment, Stephen was happy enough with that explanation. But later, when he was tucking his son up in bed, Stephen said to him sadly, 'Why do so many sad things happen? First Mummy left and now Benjy's died. Do you think it's my fault? Maybe I'm too naughty.'

'Oh, Stephen,' Gabriel gave his son a hug. 'Of course it's not your fault. Who told you that?'

'Nathan,' said Stephen.

'Well, I shall box Nathan's ears next time I see him,' said Gabriel. 'Don't you ever listen to such nonsense again.'

'Why did Mummy leave then?' said Stephen.

'Mummy's very sick,' said Gabriel. 'It makes her sad sometimes and she can't help it. I wanted to help her, but I couldn't either. Sometimes sad things just happen. But good things happen too.'

'Like what?' said Stephen.

'Like I saw Shaun today and he's growing into a fine

big sheep and it will be time to shear him soon,' said Gabriel.

They'd christened the sheep they'd rescued Shaun, and let him out on the hills when he'd grown strong enough. Gabriel often spotted him on account of his black tail.

'Oh, yes, that's good,' said Stephen sleepily. 'But I think it would be really good if Mummy came back.'

'That may not happen,' said Gabriel, and hesitated. Was now the moment to mention Marianne?

'But it might,' continued Stephen. 'I shall make a wish on a star tonight and every night for Mummy to come back home.'

Now was evidently not the time. Gabriel drew the curtains with a heavy heart and kissed his son goodnight. How was he going to prevent Stephen from facing heartbreak all over again?

Chapter Twenty-Four

Cat was in a lunchtime meeting, discussing the layout of the Christmas edition over sandwiches and sparkling water. The plan was to announce the winner of the Nativity competition the first week in December and to print the article about the Nativity in the January issue.

'Come on, people, I've got a really good vibe about this,' Bev was saying as they pored over layouts.

Even Cat had to admit, unenthusiastic as she felt about Christmas given that it was the middle of July (*and* she still had the summer holidays to get through without a family holiday as their finances were so stretched), that it was looking good.

The phone in the meeting room rang and Bev picked it up, 'Yes, she's here,' she said. 'Cat, it's for you.'

Cat picked up the phone. 'Hello, Catherine Tinsall here,' she said.

'Mrs Tinsall? Staff Nurse Tully from Homerton Hospital here. No need to be alarmed but I'm afraid I've got some bad news,' said the impersonal voice at the other end of the phone. 'Your mother's had a fall and is in hospital.'

Cat felt the colour drain from her face. She felt dizzy and sick. She sat down and asked, 'Is it serious?'

'We don't know yet,' said the woman on the other end, 'but she is very distressed and asking for you.'

'Of course, I'll be there right away,' said Cat. She put the phone down, and turned to Bev. 'I'm really sorry, but I'm going to have to go. My mother's in hospital.'

'I'm so sorry,' said Bev, putting a sympathetic arm on her shoulder. 'Yes, off you go, scoot.'

Cat ran to get her things and rushed out of the building, ringing Regina to ask her if she'd mind picking the kids up as an emergency. She had no idea how long she'd be.

By the time she got to the hospital, Mum was asleep. Her face was bruised, and her ribs were cracked but otherwise the cheerful doctor, who looked about ten, declared her to be fit as a fiddle.

'Though, of course, with her medical condition being what it is,' he continued, 'she's very unlikely to be able to continue in her own home. You're going to have to consider an alternative.'

'What do you mean?' So far no one had actually told her what was wrong with her mother, only that they were waiting for the test results.

'Well, as I'm sure you are aware, the fact that your mother is suffering from dementia is probably one of the reasons she fell.'

'It's definite then?' Cat's voice came out in a squeak. 'Mum has Alzheimer's?'

The doctor looked stricken. He was obviously quite junior and not used to having to break this kind of news.

'I'm so sorry,' he said. 'I assumed you knew.'

'Suspected,' said Cat, 'but no one's told us for definite. We hadn't had any test results.'

'Well, technically, there are no tests to diagnose Alzheimer's,' said the doctor. 'It's more a case of ruling things out. The MRI scan shows your mother has suffered from one or two TIAs but her other symptoms clearly point to

Alzheimer's. I wish I could have something more positive to say.'

'It's all right, Doctor,' said Cat. 'In a way it's a relief. At least we know now.'

And now the axe had fallen, she could start planning for the future. She shivered at the thought.

'What do you think will happen now?' she asked.

'It depends how quickly the disease progresses,' said the doctor. 'Realistically, you are going to have to brace yourself for more of this kind of thing. The memory loss and mood changes are likely to get worse, and your mother will be less and less able to manage. I'm so sorry, but it can only go downhill from here.'

Marianne was feeling rather nervous. At Diana Carew's insistence, she'd been dragged into the first meeting of the year for the Village Nativity. Quite why they needed to get on with it in July, she wasn't clear, but Diana had been most insistent that the sooner they started the better.

'Christmas will soon be upon us, you know,' said Diana, 'and, with all the chaos this year, we can't afford to get behind.'

As the village hall was still out of action, the meeting had been called at Diana's house. Fortunately she had a large house situated in a road just off the High Street, halfway up a hill, with a massive lounge that had splendid views of the Shropshire hills. It was a balmy evening so Diana had thrown her patio doors open, letting in the sounds of distant baaing and the odd car. It felt extremely odd to be sitting here discussing the Nativity.

'Right, first things first,' said Diana. 'Here's this year's script, hot off the press from my own fair hand or, should I say, computer.'

She solemnly passed round the scripts. Pippa, who was

sitting next to Marianne, whispered mischievously, 'Bet it's exactly the same as last year's.'

When the scripts arrived on Marianne's lap she realised with a groan that Pippa was right. Apart from a few updates to mention the credit crunch and the flood, the script was word for word the same as last year's, right down to the pesky elves.

'I think you're forgetting something very important,' Miss Woods said huffily.

'And that is?'

'As we don't currently have a village hall, where exactly are you planning to put on your great oeuvre?'

Diana shot a poison-dagger look at Miss Woods, before declaring: 'The Vicar has kindly said we can use the Parish Centre. Moving swiftly on—'

'It's too small,' said Miss Woods bluntly. 'You know how packed the Nativity gets. The Parish Centre's all right for your average Sunday when three people and his dog turn up. It cannot possibly cope with all the grannies and aunties and uncles and cousins who come out to watch the Nativity on Christmas Eve.'

'Well . . .' Diana looked utterly flummoxed for once.

'I've got a suggestion,' said Marianne shyly. 'Why don't we use the chapel at Hopesay Manor? It's beautiful, very simple, and probably the perfect place for a Nativity.'

Diana, looking disconcerted that someone else had made a suggestion, let alone someone as new to the village and as young as Marianne, looked on the verge of pooh-poohing the idea. But Pippa jumped in with, 'I think that would be wonderful', and Miss Woods said, 'I'm sure Ralph would be delighted to host it.' The rest of the committee nodded their agreement, so Diana had to reluctantly concede to Marianne's suggestion.

Emboldened by her success, Marianne ventured, 'I've got

another idea. Which might help us all. Has anyone seen this?' She produced the issue of *Happy Homes* that featured the Nativity competition. 'I thought we could enter it and, if we win, put the money towards a new village hall, which could become our community centre too, from where we could run the post office and shop. What does anyone else think?'

'That's an excellent idea,' said Diana, snatching the magazine out of Marianne's hand. 'The Parish Committee are already thinking we need the village hall to offer services for the elderly as well as being a meeting place. I shall look into it straightaway. Luckily we already have our script in place. I'm sure that will steal a march on our competitors.'

'That wasn't quite what I meant—' muttered Marianne. She felt as if she'd been steamrollered by an enormous truck. Whatever chance Hope Christmas might have had in the competition, they didn't stand a chance of winning it now.

'So, as you can see from the pictures I've taken,' Noel was concluding his presentation to the GRB board 'the eco town is not a sensible way forward. And in the current economic climate, I would venture to add that it would be an economic disaster to continue on this path. May I remind you of the original plans I made for sustainable housing on the Hopesay Manor Estate? There is lots of potential for this kind of development in the area, which would fit much better with the local community and provide a long-term plan that we could feel proud of being involved in.'

'Let me just stop you there, Noel,' said Gerry Cowley. 'I think we've seen enough. Matt, have you anything to add?'

'Yes, I have,' said Matt, 'I think Noel is painting far too gloomy a picture of the situation. From what I understand from Luke Nicholas, his investors are perfectly happy to stay on board with the current project, so long as we go ahead with plans to divert the river. I'm doing a feasibility study on that as we speak, and it's looking like the best solution. Given how much money we've already invested in this project, it seems utterly foolhardy to leave it now. I think it offers the best solution currently, as well as in the long term. There are many residents of Hope Christmas whose houses have been affected by the flood. Some of them may well be interested in investing in property with state-of-the-art flood defences. We are currently looking into ways we can make the option more attractive for them.'

Noel knew he'd been wasting his time, even before Matt started speaking. He turned over the card in his pocket that Ralph Nicholas had given him. Did he dare go freelance? Could he afford to do that to his family?

'Noel, a word,' said Gerry as the meeting broke up. Noel stayed where he was, wondering what was going to come next.

'I think we can safely say the Hope Christmas project hasn't been working out as planned,' said Gerry. 'So I've come to my decision. With regret, Noel, I can't keep carrying you any longer. This time I'm going to have to let you go.'

Gabriel and Dan were in the barns shearing sheep. Stephen loved nothing more than coming home from school and leaning over the pens, watching his dad and Dan at work. Gabriel enjoyed it too. He loved the feel of the wool coming off the sheep's back and watching the ridiculous expressions on their faces as they wobbled off, looking distinctly spooked about being naked.

Stephen had seemed much happier over the last week and, though he clearly missed Benjy, as Gabriel did, he had come to terms with his loss remarkably quickly. Gabriel wished he could accept it so readily. He needed to get a new dog soon, a sheep farmer was useless without one, but

Benjy had felt like so much a part of him, he couldn't quite bear the thought of a replacement yet.

He'd also been so busy helping out at Pippa and Dan's, shearing sheep, and taking this year's lambs to market, he and Marianne had had scarcely any time alone. Probably just as well really, he reflected, as he still hadn't quite worked out how to tell his son, following Stephen's revelations. Pippa assured him it would only be a matter of time before Stephen finally accepted that his mother wasn't coming back, but Gabriel wasn't so sure. For all her flakiness, Eve had always shown Stephen great tenderness in the times when she'd been well enough to. And Stephen was an incredibly loyal child. Gabriel had the feeling that, whatever she threw at him, Stephen would always accept her back. He still felt a twinge of guilt for not having told Stephen his mum had been with his grandmother at Easter. Maybe that hadn't been the right thing to do after all.

'Right, all done for today,' said Gabriel, as the last sheep ran off to join her naked friends, baaing indignantly. 'Want a cuppa?' he asked Dan.

'Not today,' said Dan. 'I still need to get rid of the rotten floorboards in the lounge. It's going to be months before we're straight again.'

Luckily for Dan and Pippa, her parents had a large farmhouse on the outskirts of Hope Christmas, so the whole family were currently ensconced there, but the clear-up operation was likely to take, as Dan had said, months. Gabriel had had a lucky escape.

He said goodbye to Dan and he and Stephen headed home. When they got in, Gabriel ran a bath and jumped into it while Stephen watched TV. He was having a rare moment of relaxation when he heard the doorbell ring. Damn. Stephen was under strict instructions never to open the door to strangers. Gabriel leapt out of the bath and, searching for any clothes that weren't filthy and smelling of sheep and finding there were none, he threw a towel round his waist and went down to answer the door. Maybe it was Marianne, she'd said she would call.

'Well, aren't you a sight for sore eyes and no mistake.' Standing in front of him, looking remarkably cheerful and even prettier than he remembered, was Eve.

'Aren't you going to invite me in?' she said.

Part Four

Someone Special

Last Year

December 24/25

Marianne took a deep breath and looked around her. The hall at Hopesay Manor was thronged with people sipping champagne and eating canapés. By the staircase stood the most massive Christmas tree Marianne had ever seen, sparkling with white lights that segued through the colours of the rainbow and back to white in a way that would have looked tacky if they'd been attached to the outside of a council house in Peckham, but here looked immensely graceful. Marianne found herself mesmerised by them. At least it gave her the pretence of something to do. After a perfunctory introduction to half a dozen people Marianne had never met before, Luke had deserted her. Establishing incredibly quickly that she had absolutely nothing in common with the two women he'd left her with (Clarissa, who cared for nothing except her horses, and Stella, who wanted only to talk about hedge funds), Marianne had made her excuses and disappeared into the crowd.

She'd wandered about forlornly before hiding herself by the fire in the corner of the vast drawing room, trying not to look too much like a wallflower, wishing that Luke wasn't proving so elusive. The tight knot of worry that had been building in her since yesterday's disastrous family lunch was getting bigger by the minute. For some reason, she suddenly had a very bad feeling about this evening. Luke seemed so on edge around her and, if she hadn't known better, she might have thought he was avoiding her.

'My rogue of a grandson not looking after you again?' Ralph Nicholas had appeared at her side. He had an uncanny knack of doing that.

'Oh, I expect he's got lots of people to catch up with.' Marianne felt utterly feeble for trying to excuse the inexcusable, but she couldn't bear to admit to this kind man how desolate and abandoned she was feeling. To make herself look slightly less pathetic, she turned her attention to the impressive stone fireplace that dominated the room and pretended that she was concentrating on a detail in it. It was carved out with fleurs-de-lys, and cherubs flew from the corners of the mantelpiece. Above the fireplace hung a massive oval mirror with gilt edges and, above that, carved into the stonework, was a coat of arms with a Latin motto.

'What's the writing above the fireplace?' she asked, squinting at it.

'It's our family motto,' said Ralph. '*Servimus liberi liberi quia diligimus.*'

'What does it mean?' said Marianne. 'I never studied Latin.'

'Freely we serve, because we freely love,' said Ralph. 'It's a code I've always tried to live by.'

'Freely we serve, because we freely love,' Marianne repeated slowly. She vaguely remembered Luke quoting it at her, on her first trip to Hopesay Manor. 'I rather like that.'

There was a pause, during which Marianne wondered how soon she could politely make her excuses, when Ralph suddenly asked, 'Has Luke ever shown you round the place properly?'

'Well, only that first time, when we met you,' said Marianne.

'Let me give you the guided tour, then,' said Ralph.

'What about your guests?' enquired Marianne.

'Do you think they'll even notice if I've gone?' said Ralph.

Marianne laughed and followed Ralph through the house back to the hallway with its amazing oak staircase. It was even more magnificent than she remembered. She remembered the black and white marble paving in the hallway, but had forgotten just how ornate the carvings in the ceilings were. More flying cherubs graced the corners of the room, and the ceiling high above them was dominated by a painting of the world on which an angel stood, plunging a giant sword into a writhing serpent.

'St Michael casting Lucifer out of heaven,' said Ralph.

Ralph led her upstairs and guided her through various bedchambers, many of which had four-poster beds made of oak.

'They're so small,' marvelled Marianne. 'Were people dwarves in the olden days or something?'

'Ah, a common misconception,' said Ralph. 'People in the sixteenth century discovered by trial and error that if they didn't sit up in bed they were likely to suffocate with the smoke as their fires went out, so they slept sitting upright in bed.'

'Well, I'd never have thought of that,' said Marianne, marvelling at the rich tapestries on the walls depicting hunting scenes, mythological creatures and pastoral idylls. Ralph was a wonderful guide and took the trouble to explain every detail.

The connecting corridors between the rooms were often low and panelled in oak, and round every corner there seemed to be a new surprise as Ralph took her past nooks and crannies, and then, to her delight . . .

'We have at least three, but I've only found two,' said Ralph, as he took her into a smallish, rather Spartan-looking room with a wooden seat and small table in one corner. 'Just lean on that panel there for me, would you?'

Marianne duly leaned on the panel and suddenly there was a click and the whole thing swung open to reveal a tiny little chapel.

'It's a priest hole,' she cried in delight.

'Indeed it is,' said Ralph. 'This is where my ancestors used to have mass said by their priest during Elizabeth I's time.'

'This house and everything, it's so amazing,' said Marianne as she followed Ralph back down the corridor to a minstrels' gallery above the Great Hall where the party guests were thronging.

'Glad you appreciate it,' said Ralph. 'But my absolutely favourite part of the house is here.'

They came down the main stairs back to the hall, and he led her down a dark side passage. He opened a small wooden door and Marianne gasped. They were in a wonderful little chapel, where the organist from the village, Mr Edwards, she thought his name was, was playing 'Silent Night'.

'Sorry, Ralph,' he said. 'I couldn't resist.'

'Carry on, carry on,' insisted Ralph.

The chapel was very plain, with whitewashed walls and a simple altar underneath a stained glass window. It was lit with candles and the pews were dark oak. In the furthest corner she could make out the tomb of a mediaeval knight. 'One of my ancestors,' said Ralph, 'he was a Templar. His father's buried in the Temple Church in London.'

'It's wonderful,' said Marianne, looking round her in awe. 'So simple, yet beautiful. How old is it?'

'There's been a chapel of some sort here since mediaeval times,' said Ralph. 'I'm glad you like it.'

'I love it. Thanks so much for showing me,' said Marianne.

'My pleasure,' said Ralph.

Marianne stood in silence, drinking it in as Mr Edwards played the haunting notes of the 'Coventry Carol'. It was the perfect setting for such ancient music, which seemed to hang in the air somehow, and Marianne was momentarily transported to another place, another time. In her mind's eye she could see Ralph's ancestors standing here in this very same chapel, listening to the same ancient song of praise. The carol came to an end and Marianne shook herself from her reverie, before glancing at her watch.

'Oh my goodness, is that the time? I'd better see where Luke's got to.'

'Of course,' said Ralph. 'Don't let an old duffer like me stop you having fun.' He stopped to chat to Mr Edwards, while Marianne made her way back to the party. Luke would be wondering where she was by now. She was heading back for the hall when she heard whispers and giggling round the corner. Was that Luke's voice? Who on earth was he with?

Marianne walked down the corridor with a sinking heart. She turned the corner, to see her fiancé with his tongue stuck firmly down Clarissa's throat.

'That's it.' Cat kneeled back on her heels. She'd sorted all the presents into piles of those to go under the tree and those to go into stockings. James, who'd been up and down the stairs like a yo-yo, had been sent back to bed with stern warnings that if he came down one more time Santa certainly would not be coming. Paige, who had just woken up, burst into tears when she heard her brother declare loudly that there was no such thing as Santa, but Cat had managed to pacify her in the end.

'Drink and one present before bed?' Noel came into the lounge proffering a bottle.

'What a good idea,' sighed Cat.

She leaned back into the sofa and snuggled up next to Noel, grateful that Angela had gone to bed hours earlier.

'Happy Christmas, sweetheart,' she said, 'and thanks for all your help today.'

'I didn't do anything,' protested Noel.

'Yes you did,' said Cat. 'I wouldn't have got anything done without you.'

'Right, presents,' said Noel, putting his glass down.

'Mine aren't desperately exciting, I'm afraid,' said Cat.

Noel got up, went over to the Christmas tree and picked up one of his to give to her, and Cat scrabbled under the Christmas tree for something halfway decent. She found him a couple of CDs she knew he'd like.

'Great, thanks,' he said and kissed her on the top of her head. 'Go on, open yours. You're going to love it.'

Cat ripped open the gossamer-thin paper wrapped round what looked like – was – an envelope. She opened it curiously. Noel clearly was expecting her to like it as he was jumping up and down like a demented chicken.

'A day at the Sanctuary? Noel, that's fabulous! But can we afford it?' said Cat.

'Shh,' said Noel putting his finger to her lips. 'You never do anything for yourself. I think you deserve a treat.'

'I feel terrible, none of your presents are nearly that generous,' said Cat.

'I know a way you can make up for it,' said Noel mischievously.

'We've got to do the kids' stockings first,' warned Cat.

Noel went up first to check everyone was finally asleep and, giggling like schoolchildren, they went round the house putting presents in stockings. This was the best bit of Christmas Eve as far as Cat was concerned. She loved the sound of rustling presents, and the sight of the children softly asleep, knowing how excited they were going to be when they woke up. It took her right back to her own childhood.

They tumbled into bed and made gloriously satisfying love. Cat went to sleep with a smile on her face, and woke up a few hours later with one too. This was going to be the perfect Christmas. The best ever.

The morning didn't start quite smoothly though.

'Don't you have any muesli?' Angela asked querulously at breakfast. 'You know I always have it for breakfast.'

Actually Cat hadn't known. Angela had been insisting on prunes for breakfast since she'd arrived, and to Cat's knowledge had never had muesli when staying with them in her life.

Ruby turned pale at the sight of breakfast and promptly threw up. At which point Cat discovered she'd eaten every single piece of chocolate that Santa had left in the selection box in her stocking. Cat had been planning for the whole family to go to the nine thirty Family Service, but Noel used Ruby being sick as an excuse not to go, and Angela cried off too, leaving Cat with the other three who moaned all the way. Cat had only gone for the carols, and was disappointed not to get any, apart from 'Hark the Herald Angels Sing' at the end. It didn't feel like Christmas at all.

By the time they got home, Mum had arrived with Great Uncle Paddy, who demanded that they find him a straight-backed chair to sit in then complained because it was too uncomfortable. In the end Noel brought down his office chair and shoved a cushion behind it, which seemed to do the trick, but the tone was already set.

Then Auntie Eileen arrived to provide some festive cheer in the shape of gin, which she insisted on everyone sharing. Cat suspected Auntie Eileen had already imbibed a fair bit before she arrived. Her red nose was worthy of Rudolph.

Finally Soppy Sarah turned up late, flustered and apologetically twittering about how long the vicar went on today. She took one look at Ruby dressed in the Santa outfit she'd got for Christmas, pronounced her 'totally adorable', and promptly burst into tears. Cat had to kick both James and Mel in the shins to stop them laughing out loud. They ran off up the stairs in fits of hysterics. Cat rubbed her forehead, where the glimmerings of a headache were beginning to form. She had a feeling it was going to be a very long day. At least she could escape to the kitchen.

Noel, who appeared to have taken Auntie Eileen's offers of gin as a good enough reason to start drinking rather earlier than Cat would have liked, was clearly being driven insane by his mother as he kept coming into the kitchen and annoying her.

'Will you get back out there with our guests?' she hissed.

'You invited them all,' said Noel, 'you go.'

'No-el,' said Cat warningly.

'Okay, okay, I'm gone,' said Noel.

Lunch was eventually served about an hour after she'd intended, as always seemed to be the case on Christmas Day. By now Auntie Eileen had really lost the plot and was humming Christmas carols out loud, which of course was too much for Mel and James who, despite Cat's warning looks, spent most of lunch in fits of hysterics. Meanwhile Soppy Sarah and Great Uncle Paddy had made the mistake of talking politics. As Sarah was the most liberal of wets and Great Uncle Paddy the most right-wing of fascists, this was not going down too well. Thankfully Granny Dreamboat was doing a sterling job of playing referee.

Angela took advantage of this to spend the whole meal quietly needling Noel about his job.

'Is it going to survive this credit crunch, do you think?' she kept asking, till even Cat was sick of it.

'Mum, will you just leave it,' Noel ended up exploding. 'I don't want to talk about work on Christmas Day.'

At that, Angela got up and rushed off in floods of tears, so Cat felt duty-bound to follow her.

'Way to go, Noel,' she said, wondering why, when it was always Noel who made his mother cry, it was she who picked up the pieces.

'How are you doing, cuz?' Pippa found Gabriel in the garden, once again fruitlessly sending a text message to Eve. 'Do you know, if you're not careful, I'm going to smash that phone up and throw it in the midden.'

'You'd probably be doing me a favour,' said Gabriel ruefully. 'You're right. I'm wasting my time. I just keep hoping. It's bad enough for me, but how can she do that to Stephen?'

'I think,' said Pippa carefully, 'that Eve's been in a very very dark place for a long time, and I don't think you can judge her actions right now the way you can a normal person's. And in a way, she may have done the best thing by leaving.'

'How can it be the best thing?' said Gabriel, shivering in the cold. There was still a smattering of snow on the ground, and though the sun was bright in the sky it was hardly warm.

'Don't take this the wrong way, Gabe,' said Pippa, 'but I don't think you help her. I know, I know. You want to. And you've cared for her brilliantly all these years. It's your special skill, that, caring for others. But sometimes people need to stand on their own two feet.'

'And you think Eve is better off without me?' Gabriel knew in his heart that Pippa was right. All his caring for Eve had been useless. He couldn't get inside her head and sort it out, only she could do that.

'In a way, yes. She's just like all those birds with broken wings you tended when we were kids,' said Pippa. 'Only you've never let her have the opportunity to fly. Maybe if you do, she'll come back better, and you three can move forward towards some kind of normal life. You couldn't have carried on the way you were.'

'I know,' Gabriel kicked a toe against the ground. It broke his heart to say it, but Pippa was right. 'I've known for years that things weren't working. I just wanted it so badly to be okay, for all of our sakes. But especially for Stephen's.'

'He's got you,' said Pippa, 'and us. Stephen will be all right. We'll make sure of it.'

Gabriel gave his cousin a grin. 'I'm not the only one in the family with a weakness for lame ducks,' he said. 'Thanks, Pippa. For everything. At least Stephen's had a halfway decent Christmas. He'd have had a rotten time with just me.'

'You are not a lame duck, Gabriel North,' said Pippa sternly. 'Now let's get inside before we freeze to death. I think it's time we started on the mulled wine, don't you?'

The turkey eaten, the Christmas pudding burnt, this should be the time on Christmas Day when Noel should have been feeling at one with the world. But he most definitely wasn't. It was partly because his mother had been nagging him so much. She never knew when to stop, and then always made things worse by crying. He felt lousy that he'd made her cry, but didn't know how to make it better. He'd never known how to do that, so always left it to Cat.

There'd been a brief moment last night, when Noel actually thought they might have something approaching a decent Christmas. But, despite feeling petty about it, he'd had to admit that he was disappointed by the minimalist nature of her present. It was as though she'd used up all her energy on everyone else and had no time for him. This feeling was exacerbated when, in the orgy of present-giving after lunch, he'd variously opened a couple of books, some socks, a shirt, a jumper and . . .

'Good God, Cat, what on earth have you given me a manbag for?' Noel's voice was sharper than he intended.

'I thought you'd like it,' Cat looked stricken, and he immediately felt like a toad. Great. Now he'd made *her* cry. Two for the price of one. Happy bloody Christmas. He grumpily helped himself to another drink and got into bad-tempered conversation with Cat's Great Uncle Paddy about the rights and wrongs of the Iraq war.

Cat started to gather up the table things, helped by her mother, who as usual was quietly going about her business, keeping people happy and entertained and smoothing over rough edges. What would they do without her? For a shameful minute or two Noel was swept with a burning resentment that he got Granny Nightmare for a mother while Cat got the Dreamboat. It didn't seem fair.

The kids had all escaped to the lounge to watch their new DVDs and the oldies, as Cat called them, all seemed to be set for the day chatting about the Good Old Days. Noel went into the kitchen to see if Cat needed some help.

'I'm sorry about the bag,' she said, but she was crashing the crockery round so much, he could tell she didn't mean it.

'Sounds like it,' said Noel.

'What's that supposed to mean?' Cat flung back at him.

'Oh, come on, Cat, I can see how little time you spent choosing presents for me,' said Noel. 'Everyone else got just exactly what they wanted and I, I got precisely zilch.'

'Oh, for God's sake grow up, Noel,' said Cat between clenched teeth. They were conducting the argument in whispers so as not to alert their guests, but anyone walking in the room right now could have cut the atmosphere with a knife.

'If I behave like a child maybe you'll pay me some attention,' said Noel, 'you pay the kids enough.'

'For heaven's sake,' said Cat, 'they're children. You're a grown-up. Don't tell me you're jealous of them?'

Realising that she was right and he sounded ridiculous, but having too much pride to apologise, Noel grabbed his coat, stormed up the stairs and out of the house. 'Where are you going?' Cat shouted after him.

'Out,' said Noel, slamming the door.

It was freezing cold, and for a moment he thought about turning back, but he was so furious – he just wasn't sure exactly with who or what. It wasn't just Cat. It was everything. His work. His mum. The feeling that he was superfluous to requirements.

Inevitably he found himself walking on Walthamstow Marshes, by the river. They often went there for Sunday walks as a family, particularly when the children were smaller. It was the one place he could usually find contentment. But not today. He walked for about an hour, feeling melancholy and out of sorts, before making his way back through the little park that he and Cat took the kids to sometimes. He sat down on a bench and stared disconsolately across the marshes. A low sun was setting, casting golden shadows across a sullen wintry grey sky. Noel felt more out of sorts than he'd ever done in his life before, and at a loss to understand why. What was happening to him? He felt like everything he held dear was slipping through his fingers.

Noel sat there for so long, his feet went numb. At some point he was going to have to go home, but he didn't know whether he was ready to.

'I thought I'd find you here.' Cat stood behind him,

298

dangling the car keys. 'Come on. This is silly. It's Christmas Day and you're sitting out here freezing to death. I'm really sorry about my crap presents. I didn't know you were going to buy me such a nice one.'

She came over and sat down next to him and put her arm round him.

'What's happening to us?' she said. 'I feel like we're falling apart.'

'It's nothing,' said Noel, 'I'm just out of sorts and grumpy.'

'So you forgive me, then?'

'Nothing to forgive.' Noel reached out to Cat and squeezed her hand. Then getting up, they walked back to the car. Cat was right. It was Christmas Day. The least he could do was try and enjoy it.

This Year

Chapter Twenty-Five

'Eve,' Gabriel swallowed hard. This was so completely unexpected. 'I don't know what to say.'

'You could invite me in,' said Eve.

Gabriel stood uncertainly in the corridor, wishing that he had something more substantial than a towel wrapped round him. Familiar feelings of tenderness, exasperation and incredulity at Eve's behaviour were churning up with pleasure at seeing her again, and a deep white fury that he had been suppressing for months.

'I could,' he said stiffly. 'Or I could tell you to bugger off.'

'I wouldn't blame you if you did,' said Eve, turning her piercing blue eyes on him, bright with unshed tears. 'If I say I'm sorry, I know it's not enough, but I was in a bad way back then.'

He'd forgotten her fragility, and the breathtaking beauty of her porcelain skin, the vulnerability that she barely concealed. It tugged at his heart and he was fighting to resist the urge to comfort her, to look after her, as he always had.

'Stephen didn't deserve that,' said Gabriel, reining in his emotions. However much he cared about Eve, he couldn't forgive her yet for what she'd done to their son.

'I know,' said Eve. 'And I know I probably don't deserve a second chance—'

'You don't,' said Gabriel flatly.

'—but I do want to see our son.'

'What if he doesn't want to see you?' Gabriel knew it was cruel, but he couldn't resist the impulse to wound.

'What are you going to do?' taunted Eve. 'Pretend I haven't been here?'

Gabriel paused. He'd lied to Stephen once about Eve. He didn't think he could do it again.

'How do I know you won't hurt him again?' he said.

'I won't,' said Eve. 'I promise I won't, not this time.'

Gabriel leant heavily against the door.

'I can't be sure of that,' said Gabriel, 'you've let him down so many times before.'

'This time it's different.' Eve was pleading now, and he felt himself weaken as he saw the tears shining in her eyes. 'I know I've not always been there for Stephen, but I am his mum. And he needs me.'

Eve looked so lost and forlorn as she said this, Gabriel felt his resolve crumble, and the old urge to look after and protect her shot right through him. She was right. Whatever Eve had done to him and Stephen, she was still Stephen's mother, and he knew Stephen was capable of a great deal of forgiveness.

'Daddy, who is it?' Stephen had obviously got bored with what was on the TV and had come out to the hall. Gabriel had been shielding the door with his body and talking in low whispers.

But now Eve pushed the door open. 'Stephen?' she said tentatively. Gabriel's wavering emotions immediately veered towards protection. He knew Eve deserved Stephen's rejection, but he wasn't sure he could bear to watch if his son didn't want to see his mother.

Stephen stood uncertainly in the hallway, as if not quite sure what he was seeing.

Gabriel tensed.

'Mummy?' Stephen whispered. 'Mummy, is that you?'

'Yes,' said Eve, the tears falling now. 'I've come back to say sorry.'

'Are you really back?' Stephen said, as if he dared not believe it.

'I'm back, and I'm not going anywhere ever again,' said Eve.

Stephen ran down the hall and flung himself in her arms, and Gabriel leant back in relief that Stephen had accepted his mother's return, but felt a gnawing worry about where they went from here. For months all he'd wanted was for Eve to come back and for them to be a family again. But that was before Marianne. If he chose to have Eve back he was going to have to hurt Marianne. But if he chose Marianne, he wasn't sure his son would ever forgive him.

Noel was on his way home when Cat called with the news about her mother. Suddenly his anxieties about telling her he'd lost his job seemed meaningless. Cat sounded tearful and upset, not at all like her calm, controlled self. Noel wanted to go straight to her but knew that, first things first, he had to check how the children were.

Regina was cooking tea and organising homework when he arrived.

'Get along with you,' she said, when Noel suggested taking the children home. 'I'm fine here for another couple of hours. I think Cat needs you right now.'

Noel protested, but Regina wouldn't hear a word of it. 'Come on,' she said, 'remember the time when I'd had my Caesarean when Ollie was born, and Cat took the kids to school for me for weeks? *Weeks*. That's what we do, Noel. We help each other out when we can.'

'I'll give my mum a ring and see if she can come round,'

said Noel. 'That way at least we won't be imposing on you for too long.'

Noel dreaded ringing his mum. Normally he let Cat do it and have one of those mysterious female chats that went on for hours and which involved nothing more important than swapping recipes (he had a feeling some of Granny Nightmare's favourites were going in the cookbook, though Cat had sworn she wasn't going to call her that), or discussing *The X Factor*. If Noel ever did ring his mother, he kept it as short and sweet as possible so she couldn't start telling him about how wonderful his sister and her offspring were and how inadequate he and his were by comparison. On a normal day, he'd never have rung her, particularly when he'd just lost his job. But today wasn't a normal day. Noel loved Louise and couldn't bear the thought of her becoming ill and old. He'd been so caught up in his own problems of late, he'd thought Cat might be exaggerating the nature of her mother's illness, and now he felt ashamed of the thought.

'Hi, Mum,' he said as his mother picked up the phone. 'It's Noel.'

'I've already packed my bag, and I'll be on the first train tomorrow,' said his mother.

'Sorry?' Noel was taken aback.

'Catherine rang me from the hospital to tell me what happened,' said his mother crisply. 'You two are going to need a lot of help while Catherine's mother is in hospital. And Catherine doesn't need to have to worry about the children right now, so I'm coming to stay till you're straight again. It's all agreed.'

'Oh,' said Noel. He'd been gearing himself up for an argument about how she wasn't at his beck and call, and here she was all ready to drop everything to come down. 'That's very good of you, Mum. We both appreciate it.'

'That's what families are for,' said Mum. 'If you can't turn to me in a crisis, who can you turn to?'

Noel was still mulling over the unexpectedness of this when he got to the hospital. He found Cat by her mother's bed, holding her hand.

Louise smiled when she saw him, but seemed a bit confused. 'Catherine, you haven't introduced me to this nice young man,' she said.

'Come on, Mum, you know who this is,' said Cat. 'It's Noel. We've been married for fifteen years.'

'Of course,' said Cat's mum. 'Yes. Noel. That's who it is.' But she looked unconvinced and, by the time the nurse was calling for visiting time to be over, she seemed to have forgotten who he was again.

'I'll be in to see you tomorrow, Mum,' said Cat. 'And I'll go and get you some things from home.'

'Oh, thank you, sweetheart,' said Louise. She looked tired and unsettled. Noel found it very disconcerting to see his energetic mother-in-law looking so frail and, well, *old*, lying in the bed. How could a fall have effected such a dramatic change?

'The doctor thinks the bang on the head may have disorientated her,' Cat said as they left the hospital. 'And her blood sugar is incredibly low. She's barely been eating apparently, which can lead to confusion. I'll have to go round to sort out her place tomorrow. I don't think she'll be going back there for a while. If at all.'

'Where will she stay, then?' Noel hadn't really thought this one through.

'With us of course,' said Cat, 'where else can she go?'

'Cat,' Noel said carefully, 'I know this has been an enormous shock to you, but are you really sure this is a good idea? You've got enough on your plate as it is.'

'Are you saying you don't want to look after my mother?' Cat flared up.

'No,' said Noel. 'I'm just saying think about it carefully. Maybe she'd be better off in a home.'

'There's nothing to think about,' said Cat. 'She's my mum. And we're all she's got. I can't let her go into a home.'

Noel backed off. Now was not the time to have this argument. He put his arm around her and kissed her on the head. 'You never know,' he said, 'it might not come to that. I'm sure we'll work something out.' Though quite what, he had no idea.

Marianne was walking to school, pondering the Nativity problem, and wondering if there was any way she could wrest control of it away from Diana. Miss Woods had been immensely helpful in providing information about the old traditional Shropshire Nativity that had been handed down from mediaeval times and been played in barns and village churches right up to the turn of the last century.

'It's a derivation from an old mystery play,' Miss Woods had explained. 'I can remember taking part in it as a very young girl.'

It seemed so much more appropriate to take that traditional route somehow, particularly now they'd been given the go-ahead to use Hopesay Manor Chapel. The play itself was very simple and therefore suitable for children and, with the judicious use of some sixteenth-century carols, and the beautiful setting, Marianne felt sure they had a very good chance of winning the competition. If only she could somehow persuade Diana Carew.

'Marianne.' She heard her name being called and, turning round, saw Gabriel running up the hill after her. They'd not seen each other for a couple of days, Gabriel having been tied up with sheep shearing and Marianne having given every spare minute to helping Pippa. Even when Gabriel had been helping out at Pippa's they'd not had a lot of time to spend together, and since Benjy'd died Gabriel had been warier of letting Stephen know what was going on between them. She hoped that wasn't an excuse and he wasn't getting cold feet. On the night of the flood, Marianne had really felt they were beginning to establish something together. She didn't want to see their fledgling relationship wither and die before it had even properly got going.

'Gabriel!' she said gladly. She'd have loved to have given him a peck on the cheek, but was aware that hundreds of eyes were probably twitching behind the curtains as it was. Miss Woods and her cronies never missed a trick in Hope Christmas, even when their houses were recovering from flooding.

Marianne waved as Miss Woods went whizzing past. She'd noticed earlier, to her amusement, Miss Woods was taking her electric buggy out again. Since the flood they'd seen less of it than normal as the roads had been too slippery and dangerous.

'Is it just me,' said Marianne, 'or does she get faster on that thing?'

'She's probably gearing up for next year's Grand Prix season,' grinned Gabriel. 'Marianne, I wanted you to hear this from me before anyone else told you—'

'Sorry, what were you saying?' Marianne was distracted for a moment as she saw Miss Woods' buggy topple sideways slightly, before she righted it. 'For a minute there I thought she was going to have it over.'

Gabriel looked incredibly nervous. Suddenly Marianne's heart was in her boots. She had the panicky thought he was about to tell her it was all over. Marianne felt a cold rush of reality flood over her. The most lovely man she'd met in her life, and she'd stalled at the first corner. When was she ever going to get this love thing sorted?

'Marianne,' Gabriel said clearing his throat.

There was a sudden screech of brakes, a thud, and a lot of shouting.

Marianne began to run to the top of the hill, and stared in horror over the other side. Miss Woods' vehicle was lying on its side; she was emerging from it grumpily waving her stick.

'Didn't you see me?' she demanded of a rather woebegone-looking Diana Carew, who was sitting on the floor nursing her shoulder.

'Well, if I'd seen you, I'd not be sitting here like this, would I?' was the acerbic reply.

Marianne and Gabriel went to see what they could do, but Diana waved them away.

'I'm fine,' she said tetchily. 'No thanks to that ridiculous woman.'

'It was an accident,' said Miss Woods to no one in particular. 'If people will not look where they are going...'

Stifling a grin, Marianne tried to make Diana more comfortable till medical help arrived, which luckily it did in the form of the local GP who happened to be passing. Breathing sighs of relief, Marianne and Gabriel beat a hasty retreat, as their presence clearly wasn't needed.

'What was it you wanted to say to me?' said Marianne, not entirely sure she wanted to know the answer.

Gabriel swallowed hard.

'There's no easy way to tell you this,' he said, 'but Eve's back. And I think she wants to come home.'

Cat stared in dismay at her mother's kitchen. Noel had offered to do the school run so Cat could go and get some things for Mum. While she was there, Cat had thought she might as well see if Mum had any food she could take in to the hospital. Louise's kitchen, like the rest of her home, was normally pristine. One of the constants in Cat's life had been that calm, orderly home, always a haven of peace where she would come and recharge her batteries. It had been like that her whole life.

Now there was days-old washing-up in the sink, and a nasty smell coming from the dishwasher. Cat went into the cupboard under the sink for some dishwasher tablets, and found Mum had put the salt there, but no tabs were to be found. Rootling around in the other cupboards, Cat discovered Mum had for some inexplicable reason been storing up tins of cat food, though she hadn't owned a cat in years.

Eventually Cat discovered the dishwasher tablets in the cupboard where her mum kept the flour, but not before uncovering everything in a state of complete and utter disorder. Not only that, half the contents of the cupboards were past their sell-by date, and by the time Cat dared venture into the fridge, she wasn't at all surprised to see it covered in mould, with cheese and ham dating from weeks back, and at least two pints of milk that gone off. There could be no more poignant display of her mother's infirmity. Cat wanted to weep for what had been lost.

Memories of her childhood years poured over her in a torrent. Cat sitting at this very kitchen table drinking milk while her mother listened to the radio, making Christmas decorations, doing her homework, while Mum pottered around her. So much of her life had been spent in this kitchen. All of her life spent knowing there was one solid certainty in it. That, whatever happened, however rough things got, there was one person who would never let her down. Whenever she fell her mother had been there to pick her up. And now that certainty had gone forever. From now on she'd have no one to pick her up but herself. She was overcome with an irrevocable sense of loss. Nothing was ever going to be the same again.

This would never do. Cat felt compelled to do something,

anything, to take her mind away from the hopelessness of the situation. Her mother had looked after her for her whole life, and now it was Cat's turn to return the favour. First things first, she could begin to sort this chaos out. Cat set off on a frenzy of cleaning. She cleared out the entire contents of the freezer; she cleaned the fridge; swept the floor; rearranged cupboards; and only when she'd done all that did she sit down and put her head in her hands. Mum had clearly been hiding the extent of her problems from Cat and Noel for months. There was going to be no way she could come back here. She'd have to come to them.

Noel hadn't seemed enthusiastic about the idea, it was true. Cat frowned – surely he couldn't really believe Mum should go into a home? He must see it as she did. Mum had done so much for them, now it was time to look after her.

'But you must promise me that if I get really bad, you'll sell this place and put me in a home.' A sudden vision of Mum swam before her eyes, the last time they'd sat in this kitchen together. Her mother was very stubborn, Cat knew, but Cat could be stubborn too. She sat surrounded by memories of growing up in this place, of coming home with scraped knees, and reading books. Her mother had always been there, an oasis of calm in her turbulent world. Her mother *had* been her world growing up. Cat looked round the kitchen once more. Whatever happened now, however much Mum and Noel might think it was a bad idea, Cat had no intention of abandoning her mum. No intention at all.

Chapter Twenty-Six

'So Eve's back for good?' Pippa whistled sympathetically. Marianne hadn't bothered to go home after work. She couldn't bear the thought of being alone in the little house that had seen so many tears when Luke left her. She knew it wasn't Gabriel's fault. She understood why he was doing this. Why he had to at least give it a go for Stephen's sake. But there was a part of her that was reacting like a child in the playground, stamping her feet and saying, 'It's not fair!'

'Excuse the chaos by the way,' said Pippa, who was folding laundry in the old-fashioned farm kitchen. 'My parents are wonderful to have us here, but there isn't a lot of room. Thankfully now they're retired they do like going off to Spain periodically, so we've got the place to ourselves for a bit.'

Marianne could hear the boys whooping wildly in the haybarn.

'It certainly gives me a break,' she said, wiping her eyes. 'I can't wait for us to get straight again. Living out of bags is so exhausting.'

Marianne felt a pang of guilt. Here she was, wittering on about her paltry problems, when Pippa had so much more to deal with than she did.

'I'm sorry,' she said. 'I've been going on too much.'

'Don't be,' said Pippa. 'Come on, have a cup of tea, and we can put the world to rights. You can tell me all about Diana Carew. Is she going to be all right?'

'I think so,' said Marianne. 'Apparently she's put her shoulder out, though. I shouldn't laugh really, but it was a funny sight seeing Miss Woods take off like that.'

'I bet,' said Pippa. 'If I was more suspicious, I might think she'd done it on purpose.'

'Oh, I can't think she'd do that, would she?' Marianne stifled a giggle at the thought. 'I mean, I know they don't see eye to eye, but that's a bit drastic.'

'It will certainly make it difficult for Diana to run the Nativity,' said Pippa.

'Maybe that's why Miss Woods did it.'

'Pippa, you are a wicked, wicked woman,' said Marianne, laughing. 'Still, you've done me some good, I can face going home now.'

'You never know, Eve might not hang about,' said Pippa, as she saw Marianne out.

'Gabriel seemed to think she would,' said Marianne. 'She says she's much better apparently. She's been undergoing some kind of therapy and now she wants to sort out the relationships in her life, whatever that means.'

Pippa snorted. 'I think staying away would be the best way to do that.'

'Actually, I think she is doing the best thing,' said Marianne. 'This way, Gabriel gets to have some kind of closure if it goes wrong again. At least I think she is . . .'

'I sense a but here,' said Pippa.

'Why the bloody hell did Eve have to turn up now, just when things were going so well with me and Gabe?' Marianne burst out. 'I do understand they've got stuff to sort out, and I'm really trying to be generous. But bloody hell. It's going to get so messy. I'm not sure

311

I want to or even should get involved. Perhaps I should just back off.'

'Don't do that,' said Pippa, 'I know Gabe really likes you. I can't see that he'd go back to Eve now.'

'Yes, but what about Stephen?' said Marianne. 'It all boils down to what's best for him in the end, doesn't it? And let's face it, we all know what's best for him is his mum coming home. I can't ever compete with that.'

'I think that's very altruistic of you,' said Pippa. 'In your shoes I'd be tempted to claw Eve's eyes out.'

'What good would that do?' said Marianne. 'I can't make Gabriel choose me. And I don't want to if it's a question of Stephen's happiness. I just have to wait and see what happens. And hope that somehow, miraculously, everything will work out for the best.'

'Thanks so much for all your help,' Cat said to her mother-in-law with gratitude. 'I really don't know what we'd have done without you.'

'I'm glad to help,' said Angela. 'I always felt bad that I couldn't do more when the children were small. I was too wrapped up in myself after Bill died to think about anyone else.'

'Oh, right.' That was unexpected. 'Maybe you could tell Noel that sometime.'

'Do you think he'd want me to tell him that?' Angela looked so genuinely puzzled that Cat nearly burst out laughing. How was it that Angela and Noel were so incapable of understanding one another?

'I know he would,' said Cat. 'Anyway, that's in the past, you're here now and we're both incredibly grateful.'

It had been two days now since her mother's fall, and Angela had moved in with a vengeance. But, for once, Cat was thankful for the forceful personality, which ensured that things got done. The kids were far more in awe of Granny Nightmare than they were of Mum and Dad, and Cat was amazed at the difference in their attitudes towards room tidying. Angela had even prevailed on Mel and James to help out with household chores, and during the day when everyone was at home, she'd taken it upon herself to give the whole house a spring clean. Under normal circumstances, Cat would have bristled at this invasion of her house but, right now, she was so exhausted and shocked by the rapidity of what was happening to her mother, she was just grateful to come back to a house that was tidy and to a meal that she hadn't cooked. Soon she was going to have to check her emails and see how things were at work, but she hadn't quite got the energy for that.

'It's a pleasure,' said Angela. 'Your trouble is you take on too much. You don't have to be Superwoman, you know.'

Cat sighed 'It's quite a hard habit to break,' she said. 'Once you're used to doing things, it's difficult not to keep feeling you *should* do them.'

'Any news on your mother?' Angela asked. Again, her quiet sympathy had been much appreciated. All these years of moaning about her, and Angela was turning out to be a great support in Cat's hour of need. Better even than Noel, who seemed to be in some mental slump and unable to cope with anything. Cat knew they were both under pressure, but living with Noel at the moment was like walking on eggshells. Although he'd taken a couple of days off, he was now saying he was needed in the office. Which was fair enough, Cat supposed. It wasn't Noel's mum who was ill, and she knew they both couldn't take time off indefinitely, but she just wanted him to be around, to feel that, if she needed to, she could howl on his shoulder. The worst thing about the collapse of her mother was the sudden realisation that her days of being mothered were over. Now it was up Cat to take care of everyone else.

'They're holding a case conference later in the week,' said Cat. 'It turns out she has had a couple of TIAs on top of the Alzheimer's, and they think she can't really manage at home anymore. And I think that too, if I'm honest. I'd hate her to burn the place down or something.'

'So what will you do?' asked Angela.

'She'll come here, of course,' said Cat, shocked that Angela could even think there was another option.

'Oh.' Angela looked disconcerted by this news, and Cat geared herself up for the inevitable lecture. 'I really meant for the long term. She can't stay here indefinitely.'

'Why not?' Cat said. 'She's my mother, and I'm all she's got. I'm going to look after her as long as I'm able to.'

Angela looked gently at her daughter-in-law.

'Cat, I know you think that now. But believe me, I've seen how hard it is for families caring for Alzheimer's patients. You think you'll cope, but it's going to put a strain on everyone. On the children. On Noel. But most of all on you. Do you think that's really fair? You should really think about that, you know.'

'I have thought about it,' said Cat, 'and there's no way my mum is going into a home. She's coming home with us and that's that.'

Noel was meeting a former colleague in a pub in town, who claimed to have some work for him. Now that GRB had finally given him the push, Noel decided he might as well try and get some consultancy work. But his colleague, a lanky engineer called Will, was pessimistic about Noel's chances of success.

'A year ago, yes,' he said. 'You'd have been calling all the

314

shots and been in high demand. But now, with the down-turn in the economy . . .'

He didn't need to spell it out. Noel had been a young engineer fresh out of uni in the early nineties. His first job had lasted eighteen months and, as he was last in, he'd been first out that time. It had taken him another year to find permanent work. But that was before Cat, and the children. He'd been on his own with no family to support. It hadn't mattered that much if Noel didn't work for a bit. Like Mr Micawber, he'd felt something would always turn up.

Noel sank his pint with something akin to despair. In his youth, he'd had that happy-go-lucky feeling that things would work out for the best somehow. More and more he now had the feeling that they *wouldn't*. He knew his outlook was becoming increasingly pessimistic, but it was as if a malaise had taken over his soul. All those years of working so hard to achieve a home of his own, to be able to provide for his family, and now he'd lost his job, and wasn't at all sure of getting another one. Although his redundancy money had given him a cushion, Noel was also worried about their financial situation, which was going to be looking distinctly dodgy if he didn't get another job soon.

He was conscious also that Cat needed him at the moment and yet he found he couldn't be the support to her that she deserved. Noel despised himself for his inability to help her, but yet he seemed powerless to prevent it. If only he could articulate some of what he was feeling, but Noel wasn't good at that at the best of times. This wasn't how he'd planned his life. He felt that everything was shrinking, becoming less. And he was becoming less with it.

Will had to get back to work, promising to give Noel a call 'if anything came up', but they both knew it was mean-ingless. Noel went for an aimless wander round town, before heading home on the bus. No point looking at electronic

315

gadgetry on Tottenham Court Road when you didn't have any money to buy anything.

He felt in his pocket for change for the bus. His season ticket had just run out, and he wouldn't be renewing it in a hurry. Noel still hadn't told Cat about his change in circumstances. With the situation with her mother so tricky, it still didn't feel like the right time. He found a card in his pocket, and pulled it out to look at it.

> *Ralph Nicholas*
> *Hopesay Manor*
> *Hope Christmas*
> *Shropshire*

There was a phone number and an email address. He thought back to their conversation and picked up his mobile.

'So, how do we do this?' Gabriel said, as he sat in the kitchen with Eve, feeling awkward. 'We haven't had any communication for six months, and I'm not sure where to even start. I know you've been very very ill but, Eve, I can't help feeling angry about what you put us through. You have to know that. If we're going to have a future together, I think we need to clear the air.'

Eve sat in silence for a moment.

'You're right,' she said eventually. 'But I can't undo what I've done. I left because I felt you were suffocating me with your love.'

Gabriel bristled.

'I know, I know, that sounds harsh, but it's true. All the time I was with you, I wasn't getting any better. Because you wouldn't allow me to.'

It was Gabriel's turn to fall silent. He found himself

chipping away at a splinter in the old kitchen table that had sat in his parents' farm when he was growing up. Pippa had said more or less the same thing to him. And in recent months, he couldn't deny it had felt like a huge relief, not to have to think about Eve and what she was doing every waking minute of the day.

'And are you better now?' He didn't look at her when he said this and his voice came out tinny and harsh.

'I think so,' said Eve. 'The therapy has certainly helped. I've realised that I have a lot of security issues relating to my mother, which I can't do anything about. But I also realise that I can change things for the future. So I want to make some big changes in my life. Starting right here.'

'Such as?'

'Gabe, I don't know how to say this.' Eve did look very distressed, but Gabriel knew of old that she was good at putting on emotions to get her own way. 'But whatever you might have thought, I'm not here to ask to come back. I think I've realised that that part of my life is over. I'm sorry. You deserve so much better than me. I wish I could have been the farmer's wife you wanted, but I can't, and it was killing me. And coming back here and staying in that damp cottage I'm renting has confirmed I'm really not cut out for country living.'

'Oh.' A wave of pain washed over Gabriel. Despite it all, there had been a forlorn hope that somehow they could put the past behind them and move on, but she'd killed even that. Stephen was going to be devastated. *But you're free to be with Marianne,* a voice whispered in his head, and suddenly he knew that whatever else happened it was okay. Eve had hurt him for the last time. She had no power over him anymore.

'However, there is something else,' said Eve. 'I realise that at times I've not been the best mother to Stephen, but I am his mother.'

'I would never stop you seeing him,' said Gabriel. 'You left him, remember?'

'And it was a dreadful mistake,' said Eve. 'Of all the things I've learnt in the last few months, I know that for sure. Stephen is my son. And I want him back. And you can't stop me getting him. Which is why I'm going to be suing for custody.'

Chapter Twenty-Seven

'Can she actually do that?' Pippa demanded a few days later, when Gabriel came round to tell her what had happened.

'Apparently she can,' said Gabriel as he sat down heavily in Pippa's cosy kitchen. 'I don't know what to do, Pippa. What if Eve takes Stephen away from me?'

'But would she be granted custody with her mental health history?' said Pippa.

'I'd have to bring that up,' said Gabriel. 'I don't know that I want to do that. I don't even want it to go to court. It wouldn't do Stephen any good to think we were wrangling over him like two dogs with a bone. Particularly as Eve seems determined to dwell on the fact that I wouldn't let Stephen speak to her at Easter. God, I wish I hadn't done that.'

'What does Stephen think?' Pippa asked.

Gabriel looked out of the window and sighed.

'I haven't figured out a way of talking to him about it yet,' he admitted. 'He's so excited his mum is home, I can't bear to tell him he might have to choose between us.'

'He might not have to,' said Pippa.

'Eve seemed pretty determined to get him back,' sighed Gabriel. 'She says she really wants to make it up to him for the times she's let him down.'

'But is that wise?' argued Pippa. 'Eve is so fragile, who's to say she won't have another relapse?'

'She does seem much better,' said Gabriel. 'I think she was probably right, I didn't help her. She's got herself a job and a flat in London, and has been seeing a therapist who seems to be helping.'

'What?' Pippa looked at him in horror. 'You don't mean she's planning to take Stephen back to London with her?'

'I do,' sighed Gabriel. 'But if he wants to go, what can I do? She's his mum after all. I can't stand between them. Besides, Stephen's pretty cross with me right now. He found out that Eve was at her mum's at Easter when I told him she wasn't. He's saying that he wants to go and live with her and not me.'

'Gabriel North, sometimes you're too soft,' said Pippa. 'Sure Stephen's cross with you, and rightly so, but you can't just let Eve waltz back in and take him back. You have to fight. Have you talked to a lawyer yet?'

'No,' said Gabriel. 'I keep hoping it won't have to come to that. I just wish we could find a way of solving things so that we're all happy. But most of all, I don't want Stephen to suffer any more than he has already. Ultimately, it's up to him. If he wants to go and live with Eve, I won't stop him.'

'There you are, Mum,' Cat led her mother into the lounge and sat her down. 'Let's get you a nice cup of tea.'

'I want to go home,' Mum looked determined – a look Cat was coming to know well.

'Mum, you know that's not possible right now,' said Cat soothingly. 'We talked about this in the hospital, remember?' Why was she even saying that, she knew her mother wouldn't remember. The speed at which the memory loss was progressing was frightening. Although sometimes it seemed as if Mum was totally *compos mentis*, an hour spent in her company was enough to make Cat realise how ill-equipped she was now to look after herself. After a while the conversation would become circular, and Mum would repeat whatever they'd been talking about earlier, as if it had never been mentioned before. Or she would stare off into the distance. But then, weirdly, she'd launch into a tale from Cat's childhood with the clearest of detail. It was as though parts of her brain had just shut down, like a power plant running on the spare generator.

'But I want to go home,' Mum was starting to get agitated. 'I don't like it here. Why won't they let me go home?'

At that point Noel came in. He looked unkempt. Cat had been aware that he had been up half the night tossing and turning, and he'd muttered something about not feeling too great this morning so hadn't gone into work. But she'd been so tied up with Mum, she hadn't got to the bottom of his misery. Making a mental note that she really really must spend some more time with her husband, Cat smiled more brightly than she felt and said, 'But we want you to be here with us, don't we, Noel?'

'Of course we do,' Noel said with a smile, which somehow didn't reach his eyes. He seemed awkward and ill at ease and Cat, remembering how unenthusiastic he'd been about Mum coming to stay with them, suddenly had a panicky feeling that he wasn't as supportive of her as she wanted him to be.

But then he moved round swiftly helping Mum with her coat off, and sitting her down and making her a cup of tea, and charming her in a way only he could. Noel had always loved Mum, and she him. Cat felt a warm rush of gratitude and love for her husband. Not everyone would cope so well with this difficult situation. Soon Mum was much calmer, and had forgotten all about going home.

'Do you want me to do the school run?' Noel asked.

'Crikey, is that the time?' Cat looked at her watch in dismay. Just getting Mum home and settled down had taken the best part of an hour. How on earth were they going to manage every day?

You manage because you must, Mum's mantra from her early childhood popped into her head. It's what she always said when people asked her how she'd coped being left on her own with Cat when her father had left.

'That would be wonderful, thanks, Noel.' She shot him a grateful look and, as he went to get his coat, got up and gave him a hug and a kiss. It felt like ages since she'd been so spontaneous with him. She needed to make more time for Noel. That was a given. And how would they manage with everything? Well, they would, because there was no other choice.

Marianne was scouring the Internet, looking for a decent modern translation of the Shropshire Nativity play. Miss Woods had given her a version that was rather too full of mediaeval Shropshire dialect, which no one was going to understand.

'Aha! Gotcha,' she said as a search engine took her to a site based on mediaeval Mystery Plays. Here it was. *A Shropshire Nativity* translated by Professor A. Middleton. Perfect. Just what she needed.

Marianne printed off the copy that she'd found and started to pull together a list of carols. She'd found a CD of old-fashioned carols, and listening to 'I syng of a Mayden' had brought tears to her eyes, as had the beautiful 'Balulalow' by Britten. She wondered if Gabriel would object to Stephen singing it as a solo. He had such a beautiful voice. She'd also listed the 'Sussex Carol', the 'Coventry Carol', 'Silent Night' and 'It Came Upon the Midnight Clear' and Christina Rossetti's achingly beautiful 'In the Bleak Midwinter'. What she was after was simplicity and purity, and all of those carols fitted the bill perfectly. She just hoped the committee would be as enthusiastic as she was. Marianne knew that here was an opportunity to put on a very special Nativity play and maybe if they were lucky enough to win the competition, give something back to the village that had helped her over the last year.

She started reading through what she'd printed off and making notes, and then decided to go and see Miss Woods, whose knowledge of this kind of stuff was not only encyclopaedic but, being Shropshire born and bred, was very likely to know more about how to put on something like this. In fact, it was Miss Woods talking about how there had been a mediaeval mystery play at Hopesay Manor in her youth that had first put the idea in her head.

Gathering her things and putting her jacket on, she made her way into the village.

She was coming up to Miss Woods' house, when she saw – oh my God, it couldn't be . . . There was Luke pinning up a notice outside the Parish Centre. She hadn't seen him in months, and annoyingly she felt a little knot of inner tension form as she approached her former fiancé.

'Luke,' she said stiffly, 'it's not often we see you in the village.'

'Marianne,' that dazzling smile again. 'You look lovely as ever.'

'Thanks,' said Marianne feeling wrong-footed. Luke was being much friendlier than the last time they'd met. 'What's that you're putting up?'

'I'm inviting people to a public meeting,' Luke said. 'The vicar's kindly let me use the Parish Centre. I wanted to explain

323

to people about the opportunities afforded to them by the eco town. Now that Hope Christmas appears to be in danger of flooding regularly, I thought people might like to know about the alternatives offered by living somewhere that is both environmentally friendly and capable of dealing with nature's extremities.'

'But I thought your village is on a flood plain?' Marianne frowned. Pippa and Gabriel had been most vocal about that.

'Not anymore,' said Luke. 'Our engineers are looking at ways of diverting the river. You'd be surprised what can be achieved nowadays.'

'But won't that be at the expense of something else?' said Marianne.

'Not a bit of it,' said Luke. 'We're just sending the water in a different direction over the hillside, and providing people with a better class of home. I mean, look at this place.' His arm swept across the High Street, which still looked distinctly dirty and shabby. 'Why would anyone want to live in one of these old damp houses, when they could have the convenience of the latest gadgets, a brand new leisure centre and a new hypermarket on their doorstep?'

'Why indeed?' said Marianne drily.

'So, can I expect to see you at the meeting?' he asked.

'I doubt it,' said Marianne.

'Pity,' said Luke. 'We're offering great rates for first-time buyers, and for key workers. You never know, you could qualify for a great discount.'

Marianne smiled at the thought that Luke might actually be doing something altruistic for once. 'I'll bear it in mind,' she said. Discounts for key workers. She loved Hope Christmas, but she was never going to be able to afford to buy here. Suddenly living in the eco town seemed a more tempting prospect. She dismissed the thought almost as soon as it entered her head with a wry smile – anything Luke was involved in was bound to have a catch in it.

Noel stood in the school playground freezing his backside off. It was the sort of grey damp wintry day where the cold got into your bones and the gloom of winter rotted your soul. He had a sudden desperate urge to be in Hope Christmas, which he instinctively knew would be cosy and cheerful at this time of year. He missed his trips up there so much that he'd eventually plucked up courage to ring the number Ralph had given him, but, when the phone was answered by Luke Nicholas, Noel had lost his nerve and hung up. Maybe Ralph was just being polite. Noel couldn't quite muster his courage to ring again.

He stamped his feet to try and get them warm. Why did they always let them out late on cold days? He hated doing the school run at the best of times. Though it was true that there were a few more dads in the playground than when Mel had first started school, there was something about being surrounded by the Mum mafia that made him feel very nervous. Luckily he spotted Regina standing by Ruby's classroom, so went over to say hello.

'Am I glad to see you,' he said. 'I was just trying to keep a low profile and hoping no one was going to accuse me of being the pervert in the playground.'

'Oh, come on,' said Regina, 'they do know you by now.'

'I know,' said Noel. 'I just always feel as though all the mums I don't know are looking at me as if I'm some kind of paedophile.'

'The times we live in,' said Regina, shaking her head. 'No work today?'

'No,' Noel hesitated. He'd spent most of the last week getting up, putting on a suit, and pretending to go to work

325

as normal. He knew he couldn't go on doing that, but he didn't now know how to tell Cat.

'The thing is,' he said, 'Cat doesn't know this yet, but actually I've lost my job.'

'You what?' said Regina. 'Oh, Noel, I'm so sorry. But why on earth haven't you told Cat?'

Noel shrugged.

'I was going to, but what with her mum and everything, it's been difficult.'

'You can't keep it a secret anymore,' said Regina. 'For heaven's sake, Noel, she needs to know the truth. She deserves the truth.'

'I know,' said Noel. He couldn't explain the apathy that seemed to be afflicting him of late, or the sheer unmitigated terror the thought of telling Cat was causing him. He knew it wasn't rational, but he hadn't felt rational for months. 'And I will. Soon.'

'Soon?' Regina said. 'You should tell her now, really you should.'

'Yes, you're right,' said Noel, turning to greet Ruby who'd come running out shouting 'Daddy!' excitedly. A definite bonus of the school run was the delight with which his children greeted him.

'Tell who what?' Ruby asked as Noel swung her in the air.

'No one anything, you nosy thing,' he said, kissing her on the nose.

As he walked home with the children, making small talk with Regina, Noel was wrestling with his conscience. Regina was right. Sooner was much better than later.

He walked in to find Cat cooking while her mother was dozing in the lounge. The children dropped coats, bags and lunch boxes and proceeded to badger their mother with accounts of their day. Eventually Noel managed to shoo them all into the family room, from where Paige called, 'The shelf's fallen down again', before settling into watching *Tracy Beaker*.

Taking a deep breath, and feeling sicker than he'd ever felt in his life, Noel went over to Cat and took her in his arms.

'There's something I've been meaning to tell you,' he said.

Chapter Twenty-Eight

Cat was flicking through entries for the Nativity competition. They'd had so many Bev had decided to split them into batches for everyone to sort through. Cat was busy putting hers into piles of no hopers, possibles and definite maybes. The pile of no hopers was depressingly large, and she had a sneaky feeling that the possibles pile had grown larger over the last hour or so as a sense of desperation crept in. She only had three choices on the definite maybes.

The trouble was that most of the entrants hadn't followed the brief properly. They hadn't asked for a Nativity with bling (roughly a third of the no hopers were Nativity plays awash with bright lights and flashing Santas), nor for the PC ecumenical versions favoured by the sort of schools Cat's children went to (she'd read some entries that lacked a single mention of the baby Jesus). Cat was ambivalent about religion, but surely the whole point of the thing was that you had to mention the birth of the Son of God. Didn't you?

The three that Cat had picked off the pile hadn't exactly filled her with excitement – the one from the Cornish village of Treadlightly had sounded quite sweet on a first read, but now she was feeling dubious about the thought of watching a Nativity outside in a barn, complete with animals and newborn baby (provided one was helpfully born in the village that week). Hadn't they heard the old adage about working with children and animals? Still, it sounded better than the Clevedon Preschool calypso version, which had only caught her eye because it sounded lively, or the rather po-faced traditional (she had wanted tradition, Cat reminded herself) Nativity offered by the straight-laced sounding Arlington School for Girls. Cat told herself off for allowing a prejudice against public schooling to prevent her accepting that they might actually come up with the goods.

None of them inspired her enormously. What was it she'd been after exactly? Cat cast her mind back to last Christmas and thought about that moment in Sainsbury's when she'd suddenly been heartily sick of it all. What Christmas was missing these days was simplicity. Simplicity and any sense of the spiritual. It was all about greed and excess now.

Feeling rather depressed, Cat got up and headed out for an early lunch, and the chance to do some Christmas shopping. She'd never been so behind at Christmas before, but what with Mum's illness, and now Noel losing his job, Cat was finding it hard to summon up any enthusiasm whatsoever for the festive season. She was still reeling from the fact that Noel had been unable to tell her about his job. Since last Christmas it felt like their lives were unravelling, and now he'd shut her out at a time when he had needed her most. Cat felt powerless to help Noel, but somewhere deep in his soul she feared there was a terrible problem.

Cat mooched miserably down Oxford Street, wandering into shop after busy shop piled high with tat, blaring out 'I Wish It Could Be Christmas Every Day'. The streets were packed, people spilling off the pavements, till Cat felt sure it was only a matter of time before someone went under a bus. At Oxford Circus there was the inevitable bomb scare,

329

rendering the tube station shut and an influx of yet more people into an already overcrowded area. Giving up in disgust, Cat returned empty-handed to the office. As she was about to go through the revolving glass doors, an elderly man who looked vaguely familiar appeared as if from nowhere and tapped her on the shoulder. He was clutching a brown envelope in his hand.

'Catherine Tinsall, I believe,' he said.

'Yes,' said Cat with a frown. 'How did you know?'

'I make it my business to know everything,' said the man, touching his nose. 'I believe you're looking for entries to a Nativity competition.'

'That's right,' said Cat cautiously.

'Of course you want to know why I ask,' said the man. 'Quite right too. Here's our entry. The Parish Committee was terribly worried about the Christmas post, so as I was coming to London, I said I'd hand-deliver it.'

'Well, thank you very much,'

'My pleasure,' said the strange man. He doffed his cap to her and vanished into the crowd as mysteriously as he'd appeared. One minute he was there, and then he was gone.

Cat went back into the office, made herself a cup of tea, and sat down to read the entry. It could hardly be any worse than anything she'd seen so far. It was from a village called Hope Christmas. Appropriate, she thought, smiling, trying to work out where she'd heard the name before. The accompanying letter was from a Marianne Moore, who was a teacher at the village school. Hope Christmas? The name was familiar. It was only when she got to the end of the letter and discovered that, if Hope Christmas won the competition, they were planning to rebuild their village hall, which had been destroyed in the recent floods, that the penny dropped. *Of course.* It was near where Noel's company had been building the eco town. The letter ended with an eloquent plea citing the importance of the village hall, which was at the heart of the community, especially now the village was losing its post office.

Cat turned to the accompanying script. It was laid out professionally – typed with double spacing as requested, which made a change. As she read it, Cat nearly punched the air with delight. Here at last was a simple retelling of the Christmas story. Marianne had gone back to an original Nativity from an early version of a Shropshire mystery play. She'd included a funny scene where Joseph sought out two midwives to attend the labour, and a charming moment with dancing shepherds who were unsure how to take the angels' news. Cat liked the sound of Marianne. But the moment when the baby was born was pure and simple and just what she'd been looking for. Accompanying the script was a carefully selected set of carols, some of which Cat was unfamiliar with but others, like the 'Coventry Carol', were guaranteed to bring a tear to the eye. This was perfect.

She rang home to ask if Noel knew anything about the suggested location, a small chapel to the side of Hopesay Manor, clearly a local stately home.

'Hopesay Manor?' said Noel. 'Yes, I've been there. I don't know about the chapel, but the estate itself is fantastic. I wanted to revitalise the old houses on the estate but was overruled. Remember?'

Cat guiltily cast her mind back to something Noel had been moaning about months ago. She felt constantly guilty around him these days. In the fortnight since he'd come clean about his job, he'd been so tense and unhappy Cat never knew what mood he was going to be in. The only good thing about the current state of affairs was at least he could help keep an eye on Mum, though she felt guilty about that too. It didn't seem fair to impose that on Noel. But she was constantly feeling torn between the responsibilities of the workplace and those of her home. One day she might even work the balance out right.

'Can you come home soon?' Noel said. 'Your mum's getting agitated again and I can't calm her down.'

'I'll try,' promised Cat. Maybe Bev, whose patience with Cat's domestic arrangements was reaching its limit, might be a little more tolerant when she knew Cat had found their Nativity. Maybe. Cat had a horrible feeling that a moment of reckoning was drawing near. She was facing some tough choices but, with Noel out of work, she couldn't possibly think of quitting her job.

'Stephen, what's the matter?' Gabriel had come in from checking on the ewes, who were about to be bred for spring lambing, to find his son sobbing uncontrollably while Eve looked helplessly on. They'd spent the last few weeks cautiously dancing round the issue of what was to happen next. Eve had gone back to London for a little while, apparently to consult a solicitor. Gabriel still hadn't been able to bring himself to find one. He kept hoping that they could resolve this another way. Until then, he had pleaded with Eve not to let Stephen know what was happening, but clearly she'd been unable to keep it secret any longer.

'I thought he'd be pleased,' she kept saying. 'I thought he'd want to come and live with me. All I want is to put things right.' She paced the kitchen, getting ever more frantic. Gabriel recognised this behaviour of old. In a minute, she was going to sit down and start shredding a beer mat or whatever else was to hand. Gently, he sat her at the table, uttering soothing noises, but inside he was seething. Why did she always have to be so destructive? Then he went to their son.

'I don't want to live with her,' Stephen spat out, between sobs. 'I don't have to, do I?'

'You don't have to do anything you don't want to do,' said Gabriel. 'I'm sure we can find a way of working this out.'

'But you said Mummy was back, Daddy.' Stephen raised a tear-stained face and Gabriel's pain shot through his heart. His inaction over the last few weeks had led to him betraying his son yet again. 'I thought we were all going to be together again.'

'I thought so too,' began Gabriel. 'But Mummy and I, well, we've been talking and we don't think we can live together anymore. So we're trying to find a way that you can live with us both. I know it's not ideal, but we think it's for the best, don't we, Mummy?'

Eve was sitting rocking back and forth saying, 'Why do I always get it wrong? I just wanted to make up to him. Why does he hate me?'

'Eve, have you taken your medication?' Gabriel was seriously alarmed. This was the worst he'd seen her for a while.

'No, no, you're right, I should,' Eve looked confused for a moment, and then got up and went to her bag, and found some pills.

'And you lied to me, Daddy.' Stephen said suddenly.

'Stephen, we've already been through this, I didn't lie—' began Gabriel.

'You told me Mummy wasn't at Granny's house when she was,' said Stephen.

'I know I did,' said Gabriel, 'and I've already told you how sorry I am. I just didn't want you to be upset.'

'That's not true,' said Stephen. 'You're a big fat liar and I don't want to live with you either. I want to go and live with Auntie Pippa.'

With that he pushed Gabriel aside and ran upstairs in floods of tears. Gabriel sat back in dismay. Eve seemed to be calming down a bit but was totally unaware of the chaos she had caused. How on earth were they ever going to resolve this?

'Crikey, it feels good to be home,' said Pippa, as Marianne helped her pull the last bit of furniture back into place. She and Dan were moving back in at the weekend, and Marianne had popped in after school to help her sort the house out while the children stayed with Pippa's parents.

'What's the long-term damage?' Marianne asked.

'I think we've been very lucky,' said Pippa. 'These houses are pretty solid and, fortunately for us, the flood swept through quite quickly, and subsided fairly smartly too. It was worse for the houses on the High Street.'

'Do you think those places will recover?' said Marianne.

'Hard to tell, isn't it,' said Pippa. 'Some of them are very badly damaged, and it will be hard now for those properties to get insurance.'

'So you're not tempted by Luke's offers of new housing?' said Marianne.

'Not a bit of it,' said Pippa. 'I know you were going to marry him, but I don't trust that man as far as I can throw him. I'm sure that eco town will still flood, whatever he says.'

'They're offering some pretty good deals,' said Marianne wistfully. 'Even I could afford one.'

'Marianne, please tell me you haven't,' said Pippa.

'No, no, I haven't done anything,' said Marianne. 'I did go and look at the mocked up showhome. And it is very nice. But the ground is very damp still. It would be like living in a bog. I can't see that changing in a hurry. It's just that I'll never afford to buy around here otherwise.'

'I'm sorry,' said Pippa. 'That was insensitive of me. I'm

lucky, I don't need an eco house. But if I did, I can see where you're coming from. Maybe he has really sorted things out.'

'Oh, yes,' said Marianne. 'Maybe he has.'

They both looked at each other and laughed.

'On the other hand,' said Pippa, 'leopards don't change their spots.'

'How's Gabe?' Marianne had been trying very hard not to probe, but it was impossible not to at least ask Pippa how he was. She'd barely seen him since Eve had come back. Only fleeting glances and nods down the High Street. Gabriel always looked pleased to see her when she said hello, but Marianne felt so shut out of his life now, she wasn't sure if he meant it or not.

'Fine, I think,' said Pippa. 'To be honest, I haven't seen that much of him myself. I've been so busy sorting everything out here. And I know he and Dan have been working all hours tupping the ewes and getting the winter feed sorted out. None of us has had a moment.'

'Yes, of course,' said Marianne. 'Silly of me.'

'You could phone him,' said Pippa. 'I'm sure he'd be glad to see you.'

'I'll think about it,' said Marianne, but she knew she wouldn't. This was just too complicated and painful. It was better if she stayed away.

Noel sat at his keyboard and stared into space. He was meant to be tarting up his CV, which was why he was actually playing Minesweeper. Like so many things these days, it felt like a huge effort. Just the thought of getting on the Internet and starting to look at jobs was filling him with despair. He had managed to sign on at a job agency but, as Will had predicted, work was very lean. He thought again about Ralph Nicholas' offer. It was wildly impractical.

335

So long as Cat's mum was with them, he couldn't even contemplate a job that took him out of London. He couldn't see what was going to happen, or how they were going to manage. All that he knew was, while the present was uncertain, the future was on hold.

'Noel!' His mother-in-law called plaintively from the lounge. Noel sighed. What did she want now? Noel could feel all his good will towards Louise leaching away as she became more and more dependent on him and Cat. Cat had no idea of how incredibly difficult it was being here in the day with her. No, that wasn't true, Cat did know, because as soon as she came in, she took over, and she was arranging work as much as possible to be at home as often as she could. But one of them had to go to work.

He went into the lounge and his heart sank as he realised that his mother-in-law had had another accident. They'd said it was likely to happen, and now it was happening more and more frequently. She was still just (thankfully) thought Noel, capable of sorting herself out enough for him not to have to clean her up, but these daily incidents were mortifying for both of them.

Cat chose that moment to return from work. He'd called her earlier when her mother had got agitated, but then she'd calmed down, so Noel had phoned back to say it was okay. Cat evidently had decided to come back anyway.

'Oh God, not again,' she groaned, when she saw what had happened. 'It's all right, Noel, I'll deal with this.'

Noel retreated thankfully into the study, and tried to concentrate again on his CV.

A sudden shout pulled him out of himself.

He raced to the bathroom, where he found Cat hysterically screaming at her mother. 'Why can't you just get dressed? It's so simple. Why can't you do it?'

Noel stood looking at Cat in shock. His normally calm

wife was totally out of control, while his mother-in-law stood in her underwear, crying and saying, 'Please don't be angry with me, please don't be angry.'

Cat's face suddenly crumpled and she ran out of the bathroom. Noel grabbed a dressing gown hanging on the side of the bathroom, wrapped it gently round his mother-in-law, and eased her into her bedroom.

Then he went to find Cat who was sitting bleakly on the end of their bed.

'I know, I know,' she said heavily. 'Any more of this and I'm going to end up as a parent abuser.'

Noel sat down next to her and put his arm tentatively round her shoulder.

'You do know we can't go on like this, don't you?' he said.

'I feel like I've failed her,' Cat whispered.

'You haven't failed her,' said Noel. 'Alzheimer's is a ghastly disease. You just have to accept you can't beat it. You're going to hate me for saying this, but I don't think this is working. Your mum needs to go into a home.'

Catherine leant against him and wept.

Chapter Twenty-Nine

Marianne entered the Parish Centre where an impromptu meeting of the Save the Post Office Campaign was being held. The news that the post office was going to shut had been followed swiftly by the flood and the campaign had faltered, only to come back with a vengeance now. Marianne had missed the last couple of meetings, but she'd gathered from Pippa that the idea to have a One Stop Village Shop, which would be manned in part by volunteers from the village and would sell Pippa's, Dan's and Gabriel's local produce, as well as offering post office services, was gaining ground, as was a distinct groundswell of opinion against the eco town. Luke's attempts to win the villagers over had backfired badly and, as far as Marianne was aware, he had yet to sell a single house to an inhabitant of Hope Christmas. That didn't mean he wasn't going to be able to sell them to incomers, but word on the street was that, with recession beginning to really bite, those urban dwellers looking for a good life in the country were somewhat more reluctant to bite the bullet than they had hitherto been. It was beginning to look as if Luke had a huge white elephant on his hands.

'So we're agreed that the next task is to start fundraising for the village hall and shop?' Vera Campion was saying. 'Albert has already drawn up a battle plan.' She blushed when she said this. It was not a very well kept secret that since the flood she and Mr Edwards had finally become an item.

'I've got some really good news about that,' Marianne stood up waving an envelope she'd brought with her. She came to the front of the room. 'I believe some of you already know this, but I entered Hope Christmas for a competition to find the perfect Nativity in *Happy Homes*. And, I found out today that, incredibly, we've won. So this Christmas, a team from the magazine are coming up to photograph the Nativity, and write a feature on us. We may even get on TV. But the best bit is the prize money is ten thousand pounds, which I'm sure you'll agree will help the campaign enormously.'

'That's fantastic,' said Vera, leading the applause. 'I think I speak for us all when I say how grateful we are to you, Marianne.'

'Miss Woods was a great help,' said Marianne, acknowledging the old school teacher who nodded graciously, 'and without Sir Ralph promising to let us have the chapel at Hopesay, I'm not sure we would have won it.'

'I hope you are going to direct it yourself,' said Miss Woods, 'as Diana Carew sadly won't be able to help this year.'

Diana Carew was still out of action as her shoulder had been dislocated in the accident. Even she had realised that it was going to be impossible for her to run things this year, and she was grumpily ensconced at home discovering the wonders of the shopping channel.

'I'd love to,' said Marianne. She looked around her at the excited, enthusiastic faces. Luke didn't understand anything about the community here. No wonder his houses hadn't sold. People didn't want to live a lifestyle, they wanted to live a life. For the very first time since he left her, Marianne felt truly glad he had.

* * *

'Each of our guests is treated to the best care possible,' the smartly dressed owner of the Marchmont Rest Home was saying as she showed Cat and Noel around. The place was much brighter than Cat had imagined, and a huge step up from the previous two places they'd looked at, neither of which was fit for a dog to live in, let alone her mother. The Marchmont was light and airy, the rooms luxurious, the carpets soft and springy.

'Mum will feel like she's staying in a hotel here,' said Cat. She still felt terrible about what she was doing, but both Noel and Angela had been very firm with her, pointing out the destructive effect Mum's presence was having on their family life. Cat had tried to talk to the children about it and, while they all understood that Granny Dreamboat was very ill, none of them could cope with the fact that their beloved granny kept forgetting who they were, or that she was so fretful and tetchy a lot of the time. Paige and James had been particularly difficult about it and Ruby, being so little, didn't quite understand what was happening. It was only Mel, whom Cat had thought would find it harder, who seemed to have grasped the complexity of the situation with a maturity of which Cat was incredibly proud. She was becoming a great help with Mum, bringing her a cup of tea in the mornings, patiently going over the same cross-word puzzle in the evenings. But even so, Cat could see how upsetting it was for them all.

But the clincher had been the conversation she and Mum had had after Cat had screamed at her in such an unseemly fashion. Immediately after the incident, Mum appeared to have forgotten all about it. But a day or so later, she'd suddenly said, as Cat was putting her to bed, 'I'm sorry, sweetheart, for being such a burden to you.'

Cat sat on the edge of the bed and held her mother's hands. When had her skin become so paper-thin?

'Mum, you could never be a burden,' she protested. 'I'm so sorry that I'm not as tolerant as I should be.'

Mum squeezed Cat's hands and said, 'Cat. I know what I am becoming. I know how I can be. It frightens me.'

'Which is why I want to look after you,' said Cat.

'And why you'll end up hating and resenting me,' said Mum. 'I won't let you put yourself through this anymore. I want you to promise me that you will sell my house and find a home for me. I'm not going to be able to make that decision soon, so you have to make it for me.'

'Don't,' said Cat through her tears.

'Cat, you know it's what has to happen,' said Mum. 'We'll manage because we must.'

They'd both cried then, Mum for the loss of independence, Cat for the loss of her mum.

Since that moment, there had been precious few times when Mum had shown such lucidity, and Cat knew that she couldn't put it off any longer. By dint of dropping the price to suit market conditions, her family home had sold so quickly Cat had had to come to terms with yet another blow to her bruised and battered heart.

Clearing out the house had been the worst thing she'd ever had to do. She and Noel had only had a week to pack things up, and in the end were reduced to shoving things in boxes without paying any attention to what was there. In the confusion, Cat belatedly realised she'd accidentally thrown out her mother's favourite earrings, and a family Bible belonging to her grandmother. But the worst of it was the systematic stripping down of everything that she'd known since childhood, of everything that had made her mother the person she was. Somehow it diminished Mum in a way. Apart from the piano on which Cat had bashed out 'Chopsticks' as a child, her mother's battered old furniture had gone to the charity shop; the bed that Cat was born in, so battered and old, had ended up on a skip; the grandfather clock just wouldn't fit in anywhere and had to go to an antiques shop; while the new owners had carelessly and unwittingly poured hot coals on Cat's head by casually talking about getting rid of the Aga ('So 90s,' they'd declared), and putting in a shiny new stainless steel kitchen. Cat knew it had to happen but, as a symbol of the loss of all her memories, it seemed the most potent. Now when she thought of her childhood home, it was tainted with the memory of the way she'd last seen it, stripped bare, and denuded of all comfort.

But at least now they had the money to look after Mum and, of all the homes they'd looked at, the Marchmont was certainly the best they'd seen.

'What do you think?' She was pulled out of her reverie to discover that she was being required to give an opinion. Even now, a part of her wanted there to be another way to solve this. She looked at Noel, who gave her a small grin and the thumbs up.

'You don't have to make a decision straight away,' the owner was saying, 'your mother could come and try it out for a day, see how you all feel.'

Taking a deep breath, Cat said, 'I think that would be perfect. When can we arrange for Mum to come for a visit?'

Gabriel was coming out of the solicitor's office, one of the few buildings on the High Street not affected by the floods. He'd been so angry with Eve that, the day after she'd told Stephen what was happening, he'd immediately booked an appointment with a solicitor. He should have done it months ago, when Eve first left, to consolidate their position, but there was something about his relationship with Eve that had the effect of stultifying him, making it impossible for him to act. With the benefit of distance and hindsight, he was beginning to see how bad they'd both been for each other.

It would be better with Marianne, a voice whispered in his head. Gabriel knew he could have a thoroughly normal relationship with Marianne, had even dared hope that in time Stephen might come round and they could make a fist of a proper family life. But now? He stopped and sighed. Stephen was speaking to him again, but had retreated somewhere deep inside himself. He appeared to have forgiven Eve too and seemed to enjoy the time he spent with her at the cottage she was renting. Gabriel had offered to pay but she declined, making him wonder how she could afford it. True she'd mentioned a job in London, but Eve had been in Hope Christmas a month now, and there was no sign that she was going back to work anytime soon.

Gabriel's solicitor had been confident that he would win custody. 'With your wife's history of mental illness, not to mention the abandonment issue, we have a very strong case,' the lawyer had advised. 'Are you ready to start proceedings?'

Gabriel couldn't give him an answer. Eve's solicitor hadn't written the letter she'd been promising him was on its way. It was like the sword of Damocles hanging over his head. She seemed to him increasingly skittish and erratic, and he was on the verge of suggesting she go back to their doctor, but now he felt in some odd limbo, where he felt he couldn't be so involved.

'Penny for them.' As he walked down the High Street, Marianne was walking up, laden with books. Her eyes were sparkling, her long dark curls tumbling over her shoulders, the cold autumnal air giving her cheeks a healthy glow. It had been weeks since he'd seen her. And suddenly she was there, lovely and natural, and for the moment completely unattainable.

'Marianne,' Gabriel felt suddenly awkward; she must think he'd totally lost interest in her. 'I'm sorry I haven't been in touch.'

'I know it's been tough,' Marianne's ready sympathy was like a balm to his battered soul, but she looked as awkward as he felt. 'Pippa told me what's been happening. Is there anything I can do?'

'Nothing,' said Gabriel. 'But thanks.'

There was an uneasy pause, then he said, 'You've got a lot of books there. I didn't realise teaching reception was so academic.'

'It's not,' laughed Marianne, slightly more at her ease. 'No, these are research. Courtesy of Miss Woods.'

'Research?' Gabriel was puzzled. He'd completely lost touch with what was happening in Hope Christmas over the last few weeks.

'Didn't you hear? We've won a competition to put on the perfect Nativity, and yours truly is running the show.'

'I hope you're going to keep the elves,' said Gabriel, his mood lightening.

'Of course,' said Marianne mock seriously. She paused and then said: 'I realise this might not be the best time to ask this, but do you think Stephen would like to do a solo? He has such a lovely voice, and I thought he'd be perfect to sing "Balulalow".'

Gabriel was suddenly hit by a pain so intense it nearly stopped him breathing. Stephen might not even be with him at Christmas. Besides, he was so fragile, it didn't seem right to put him through that, even if he were here.

'Now's not the best time,' said Gabriel. 'Sorry, the answer's no.'

'But—' Marianne started to protest.

'I said no,' said Gabriel. 'Stephen has enough to cope with.'

'It might help,' said Marianne, 'give him some confidence. You saw how much he enjoyed it at Easter.'

'Marianne, I know you want to help,' said Gabriel stiffly. 'But I can assure you I know what is best for my son. And right now singing in your Nativity isn't. Please let's leave it at that.'

'Fine,' said Marianne equally stiffly. 'But just suppose you're wrong. Stephen has a rare talent. I think it should be encouraged, not stifled.'

'Like I said, he's my son,' said Gabriel. 'Don't ask me again.'

'I think you're being very unfair,' said Marianne, but Gabriel didn't answer, and strode off down the hill, unable to articulate further the rage that was coursing through him, but dimly aware that somehow he'd managed to direct it at entirely the wrong person.

Noel looked at his email inbox. Another slew of rejections to match the ones that seemed to be dropping through his letterbox at a phenomenal rate. He couldn't imagine that he would ever get another job again. Maybe he *could* commute to Hope Christmas and back.

'Cup of tea?' Cat had come in silently. She'd barely spoken all the way back from the visit to the care home. Noel didn't blame her. It was nice as these places go but, however the dedicated staff dressed it up, it was an institution and, judging by the majority of its inmates who had sat rocking silently in chairs in front of the TV, the residents were swiftly institutionalised. It wasn't a fate he'd wish on anyone, not even his mother in her worst moments. Although miraculously of late she seemed to be a lot more helpful than she'd ever been, even turning up today to make sure they could go out together to visit the care home. Cat had told him what she'd said about not helping out before, and for once Noel was prepared to admit that maybe he too had got it wrong, and he'd actually managed to tell her so.

'That's all in the past,' his mother had said to his astonishment. 'For now, Cat needs you,' she'd admonished, and he knew she was right. Cat did need him. Cat was so gorgeous and vivacious, Noel had always felt slightly amazed he'd caught her eye all those years ago when they'd first got together, and now, with his confidence at rock bottom, he wasn't sure that he could keep it.

'Tea would be great,' said Noel. 'How's your mum?'

'Asleep,' said Cat with a sigh. She looked tired and worn out.

'Fancy going out tonight?' he said. 'I mean, my mum's here, we could manage a curry or something.'

'I'd love to,' said Cat, 'but I'm so behind. I've got to write up some Christmas recipes for *Happy Homes*, and work on the book a bit more. My agent thinks she's got someone interested, and she's pushing me to finish it.'

'Oh.' Noel was absurdly disappointed. He knew – thought he knew – she wasn't rejecting him, but she had a way of looking straight through him, as if he wasn't there. It was hard not to take it personally.

'Sorry, Noel,' she said. 'I'm just feeling a bit overwhelmed with everything, what with Mum and you not working. I haven't even started on Christmas yet. Normally I've bought half the presents by October. I just somehow don't have the energy for it this year.'

Noel felt a little bit resentful. Cat had a knack of making him feel like that. *What about me?* He wanted to say, can't you see beyond yourself to me?

'You have had a lot on your plate,' Noel said. 'Why don't you let me help you? After all, I don't have anything else to do with my time.'

'I'm not sure I can trust you with the turkey,' Cat said lightly, but it made Noel bristle.

'I'm not a complete idiot, you know,' he snapped.

'I never said you were,' said Cat, looking shocked at the venom in his tone.

'Stop treating me like one, then,' said Noel. 'I am capable of ordering a turkey. You just need to learn to delegate more.'

Cat looked as if she might spit something back, but then thought better of it.

'You're right,' she said, 'and I'm sorry. I am going to need your help. By the looks of things I'm going to have to be up in Hope Christmas on Christmas Eve for this wretched photo shoot. I wish I'd never suggested a sodding Nativity competition.'

'You just leave everything to me,' said Noel, a sudden brilliant thought burgeoning in his mind. 'I think, if you let me, I could sort Christmas out very well indeed.'

Chapter Thirty

'Hello, is that the Woodcote Lodge Hotel?' Noel was enjoying a certain amount of secret squirrelness about his plans for Christmas. It was going to be expensive, he knew, but GRB had at least sorted out a reasonable redundancy package for him and, despite their stretched finances, he was sick to death of being careful. For once he was going to throw caution to the winds. They might not get a chance like this again and, with Cat working herself to the bone at the moment, and all the worry she'd had with her mum, Noel didn't want her to have to think about Christmas at all. So he'd found some hotels offering festive deals in the Hope Christmas area and, to his amazement, the place wasn't booked up.

'Lost a lot of custom because of the flood, see,' the warm Shropshire burr on the other end of the phone informed him, reminding Noel again that he'd love to make his home in such a comforting place. If only they hadn't got Cat's mum ensconced in the Marchmont. There was no way Cat would leave London now. She still felt so guilty about her mother, which was ridiculous as they'd done everything they could for her. She didn't even recognise them anymore. Noel knew it was wrong to think it, but he couldn't help wondering if it would matter if they left. Louise was lost in her own world anyway. They knew she was cared for – would she actually notice they'd gone?

But he couldn't do that to Cat. It would break her heart.

Noel made the booking for all of them to arrive on Christmas Eve and stay for the whole week. They all deserved a holiday. He wasn't sure Cat would go for leaving her mother that long, but he'd had a long chat to the woman who ran the Marchmont and she'd been most insistent that Cat took a break.

'Families always feel guilty,' she said, 'but you can't look after people if your own batteries aren't recharged. Go on, have a good time and we'll make sure that your mother-in-law will have the best Christmas she's ever had.'

Noel doubted that somehow, thinking back to the first Christmases when he and Cat had been married and spending their time in between the two sets of parents. In the end, Cat had felt so guilty about her mother being on her own, they used the excuse of a new baby and a bigger house to have everyone to them. They had been happy years when the children had been small and cuddly and not older and spiky, when he'd felt confident in his job and his marriage. He stared out the window at the greying November sky. Things seemed to have changed so much since then. He still had Cat, it was true, although he felt he only got half of her most of the time. And the children were wonderful, he had to remember that. But he'd lost his job, his father, and now he was losing his wonderful mother-in-law. He felt more weighed down by cares and responsibilities than ever before in his whole life and where once the future had looked rosy, now it simply looked bleak.

This would never do. He turned over the card that Ralph Nicholas had given him all those months ago. Dammit, he would try to ring him again. Maybe there was some way he could do the job and commute. What was the worst that could happen? Ralph could only say no.

* * *

349

Marianne was making a snowman frieze with a bunch of reception children, and trying not to think too much about Gabriel. She hadn't seen him since their disastrous meeting on the High Street and, although she understood that his life was peculiarly difficult right now, she was frustrated at his inability to see that Stephen might be helped by singing in the play. His teachers reported that Stephen, never an outgoing child, was growing more and more withdrawn. Marianne's heart went out to him. It must be so difficult for a child to be caught up in things he didn't understand. And, despite being still cross with Gabriel, her heart went out to him too. Pippa reported that he wasn't eating or sleeping, and that the stress of the situation was making him ratty as hell. Marianne had thought on so many occasions that she should go and comfort him, but didn't know if she'd be welcome.

'Miss Moore,' said Jeremy Boulder, at five years old the eldest and liveliest child in her class. 'Need the toilet, Miss Moore.'

'Off you go then,' said Marianne. She watched him go out of the door at the back of the classroom.

'Miss Moore, look.' Jeremy was jumping up and down and pointing with glee at the glass door opposite her classroom that led to the playground.

'I don't believe it,' Marianne laughed out loud, completely taken aback by what she was witnessing. 'There are sheep in the playground.' She'd never had to deal with *that* in London.

'Where, where?' the children clamoured around her. Marianne led them out onto the corridor. She could see that the fence in the field next to the playground had come down. There'd been high winds last night, presumably that was when the damage had been done. The sheep had strayed across into the grassy area at the far end of the playground, and were now wandering aimlessly on to the concrete area where the children played. They hadn't seemed to work out that they needed to go back the way they came.

'Can we go and look at them, Miss?'

'You'd better not,' said Marianne, thinking of health and safety: then thought, don't be ridiculous, what could sheep do to children?

She called Jenny, her colleague in the next classroom, and together they shooed the sheep back the way they came while the children lined up by the school wall laughing.

The sheep were baaing and running around piteously, but none of them seemed to know where they were going.

'I hadn't realised how much hard work it was being a sheep dog,' Marianne laughed, as she unsuccessfully chased another sheep away from the school entrance where it had stopped to chew the winter pansies Year 3 had planted for Environmental Club.

Suddenly she heard a whistle and a black and white speeding bullet flew across the playground and started rounding the sheep up. She looked up to see Gabriel ordering his dog this way and that until, finally, all the sheep were firmly over the right side of the fence.

'You've got a new dog,' she said.

'Yes, this is Patch,' said Gabriel, 'grandson of Benjy, so even Stephen has taken to him.'

'I hadn't realised it was your sheep in that field,' Marianne added.

'They're not normally. I rotate them during the mating season, so the ewes get enough to eat. They don't breed well if they're too thin. I'm going to have to move them to another field now till I sort out this fencing.'

'Right,' said Marianne, suddenly remembering her class. 'Best get on. Children to teach and that.'

'Marianne,' said Gabriel. He paused, looking awkward. 'I owe you an apology.'

Marianne said nothing, wondering what was coming next.

'I was rude about Stephen and singing the solo,' he said. 'It's just been so hard, and Stephen is so unhappy, and I don't know how to help him.'

'Then let him do this,' Marianne came up and touched Gabriel lightly on the arm. Never had she wanted more to take away someone's pain. 'He's so quiet at school. If he could only do this, I think it would really help bring him out of his shell.'

'Do you? Really?' Gabriel looked at her intently, those dark brown eyes searing into her soul.

'Yes, I do,' said Marianne.

'I'll think about it,' said Gabriel. 'But right now I'd better get these sheep away before you have another invasion.'

'It's given the kids something to giggle about,' laughed Marianne.

'Marianne—' said Gabriel, as she turned to go.

'Yes?' said Marianne.

'Oh, nothing,' Gabriel said abruptly, and turned back to his sheep. Marianne walked back to the classroom feeling crushed. For a moment there, she'd hoped Gabriel was going to ask her to come back. For a moment. But Eve was still here. Nothing had changed. It was foolish of her to expect anything else.

'Hi, Mum, I bought you the paper,' said Cat as she came into her mother's room. Mum was still in her nightie, sitting in her chair rocking back and forth. Cat had come to expect this, and also come to accept any little sign that her mother knew she was there with gratitude. If she didn't, she'd go mad with this. How could it be that her once bright, bubbly mother was reduced to this shell sitting mumbling in a corner?

'That's nice, dear,' her mother said. 'I'm waiting for my daughter. Do you know when she's coming?'

'It's me, Mum,' said Cat, tears springing to her eyes. She still couldn't get used to the fact that Mum didn't recognise her at all anymore but, if she made a fuss about it, Mum only got upset. 'Shall I wash your hair for you?'

The care in the home was patchy. Sometimes Mum was dressed when she came in, sometimes she wasn't. When Rosa was on, Cat always felt relief. Rosa clearly loved Mum and was gentle and tender with her, but then there'd be days when Rosa wasn't there, and the care assistants that Cat referred to as The Lazy Gits would be there instead, sitting down at every opportunity, delighted by Cat's arrival because it relieved them of their responsibility. Cat preferred to wash her mother's hair than let them do it – she'd seen how rough they could be. Though she'd complained to Gemma, the owner of the Marchmont, nothing much seemed to get done. As ever, there was a gnawing guilt about whether she'd done the right thing. But what, as Noel said, was the alternative?

Gently, Cat led her mum to the sink in her bedroom and got her comfy, then ran the water through her mother's hair. Once Mum had done this for her; Cat could still remember the comfort of having her hair washed as a child. Once Cat had done it for Mel, who now wouldn't dream of letting her mum get involved in the ritualistic hairstyling of the preteen. Now, here she was, the child becoming the mother, the mother whose child was needing her less and less. Cat was at a loss to know what her role was anymore. Never had she felt more lost and in need of her mum, and never had the strength of that loss felt more heartbreaking.

She finished washing her mum's hair, and dried it with a towel. Then she sat Mum in front of a mirror, and slowly curled her hair the way she knew she liked it. It was gently soothing to do this task. There was so little she could do for her mother, but she could do this one thing.

When she'd finished, she said, 'There, don't you look nice.'

Mum smiled at her, and patted her hand.

'You're a good girl,' she said. 'Just like my Cat. She's a good girl too, I can't think why she doesn't come.'

It never ever got any easier, but Cat had learnt that repeating that she was there only got Mum more agitated. 'Shall we have a cup of tea?'

'Yes, a nice cup of tea and a biscuit would be lovely,' Mum said. 'I'm glad you're here. You always look after me so nicely. I shall tell Cat when she arrives what a good girl you are.'

Blinking away the tears, Cat went to ask the staff for a cup of tea.

She came back and sat down next to her mother again, taking her hand and squeezing it tightly.

'I'm glad I'm here too,' she said. Even if her mother didn't recognise her, at least she knew she was here to look after her. That was the most she could hope for now.

Gabriel came back to the house to find it in darkness. Eve had taken to picking Stephen up from school every day and taking him home for tea. It was an uneasy arrangement, but so far had worked without incident.

His heart was in his mouth as he turned on the lights, calling Stephen's name. Where were they? Eve hadn't mentioned that she was taking Stephen anywhere.

'In here.' Eve was sitting alone in a darkened kitchen. The last rays of a wintry sun were setting across the valley.

'Where's Stephen?' Gabriel had a sudden shocking thought that she might have hurt him in some way.

'He's with Pippa,' Eve was twisting a cup round and round. Suddenly Gabriel had a feeling he knew what she was going to say.

'You shouldn't be sitting here in the dark,' he said gently. 'What's the matter?'

Eve was silent for a moment.

'It's me,' she said, 'it's me that's the matter.'

'What do you mean?' Gabriel felt the need to proceed with caution.

'I've made a mess of everything. Of life with you. Of life without you.' Eve was shaking. 'I've been a lousy mum to Stephen. I am a lousy mum to Stephen.'

'You're not,' said Gabriel. 'He loves you to pieces. It's done him so much good to have you here.'

'Has it?' Eve stared at him with a look of such painful intensity it pierced his soul. 'All I've done is brought him more heartache. I thought I could do it, I really did. But I just can't do this school run thing and being a mum. I do love Stephen. Really I do. I'm just not cut out to be a mother.'

Gabriel sat down next to her and put his arm around her.

'Eve,' he said, 'you've made such great strides. You've done so well. Don't give up on yourself or on Stephen. He needs you, you're his mum.'

'No, he needs you,' said Eve. 'I realise that now. You're mother and father to him in a way I can never be. It was selfish of me to come here and try and take him away from you and I'm sorry.'

'Don't be,' said Gabriel. 'You can't help who you are. But you can help your son. Go if you have to. Don't have him living with you if you don't think you can. But never forget you're his mother. He needs you and you need him. I've seen how happy he's been around you. We can build on that, all of us. Just not in a way that might be terribly conventional.'

'What on earth did I do to you, all those years ago, Gabriel North?' said Eve with the inkling of a smile. 'I bet you wish you'd never met me.'

'If I hadn't, I wouldn't have Stephen,' said Gabriel. 'We might have messed everything else up, but we did that right. If you drop your battle for custody I'll never stop you from seeing him. He needs you in his life.'

'And you need me out of yours,' said Eve. 'I'll explain everything to Stephen this evening. I've booked a train to London tomorrow. But this time I promise I'll come back.'

Gabriel kissed her on the head, and sat back with relief. He was going to keep his son after all.

Chapter Thirty-One

Cat sat down at the computer. She'd barely blogged for weeks now. She had so little time and energy for anything. She'd never been this behind for Christmas. Every time she thought about it a sick feeling entered her stomach, and she felt paralysed. Nothing was going to be ready on time, but for once she didn't care. Dimly she was aware that Noel seemed to be taking it on himself to read through the Christmas lists and bring home bulging bags of goodies from Argos but, for the first time in her life, Cat couldn't get at all enthusiastic about the festive season. She just wanted to curl up in a ball and hibernate till it was all over. She hadn't even managed to rustle up any energy for decorating the Christmas tree, which was normally her greatest pleasure.

Normally, Cat would have found herself blogging amusingly about the varied exploits of her offspring at Christmas: how do you make a camel costume, anyone? But this year, she didn't even have the heart for that. She was heartily sick of the Happy Homemaker. Seeing Mum in the home had made her realise she had to make some changes in her life. It might mean difficult times ahead for her and Noel financially, but they simply couldn't carry on as they were.

I realise I've been a bad blogger of late, she began, *but real life has interfered in a way I could neither foresee or imagine. Some of you may have realised by now, but the Happy Homemaker blog is a façade. It's a cover for my real life and, as I'm sure is the case for a lot of bloggers, it's a carefully constructed edifice – a pretend version of my life, if you like. I hope I'm not going to disappoint any of my readers by saying this, as I'm grateful to you one and all, but I can't keep the façade up any longer.*

Put simply, my life isn't perfect, it never was. I am a mum of four whose domestic life is usually chaotic. I started this blog to stop me going mad when my children were small, and then it ended up taking over my life. Recently, I felt, to the extent that I started forgetting my responsibilities, neglecting my family and in particular not supporting my husband. Events in my life right now have led me to rethink things. My mother has just been diagnosed with Alzheimer's . . .

Cat paused, could she be this honest in her blog? She'd never given away a real thought or emotion before, but somehow the blog seemed to be writing itself. She poured out all her heartache and sadness about the change in her mother, about the way the loss of her mother had made her feel. It was cathartic and necessary. There were no doubt readers who were going to feel cheated about what she'd done, and Bev was going to hit the roof when Cat told her. But Cat didn't care anymore. The Happy Homemaker had to go, and with her, Cat knew her days as features editor at *Happy Homes* were also numbered. She was going to hand in her notice and go freelance. From now on, her family came first.

'Yes, shepherds, if you can dance about like you're cold that will work very well.' Marianne was directing her ten-year-old shepherds, chosen for their comic abilities, as they kept themselves warm waiting for the angels to arrive. She consulted her script. 'Right, then we'll lead into "The Angel Gabriel From Heaven Came", and the angels come in.'

The angels – three fair-haired girls and one brunette (chosen because Marianne felt sorry for her after overhearing her complain she never got to be an angel) – came forward and took their positions.

'We bring glad tidings,' the chief angel said, 'of great joy to all mankind.'

This was going better than she'd expected. Marianne was really enjoying herself. The script that she'd adapted from the mystery play with a little help from Miss Woods (carefully ensconced on a chair in prime position as assistant director) was simple and clear, just as she'd hoped, and the children had all risen to the occasion beautifully. It was less than a week to go till the Nativity. She had a feeling that it was going to be a really special evening.

'Is it too late for Stephen to take part?' Gabriel poked his head around the door just then, looking nervous.

Resisting the urge to run up to him and throw her arms around him, Marianne welcomed them both into the room.

'Stephen, would you like to sing for us?' she said. She'd dropped "Balulalow" in favour of "Away in a Manger" for the crib scene, but she'd happily reinstate it if it meant Stephen singing.

'I've been practising at home,' said Stephen shyly.

'Just sit there for now,' said Marianne, 'and we'll get you to do your piece as soon as we get to the baby being born.'

The rehearsal went on and every fibre of her being was conscious of Gabriel at the back of the room, but she didn't dare look over at him.

'And so it came to pass that Mary gave birth to a son named Jesus,' intoned the narrator, 'and she wrapped him in swaddling clothes and laid him in a manger.'

Mary and Joseph (both chosen by virtue of being the

children of the only two sets of parents who *hadn't* tried to bribe Marianne to give them the role) moved forwards and placed the baby in the crib.

'Wonderful,' said Marianne. 'Now, Stephen, if you just come round to the front. Mr Edwards will give you a note.'

Mr Edwards, who was practising on the ancient piano in the Parish Centre instead of the wonderful organ in the Hopesay Manor chapel that he'd be playing on Christmas Eve, sounded a note. Stephen stepped forward, and began to sing.

'But I sall praise thee evermoir, With sangis sweit unto thy gloir,' Stephen sang and the whole place froze. You could have heard a pin drop as he reached the high notes.

Marianne sat back in delight. She'd been right to get Stephen to sing, she knew it.

'And sing that last rycht Balulalow.' Stephen finished off the last note, which lingered softly in the air.

The cast spontaneously burst into applause. Stephen shyly smiled, and Marianne looked across at Gabriel.

'Thank you,' she mouthed. Now she knew she had the perfect Nativity.

Gabriel waited at the end of the rehearsal for Marianne.

'It's going to be fantastic,' he said. 'You've done brilliantly.'

'Thanks,' said Marianne, 'and I'm glad you brought Stephen. He's going to bring the house down.'

'I have to admit he had me going,' said Gabriel. 'You were right. Singing *is* good for him. I could see how much it's brought him out of himself.'

'I'm glad,' said Marianne. 'He has a rare talent, and it needs to be nurtured.'

There was a pause and Gabriel wondered how to fill it, before suddenly being unable to stop himself from saying: 'So do you.'

360

'So do I what?' Marianne looked confused.

'Have a rare talent. You've made such a difference to Hope Christmas.' Gabriel paused and looked shyly down at his feet. 'You've made such a difference to me.'

'Oh,' she said, looking stunned.

'Pippa's having mulled wine tonight, I believe,' said Gabriel, looking up at her now, his brown eyes twinkling.

'But what about Eve?' said Marianne. 'Aren't you going with her?'

'Marianne Moore, where have you been? The village hotline must have got the news out by now, surely?'

'What news?' Marianne was puzzled.

'Eve's gone back to London. She's decided she couldn't cope with Stephen and that it's for the best.'

'I'm sorry,' said Marianne. 'I thought you'd be able to work things out.'

'I'm not,' said Gabriel. 'Really, this is for the best. Stephen understands his mother is ill, and he knows we can't be together now. Which means . . .'

He left the rest of the sentence hanging but the broad grin that lit up his face left Marianne in no doubt about his intentions.

'You know you look so much better when you smile,' said Marianne. 'You don't do that nearly enough.'

'I haven't had much to smile about recently,' admitted Gabriel. 'But since I found out Eve's not suing for custody of Stephen, I haven't been able to stop grinning.'

'I bet,' said Marianne. 'And Stephen is really okay about this?'

'Better than I thought he'd be,' said Gabriel. 'He was distraught at the thought of going to London, and I think he understands that Eve can't look after him. Apparently all she ever gave him for tea when he was staying with her was cheese on toast. But she's not going to leave him for good like she did last time. In fact she's coming for Christmas at Pippa's. Weird, I know. But better all round for Stephen.'

'I'm so glad,' said Marianne. 'Really I am.'

'So what about Pippa's and mulled wine then?'

'Yes, right, great idea,' said Marianne. She followed Gabriel and Stephen out of the Parish Centre, down the High Street and to the lane that led to Pippa's house. Snow was gently falling as they entered the lane.

'Magic!' said Stephen and ran up the lane whooping in delight as he tried to catch snowflakes on his tongue.

Marianne linked her arm in Gabriel's. It felt right and natural to have it there. He squeezed it tight.

The short walk to Pippa's was all too brief, and before long Gabriel found himself separated from Marianne in a whirl of Christmas bonhomie. But he was always aware of her presence, following her round the room. Lighting up when he caught her eye.

Eventually they caught up by the mulled wine.

'We must stop meeting like this,' said Gabriel.

'Must we?' The mulled wine had made Marianne flirtatious, and he suddenly had a vivid remembrance of the first time they'd met.

'Well, are you going to kiss her or what?' Stephen appeared next to him with his arms firmly folded, looking very disapproving.

'Um—' Gabriel was totally thrown off his stride. 'Are you saying you wouldn't mind if Marianne and I were together?'

'Duh, *nooo*, of course I wouldn't,' said Stephen. 'Anyone can see you're made for each other. Parents. What are they like?'

Gabriel and Marianne laughed.

'Look, Auntie Pippa even put some mistletoe up there specially for you,' said Stephen. 'Some people are so dense.'

'Happy Christmas, Marianne,' said Gabriel, and bent down and kissed her on the mouth. 'I believe I owe you a drink.'

'I do believe you do,' said Marianne responding more enthusiastically than he would have dared imagine.

'You've done what?' Noel couldn't believe his ears. Cat had just walked in and told him her news. 'Why the hell didn't you ask me about this?'

'You never told me about your redundancy,' Cat said reasonably enough. 'I thought you'd be pleased. In the New Year you can get another job, and I'll go freelance. It will be fine. You'll see.'

'I don't know whether you've noticed,' said Noel, 'but the job offers aren't exactly falling from the trees. Let's face it, I'm a tired, washed-up has-been.'

'Oh, don't be ridiculous, Noel,' said Cat. 'Now you're just feeling sorry for yourself.'

Noel couldn't respond to that because part of him knew it was true. But how could she have handed her notice in without consulting him? It made the Christmas hotel a luxury they could barely afford, let alone the presents he'd bought in a fit of generosity, figuring that he wouldn't have a redundancy package every year and, while Cat was still working, it wouldn't matter if he blew a little of it.

'And why shouldn't I feel sorry for myself?' Noel spat out. 'I've sat here at your beck and call for the last few months feeling like a stranger in my own home. You barely acknowledge me, the kids probably wouldn't care if I was here or not. What is the bloody point of me existing? I barely know anymore.'

'Noel.' Cat looked shocked.

'Daddy, the shelf has fallen down in the family room again.' Ruby bounced in exuberantly. 'Can you mend it?'

'No, I bloody well can't,' said Noel. 'Let your mother mend it. See how well she can do it.'

Ruby burst into tears.

'Noel!' said Cat. 'That was so unkind.'

Appalled at what he'd done, Noel got up and, without a word, picked up his coat and left the house. It was cold out and the wind whipped through him as he walked and walked through the sleet-ridden streets of London, through busy roads bustling with commuters going home to their loved ones, and Christmas revellers sharing the festive spirit. He barely knew where he was going. Only that he had to get away.

Almost without knowing how he'd got there, he found himself on a bus heading into town. His mobile rang. He ignored it. It rang again. So he switched it off. Eventually the bus stopped, and he got off, for a moment unsure of his surroundings. Then he walked for a while until he found himself by Waterloo Bridge. It was brightly lit and on the far side of the river he could see the glow of the National Theatre proclaiming something by Chekhov showing, while below twinkling blue lights gave the trees on the South Bank a festive glow, and the slow ponderous movements of the Millenium Wheel shone out against a dark wintry skyline.

People flitted from one side to the other, full of Christmas cheer, ready to spend a night on the town or go back home to their loved ones. Noel was filled with an overwhelming sense of hatred for them, but it was coupled with a self-loathing he couldn't escape. How could he have been so cruel to Ruby? And to Cat for that matter. She'd been through such a lot lately. Maybe she was right. Perhaps she should be at home more, but how could they manage on her freelance salary and without any income from him? She'd be better off if he were dead. At least the insurance would pay for the house.

He walked over to the side of the bridge. And looked down into the dark whirling waters below. They looked somehow inviting. He'd never contemplated ending it all before, but he'd never been this miserable either.

Cat would be better off without him. Noel had nothing to offer her or the children anymore. He stared into the darkness below. It seemed to call to him. To tease him. To welcome him home.

Chapter Thirty-Two

'Well, go on, if you're going to,' a slightly testy voice came from behind him. 'It's a cold night and I'm not as young as I was. So go on. Do it.'

'Do what?' Noel turned round as the wind whipped his face and stared bemusedly into the twinkling eyes of Ralph Nicholas. 'What on earth are you doing here?'

'First things first,' said Ralph. 'I take it you *were* planning to jump off the bridge, weren't you? So what's stopping you?'

Noel paused. What was stopping him? A minute ago it had seemed like the answer to his prayers. The temptation to end it all had been enormous. But suddenly a picture of Cat swam before his eyes. And a vision of her dressed in black surrounded by the children. Financially she'd be better off without him, but would she *actually* be better off? Wasn't the act he was contemplating supremely selfish?

'My thoughts exactly,' said Ralph. 'Never seen the point of suicide. So unkind to the people left behind. I always make a point of trying to stop them.'

'What do you mean, you always try and stop them?' Noel was reeling, trying to make sense of this.

'Let's just say it's part of my job description,' said Ralph. 'Besides, you can't go topping yourself. Not when I have a job to offer you.'

'What job?'

'Well, I was rather hoping that you'd have the sense to ring me up yourself. I've been waiting for you to, you know. But since the mountain wouldn't come to Mohammed . . .'

'Right,' said Noel, sheepishly. 'But how did you know I'd be here?'

'It's my business to know that kind of thing,' said Ralph, which was about as clear as mud. 'Now, chop chop, I've a few things to show you before you go home.'

Noel found himself following Ralph through the London streets in a daze. For an old man he moved remarkably quickly. Suddenly they were on the Embankment.

'Fancy spending Christmas like them?' he said quietly, pointing to the tramps camped outside Embankment Station.

'No,' said Noel, feeling ashamed of his earlier outburst. How could he feel he had nothing when these people had so little? Normally he walked past the tramps in the street, but now he went up and offered one his coat. Weirdly, he didn't feel cold. In fact, he felt warmer than he'd ever felt in his life.

'Better,' said Ralph approvingly. He led Noel away from the streets into the cloistered seclusion of the Middle Temple, and towards the Temple Church. Noel had been here once before. It was a haven, a sanctuary not far from the hustle and bustle of the London streets. 'Now, shall we go in?'

Noel walked into the back of the church feeling awkward.

'I know, I know, you only come into these places about once a year,' said Ralph. He nodded at the crucifix high above the altar. 'Do you think He minds about stuff like that? Blessed are the pure in heart, theirs is the Kingdom of Heaven. That's what it's all about.'

Noel sank into a pew and stared ahead of him. Candles had been lit and a boys' choir was practising for a carol service. The sound brought tears to his eyes.

367

'Remind you of anything?' said Ralph.

'When I was a boy, I sang in a choir just like that,' said Noel. He'd forgotten the simplicity and the joy of standing in the choir, belting his heart out. Once his voice had broken, he'd given up.

'See the one on the left?' Noel looked where Ralph was pointing, at a ten-year-old boy who was struggling to sing through his emotions. 'His father died last Christmas. Do you want your son to be feeling like that next Christmas?'

'No,' whispered Noel quietly.

'And see that old woman in the corner?'

Noel looked and saw a bag lady, rocking back and forth against her shopping trolley, muttering to herself slightly madly.

'She used to have a family. Once,' said Ralph. 'But she lost them one by one, and then, eventually, she lost her wits. And now here she is. Every Christmas she comes here because she remembers the carols from her youth. The clergy here give her something to eat, but though they try to set her up in a hostel, she'll never stay. It seems she's forever fated to wander the streets of London.'

Noel looked at the woman, who couldn't have been much older then he was, but her lined face belied her years, and her unkempt appearance betrayed her suffering. Whatever he'd struggled with, was nothing compared to what this poor woman had gone through.

'Still feeling sorry for yourself, are you?' Ralph looked at him kindly. 'Everyone loses their way sometimes. It's whether you can find it again that counts.'

Noel looked back up at the choir.

'I think I want to go home,' he said.

'Excellent idea,' said Ralph. 'I have a feeling your wife might have some very good news for you.'

* * *

368

Gabriel put Stephen to bed and read him a story. It had been a long time since they'd shared a moment like this. Stephen had spent the whole time Eve had been there withdrawing into himself, and somehow they'd got out of the habit of spending time like this together.

'So you're sure you don't mind about Marianne?' he said.

'She's really nice,' said Stephen, looking suddenly shy, 'and, I know this sounds awful, but I have more fun with her than I do with Mummy.'

'You do understand how ill Mummy is, don't you?' Gabriel said with a sigh. 'She loves you, but she can't look after you the way she'd like, or the way you need.'

'I know,' said Stephen, 'but it doesn't matter, because you can do it for her.'

Gabriel kissed his son and went downstairs, where Marianne was waiting for him.

He took her in his arms and kissed her with a long deep sigh of contentment.

'I can't tell you how long I've been wanting to do that,' he said.

'Nearly as long as I have,' said Marianne, with a smile.

'You realise that we'll have to take things slowly, though, don't you?' said Gabriel, 'for Stephen's sake. And for mine.'

'Gabriel North, we can take things as slowly as you like,' said Marianne, 'After all, we've got the rest of our lives to get to know one another better.'

'We have, haven't we?' said Gabriel. He put on a CD, and poured her out a glass of wine. 'Come on, let's dance.'

Marianne burst out laughing as the first words played while they danced slowly in front of the fire.

'"Last Christmas"?' she said. 'I didn't know you had a penchant for cheese.'

'I've always had a soft spot for those Wham boys,' said

369

Gabriel, pulling her to him. 'But first things first. Do you have plans for Christmas?'

'Well, I was going to my parents', but they've decided to go on a last-minute skiing holiday, so I don't actually have any.'

'Good,' said Gabriel, 'because this year, I want to spend Christmas with someone special, and I'd really like it to be you.'

'What about Eve?' said Marianne.

'She's coming on Christmas Eve to see Stephen sing,' said Gabriel, 'and she'll be there for lunch, but she's not staying. You, on the other hand, I rather think are.'

'I rather think I am,' said Marianne, and fell into his arms.

Cat paced up and down the kitchen, wondering at what point she should call the police. Noel had been gone for hours. She'd dispatched the children to bed, even Mel, who had hovered about uncertainly, till Cat had made up some nonsense about Noel going out with one of his friends for a drink. She wondered whether she should go looking for him, but where to start? And she could hardly ask Regina to have the children in the middle of the night. There were limits to even the strongest of friendships.

This was like Christmas Day all over again. That time Noel had only gone AWOL for an hour. But she'd known how miserable he was. She'd had the feeling for months that he'd been suffering from some kind of depression, and she'd done nothing about it. She'd failed him. And now maybe she'd lost him.

'No, you haven't.' The front door banged shut, she heard footsteps on the stairs and suddenly an old man was standing in her kitchen. There was something familiar about him. 'I hope you don't mind, the door was open, so I let myself in,' he said.

'Who are you?' Cat was astonished by the appearance of this stranger in her kitchen.

'My name's Ralph Nicholas and I'm a friend of your husband's,' said the man, 'and you most emphatically haven't lost Noel. He's on his way back now. By the way, I don't think you've listened to your answerphone messages this evening. One of them is quite illuminating.'

Cat went to the phone and pressed playback.

'Hi, Cat, this is Sophie here.' Cat hadn't heard anything from her agent for a while, she'd almost forgotten about the cookery book. 'Great news. I've got a brilliant offer for you from Collins, they're really keen to do a big number on you, and it looks like we might have a TV series to go with it.'

She named a figure that was staggeringly high – certainly enough to make up for the loss of income from handing in her notice. Cat sat down with a thump. She turned back to Ralph, suddenly realising where she'd seen him before. 'Wait a minute, aren't you—' but she was addressing the empty air. 'What on earth is going on?' she said out loud.

Cat was still sitting there slightly bemused when Noel came back in.

'Cat,' he said hesitantly. 'I'm sorry. I'm so so sorry.'

'No, I am,' Cat ran to him. 'I've been so wrapped up in myself I didn't realise how unhappy you've been.'

'I thought I'd lost you,' said Noel, pulling her close.

'I thought I'd lost you,' said Cat.

'Never,' said Noel. 'Remember that Bryan Ferry song? We should stick together, whatever it takes.'

'I know,' said Cat. 'I know.'

They stood holding each other for a few moments, and then Cat suddenly said, 'Oh, I nearly forgot, I've got some great news. My book's been accepted.'

'That's fantastic,' said Noel. 'Ralph told me you had some good news.'

371

Cat pulled apart and said in puzzlement:

'But that's weird, he was here as well.'

'Who?' It was Noel's turn to look bemused.

'Your friend, he came ahead of you to tell me you were coming home,' said Cat. Come to think of it, she didn't remember him leaving.

'That's odd, he was with me for some of the way home and then I lost him,' said Noel. 'But it's been an odd evening all round.'

'Hasn't it just?' said Cat. She pulled back from Noel, frowning. 'Where's your coat?'

'Uh, I gave it to a tramp,' said Noel.

'Wonders will never cease,' said Cat.

'Yeah, well, like I said, it's been an odd evening,' Noel paused, then said hesitantly, 'Listen, Cat, you can say no to this, but I've been offered a job. The only drawback is that it's up in Shropshire. I know, I know, you won't want to leave your mum, but can we at least think about it? I'm sure we can find her a good home in Hope Christmas. And Ralph tells me there's a lot more support for the elderly up there. In fact, one of his plans is to build a new community centre, where Alzheimer's patients can go and spend time during the day. It would mean your mum might have some kind of life. So what do you think?'

'Six months ago I'd have said go boil your head,' said Cat. 'But I've realised my priorities need to change. Besides, though the Marchmont is doing its best, it's not good enough. So long as we can find Mum a better home in Hope Christmas, I'm up for it. The important thing is we're all together. Nothing else matters.'

Marianne sat in the back of the candlelit chapel as the audience came quietly in. She'd had a flurry of excitement earlier in the day when she'd finally met Catherine Tinsall, aka the

Happy Homemaker. 'Though not for much longer,' Catherine had confessed. 'I've handed in my notice and we're thinking of relocating up here. My husband's been offered a job by Ralph Nicholas renovating some old cottages.'

'I know,' said Marianne grinning. 'The eco town wasn't a popular option round here. Everyone's been buzzing with the new plans.'

Catherine had looked a bit startled that everyone knew her business already, so Marianne added, 'Welcome to village life, you no longer have any privacy . . .'

Luke, it turned out, had been voted off the board once it came to light that he had yet to make a single sale in the eco town. The political tide was turning against the whole idea too and, from what Marianne had heard, he'd departed for sunnier climes in a hissy fit. No doubt he'd soon be selling luxury apartments in the Bahamas.

'Good luck, my dear,' a voice said behind her. She turned gladly to see Ralph Nicholas.

'I don't think I'll need it if you're here,' she said, 'you've brought me nothing but luck this year.'

'All part of the remit,' said Ralph, bowing his head before going to take a seat next to Miss Woods.

The chapel darkened and silence fell, and a little boy got up to sing of a mayden that was makeles. Marianne hadn't been able to resist using Stephen for more than one song and, judging by the rapt atmosphere in the chapel, she knew she'd made the right choice.

The audience were suitably amused by the shepherds' antics, and they sat in silence as the narrator told the ancient tale, and Mary and Joseph came to rest in the stable in Bethlehem as they had done on so many occasions in so many plays throughout history. But none in quite such a magical setting as this, thought Marianne. Stephen's rendition of 'Balulalow' predictably had the women in the audience sobbing into their hankies – even Diana Carew, Marianne was amused to note. Diana had only come along reluctantly at the last moment but, in the end, Marianne suspected, she couldn't quite bring herself to stay away. The wise men, who in rehearsal had kept forgetting their lines, managed to be word-perfect and the whole thing ended with a rousing version of 'Hark the Herald Angels Sing'.

'That was magnificent, thank you so much.' Catherine Tinsall was the first to congratulate her. She was joined by her husband and four children, the youngest of whom was swinging on her dad's arm saying, 'Can we go back to the hotel now, Daddy? I don't want to miss Santa.'

Catherine laughed. 'Be patient, Ruby,' she said. 'It's hours till bedtime.' She turned back to Marianne. 'I'm so glad we chose you, even though I'm not working for the magazine anymore.'

'Well done, my dear, well done.' Diana Carew's bosoms bore down on her. 'I've been saying for years that we needed some new blood to shake things up around here, but no one would listen.'

'I bet,' said Marianne.

'That was wonderful,' said Gabriel, 'but then I knew it would be.'

'Of course it was,' Miss Woods stumped up with her stick. 'She had me to teach her.'

'And I was very grateful for the help,' said Marianne.

'Marvellous effort, my dear.' Ralph Nicholas appeared, as he always did, as if by magic. 'I do hope you're all coming over to the house for mulled wine and mince pies?'

'This is fantastic,' Catherine Tinsall said as they walked from the chapel into the Great Hall, evidently as awed by the fabulous Christmas tree in Hopesay Manor as Marianne

374

had been a year ago. 'Noel never told me how wonderful this place was.'

'So you're staying then?' Marianne asked.

'It looks like it,' said Catherine, grinning at her husband.

'Who's staying?' Gabriel came up and half-inched a mince pie from Marianne's plate.

'Catherine and Noel,' said Marianne, 'this is Gabriel North. Gabriel, meet Hope Christmas' newest inhabitants.'

'Whereas, I, on the other hand, must depart,' Ralph came up to them and smiled enigmatically.

'What do you mean?' Marianne said, 'you're not leaving us?'

'I'm afraid so,' said Ralph. 'My job here is done for the time being. Until the next time, of course.'

'Next time?' Noel looked puzzled.

'There's always a next time,' said Ralph. 'I believe I can leave the renovation of my cottages in your capable hands, Noel. Oh, and if you're interested, I do believe there's a rather fetching old grandfather's clock in the antiques market, which will look perfect in the hallway of that lovely old farmhouse you are going to buy.'

'How did you know?' Noel looked incredulous.

'Haven't you worked out yet that I know everything?' said Ralph with a twinkle. 'But I have to go where I'm needed and, from what I hear, my grandson is causing merry mayhem in Barbados. I live in hope of bringing him on side, but he tries me sorely. But then, of course, as his father is adopted, he's not really a St Nicholas.'

'I thought your name was Nicholas?' said Marianne.

'It is, but we dropped the St because it sounded too pretentious,' said Ralph. 'Now, really, I must be going.'

'Why?' said Marianne, suddenly feeling desolate at the thought that Ralph was leaving.

'Because that's just the way it is,' said Ralph and, in a

familiar gesture, doffed his cap. He walked off down the drive to a waiting taxi, and the snow gently fell on the path.

'St Nicholas?' Noel said. 'You don't suppose – no, I'm being daft.'

'What?' said Catherine.

'It's just occurred to me that Ralph is something of a modern-day St Nicholas, or at the very least a guardian angel. But that's daft. There's no such thing as angels.'

Marianne looked down the drive – the car, and Ralph, had already disappeared into the night.

'Do you know, I'm not sure that it is so daft,' she said, linking arms with Gabriel. 'I think Ralph's been like a guardian angel to me.'

'And to me,' said Catherine. 'Besides, you do know what his name is short for don't you?'

'No.' Marianne looked puzzled.

'He told me his name is Ralph, pronounced Rafe. It's short for Raphael. Which happens to be the name of the angel in Milton's *Paradise Lost* who comes to warn Adam and Eve about Satan.'

'And your point is?' said Noel, puzzled.

'Look above the door,' said Cat. 'I noticed it as soon as I came in. *That thou are hapie, owe to God; That thou continu'st such owe to thyself.* And that Latin inscription, *Servimus liberi liberi quia diligimus—*'

'It means *Freely we serve, because we freely love,*' said Marianne. 'Ralph told me.'

'And they're both quotes from *Paradise Lost,*' said Cat triumphantly. 'From when the angel Raphael comes to warn Adam and Eve about Satan. I know because I did it for A level.'

'And look at all those angels,' Marianne said, with sudden wonder. She pointed above the door, and suddenly they all saw the cherubs flying in the corner, the angel on the door knocker, and remembered all the angel motifs dotted around the house. 'It was right in front of our noses all the time. Ralph *is* an angel.'

'And you know who St Raphael is the patron saint of, don't you?' said Catherine.

'No, I don't,' said Marianne.

'Lovers,' said Cat.

'Whatever he is, I think he's done rather a good job, don't you?' said Gabriel, raising his glass. 'To all of us. Merry Christmas.'

'Merry Christmas' came the instant response, and they chinked glasses to the soft strains of 'God Rest Ye Merry Gentlemen', while they watched the snow fall softly on Hopesay Manor lawn.

Epilogue

A Merry Christmas to my blog readers, one and all. Cat squinted at the screen on her laptop.

'Come to bed,' said Noel plaintively. 'I've got the champagne on ice and everything.'

'Just coming,' said Cat who, thanks to Ralph's generosity, felt she'd probably had enough champagne for one night, but it was Christmas after all.

And thanks to the many readers who've kindly commented on my last post and given me such thoughtful and supportive advice. It reminds me what a powerful thing the Internet is and, at its best, what a positive force for good. I have been hugely touched by the outpouring of emotion my post caused, and am deeply grateful to those of you who've kindly requested that I stay. However, I think enough is enough. As of tonight, this blog is, like a rather famous parrot, no more. Although, never say never and, like Arnie, I may well be back in another form. Who knows? In the meantime, thanks for reading, and I wish you all a very happy and peaceful Christmas. I hope that, like me, you find the peace you deserve.

Cat pressed send, then powered down the computer and climbed into bed where her husband was waiting for her. He presented her with a glass of champagne.

'To us,' Noel said, 'and to our future. Merry Christmas, Cat.'

'Merry Christmas, Noel,' said Cat. 'It's going to be the best one yet.'

In a car speeding off in the darkness, Ralph St Nicholas sat back and smiled.

Acknowledgements

As usual, I have lots of people to thank for the help they gave me when writing this book.

First and foremost, thanks as ever are owed to my brilliant editor, Maxine Hitchcock. When she suggested I write a Christmas book I had no idea how much fun it was going to be. I'd also like to thank Keshini Naidoo and Sammia Rafique at Avon for their continued hard work and enthusiasm on my behalf. Very much appreciated, ladies!

And without the enthusiasm and support of my lovely agent, Dot Lumley, I'd have given up on this writing malarkey years ago, so thank you again for all the help.

Juggling writing and a school-run can be a tricky task. Thanks to my lovely friends, Dawn and Clive Pearce, who picked the children up for weeks while I was writing this book. I can honestly say this book wouldn't exist without their help.

I'd like to say a special thank you to my sisters Paula, Lucy and Virginia for sharing their different experiences of the school-run in town and country, with a particular shout out to Ginia for telling me about the escaping sheep – genius. And my very clever brother John providing me with a Latin translation, which was a much better result than me trying Google translator.

I'd like to thank Nicola Rudd who has been an enthusiastic follower of my blog from the start and whose blogging about Nativity plays was part of the inspiration for this story; all the long-suffering teachers who have put on the many Nativities I've seen over the years; Kate Whalley for enormous help with mental health issues; Chris Montague for helping me out on engineering matters and Heather Choate for giving me background information about Shropshire sheep farming. Any mistakes are entirely my own.

A special thanks goes out to Cath Hicks for sharing her hilarious anecdotes about the pitfalls of having an au pair, although nothing I made up could be nearly as funny as the real thing.

Blogging is something I started to do as a bit of fun, but is now a very necessary part of my online life. I am grateful to Bea Parry Jones for sharing some of the occasional downsides to blogging. However, on the whole I have found blogging to be a positive experience, and over the last year have had much fun, usually David Tennant-related, with the following people: Rob Buckley, Leesa Chapman, Marie Phillips and the elusive but extraordinary Persephone. Thanks guys, it's been a blast. To follow my blog go to http://maniacmum.blogspot.com.

Over twenty years ago, I had a fabulous time taking part in the Chester Mystery Plays Nativity, which was the inspiration for Marianne's play. To all the gang who were there in '87, I bet you never knew then it would end up in a book! Thank you also to the enthusiastic and lovely ladies who run Burway Books in Church Stretton. Quite possibly the best bookshop in the world.

Shropshire has had a hold over my imagination since I was a child and read *The Lone Pine Adventures*. I'm immensely grateful to my parents for choosing to go and live there so I could get to write about it too. Thanks especially to my amazing mother, Ann Moffatt, who told me about Plowden Hall, which is the inspiration for Hopesay Manor, and whose own cooking exploits first got me started in the kitchen.

I'd like to give a special thanks to my former English teachers, Keith Ward and Susan Roache for their inspirational teaching, which in part has led me to where I am today. I had no idea when I was studying *Paradise Lost* all those years ago it would come in so handy!

It seems lucky to have one family you get on with. It seems positively greedy to have two. But that's the fortunate position I find myself in. So for both my families, I'd like to say a big thank you for all the Christmases, past, present and future. Here's to many many more.

Read on for exclusive Christmas Tips from Julia Williams
to help you through the festive season

Christmas Tips

- Defrost the turkey in time.

- Try and buy a few presents every week.

- If you're making a Christmas pudding use Marguerite Patten's recipe, which can be done the day before.

- Try to remain calm. It's only a day.

- Don't invite feuding family members.

- Try and invite only people you like.

- Get those people you like to help you by preparing vegetables.

- Set the table the day before.

- Don't leave present wrapping till Christmas Eve.

- Don't leave present buying till Christmas Eve.

- Ignore any child that wakes up before 7am.

- Try and eat in the evening avoiding early morning putting-on-the-turkey rises.

- Most of all . . .

DO NOT STRESS!!!

Read on for an exclusive extract from Julia Williams's new novel, *The Bridesmaid Pact* coming next year.

It was Doris' idea of course. Everything back then tended to emanate from Doris. She was the glue that bound us all together. She was the sticky stuff that made us all friends. Without Doris we were nothing. And even then we knew it.

'It's on, it's on,' she said, proudly brandishing the new video control of her parents' state of the art Beta Max video machine. Though of course we didn't say state of the art then. Nor did we realise that Doris' parents ahead of the trends as ever, had invested in a bit of technology which was going to be obsolete in a few short years. At eight years old, we were still marvelling at the idea of being able to watch our favourite TV moment of the year, again, and again.

'Go straight to the kiss,' Caz demanded. She was always the most impatient one.

'No, we have to watch it all,' Beth was most emphatic on that point. Her serious little face peeped up from under arms. 'I didn't get to see it because my mum and dad are anti-royalsomething.'

'Royalist,' interjected Doris.

'They don't like the Queen,' said Beth. 'So I wasn't allowed to watch any of it.'

Silently we all marvelled at this. All term we'd talked about nothing but the wedding. About what she'd wear, and who the bridesmaids would be. We'd even had a day off school to watch – Doris' mum and dad had taken her up to London and they'd camped out outside St Paul's Cathedral and watched it on the day – and poor Beth hadn't seen any of it.

'Luckily my mum and dad videoed it then, isn't it?' said Doris. 'Now sssshhh.'

We all settled down on the beanbags and cushions in the room that Doris' American professor dad called the den. Doris' house was like nothing the rest of us had ever seen. It was massive, with huge airy rooms and en-suite bathrooms for every bedroom. Imagine that. Even Doris had one. For me who shared a tiny suburban three bedroomed semi with my parents and three siblings, it seemed like a fairy palace. I still kept pinching myself that Doris had allowed me into her inner sanctum. It would have been easy to hate her, with her little girl ringletted beauty, her film star mother, clever professor father, and amazing house, but somehow, it was impossible to hate Doris. She was kind and generous and dappy and funny, and hid her cleverness (inherited from the professor father) under a carefully cultivated dizzy blondeness – except of course, she wasn't blonde.

The posh voice of the commentator was describing the guests as they arrived, and pointing out Prince Charles waiting with Prince Andrew for Diana to arrive. We all oohed and aahed as the carriages pulled up bearing the Queen and Prince Philip.

'I have to have that dress when I'm a bridesmaid next year,' Doris paused the tape so we could ogle the bridesmaids. After some critical discussion, we all agreed that Doris was much prettier then India Knight, and would suit the dress better. It never even occurred to the rest of us to think about any of us wearing the dress—

'Why is it always you?' Caz burst out. Her eyes pinpoint dark, and two bright points of red flaming her cheeks, her attitude as ever, spiky and pugnacious. 'Why can't the rest of us get to wear that dress? Just because you're rich and we're not!'

'That's not fair!' Doris leapt up and shouted. 'Don't I always let you have my stuff and invite you over?'

'So you can feel good,' spat back Caz. 'I know you only have me here because you feel sorry for me.'

'That's not true,' said Beth, ever the peacemaker. 'Caz I think you should say sorry.'

As Caz's best friend, I felt duty bound to take her part, though I didn't think she was being fair either. As the prettiest, richest one of us, and the only one who was going to actually be a bridesmaid, I felt that Doris was quite within her rights to lay first claim to India Knight's dress. After all, even she with all her wealth wasn't going to wear that exact dress.

'Doris, it is true that you always take the lead,' I said reluctantly. Like Beth, I always hated confrontation. And a part of me seethed that just as I'd got to being accepted by Doris, here was Caz trying to muck it up for me again. As she always did. I loved Caz to bits, but why did she have to be so angry all the time? Doris was the one person she didn't need to be angry with.

'Do I?' Doris looked stricken, and I felt even worse. 'I don't mean to. I'm really sorry, Caz, I didn't mean to upset you.'

Seeing her lower lip begin to quiver, and tears dangerously start to wobble down her cheeks, Caz for once softened uncharacteristically. Perhaps even hard as nails Caz couldn't resist Doris' charm.

'It's ok,' she said sulkily. 'I didn't mean to upset you either.'

Relieved that everything had gone back to normal, Doris ran to the huge kitchen and produced ice creams for all of us as we settled down to watch as Diana finally emerged from her carriage, to instant oohs and aahhs and squeals from the four of us.

'Isn't she like a fairy princess,' breathed Beth.

'She's beautiful,' I agreed.

'I'm going to have that dress when I get married,' announced Doris solemnly.

'I think she looks like a marshmallow,' said Caz, who didn't have a romantic bone in her body.

We all threw our ice cream wrappers at her, and settled down in blissful silence to watch as Charles Windsor took Diana Spencer to be his lawful wedded wife—

'To have and to hold, for richer for poorer, in sickness and in health, till death do us part,' we chanted the vows in unison.

'That's so romantic,' said Doris. 'I want to marry a prince when I grow up.'

Caz snorted, so we sat on her. By now we were getting bored of the video, so Doris fast forwarded to the kiss, which we watched over and over again, ecstatically imagining what it would feel like to have a boy kiss you on the lips like that. I thought it must feel very rubbery.

'We should make a pact,' Doris suddenly said. She was like that. Full of odd ideas, that seemed to come from nowhere.

'What kind of pact?' I said.

'We should promise to be friends forever and make a pact that we will be bridesmaids at each other's weddings.'

'I'm never going to get married,' declared Caz firmly.

'You can still be a bridesmaid though,' said Doris. She was impossible to resist, so even Caz was persuaded to stand in a circle. We all raised our hands together and held them up so that we touched.

'We solemnly declare,' intoned Doris, 'that we four will be friends forever.'

We looked at each other and giggled.

'Go on,' she said, 'say it after me.'

So we repeated what Doris had said, and then all four of us said, 'and we promise that when we get married we will only have our three friends as bridesmaids. And we promise that we will be bridesmaids for our friends.'

'From this day forth, forever and ever, shall this vow be binding,' said Doris. And then she made us cut a lock off each of our hair, and bind them together. She put the locks of hair, together with a written copy of the words we'd said, which we all signed, and then put it away in her special box.

'There,' she said, with satisfaction. 'Now we've taken an oath, and we can never ever break it.'

August 1996

Caz

Billy Idol was screaming out it was a nice day for a white wedding, which seemed appropriate in a bar in Las Vegas. I couldn't resist the craving for the next drink, though I knew I needed it like a hole in the head.

'Oi, Charlie boy, gezza another drink,' I was aware vaguely in some dim dark recess of my brain that I'd probably had enough and I was definitely slurring my words. The sensible thing would be to go to bed right now. Call it a day with these very nice and fun-loving work colleagues with whom I'd spent a couple of days bonding in Las Vegas on the first solo photo shoot of my burgeoning career as a make-up artist, and probably the most exciting job I'd had to date. But sense and I didn't go very well together. My sensible head never won over my drunken one.

'What are you on again?' Charlie looked in about as good shape as I was. He had wandered up to the bar. He turned to look at me as he said this, and leaned rather nonchalantly against the bar. He missed, narrowly avoiding smashing his chin on the bar, before righting himself.

'Vodka and coke,' I said, giggling hysterically. Our companions, Charlie's boss Finn, and Sal, the PA to the spoilt model whose photos we'd all been involved in taking for the past couple of days were nuzzling up to each other in one of the deep red heart shaped sofas that littered the bar. It had not been a very well kept secret of the week that they were shagging the pants of each other, despite Finn's heavily pregnant wife at home. I wasn't quite sure how I felt about that. I was no angel it's true, but shagging someone who was hitched with a baby on the way seemed like a complication too far to me. I wondered if he was worth it. Then looked at his rugged, wrinkled face and decided he wasn't. Finn must be nearly twenty years older then Sal. What on earth did she see in him?

Now Charlie on the other hand. He was a bit of alright. Tall, dark, conventionally good looking with a rather fetching quiff that fell over his eye, and which he brushed off with a rather shy movement which I found at once attractive and endearing. Charlie was rather lovely. And might be just the thing to take my mind off the humiliation of being turned down by Steven.

I'd always known Steven would go for Sarah, in the end, despite all his flirting. They always did. Her pretty girl-next-door looks always won them over, even if they were initially attracted to my wildness. My spiky aggressiveness, was in the main too much for most of the men I encountered. Far too toxic, as I'd been told on more then one occasion. They enjoyed the shag, but they never hung around long enough to keep their spare pyjamas in my cupboard.

When we'd met him out drinking in Soho, it was obvious that a cityboy slicker like him would go for Sarah, the safe bet, rather then her more wild and unpredictable friend. Not that it stopped him flirting with me mind, and making lewd suggestions about what he'd like to do with me when Sarah wasn't around. I'd bet a million dollars he never said anything like that to her. I should have been a better friend to her. I should have warned her about what he was like. But annoying prick as he was, Steven also happened to be one of the most gorgeous guys I'd ever met. And when

397

he was flirting, boy did he make you feel good about yourself. And I, despite all my chippiness and bravado, needed a morale boost from time to time. Not that I'd ever admit it to anyone, of course.

So when he finally moved things up a notch, one night when I bumped into him without Sarah, I didn't even think about her and went along with things. And after we'd danced and snogged and gyrated our way round the dance floor, I'd assumed we were going back to his. I was so unprepared for that knockback. I hated the feelings of churned up misery he'd stirred up in me. It made me furious to feel so weak. After that he and Sarah became more of a permanent item. And I was left alone. Bruised and sore. And not a little jealous.

Yes, I could do with Charlie to lighten things up. And he seemed to like me . . .

'What time is it?' I jerked awake, and suddenly realised I had dozed off on Charlie's shoulder. There was no sign of the other two. Presumably they'd gone off to consummate their passion. Well good luck to them.

'Three a.m.,' said Charlie, 'but hey, the night's still young. We're in Vegas don't forget. Ever played black jack?'

'No,' I said, 'but there's a first time for everything.'

So suddenly we were out on the streets, when sense dictated we should have been tucked up in bed, running through Vegas like a pair of school kids. It was such an outrageously extravagant place, I felt right at home. I could be anything I wanted here. Anything at all.

It wasn't difficult to find a casino, and soon we were betting money we couldn't afford on a game I barely understood. I was drinking vodka like it was going out of fashion, but here, in this atmosphere, I felt alive in a way I never had, and carried away on a feeling of indulgent recklessness. Charlie was lovely too, really attentive in a way none of the guys I'd ever been with had ever been before. I was enjoying the sensation so much, I let my guard down. And it felt great.

'Hey, look over there,' I nudged Charlie, 'there's a wedding couple.'

'So?' said Charlie, who was looking at his hand trying to work out if he was going to make 21 or have to go bust. His last five dollars were riding on it. I'd had to give up a couple of hands before as I'd run out of money. I wasn't quite reckless enough to go into debt.

'Isn't it cute?' I said, suddenly fascinated with this couple. They seemed to represent something I never thought I'd have. 'I bet there's a little chapel next door where you can get hitched just like that.'

'There is honey,' a Texan blonde with a pink rodeo hat and tassled pink denim jacket next to me, drawled. 'It's called Love Me Tender, and they've got an Elvis impersonator who'll marry you for a few dollars.'

'What a hoot,' I said. I nudged Charlie. 'We should do it.'

'Don't be daft,' said Charlie.

'Come on, where's your sense of adventure?' I said.

'I think marriage should be a bit more serious then that,' said Charlie.

'Oh, don't be so boring,' I said. 'Think what fun we've had tonight. We're made for each other. We'll get married tonight and go home and make a little Las Vegas baby.'

I didn't know what I was saying. I hated babies. I certainly didn't want one now. But somehow, I felt certain of one thing. Charlie and I had connected tonight, in a way I'd never connected with anyone. We should be together.

'You're mad,' said Charlie. He gave me a quizzical look, as if weighing something up. 'Did you mean all that?'

'Course I did,' I said. 'If you win this game, then we get married?'

'Ok,' said Charlie, 'but I don't think I'm going to win.'

Everyone had stuck apart from Charlie. He turned over his hand. Twenty-one. He'd won. Over two hundred dollars. It seemed like a fortune.

'Go on,' I said. 'Now you have to do it. A deal's a deal.'

An hour later, fortified by more vodka and a promise of a singing Elvis – Charlie it turned out was a closet Elvis fan – and we found ourselves in front of the Love Me Tender chapel. The door was heart-shaped, and the outside of the chapel was a sickly pink which reminded me of the terrible blancmanges my grandmother used to make when I was little and Mum was having one of her funny 'turns'. We giggled as we saw it. We'd come armed with our marriage license, which bizarrely in Las Vegas you could buy at any time of the night or day over the weekend, and the sun was just rising above the city, which seemed just as busy now as it had done when we'd embarked on our drinking spree all those hours earlier. I had a moment of panic then. This wasn't how I'd planned my wedding day. I'd always pretended I didn't want to get married, but now I was here, I could admit to myself I wanted the real deal, not this ghastly parody, with a boy I barely knew. I thought of Doris with a pang. She'd be furious with me for not fulfilling her silly pact.

'Come on then,' Charlie grabbed my hand, and pulled me through the door. We were met by an Elvis impersonator who was apparently the official who was going to marry us. It also transpired that he was going to give me away. So I walked down the aisle to the tender strains of *Love Me Do* and then in a few easily spoken words we were hitched. It felt surreal. This wasn't the way I'd ever imagined it was going to be.

We then took a cab out to the desert and held hands as

we watched the sun rise. It was the most romantic moment of a bizarre and weird evening. Charlie kissed me on the lips and said, 'Happy Wedding Day, Mrs Davies. Come on, let's go home.'

We got back to the hotel, and then shyly, I followed him up to his room. It was strange. We'd been behaving so recklessly all evening, and now I felt like a fool. I could legitimately sleep with the guy and suddenly, now I was here, it felt all wrong. In the end, we just stumbled into bed, and collapsed cuddling on the bed from exhaustion and over consumption of alcohol.

I woke at midday. The sun was streaming through the window, and Charlie was still snoring next to me. *Charlie*. I sat bolt upright and looked down at him, the events from the previous night flooding back with sudden and vivid clarity. Oh my god. I'd got married to a guy I barely knew. What on earth had I been thinking? Of all the wreckless things I'd ever done, this had to be the most stupid.

Snapshot: Caz

I knew even as I sat down at the bar with him, I was doing the wrong thing. But a combination of anger at Sarah, and recklessness from having had too much to drink, and a sort of self-hatred which has always been my fatal flaw, led me not to care. Besides. He was here with me. Not with her. I knew it was wrong to want him as much as I did. But I had wanted him from the first time we met. And he chose Sarah, as they always did. I was the one they shagged. Sarah was the one they chose for the long term. And this time, he'd really made it clear he was playing the long game. This time, I'd lost him for good.

Except. Here he was, newly affianced, in a bar with me. Playing footsie under the table, looking at me with lascivious eyes, accidentally touching my hand when there was no need.

I could lie and say I was so drunk I didn't know what I was doing. I could pretend that 'it just happened', like they always say in the problem pages. But it wouldn't be true. These things don't 'just' happen. You have to lose control of the bit of you that's screaming that this is so so wrong, you have to let go of your moral compass and go on a journey into a morass of grubby decisions that you'll later regret. You have to choose all that. It doesn't just happen.

Even at the moment I let him into my flat, I could have just ended it then, after the coffee, before we'd gone too far.

But I was drunk on power, and lust and the feeling I'd got one over on Sarah for once. Besides, I wanted to know what he was like, this golden boy, whom I'd adored for so long.

And once we'd kissed, and cuddled, and got down and dirty, then there was a point, a moment when I could have said, no, this is wrong, we mustn't go any further, but I didn't say it. I didn't try to stop the inevitable, and I could have. Because drunk and all as I was on lust, tantalising as every touch was, I knew exactly what I was doing. But still I continued, carried on a wave of passion into a world where there were no commitments, and I didn't betray the people I loved, and the man I was with loved me for myself, not for the undoubted quick bit of fun I undoubtedly was.

It was only in the morning, when I woke up, and saw him already dressed, already distancing himself from me, that I felt ashamed. I didn't know how I was ever going to face Sarah again. I didn't know how I was ever going to face myself. I felt wrong and dirty and so very, very bad. A sudden vision of my mother, in her worst vengeful mode swam before my eyes. 'You're a dirty little whore,' she hissed in my ear. 'I always knew you'd turn out to be no good.' I turned my face to the wall and wept.

I turned the invitation over and over in my hands, despite the feeling of nausea rising up from the pit of my stomach and the sheer panic that seeing that handwriting for the first time in what, over four years, had engendered in me. You had to hand it to Doris, she certainly knew how to break the ice. Only she could have sent me an invitation to her hen weekend on Mickey Mouse notepaper.

Dorrie and Daz are finally tying the knot, it read, and I snorted with laughter. Trust Doris to make her forthcoming nuptials sound like some kids' TV programme. I was glad she was finally getting hitched to Yakult Man (so called because of his obsession with cleanliness). They were made for each other. *You are invited*, it said, *to Dorrie's extra special hen weekend at Eurodisney. Fab four members only. One for all and all four one* – trust Doris to remember that stupid tag line we'd had as kids. But then, she'd probably been the one to think it up. At the bottom, Doris had scrawled in her unforgettably untidy handwriting (amazing how someone as beautifully presented as Doris could have such terrible writing, but then, that was Doris all over. A mass of impossible contradictions.), *Please come. It won't be the same without you.*

Doris. What a bloody stupid name. How could her parents have been so unkind? She always claimed it was because her mum was a fan of Doris Day, but it seemed like, for once in her impeccably toned and manicured life, Doris' mum had got it wrong and caused a major *faux pas*. Not that Doris seemed to mind. She'd inherited the happy-go-lucky nature of her screen namesake, and took *que sera, sera* as her motto. And because she was just so bloody wonderful, and fabulous, no one ever seemed to even tease her about her name. Now if it had been me . . .

I turned the invitation over in my hands once again. Should I go? It seemed to me, Doris was offering me another chance. Typical of her generosity that. And I didn't deserve it I knew. Last time we'd met, she'd tried to bridge the gap between me and Sarah and guilt and hurt and anger had led me to be unforgivably rude to her. Even Doris had been unable to forgive that for a while. But now it seemed like she had.

But what of the others? Could Beth and Sarah ever forgive me, for what I'd done to them? We grew up in a culture that taught us that redemption is always possible. But I'd been around in the world enough to know that it didn't happen as often as our teachers told us. Besides. You need to earn redemption. To gain forgiveness, you need to be truly, truly sorry. And even now there's a self destructive bit of me which isn't sure that I am . . .

The plane touched down at Charles de Gaulle airport and I took a deep breath. Well, here I was. Finally. It had taken all my courage to come – I'd been tempted by a job in Greece where a famous model was attempting a comeback shoot for M&S. It would have been a great job. Glamorous. In the sun all day, and time in the evenings for some unwinding and Greek dancing in the local tavernas. But Charlie persuaded me otherwise. Charlie was my favourite photographer on the circuit. Down to earth and easy going, he had the most amazing ability to tease the best out of the subjects he shot. Working with Charlie was always a breeze. And he was fun to socialise with too. Not since that mad moment in Las Vegas, that we'd ever been anything other then friends, mind. He was firmly hitched to his live-in girlfriend and attractive as I found him, I wasn't about to go upsetting any apple carts. I'd learnt my lesson too well last time.

I emerged blinking from the airport into the pale March Paris sunshine. I always loved coming to Paris, but it was the cafe culture, museums and walks along the Seine which were the usual attraction for me. Without Dorrie's invite, I doubt I'd ever have visited Disneyland Paris, but here I was on a train out of Paris, bound for Mickey Mouseville. Doris was the only person who could have ever persuaded me to come.

The shuttle service to Marne la Vallee proved surprisingly quick, and I had barely time to get my head together and think what on earth I was going to say to everyone when suddenly there I was, being deposited in front of Woody's Cowboy Ranch – *Toy Story* being Dorrie's favourite

Disney film, she'd insisted we stay here. Suddenly my heart was in my boots, and I was eight-years-old again, being invited for the first time to Dorrie's mansion. It had felt like such a privilege, back then to be entering Dorrie's inner sanctum, and yet in the self-destructive way I have, I'd pretty much blown the chance of making the most of the opportunities being friends with Dorrie and the others had afforded me. I didn't even know if they'd want to see me again, let alone forgive me. Knowing Dorrie, I bet she hadn't told them I was coming.

I checked in at the desk, my nerves making a mash of my school girl French. The unsmiling receptionist responded in perfect English with a look of such sneery disdain, I wanted the ground to swallow me up whole. Giving up on any attempt to speak her language, I said, 'I'm meeting friends, a Doris Bradley?'

'Ah oui, Mademoiselle Bradley is next door to you. I will let her know you have arrived.'

I took my bags and made my way to the third floor, shaking like a leaf. Suppose the others didn't want to see me. Suppose I ended up ruining Dorrie's big weekend? This had been a dreadful mistake. I was wrong to come.

I found room 325, next door to 327. Dorrie's room. I swallowed hard. Should I dump my bags, freshen up, and then go and say hi? Or should I bite the bullet and go straight for it?

The door to 327 flung wide open, and there in the flesh for the first time in years stood Dorrie. Larger then life as ever. Welcoming me in a massive hug. I felt my worries disappear instantly. Dorrie had a way of doing that. It was her special talent.

'Caz! You came, I'm so pleased. Come right in,' she propelled me into the middle of a massive room, complete with double bed and cowboy paraphernalia hanging from the walls.

Lounging on the bed, sipping champagne, were two faces I hadn't seen in a very, very long time. They both looked up at me and registered their shock.

'You never said *she* was coming,' Sarah shot me a look of such venom, I was quite taken aback. God did she really still hate me that much?

'It wouldn't have been the same without her,' said Dorrie firmly.

'Lock up your husbands,' said Sarah. 'Sorry Doz, I know you mean well, but I'm not spending any more time with her then I have to.' She got up and stormed out of the room, pushing past me with evident hatred.

I knew I shouldn't have come.